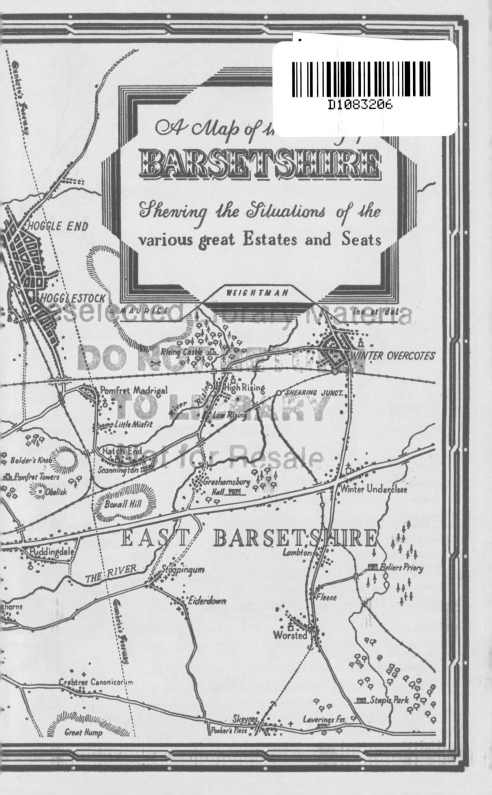

A Map of the County of

BARSETSHIRE

Shewing the Situations of the
various great Estates and Seats

WHAT DID IT MEAN?

WHAT

DID IT MEAN?

by

Angela Thirkell

NEW YORK: ALFRED·A·KNOPF

19 54

L. C. catalog card number: 54–8769

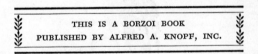

THIS IS A BORZOI BOOK
PUBLISHED BY ALFRED A. KNOPF, INC.

FIRST AMERICAN EDITION

WHAT DID IT MEAN?

WHAT DID IT MEAN?

CHAPTER 1

Mrs. Merton, she who was once Lydia Keith, and her husband, Noel Merton, K.C. since 1946 and Q.C. since England had a Queen, had lived since the end of the war in her late parents' house near Northbridge. The house and small estate had been intended for her eldest brother, Robert, but Mrs. Robert Keith, she who was once Edith Fairweather, Captain of Hockey and Captain of Cricket at Barchester High School and also Girl of Honour (for such was the headmistress Miss Pettinger's beautiful interpretation of the more prosaic Captain of the School), had a strong feeling, based on no one knew what, that Northbridge was on the wrong side of Barchester and—as a rider or corollary—that her children would drown themselves in the river at the bottom of the garden. So Noel and Lydia, by a very amicable arrangement, had bought Northbridge Manor from Robert, who had moved —or rather been moved by his wife—into the Gatherum Castle side of the county, and everyone was content.

The families were on very friendly terms. Noel Merton and Robert Keith could always talk Law, Noel reminding himself that though the bar is somehow better than being a solicitor, it is useful to have a good solicitor in the family who has his younger sister's interests at heart, while Robert was not at all unaware of the advantages of a Q.C. brother-in-law with briefs marked goodness knows what and likely to be a Sir or even a Lord in time. As for Lydia Merton and Edith

Keith, the sisters-in-law, while each knew inside herself that the other was running her life and bringing up her children on all the wrong ideas, they were on excellent terms. Edith Keith's two boys and one girl were able to patronize Lydia Merton's Lavinia, Harry, and Jessica (called after Jessica Dean, the brilliant and popular actress) to their hearts' content. Every now and then someone would say how nice it was the Mertons having two girls and a boy and Mrs. Robert Keith two boys and a girl, but on examination this statement appears to mean nothing at all.

Those who had known Lydia Keith before the war were very fond of her and had considerable respect for her capability. The very few who knew her well remembered the summer when Noel Merton, perhaps still feeling the backwash of the six years' war though on the surface this was not apparent, had for a short time chosen to consider himself in love with the pretty widow Mrs. Arbuthnot, now Mrs. Francis Brandon. His Lydia had never for a moment doubted his faith, but she had been afraid, for the first time in her life, and afraid to tell Noel her fear. Noel had been delicately set in his place by Jessica Dean and his heart had returned completely to his Lydia (whom, we may say, it had never really left). He then had the sense and the grace not to explain or apologize, and their life had been as happy as anyone has a right to hope or expect.

During term-time, or whatever it is called when Q.C.'s have to be in London, Noel would spend most of the week in their London flat where Lydia sometimes joined him, especially for the first nights at the Cockspur, for which Jessica Dean and her husband, Aubrey Clover, who mostly wrote his own plays and the music for them and acted in them with Jessica, always sent a box. But even with Noel she could not love London, and there was so much to be done about their property and the cows and the hay and the farm. Mr. Wickham, their agent for many years past, said if he kicked the bucket Mrs. Merton could run the place standing on her head.

"That is," Mr. Wickham added to Lady Cora Waring, an old friend of war days, on whom he had called with a bottle of Vanderhum, "so long as we don't get a touch of contagious abortion. There's only one person I'd trust on that if I weren't here. Mrs. Tom Grantly over at Rushwater. Emmy Graham she was, and I'd trust her with any cow, anywhere, any time. Best hands in the county," to which Lady Cora had replied gravely that she always thought that was Lady Pomfret.

"Great Jumping Jehoshophat, my girl," said Mr. Wickham, "Sally Pomfret doesn't know a B from a bull's foot when it's cows. Horses, yes, and every time," on which Lady Cora had said Wicks was losing his grip on things and Mr. Wickham said Kamerad and he was too old to have his leg pulled and he must be buzzing off because there was a meeting over Chaldicotes way at five o'clock to elect a Coronation Chairman of Committee and they were bound to make damned fools of themselves.

"Whole point of a committee," said Mr. Wickham, finishing the last dregs of one of the bottles of beer which Lady Cora had kindly provided for his tea, "is to have one person on it who knows his own mind, though it's usually her mind. Doesn't matter what you decide to do. Great thing is to decide to do it. How's the future Bart?" for Mr. Wickham took a strong personal interest in Master Plantagenet Cecil Waring (better known as P.C.), one of whose godfathers he was, though only by proxy as he had on the date of the christening a long-standing engagement to assist in the French sense at the bottling of some of the famous Audit Ale still brewed for

Paul's College at Oxford. "And when's that nice girl, though she's a bit long in the tooth for that, Margot Phelps going to get married?"

Lady Cora said she did not know. It rather depended, she said, whether her parents, Admiral and Mrs. Phelps, would consent to leave their home in Southbridge and become pensioners, as it were, of their future son-in-law, the wealthy Mr. Macfadyen, the Head of Amalgamated Vedge and many kindred concerns with a controlling interest in Washington's Vimphos, Corbett's Bono-Vitasang, and Holman's Phospho-Manuro.

"Well, their business, not mine," said Mr. Wickham. "Margot's running it a bit fine though, isn't she? Let's see. She was as near thirty as makes no odds the year war broke out, the last war I mean. Thirty-nine, forty-nine, fifty-three. That makes her about forty-three. Can do, I suppose, but it's a near thing."

Lady Cora said not to be so Gampish and how were Margot's people, to which Mr. Wickham replied that the betting was absolutely even, but if the Admiral and Mrs. Phelps meant to run the Coronation do at Southbridge, run it they would, and he must be off.

"It's no business of mine," he added, "but I did ask Dr. Ford the other day if he thought the Admiral ought to do so much with the Sea Scouts," for owing to Sir Cecil Waring's efforts the Barsetshire Sea Scouts were now on a good financial footing and during the last year had raised enough money to cover half the expense of a week's outing to the South Coast, the rest being provided by Sir Cecil, old Admiral Palliser over at Hallbury, and other benefactors.

Lady Cora asked what Dr. Ford had said.

"He said," replied Mr. Wickham, absent-mindedly opening the last bottle, "that old people must be allowed to kill themselves in their own way, and I think that's pretty sound."

Lady Cora said it depended how old, for she could never forget the day when her husband, warned by both naval and civil doctors never to strain himself on account of some bits of shrapnel which would be better undisturbed, had insisted on helping with the rush-cutting in the lake at Harefield, and would have died in agony had not Lady Cora Palliser (as she was then) driven him to the Barchester General Hospital at a speed from which several members of the county constabulary and the Automobile Association, all Lady Cora's devoted friends, deliberately averted their eyes, and so saved his life. Mr. Wickham said anyone who had been through the 1914 war was all right under Ford's ruling and he must be off, and he went away to Northbridge in the far too powerful car which he had bought in the previous year with a bequest from his old uncle over Chaldicotes way.

The whole of England was now in an orgy of Coronation Committees. Temporary differences were forgotten in the common cause. The Women's Institutes and the Townswomen's Guilds became as sisters, though always reserving the right of a sister to dislike a sister wholeheartedly. Parish Councils lay down with Town Councils, nor were the Mothers' Unions unheard. Gatherum Castle opened its gates and its grounds to any form of political, social, or religious body that wanted to express its loyal feelings. Mr. Adams gave five hundred pounds to the Coronation Fund for the Barsetshire General Hospital and was arranging a feast with a great marquee and dancing for his works at Hogglestock, which feast would certainly cost as much or more, besides the certainty, as he said to his father-in-law, Mr. Marling, that half the works would be on the sick list next day with stomach-trouble. In Barchester considerable pleasure was caused by an exchange of salvos between the Palace and the Deanery in the matter of a kind of mystery play to be acted in the crypt, the Dean (quite rightly, we feel) insisting on seeing the script of the play and refusing to have representatives of Russia, Japan, Persia, Egypt, and Communism included in the great Tableau of All Nations at the end. The Palace then issued invitations to a Coronation Garden Party, but when the news leaked out (or rather was industriously spread, via Messrs. Scatcherd and Tozer, the well-known Barchester caterers) that the entertainment was to be sangwiches and gatto on their lowest tariff, with tea and lemonade to drink, a great many people accepted out of politeness with the mental reservation that they would only stay a few moments, or not come at all.

In Northbridge there were on the whole fewer squabbles than elsewhere, for in the little town the gentry and the cottages, united for centuries by bonds of slightly despotic kindness on the one side and a finely archaic ingratitude for favours combined with a determination to take every advantage of them on the other, had come to a kind of agreement. A Joint Committee had set itself up, its first business being to elect a president. The position was offered, as a matter of form, to Mrs. Villars, the Rector's wife, who begged to be excused on the grounds of already being in charge of pretty well every other committee. There was no Great Lady in the neighbourhood; nor one in the position of Squire's wife, the nearest approach being Mrs. Noel Merton, who, though she was liked, had never been much mixed in Northbridge doings. Miss Pemberton, the Provençal scholar at Punshions, a stone cottage of considerable antiquity and even more considerable discomfort to which its owner was completely impervious, was mentioned, but there was a general feeling that she wouldn't do, as indeed she would not. There had been talk of Mrs. Marling, for Marling Hall was the nearest Landed Gentry seat to Northbridge, but Mrs. Marling, who had run more county and local committees than most people, was finding the grasshopper a distinct burden and more inclined to resign from committees than to take part in fresh ones, besides having her own village celebrations to organize.

It now became increasingly apparent to all women of goodwill (for in Northbridge, with its population preponderantly widows and spinsters, the male element was on the whole not much considered) that Mrs. Noel Merton must be the right person, whether she liked it or not, and a deputation in the shape of Mrs. Paxon and Miss Hopgood's Aunt was sent to wait upon her. Mrs. Paxon, wife of a Barchester bank-manager, had been, as our older readers may remember, a most valiant war-worker, dealing impartially with refugees, air-raid precautions, auxiliary fire service, Red Cross, billeting, de-lousing, and other activities too dull and numerous to mention. The arrival of Peace had but turned her energy in other directions. The Red Cross still claimed a good deal of her attention, and of late the revival of Civil Defence had caused her joyously to look over her wartime trousers and see which of them she could still get into. Whether she was capable of helping to organize a Coronation Pageant, with the subsidiary Treat for the Old People and Treat for the Kiddies, was not clear; but she had a strong body of supporters among those people who while anxious to work had a rooted objection to taking responsibility.

Miss Hopgood's Aunt represented on the whole the more highbrow side of Northbridge, for she was not only nearly twice as tall and twice as broad as Mrs. Paxon, but was the widow of an astronomer and had an excellent telescope through which she industriously observed the heavenly bodies on such rare nights as were not wet or misty. She also had a reputation in astronomical circles through her paper on the lesser-known satellites of Porter Sidus, a luminary discovered by her late husband when working at the Observatory in Porterville, U.S.A. (financed by Mr. Walden Concord Porter).

Accordingly Miss Hopgood's Aunt, supported by Mrs. Paxon in her Civil Defence role, arranged to visit Northbridge Manor on a nasty morning in February. The distance was not great and Miss Hopgood's Aunt liked walking; so she walked. Mrs. Paxon always bicycled if possible because she said it saved time, even if it meant wheeling her bicycle along a path, through a cornfield, lifting it over a stile, and wheeling it across a seven-acre field where several cows in an interesting condition must not be alarmed, which they would not in any case have been, as what intelligence they had was entirely devoted to eating, ruminating, and standing side by side in opposite directions (if we make ourselves clear) and swishing flies off each other's faces with their respective tails (a sentence which any reader will at once understand); so she bicycled, rather on the Ride and Tie principle except that it was Ride and Wait for a bit till Miss Hopgood's Aunt caught up. But the ladies were used to each other, each having a sincere respect for the qualities in the other which she herself neither had nor wished to possess, and what with Miss Hopgood's Aunt's steady three and a half miles an hour and Mrs. Paxon's swallow flights punctuated by stopping till Miss Hopgood's Aunt came up and then resuming her course, they got to Northbridge Manor by eleven o'clock, the hour named for their visit.

In the drawing-room there was a good fire. The French windows, which in most country houses exude death-dealing draughts owing to not fitting very well, had been made safe for human beings by well-lined velvet curtains with no nonsense about them and quite elegant wooden screens about two feet high which were firmly secured with bolts across the bottom of the windows in winter. The elderly parlourmaid,

Palmer, at the same time the mainstay of the house and the terror of such underlings as the times could afford, received Mrs. Paxon and Miss Hopgood's Aunt with a manner that but thinly veiled her contempt (though not so much for the two ladies in particular as for visitors in general) and saying she would tell Mrs. Merton, left them alone in the drawing-room, where they were able to admire a photograph of Noel Merton in wig and gown and various photographs of the children at different ages till Lydia made her appearance. We will not say that she plunged or burst into the room, for life had softened and tamed Miss Lydia Keith to a certain extent since her hoyden days; but her coming brought a not unpleasant feeling of commotion and exhilaration.

"How do you do, I'm awfully sorry I wasn't here when you came but I was down in the cowshed with Pucken," said the wife of the eminent Q.C., crushing the hands of her guests warmly while she spoke. "It's something about the Corona-tion, isn't it? Mrs. Villars rang me up and said you were com-ing. Thank you, Palmer," she added, as the parlourmaid brought in a tray which she placed on a table with a distant air, rather as if she were bestowing charity on lepers and hop-ing to avoid infection.

"Will that be all, madam?" said Palmer, asking what was quite obviously a rhetorical question.

"No," said Lydia, who had looked at the tray. "I did say the digestive biscuits. Those ginger biscuits are as hard to bite as cracking nuts."

"Very good, madam," said Palmer, at once the resigned martyr, and she picked up the offending plate.

"You needn't take them away," said Lydia. "We'll have the digestive as well. Some people," she continued, now addressing her guests, "can't manage ginger nuts except in a sideways sort of way."

"I can't," said Miss Hopgood's Aunt. "But ginger biscuits aren't what they were when I was a girl. Then there was plenty of good treacle in them and one could bite them easily."

"I couldn't," said Mrs. Paxon, "but we used to hide our ginger biscuits in our beds and next morning they were no difficulty at all."

"So did I when I was little," said Lydia, "and in the morning one could squish them up and make animals and faces with them, only nurse said not to. So I ate them before she got up. I say, what are we going to do about the Coronation?"

This question, though hardly Parliamentary, cleared the ground for the deputation, who both began to talk at once.

"Sorry. You go ahead, Mrs. Paxon," said Miss Hopgood's Aunt.

Mrs. Paxon unshipped, if we may use the term, a capacious sham-leather bag which hung aslant her body from one shoulder, and took out a sheaf of limp, dog's-eared papers.

"I've got everything written down here," she said, "only they got a bit mixed up with the Friends of Barchester General Hospital papers because yesterday was my visiting day and the old dears wanted such a lot of things that I had to make notes of."

"I don't know about the Friends of Barchester General," said Lydia.

Miss Hopgood's Aunt, who had a very civic mind, drew in her breath in an audible manner.

"Oh, it's visiting the old ladies in the part of the Hospital that won't ever come out," said Mrs. Paxon, rather confusingly reminding her hearers of the Cat that walked by himself.

Lydia asked why they wouldn't.

"Well, they can't," said Mrs. Paxon. "It was the workhouse, only then it was called the Institution and then it was called

something else, but it's really the Workhouse Infirmary and
it is called the Hospital. Some of us visit there every week and
let them talk to us, and they give us orders for little things
they want, like pink and blue ribbons and scent and powder
and chocolate and millions of ginger biscuits and pay for them
out of their Old Age Pensions or their little bit of money that
the Almoner takes care of. They are such pets. Old Mrs.
Pucken, she's really Miss but we call her Granny because she
had her hundredth birthday last year, buys chocolate and blue
hair ribbon and pink elastic garters nearly every week. She is
completely bedridden and pretty dotty."

"What does she do with the garters, then?" said Lydia the
practical.

"Gives them to the Ward Sister," said Mrs. Paxon, "and
Sister gives them back to us to sell again, so everyone is
happy," and her face shone with busy, undiscriminating benevolence.

"And now," said Miss Hopgood's Aunt, who with exem-
plary patience had bided her time, "about the Coronation."
And having delivered her mind, she sat back with the air of
one to whom a thousand ages were but a morning wasted—as
possibly in the astronomical world they are.

"Well," said Lydia thoughtfully, "what?"

Mrs. Paxon having by now sorted the Friends of Barchester
Hospital from the Coronation suggestions, began to look
through her notes.

"Here we are," she said. "No, not that one. That's the
Townswomen's Guild program from Silverbridge. They are
having a special show of Cottage Needlework and Fancy
Work to raise funds for a tea-party in Silverbridge High Street
for the Kiddies," at which dreadful word Lydia did not blench
outwardly.

"What kind of fancy work will it be?" she asked, for as the talk was obviously going to divagate in all directions, she felt she had better resign herself to drift with the tide.

"I can't imagine," said Mrs. Paxon, "as none of them can sew now. It might be Ekroo Doyleys. They are very popular."

Lydia, who thought she recognized in Mrs. Paxon's description those nasty round mats crocheted in cotton of a browny-yellow hue, said how nice.

"Not really," said Mrs. Paxon dispassionately. "Here we are. The idea, Mrs. Merton, is first a short service for the kiddies and their parents at nine o'clock to give everyone time to get back to the Telly in good time to see it all."

"But they'll have to spend *hours* looking at the television," said Lydia. "We haven't got one."

"Oh *dear*, Mrs. Merton," said Mrs. Paxon, genuinely shocked. "You can hire quite a nice one in Barchester. Surely Mr. Merton will want to see it all."

The old Lydia Keith would have said Rot, and if anyone thought a dithering picture interspersed with spots of light and flashes of lightning, sponsored (if we may use that silly word) by voices which were far too apt to say contròversy and ackcherly and "Pardon" if they coughed, they were welcome. But time had in some respects softened our downright Lydia, or taught her the wisdom of occasional conforming, so she asked Mrs. Paxon to tell her exactly what, as President, she would be required to do. This appeared to be the one question which Mrs. Paxon, usually very well briefed in any cause she took up, could not answer, and she remained silent.

"May I state briefly," said Miss Hopgood's Aunt, coming unexpectedly to the rescue, "what we would ask, Mrs. Merton? We want your name, your presence at our Coronation meetings, where I or Mrs. Paxon or Mrs. Villars will protect you, a donation large enough to show goodwill but not so large as to make other people ashamed of giving less, and your husband's name. We shall also be grateful for anything you can spare for our Dairy Produce Show and any suggestions you could make for the Kiddies' Entertainment and some kind of entertainment for the over-seventies. There will be various other items, but you can safely leave them to us. And of course we shall all go to the Rector's Coronation Service, which, as Mrs. Paxon has told us, is to be early, so as not to interfere with the television. Sic itur ad astra."

"I know that one," said Lydia. "We did a bit of Virgil at Barchester High School and somehow that came into it. But I was never very good at Latin because of all the words coming in the wrong order, and Colin—you know, my lawyer brother who lives in London—used to do most of my Latin prep for me."

"I was at the same school as Bertha Pettinger," said Miss Hopgood's Aunt. "She was very good at mathematics. I was not. She then went to college, with a scholarship, I believe. I did not. My dear parents did not believe in higher education for women. Nor do I."

"But, I say," said Lydia, still the irrepressible in spite of her years and her family, "how on earth did you do it? I mean not do it."

"My dear parents," said Miss Hopgood's Aunt, "did not wish me to go to a university and I did not wish to go either. I married my late husband quite young and he trained me to help him in his astronomical work. You know he discovered a new star while working at the Matthews Porter Observatory in Texas and I took the greatest interest in his work and typed all his papers for him. He used to call me S.W."

Even the competent and resilient Mrs. Paxon was slightly

stunned by this statement, but recovered herself to ask Why, a question Lydia had been longing to ask but wondered if it was polite.

"Star Watcher," said Miss Hopgood's Aunt, simply. "A term of endearment. But star-watching in Texas is child's play, so clear is the air. In Porterville I have often watched through my telescope the coyotes at play in the foothills fifty miles away."

Lydia expressed suitable surprise, which was a weakness rather unlike her, but she had no idea how far one ought to see with a telescope and did not want to expose her ignorance to Miss Hopgood's Aunt, nor until she was telling Noel about it afterwards did she realize what Ky-hoties really were.

"Well now," said Mrs. Paxon, who was well trained in bringing people back to the point. "About the Coronation. On the day itself there will only be the early service, because of the television, and a bonfire in the evening if it doesn't rain. On the following day a service for the kiddies and their parents at eleven, followed by a procession to the War Memorial, where wreaths will be laid by representatives of the British Legion and other bodies. After lunch there will be the Dairy Produce Show in the School Hall. We did think of a marquee, but they cost too much. We have got Packer's Universal Royal Derby—"

"Gosh!" said Mrs. Noel Merton, suddenly becoming Miss Lydia Keith aged sixteen or so. "I went on his roundabout fifteen times running at the Pomfret Madrigal Fête when I was a girl. I simply *adored* it. On a cock. Sorry, Mrs. Paxon."

"My evacuees were on it all afternoon when it came to Northbridge near the end of the war," said Mrs. Paxon. "That nice Father Fewling, though I suppose we ought to say Canon Fewling now, gave me ten shillings for them. They had a lovely time and they were all sick. Well now, Mrs. Merton, we hope the younger kiddies will be tired out and ready for bed after the Tea. We are having the Tea on trestle tables in the market-place if it is fine and the Church Hall if it isn't. I hope myself it will cloud up a bit after lunch, as children out of doors are really quite a handful. And then, Mrs. Merton, in the evening we want to have a kind of concert, or variety show, in the Town Hall, only we don't know who to ask. There's Vidler at the fish-and-poultry shop, he loves reciting. And Mr. Scatcherd at the Stores says he'll get his cousin over at Hatch End, who takes likenesses in five minutes."

Lydia, always practical, asked how long Vidler would recite and how many likenesses Mr. Scatcherd would take, and was there anyone else. Mrs. Paxon said she must think.

"Look here," said Lydia. "If you can find enough people to take likenesses and recite for an hour, I'll see if Aubrey Clover and Jessica would come down and do a little show for us."

"Do you know them?" said Mrs. Paxon, awestruck.

Lydia said quite well enough to ask them, and if they couldn't or wouldn't come they would have to think of something else and that was that.

"Then I expect that's about all for the present," she said, getting up, though in a very kind and friendly way. "Let me know when you want a real Committee Meeting and I'll come."

"My late husband," said Miss Hopgood's Aunt, "always said committees were a cardinal error. Why cardinal, I do not know, but those were his words."

"It's something to do with a hinge," said Lydia, who was getting rather tired of her guests, though she did not show it. "And I had quite forgotten, Mrs. Paxon. Noel heard that you were going to run the Coronation arrangements and he asked me to give you his contribution to the expenses," and she put an envelope into Mrs. Paxon's hand which that lady, who was very practical and in the cause of good works had no kind of shyness or reticence, at once opened.

"Ten pounds!" said Mrs. Paxon. "Oh, really, how *very* kind of Mr. Merton. I suppose he couldn't come to the entertainment in his robes and wig? It would be an immense attraction."

Lydia, who did not laugh very often, almost had an unladylike fit of the giggles, but managed to choke them back and said she was afraid the Chief Justice would not like it.

"No, I daresay not," said Mrs. Paxon reflectively. "It would be like Mr. Paxon turning up in his Masonic Robes," to which Lydia, most gratefully, said Exactly, and the ladies took their departure.

What with the talk and the refreshments, the morning was almost gone. Being a Friday, Noel Merton would be back as usual for the week-end and Lydia was going to meet him in Barchester and also collect Miss Lavinia Merton from the Preparatory School now attached to the Barchester High School. Otherwise Lavinia came by train with some other girls and walked home from Northbridge Halt.

The Preparatory School had only been started since the war, and the Governing Committee had been both wise and lucky in securing as its headmistress Miss Head, who had taken the English Literature classes in the Hosiers' Girls' Foundation School, which had been evacuated to Harefield during the war and was now permanently settled in its new buildings beyond Harefield on the Southbridge Road. Miss Head had made a very good job of organizing the Preparatory School. She was liked and respected by mistresses and girls and had also become a figure in Barchester Society, meeting the Dean and Mrs. Crawley on equal terms and holding very proper feelings about the Palace.

Outside the school, girls were coming out like the waters at Lodore. A few of the youngest looked attractive. A few of the very senior girls were already approximating to human beings. The bulk of the school gave Lydia an impression of thousands of school hats which neither fitted nor suited their wearers, though she had to admit that the wearers had distinctly more style than her own generation of girls. She got into the car and sat waiting for Lavinia to come out, and when that young lady appeared, her hat set well on the back of her head and her face rather shiny, she felt that to get her daughter to take any interest in style was beyond her. But she was a darling child, with kind eyes like her aunt Kate Carter's and dark, shining hair like Lydia's own. Certainly girls had improved since her own schooldays. Her brother Robert's Catherine at eighteen (who had also been at the High School) was extremely personable and well-mannered. Probably Lavinia would improve with time, and she was a darling, which was the great thing.

"I say, mother," said Lavinia.

"Well, darling?" said Lydia.

"I really can't help not liking arithmetic, mother. Do you and father mind?"

"Not a bit," said Lydia, "only one has to know enough to get through the exams."

"I wish arithmetic was French," said Lavinia, rather boastfully. "I like French. I'm top every week."

"Well, we'll see if we can make it French," said her mother. "Perhaps Mademoiselle Larousse would give you some extra French and you could do arithmetic in it."

"Oh, *mother!*" said Lavinia, which was quite enough, and Lydia drove on towards Barchester Central Station. The London train was late as usual.

"Let's go on the platform, mother," said Lavinia, "and see

if the chocolate machine is working," for after many years of dearth a rumour was going about that the penny-in-the-slot machines were going to work again. It made one feel very old, thought Lydia, to have a daughter who had never put her pennies into a machine for chocolate, or had a pennyworth—or was it three pennyworth—of those enchanting name-plate machines where one could emboss one's name and as much of one's address as space allowed on a strip of shining aluminium which came slithering out of the machine when you had stamped it. Even the weighing machines, with the table of the proper weight for every age (though the figures never tallied with physical facts) and the excitement of seeing the hand go quivering round till it stopped at one's own weight, seemed romantic in retrospect. Lydia's mind went back to tales her mother told her about the railways of her childhood and smart little boys with a flat basket of newspapers slung round their necks walking up and down the platform seeking custom, and the great iron footwarmer, full of boiling water, thrust into your carriage in London for twopence, to be renewed at other large stations if the journey was long. And even more nostalgically her mind went back to her own pre-war youth and the shining cleanness of the engines, now caked with oil and dirt, all their brass smeared and dull, the wheels looking as if they had been through the Serbonian bog. Stories that had floated down from the past of people lightly ordering a "special" for some party or some race-meeting, of carriages where all the cushions were clean and a lady could read *The Times* in her white kid gloves, so good and fast was the ink.

"Oh, mother," said Lavinia's voice breaking in reproachfully upon her meditations, "the chocolate machine isn't working yet. When will it?"

Her mother could not tell her, but luckily just then the London train came labouring in, hissing like a thousand drag-ons, and Noel's tall form came out of a first-class carriage. For both Noel and Lydia travelled first now, in spite of the rise in prices, simply as an insurance against more fatigue than was really necessary.

Lydia clung to her Noel for a second and then made way for her daughter, who flung herself on him with abandonment.

"Gently, darling," said Noel. "I am not so young as I was."

"Oh, father, I'm going to do arithmetic in French," said Lavinia. "It's *much* easier."

"I can't think what you are talking about, my love," said Noel.

"It was only an idea of mine," said Lydia. "I'll tell you about it later," and she put her arm through his and they went out of the station. Lord and Lady Pomfret, who must have come down by the same train, were outside, waiting for their car. Inevitably the Coronation was mentioned.

"I suppose you are going," said Lydia with the very slightest touch of envy.

"Yes, we are," said Lady Pomfret. "I wish in a way we weren't. I shall love it, but it is terribly long and tiring for Gillie. We are spending the night with an aunt of his who most conveniently lives in Smith Street, near that peculiar church with its legs in the air, so we shall only have a very short walk. I have found quite wonderful plastic raincapes for us. They are quite transparent and cover us from head to foot and fold up as small as a French roll."

"Or a marshal's baton," said Noel, at which Lady Pomfret smiled and Noel felt, as so many of her friends felt, that the countess's life was so full of anxieties for her husband and of public-spirited work in and for the county, that her real self sometimes took flight into some fastness of its own, leaving a kind smile as a mask to protect it.

"Then we come down early next morning for the festivities here," she went on. "And you are doing all sorts of good works, I am sure."

"Lydia is," said Noel. "I leave everything to her."

"Yes, one does," said Lady Pomfret, partly to herself. "Perhaps you will come and dine with us soon," and then the car came up and the Pomfrets went away. Lydia brought her car up, Lavinia got into the back, and Noel drove.

"You drive better than I do," he had once said to Lydia, "but I like driving better than you do," and Lydia only smiled, for she drove by nature and could equally by nature relax as the driven; rare gifts in the same person.

"Any news?" said Noel, once they were through Barchester.

"Only Mrs. Paxon and Miss Hopgood's Aunt," said Lydia. "They came like a kind of deputation to ask me to be chairman of the Coronation Committee in Northbridge."

"So of course you said yes," said Noel.

"Of course I *had* to say yes," said Lydia. "Mrs. Villars is a good deal older than I am and full of parish work to start with. I don't see how I could back out. Anyway I thought I might ask Jessica if she and Aubrey would be angels and help us. I know they'd love to be at the Coronation if they were Dukes or something and they would do it beautifully, but as they can't I expect they'll be at Winter Overcotes with her people."

Noel said a very good idea and in his voice there was no trace of self-consciousness, much to his Lydia's relief, who in her pelicanish way would almost rather have seen him dally with some charmer again than be embarrassed by the memory of how Jessica had made him repent his inconsiderate and quite unimportant flirtation with pretty Mrs. Arbuthnot, now Mrs. Francis Brandon.

Lavinia went up to the nursery, where her younger brother,

Harry, and her still younger sister, Jessica, were having their tea, and her parents were left in peace.

"And now, what does Lavinia mean by doing arithmetic in French?" said Noel, so Lydia told him about her not very serious suggestion that Lavinia should be coached in mathematics by Mlle Larousse. To her pleasure, Noel said he thought it quite a good plan and they must think about sending her to Paris, or Grenoble, or somewhere when she left school, to learn French properly and get to understand good cooking.

"Whenever I see Pomfret," he added, switching off to other thoughts, "I feel how lucky I am to be as well as I am. He was lunching at the club with someone on Wednesday and I thought he looked quite grey with fatigue. But he was lunching with old Dodder," which was the fine Anglo-Saxon name of a well-known Law Lord, "which would easily account for it. By the way, my love, Dodder told me something. I don't know whether you will like it or not."

"If you do, I will," said Lydia.

"It's a Coronation Knighthood," said Noel. "This was unofficial, of course. What do you think?"

"What do *you* think?" said Lydia.

"If I am a career man, and I have been accused of it," said Noel rather sententiously, "it will be a good mark in my career. Otherwise I don't mind. I shall be expected to tip more highly. On the other hand I understand that it is much easier to reserve a table at a restaurant if one has a title. I also have a feeling that under a new young Queen one should not bandy words with one's sovereign. What do you think?"

"Of course if not to take it would be being a Traitor," said Lydia, just as Lydia Keith might have said it when Noel first came to her parents' house and she was a hoyden schoolgirl, "you must take it at once. I suppose I'll have to be Lady Merton," she added.

"Yes, you will," said Noel, looking at her with amused lovingness. "You'll get used to it, you know. I admit that with the wholesale distribution of honours a knighthood is not uncommon now. I might even become a Law Lord in time."

"Oh dear, would I be a lady then?" said Lydia.

"You would, my love," said Noel. "In Scotland there was an excellent custom by which only the husband got the title with a law peerage, while his wife remained Mrs. and the children plain commoners. Here, now, the wife is a Lady and the children are Honourables, but the title does not pass to any son. Probably it will in the next generation. In fact I look forward —I mean prophetically, not with pleasure—to a time when one will be offered plain Mister as a mark of honour, owing to the appalling spread of titles."

Lydia was not quite sure whether he was serious or not and her husband looked at her very affectionately, for he always found her gravity both charming and amusing.

"But not a word, my love," he said. "I only wanted to warn you, in case I suddenly came down to breakfast Sir Noel. Tell me some more about the Northbridge doings."

Lydia said there was not very much to say. The Northbridge people seemed to want her for the Coronation Committee, so she thought she had better.

"Don't let them kill you, my darling," said Noel, who did not forget the summer when Lydia had measles and been really ill, and though her measles had nothing to do with his silly and short-lived infatuation for pretty Mrs. Arbuthnot, he would never stop feeling guilty. But his good sense and his love had told him that to keep silent was the only gentlemanly thing he could do. And he had done it; with what remorse for having wounded his Lydia only he would ever know.

Later in the evening Mrs. Villars rang up and asked them if
they would dine at the Rectory to talk about Coronation plans,
and the following Friday was fixed.

"And now, my dearest love," said the eminent Q.C., "don't
rush your fences. I cannot have you killing yourself again. It
was quite bad enough in the war, but there was a reason for it
then and there weren't any children."

"It wasn't my fault, really," said Lydia, looking away. For
in the early years of the war, while she was working in a hospital and Noel was abroad with the army, there had been a
hope which had never come to fruition; a loss for which Lydia
had always blamed herself, though no other person would or
could have blamed her.

"My dearest girl," said Noel, deeply distressed. "I never
thought of any blame. You were only doing your job too con-
scientiously, as you always do and always will. But please don't
let Northbridge over-persuade you."

Lydia came and rubbed her cheek against his shoulder and
said she would be sensible. And Noel also determined to have
a word with Mrs. Villars.

Accordingly, next Friday they drove over to the Rectory,
where they found the Rector and Mrs. Villars and a man unknown to them.

"You haven't met Mr. Holden, I think," said Mrs. Villars.
"He was billeted here in the war. He was a lieutenant then,
but really he is in Adrian Coates's publishing business. He let
me read a wonderful novel about India in typescript when
he had influenza and we both laughed till we felt ill. Was it
ever published, Mr. Holden?"

"Coates wouldn't take it," said Mr. Holden, "but someone
who was just starting took it and it had an enormous success.
It has just been filmed. There's a wonderful part where there

is a flashback to where the Colonel's wife recognizes in Major Prendergast—who was a rotter anyway and doped the subaltern's wife's husband to prevent him playing in a polo match—the man who had wronged her on a long, scented voyage across tropical seas in her youth. Glamora Tudor as the subaltern's wife who goes at night in pink chiffon pyjamas to get compromising letters about another woman from a Rajah was splendid. The Rajah had left the letter with his Prime Minister, who was a Ptarn—"

"A what?" said Noel.

"Well, a Paythan, then," said Mr. Holden. "It's one of those words I never say aloud. But most luckily the Colonel's wife, who was a Mutiny grandbaby, knew that her grandparents had been murdered by the P.M.'s family and shot him. So the subaltern's wife took his place—I mean her husband's place, not the P.M.'s—in the polo match on account of her husband being doped, and of course no one knew till her cap fell off and her golden curls fell on her shoulders, but by that time she had got the Cup from the Viceroy. You ought to have seen it."

The whole company made a vow to see it as soon as possible if it came to the Barchester Odeon.

"I didn't try to get another woman," said Mrs. Villars. "Not that I am an anti-feminist, because I think that on the whole women are more reliable than men. But somehow an odd man is easier to deal with. And we used to know Mr. Holden very well."

"And very kind Mrs. Villars was to me when I was being the licentious soldiery here," said Mr. Holden. But he did not add—or perhaps he had forgotten—that he had chosen to imagine a Platonic passion for his hostess, which had made him a great bore. Not that his passion had manifested itself before company, but he was far too apt to hover about her with cushions, and on the day when he left the Rectory had most annoyingly put her at a disadvantage when she was resting on the drawing-room sofa by coming to say good-bye, which he did at such length and with such devotion that she would have had the giggles if she had not been so tired. However, Mr. Holden did not allude to this, and as Lydia gathered during the course of the evening that he was married with three children, we cannot think that his life was seared and ruined.

"There was a good deal to be said for the war," said Mr. Villars thoughtfully. "One made so many friends that one would never have met under normal conditions."

"But after the war one often wished one hadn't made them," said Mrs. Villars. "Especially in a little place like Northbridge. I am now committed for life to being a friend of Miss Hopgood's Aunt, and even worse—for Miss Hopgood's Aunt is very intelligent though overpowering—Mrs. Dunsford and her daughter at Hovis House."

"You *will* do it, Verena," said her husband, with a kind of affectionate resignation.

"And then Gregory has to save me, which he always does," said Mrs. Villars.

"Dinner is served, madam," said Foster, the tyrant parlourmaid of the Rectory, who still kept up the standard of living in a most exhausting way.

"I cannot tell you how delightful it is to be here again," said Mr. Holden, as he took his seat, but this announcement was marred by the Rector saying: "Benedictus, benedicat; what were you saying, Holden?"

"Oh, only how nice it was to be here again," said Mr. Holden, feeling as if he had stolen the Communion plate.

"We certainly had some pleasant incidents during the war," said Mr. Villars, now again an ordinary person and a very agreeable one. "Do you remember, Holden, the evening we were discussing false teeth and those ridiculous Air Raid instructions about how people with false teeth ought to put a piece of rubber between their teeth and lie on their stomachs with their hands lightly clasped behind their heads?"

"*So* like the official world," said Mr. Holden, and then he and Mr. Villars fell into wartime reminiscences. Noel, who had been at Dunkirk and through a good deal of the war before being transferred to Intelligence in England, preferred to exchange local gossip with Mrs. Villars, while Lydia listened. Not that she felt out of it, but her nature was a silent one and she could sit quietly while people talked without feeling out of things herself or making other people feel embarrassed.

The dinner was short and good. Then Mrs. Villars took Lydia away with her.

"Tell me, my dear," said Mrs. Villars, "what I can do for you."

Lydia, with a grateful heart, said pretty well anything.

"What I really want to know," she added, "is exactly where you stop and I take over. I know you really ought to be the chairman, but Mrs. Paxon said you wouldn't."

"It's more couldn't," said Mrs. Villars. "I have a fair amount of committee work in any case and Gregory says I mustn't take on any more. What I would really like, very much, is to be a Yes Man on your committee. I can always get Mrs. Paxon to agree with me and Miss Pemberton, and I don't think the others will give much trouble. Miss Hopgood's Aunt is always on my side. She says committees are too difficult compared with the great silent spaces of the night sky, and she likes to have her mind made up for her."

"But I thought she was frightfully clever," said Lydia.

Mrs. Villars said she was, as far as anyone in Northbridge knew, a really good amateur astronomer, but that did not necessarily make her good on committees. "I have asked Miss Pemberton and her lodger, Mr. Downing, to come in for

coffee," she went on. "She is undertaking the historical episodes for our evening entertainment. I think you will find
that she and Mrs. Paxon will run everything, which will save
you a lot of trouble. I wish we had Mrs. Turner here—I don't
think you knew her—but she went to live near a married niece
in Norfolk."

"I really feel rather ashamed of not knowing such a lot of
people, considering how near Northbridge we live, but I used
to see Mrs. Turner at the Communal Kitchen at the beginning
of the war," said Lydia. "Noel is in town all week and I usually
go up for a night or two, and there are the children and the
cows and—"

"No need to excuse yourself, my dear," said Mrs. Villars.
"A husband like yours is a one-woman job. Those husbands
with public positions! Gregory is much the same. There
couldn't be a better and more useful hard-working clergyman,
but he needs me all the time in the background. That's why
I have never done as much as some clergy-wives. And I had a
surfeit of parents and people when he was a schoolmaster."

Lydia did not quite follow Mrs. Villars's reasoning, but she
felt much relieved, for she did not wish to be pushed into coming the Squire's Lady over the Rector's wife. Foster, with her
usual air of suspicious contempt for visitors, brought in Miss
Pemberton and Mr. Downing.

"How nice of you to come," said Mrs. Villars. "And here is
Mrs. Noel Merton, who is to be our Coronation Committee
chairman. Gregory and Mr. Merton are still in the dining-
room, Mr. Downing, with Mr. Holden, if you would like to
join them."

"You can join the gentlemen if you wish, Harold," said Miss
Pemberton, thus effectually stymying any such wish that her
lodger might have felt. "And now, Mrs. Merton, how can I
help you?" which words from a well-known Provençal scholar,

dressed in what looked like sacking dyed to a dirty green, shapeless from top to bottom, made Lydia feel younger than ever.

"It's really how can I help *you*—if I can," said Lydia.

"Good," said Miss Pemberton. "We shall get on together. We need help. Mrs. Villars is a tower of strength, but her health is far from good. Mrs. Paxon is full of enthusiasm and extremely willing, but with no power of concentration. I am willing to organize to the best of my power, but I cannot get about as I used to and have no car, and Mr. Downing, who lives with me at Punshions, is admirably qualified to superintend a Court of Love in Provence, but no more."

"I'm afraid I really don't know anything—I mean not anything special," said Lydia, "except Red Cross nursing."

"All the better," said Miss Pemberton. "The only thing you need to know is your own mind. Once that is made up, stick to it. If I may offer advice, I should say Follow Mrs. Paxon. She has the temperature of the town—the norm. I am organizing some historical episodes for the Evening Entertainment in the Village Hall. And we might add a Red Cross Tableau somewhere. But we will see. Mrs. Paxon was extremely good as a hysteria case when we had an A.R.P. casualty practice during the war. She used to act with the South Wembley Amateur Dramatic before she was married. Harold!" and she beckoned to her lodger, who at that moment came into the room with the men, "Mrs. Merton is organizing a Red Cross Tableau for the Entertainment. You can be a stretcher-bearer."

Mr. Downing looked depressed.

"Or the body, if you prefer," said his Egeria kindly. "You can have your head bandaged, on a stretcher."

"Very well, Ianthe," said Mr. Downing. "But you know how sick I feel in anything unsteady."

"It is a Tableau," said Miss Pemberton, with awful clarity.

"The whole point is that the scene should be static. Mrs. Merton will see to that," at which point Lydia felt she would resign the whole thing for sixpence. But one cannot.

There was a little more talk about the Coronation celebrations, the chief point of interest being Effie Bunce, daughter of old Bunce at the ferry. The Bunce family were a pure Anglo-Saxon survival, celebrated for never changing any of their clothes by day or by night. Their two daughters had appreciably increased the population of the county without any marriage lines, Effie being perhaps the best (or the worst, as you choose to look at it) of the lot but, as such ladies often are, of a very obliging disposition towards the whole human race and on the whole very kind to Miss Pemberton. Nor was her sister Ruby, at present working at Northbridge Manor, behind her in general benevolence to anything in trousers. They were both very tolerant of their employers and were even beginning to feel—or so Mrs. Villars thought—that it was time for them to settle down.

The point in question at the moment was whether Effie and Ruby Bunce would be suitable for parts in the Red Cross Tableau, which was to include, as far as possible, all nations and creeds. Lydia rather wondered why such a fuss was made about them, but the reason was made abundantly clear when Miss Pemberton, speaking as Effie's employer with authority, said June would be impossible. After a moment's silence everyone realized the implication. No one could keep from laughing, and we may add that the Misses Bunce would have laughed more heartily than any of them had they been present and probably offered in their simple way to be emergency maternity cases. Then Noel and Lydia said good-bye and went away.

"Well, that is that," said Noel as they drove home. "One does see life at Northbridge. The Law Courts are nothing to it. But do not let them kill you, my dearest love," to which Lydia replied that Mrs. Villars and Miss Pemberton wouldn't let them; in which we think she was right.

Before they went to bed they looked into the night nursery. Harry and Jessica were past the plunge of plummet in seas that not their loving parents (nor even Nurse) could sound. In the little bedroom to which she had lately been promoted, Lavinia was neatly and tidily asleep. Her parents tiptoed out again.

"And why anyone wants to bother Lavinia to do arithmetic, I don't know," said Noel, who had a weakness for his firstborn.

"Never mind, darling," said Lydia when they had shut the door. "She shall marry quite young, someone very nice, nearly as nice as you are, very rich, and have a secretary to do her accounts for her. Only it must be someone down here. I don't want her to go to London."

"On the whole I agree with you, my love," said Noel. "London is my livelihood and I like every moment of it. But then I know I can get the afternoon train to Barchester and be with you for the long week-end," which touched Lydia so much that she quickly changed the subject to the heifer of whose future offspring Mr. Wickham had high hopes, and so to bed.

CHAPTER 2

IT WOULD be idle to deny that when Lydia had a letter from Lady Pomfret asking if they would dine at Pomfret Towers on Saturday week, she felt slightly uplifted. And we think she was right. For though our aristocracy is extensive and peculiar, it is, in its better parts, a true aristocracy not only of blood but of the tradition of service, and Barsetshire was lucky in having such families as the Omniums and the Pomfrets, not to speak of the Luftons in their quiet way and even the Bonds, who in the second generation of the title were doing their duty very well. Of the Nortons we will not speak, for the present baron is always known as young Lord Norton though his father died a good many years ago, which, as Lucy Adams so truly remarked, just shows; while his widowed mother is simply known as the Dreadful Dowager.

The glory and grandeur of Pomfret Towers was now, through two wars and crippling taxation, little more than a memory. The Pomfrets could still just manage to live in part of the huge pile and to do their duty by the people on the estate, though little thanks they got for it. The West Barsetshire Hunt still met at the Towers at least once in the season, and Lady Pomfret, who as Sally Wicklow, the estate agent's sister, had the best hands in the county, still did some hacking and usually attended the Meet, though she had given up serious hunting. In the stables where at least a dozen hunters used to live, with the straw along the front of their stalls freshly plaited and woven every day and each horse's name emblazoned above its stall, there were now only her ladyship's mare, his lordship's horse for riding about the estate, and the three children's ponies.

No longer did big week-end parties drive in front of the Towers (built by the sixth Earl of Pomfret in pious imitation of St. Pancras station), up the immense ramp, and enter by the majestic portico. The family now lived at the far end of the gigantic pile in what used to be the apartments of the upper servants, while the great hall and the big reception rooms were sheeted and unfriendly. So Noel and Lydia went by the tradesmen's drive to the west wing and drew up at what used to be the entrance to the housekeeper's apartments.

The door was opened by a middle-aged woman, obviously one who had been in good service at the Towers or elsewhere. Lydia had come, according to post-war English usage, in a light woollen dress and for further security had brought a fur with her.

"I don't think you will need a fur, madam," said the attendant. "We have the central heating now," and indeed the Mertons were conscious of a heavenly feeling of all-pervasive warmth, very rare now except in the cottages where the one living-room is still gloriously stuffy.

But Lydia, though grateful for the advice, said she would keep it just in case, so the attendant took them along a passage to what used to be the housekeeper's room, now Lady Pomfret's sitting-room, overlooking one end of the formal Italian garden, where Lady Pomfret, also in a woollen dress but not with a fur, welcomed them.

"Miss Merriman you do know, I think," said Lady Pomfret to her guests, and indeed there were few people in West Barsetshire who did not know Miss Merriman, secretary and friend for some years to the former Countess of Pomfret, then secretary, friend, and almost guardian of Lady Emily Leslie, old Lord Pomfret's sister, in her last years, and now again at the Towers, at her task of guarding the family to whom her devotion had so long been given. There was hardly a day in the year when Lord or Lady Pomfret would not say, or think, What *should* we do without Merry; and we believe that Miss Merriman would have faded and pined if she could no longer be the quiet, efficient helper of the class whom it was her life's work to aid and shelter.

A tall, anxious-looking boy then came in. Too tall for his strength, was Lydia's compassionate thought.

"This is Ludovic," said Lady Pomfret. "We have him at home for the week-end, which is very nice. And I have Emily at home too for her half-term holiday. Where is Emily, darling?"

"She was down in the stables and is trying to get clean," said young Lord Mellings, shaking hands with a tired courteous manner so like his father's that Lydia could have laughed and cried. "Nurse said she couldn't come in to dinner with hands like that and company coming and all. Nurse," he added with a manner so like his father's that Noel almost laughed aloud, "was right, as she always is whether she is or isn't."

Noel, observing the scene as an outsider, thought how strong the likeness was between Lord Pomfret and his heir, and how different both were from the regular Pomfret stock. But when Lady Emily Foster, aged about fourteen, came banging into the room with an air of complete self-assurance, he saw that the Pomfret blood was running true to type in one of the family at least.

"Mother," said Lady Emily, "there's a badger down by Hamaker's Spinney and they are going to dig him out on Monday. Can I go and help? I told them it must be in the morning because of having to go back to school in the afternoon, what a bore, and Jasper is coming."

Miss Merriman thought, as she had thought a thousand times, how much Emily resembled the late Lord Pomfret, and how his lordship would have rejoiced over a Foster so exactly after his own likeness; and quite probably taught her to play first-class bridge as well as riding and estate work.

Lady Pomfret looked towards her husband. It was apparent to her that, as often happened, he was a prey to indecision. Not that his views—and his principles, if we may use so old-fashioned a word—were not strong, but even the best mind, if engaged in perpetual defensive warfare against poor health, cannot always be up to the mark. And she had for some time realized, without quite knowing how to prevent it, that this was going to make his relationship with his children more difficult as they got older.

"Perhaps," said Miss Merriman quietly, "Mr. Wicklow would be able to help us. I think I hear him," and in came the estate agent, Roddy Wicklow, Lady Pomfret's brother. In the clamour that greeted his arrival, for he was much loved by the family, Miss Merriman said quietly to Emily: "Don't bother your father now. I will get Mr. Wicklow to settle it all."

"Thanks most awfully, Merry," said Emily. "And, I say, tell Uncle Roddy Ludo doesn't want to come. He does so hate anything to do with animals being killed. I can't think why and anyway badgers are a nuisance, but there it is."

Miss Merriman said she would do her best.

"It is such a pity Roddy's wife can't come," said Lady Pomfret to Lydia, "but one of the children is measling. Alice is the daughter of Mr. Barton, the architect, and her mother writes those interesting historical novels about Italy and Popes and Cardinals."

"It's her brother who married the Archdeacon's daughter over Plumstead way, isn't it?" said Lydia. "We met them at the Deanery and liked them so much," and then Lady Pomfret said they might as well have dinner and led the way to the dining-room, the others drifting after them.

"This was the Upper Housemaids' Room," said Lady Pomfret to Noel when the company were seated; not without words between Lord Mellings and Emily Foster, who had both wanted to sit next to Uncle Roddy but had to sit on the opposite side of the table and found they had to sit together, which was even more degrading. "It was extremely lucky that my husband came into the title when he did, because there was still some money then and we had the servants' quarters completely altered and improved. There wasn't a single bathroom in this wing."

"But we must be fair to Uncle Giles," said Lord Pomfret across the table. "There was only one bathroom in our part of the house either, and it was a bedroom divided with partitions that didn't go up to the ceiling, highly embarrassing, and only the men used it as a rule. Hip baths for the rest."

"You've forgotten the bedroom that had a large bath in it," said Roddy Wicklow. "Alice had it the first time she stayed here. It was a kind of sarcophagus with steps up to it and had a screen in front of it in the daytime, and all the bottom of the bath under the taps was brown because of the water."

"Poor Alice," said Lord Pomfret with what for him was almost a hearty laugh. "I have never seen anyone look so frightened as she did the first time she came here. I remember finding her in the passage, nearly crying, because her shoes hadn't been brought up and she was afraid to ring the bell more than once."

"What did you do, darling?" said Lady Pomfret.

"I called down the stairs," said his lordship. "And when no one answered I dropped a great lump of coal down the well— it was the winding staircase in the northeast corner—and yelled for Miss Barton's shoes, and Finch came rushing up out of his boothole three steps at a time. I think it was the first time I had ever thrown my weight about."

"Father," said Emily, "can I throw a lump of coal down the stairs? I'd love to hear it crunch at the bottom."

Lord Pomfret looked at his daughter.

"Certainly," he said. "But first you will have to carry the coal up to the top yourself. They used to keep a large box on the landing to refill the bedroom coal scuttles then. And, what is more, you will have to clear up the mess downstairs afterwards."

"Thanks awfully, father," said Emily. "Ludo can help me and then we can drop quite a lot," but if she hoped to rouse her father by this slight impertinence she had met her match, as Lord Pomfret was already talking to Lydia and paid no attention to her at all.

Lady Pomfret had wondered whether Mrs. Noel Merton's rather downright manner would put her husband off, but to her great pleasure they were soon talking very comfortably.

"You were Miss Keith, I think," Lord Pomfret said. "Your brother's firm handle any legal matters about the estate, and he told me his sister had married a barrister," and the ice being broken, they got on very well, though if Lady Pomfret had heard what they were talking about she would have been surprised. But she was devoting the attention of a good hostess to Noel.

"You live at Northbridge, don't you, on that little line from Barchester?" said Lord Pomfret. "I have been on it once or twice and enjoyed it immensely. It reminded me of a film I saw —but I daresay you don't go to films."

"It depends," said Lydia. "The Barchester Odeon does have such ghastly ones. But that little cinema in Barchester, the one in Barley Street, had a heavenly one last autumn about trains. *The Titfield Thunderbolt* it was called, and I think some of it *must* have been filmed in Barsetshire, it looked so real."

"I am so glad you liked it," said Lord Pomfret, with unusual animation. "Sally and I went to it quite by chance because we had to fill up time between some meetings, and we simply adored it. I went again the next two days, and then it was off and I couldn't find out where it had gone. It was so nostalgic that I nearly cried."

"I know," said Lydia, her eyes shining at the remembrance. "It was everything that England has lost. All the freedom and people doing things for themselves and not letting officials badger them. It nearly made me cry too. My brother Colin saw it in London and he said only England could produce a film like that, because he is a barrister and knows a terrific amount about railway law. I don't know why railways have to have different laws from other people," said Lydia meditatively, "but Colin knows all about it."

"Then is your brother the Colin Keith who edited *Lemon on Running Powers?*" said Lord Pomfret, showing a depth of feeling that Lydia had not suspected. "I always loved railways, and if I hadn't come into the place when Uncle Giles died, I should have liked to be one of those men who walk up and down beside the train banging bits of it with a heavy bit of metal. I never knew why they did it, but it fascinated me. I keep your brother's book in my dressing-room."

Lydia's approval was always won by anyone who liked her dear Colin. The ice was broken and she and her host talked very comfortably about all sorts of things, and he told her how his eldest son had hated his prep school but seemed really happy at Eton and didn't care much for riding, and how Emily knew nearly as much about cows as her cousin Emmy Grantly, who helped Martin Leslie with the famous Rushwater herd, and how nothing could keep Giles off anything with four legs. But as Ludovic and Emily were present he was

careful to lower his voice, though the noise made by Emily and
her uncle Roddy Wicklow on the subject of the badger made
conversation quite safe. Lydia, whose consideration for other
people's feelings had deepened as she grew older, felt a good
deal of sympathy for Ludovic, for though she was fearless by
nature, she had never felt really happy with horses except
those on the roundabout that visited the local flower shows.
She asked how old Ludovic was. Rising sixteen, said his father,
and it would be military service before they knew where they
were, and he looked so dispirited for a moment that Lydia's
kind heart was touched, though she did remind herself that it
was not the military service that Lord Pomfret minded, but the
fact that his eldest child was already so old. Then it was time to
change partners and Lydia turned to Roddy Wicklow. Roddy,
who had a methodical mind, had taken care to be well briefed
on the Mertons before he came to dinner. To that end he had
caught Mr. Wickham, the Mertons' agent, in the County
Club, and over several beers he had got all he wanted to know.
Any employer of Wickham's was, he felt, entitled to respect.
That Merton was a Q.C. he accepted, though without much
interest; but Merton as the owner of a first-class dairy herd was
a man to be considered, and therefore his wife also. Lydia
had never really been cow-minded and made no bones about
saying so, but they quickly discovered common ground in
measles.

"Do tell me about the children," said Lydia. "How many
have you?"

Roddy said there were three. Guy and Phoebe and Alice.

"And how many are measling?" said Lydia.

"Alice and Phoebe at the moment," said Roddy, "but we
hope Guy will get it too, because he is going to boarding school
next September and we'd like to get it over. Luckily we have
an elderly Nanny, whose brother used to be butler at the Tow-

ers, but it means a good deal of work for my wife too. That's
why she didn't come. Have your family got through the measle
stage, Mrs. Merton?"

"Lavinia has, that's the eldest," said Lydia, "and what was so
silly was that I got it too. And, even sillier, Harry—that's the
next eldest—didn't get it. My youngest, Jessica, wasn't born
then, so of course she couldn't. It does save a lot of trouble to
have it together and I think you are very sensible to let them."

"My great-grandmother," said Roddy Wicklow, "had ten
children, of all ages—"

"Of course they *couldn't* all have been one age," said Lydia,
not carping, but zealous for the truth.

"I quite agree," said Roddy, amused by Mrs. Merton's downright manner. "I mean she had ten children, each one older
than the other. No, I don't mean that," he added hastily, seeing the light of argument in that handsome Mrs. Merton's
eye. "I mean—well, anyway she had ten children, all under
fifteen I think it was, and when one of them got measles she
shut them all up together in the nursery quarters to save
trouble."

Lydia, much interested, said she had heard of people doing
that but never knew it was true. And what happened? she
asked.

"Too, too mortifying, as Gillie's cousin Clarissa Graham
used to say," said Roddy Wicklow, "Clarissa Belton that is
now. Half of them got it and two of that half died; and the
other half didn't get it and they all had it again later at different times. At least it was another sort. German measles, I
think. But she had an eleventh baby afterwards. That's why
none of us have much money."

"You mean there were so many people for it to be divided
among," said Lydia, who as we know liked to get things clear.

"That's it," said Roddy. "And it mattered a good deal then.

because people were allowed to keep their money when they died."

Lydia said seriously, If you were dead you couldn't.

"You are laughing at me, Mrs. Merton," said Roddy Wicklow, though with the utmost good-nature. "I never could explain properly, except things about hunting and farming and the estate."

"I'm sorry," said Lydia. "I only meant *You Can't Take It With You*—was that a film or a story?"

Roddy said it sounded like a film, but she was right.

"And people are always trying to find a way of doing it and the Government gets in first every time. I am sure Mr. Churchill doesn't *want* to, but after the way They muddled everything I suppose he has to," said Lydia, loyal to our great statesman.

Roddy said he was afraid that was only too true and getting truer every day.

"Not even when it is gold," said Lydia, "like Browning. He knew nearly everything."

"I say, Mrs. Merton, I'm not a very literary chap," said Roddy, amused by Lydia's earnestness and also perplexed. "Where on earth does Browning come in?"

"Oh, it's a poem called a Legend of Something-or-other," said Lydia, "about a girl who was very rich and had masses of very beautiful golden hair and she died and after she was buried they couldn't find the money anywhere and years afterwards they were excavating or restoring or something in the church and managed to break open her coffin by mistake. Of course she was pretty well mouldered by then, but her hair wasn't and they found all her gold in the coffin under her long hair, which just shows," though by that time she was not quite sure if she knew what she meant, so far does speech fall short of thought.

"I say, I didn't know that one," said Roddy. "I like Browning, but only the easy bits, the short ones. I expect Alice will know it, she reads everything, bless her. I did have a go at one of the long ones when I was younger and had more time, but it never got me anywhere."

"You needn't try," said Lydia kindly. "One just can, or one can't. I can't either, at least the long ones. I still adore the short ones. Do tell me more about your children, Mr. Wicklow," upon which Roddy, nothing loath, expatiated with the false modesty of a doting parent upon the virtues of his offspring and how they all took to a pony with ease and address practically from birth, so that Lydia was able peacefully not to listen and to look at the rest of the table. Her host was talking to his daughter, very comfortably she thought, and Lady Pomfret with her tall elder son. Noel appeared to be deeply interested in what Miss Merriman was telling him, but Lydia knew very well how the consummate actor that is in most good lawyers gives them a shallow facility in seeming to listen when they are thinking of something else; or even, which is a subtle form of bad manners common to most of us, thinking far more about what one is going to say next oneself than what one's partner is saying to one. And she determined in her own mind that Lady Pomfret would do this very well, and indeed it is one of the arts that anyone in a semi-public position does well to cultivate.

"I say, Uncle Roddy," said Emily across the table in the lull that sometimes breaks out at the most easy and comfortable parties.

"You always do," said her uncle. "You are nearly as bad as Mrs. Adams with her I'll Tell You What."

"It's about the badger," said Emily, who, though very kind-hearted, inherited to the full the fine want of consideration for others which cropped up in every generation of the Pomfret line. "They are going to dig him out on Monday, down near Hamaker's Spinney. Do tell them it *must* be in the morning, because I have to go back to school in the afternoon. I think a half-term holiday is absolutely mouldy if one has to be back by Monday evening. Giles wants to come frightfully too, and we hardly ever get our half-terms together. I can't think why school's don't think a bit more."

Disregarding his niece's divagations into the general silliness of schools, Roddy, who was one of the very rare people that can think before they speak, said nothing for a moment. During that moment all the party became silent (as Virgil has put it far better than I can) and listened to hear what would happen. But unlike the pious Æneas (and why pious, as Miss Lydia Keith had rebelliously remarked aloud in class while Miss Pettinger, herself a mean Latin scholar, was endeavouring to drag the Upper Fifth through part of the second book of the *Æneid*, unless it was because he let his wife get killed or burnt or something so that he could look after his father, who any-way was no use and had to be carried pick-a-back, and prom-ised to marry Dido and took heaps of gold and things from her and let her pay for repairing his ships and then went away overnight so that she killed herself, she couldn't possibly think; upon which Miss Pettinger had given her a Conduct Mark, which was the worst the school could do), Roddy did not speak at great length in hexameters and said he didn't see why not and he would think about it.

"And if you and Giles go and dig out the badger, that will give Ludo a little peace," he said, looking kindly at his niece. "You've got an essay to do, haven't you, Ludo?"

We are not quite sure whether Lord Mellings quite realized his uncle's deliberate kindness, for he was a slow thinker and found it difficult to make his feelings clear to himself, but such a light of relief shone in his sad anxious eyes, so like his father's, so unlike the rest of the family, that Roddy felt he had done the right thing. To Lydia, sitting opposite young Lord Mellings, his relief at not having to dig out badgers was equally apparent, and she looked at Roddy Wicklow with considerable respect.

"Ludo is so dreadfully like me," said Lord Pomfret to Lydia, under cover of Emily's loud description of exactly how the badger was to be evicted from his basement flat. "I simply *cannot* enjoy sport. I know it is all wrong, but I can't. You see, I was never really meant to be Lord Pomfret. My uncle had a son, but he was killed ever so long ago in India, and my father was the next heir and Uncle Giles loathed him. My father loathed Uncle Giles too, so I never saw him till I was quite grown up and he sent for me to stay at the Towers. I must say I was terrified of it all, but Sally was there on a visit and she was such a help and she said she would marry me. If it weren't for her, I could never have managed this job. Emily and Giles are pure Pomfret and will bang their way through everything, but Mellings—" and his melancholy eyes rested for a moment upon his heir who did not want to see a badger dug out of its hole. "It is going to be so hard for him. I wish you would have a talk with him after dinner, Mrs. Merton. You would like him."

Lydia, who felt compassion for father and son, said she would like very much to have a talk with Ludovic—it was Ludovic, wasn't it?—at which moment her host interrupted to say that the name was entirely the Dowager Lady Lufton's fault because she was Ludo's godmother and the name ran in the Lufton family and he sometimes wondered if he had been weak about it.

"What would *you* have called him then?" Lydia asked.

"That," said Lord Pomfret, with his pleasant tired smile, "is exactly what I hoped you wouldn't ask. I am Giles, called

Gillie in the family. My old uncle was Giles. In fact they were mostly Giles ever since the twelfth century. I know that doesn't sound true," he added apologetically, "but it is. We are really quite an old family as families go. There was a castle more or less where this house is now, in the thirteen-hundreds. This horror was built by my great-uncle, the sixth Earl, and I hope he is sorry now."

"Is it *very* awful?" Lydia asked. "I mean, I've seen the outside and it's pretty ghastly, but wasn't it nice inside?"

"Nice is an overstatement," said Lord Pomfret. "The old agent, Mr. Hoare—who, thank goodness, retired before Uncle Giles died, as it would have been impossible to work with him —said he had calculated that each footman could easily walk ten miles a day in the normal course of his work. To get from the kitchen to the dining-room meant a dark passage about fifty yards long with two sharp corners, a flight of stone steps, and then the serving-room. But they always had plenty of servants, and the food was always hot."

"And now, the easier you try to make it, the fewer you get," said Lydia. "Still, this part of the Towers is very nice and so warm."

"It is all Sally's doing," said Lord Pomfret, looking with affection at his wife. "She and Roddy between them made the old servants' wing into this really very comfortable house."

Lydia said, rather wistfully, that she would like to have seen the Towers all the same, in the days of its glory.

"I wish you would come and see it by daylight," said Lord Pomfret. "If you would care to, I would get Sally to arrange it. It is so ghastly that it is really worth seeing. Perhaps you could come to lunch one day when the weather is a little better. The Italian garden is at its best when the hedges have their spring green. We still have a few old hedgers and ditchers about the place," and then Lady Pomfret collected Lydia's eye and took her ladies back to the drawing-room, though Emily, fearful lest the badger plan might be interfered with, firmly stayed with the men.

Hardly had Lady Pomfret, Lydia, and Miss Merriman begun to have a really sensible talk about the cost of a marquee for the Coronation Feast that the Towers was giving when the door opened and young Lord Mellings's tall, rather lanky form brought itself diffidently into the room.

"Can I come in, mother?" he said. "Emily and Uncle Roddy are off about the badger again and father is talking politics with Mr. Merton."

"Of course, darling," said his mother, with a fleeting look at Lydia which, being rightly interpreted, meant: "I know this is out of order, but poor Ludo does so hate anything to do with shooting or trapping and he is a defenceless creature and I hope you won't mind." Lydia guessed what was happening and smiled at Lady Pomfret, who thought she had seldom seen a more handsome woman than Mrs. Merton, and one who added kindness and understanding to her good looks.

"Oh, mother," said Ludovic, standing before the fire, looking, Lydia felt, so pitifully like his father, "Giles said would you come and see him in the nursery after dinner and bring Mrs. Merton with you. He wants to see her. I'll stay with Merry. May I, Merry?"

Miss Merriman wondered for a moment if she ought to push him back to the dining-room, his rightful place, but she could not, for in Ludovic she saw, so very clearly, the young Mr. Foster who had come to the Towers on approval, as it were, some seventeen years ago; the young heir, accepted as a duty by his uncle and aunt, whose only son had been killed on the field of battle; fighting his own diffidence because his unwelcome duty lay only too plainly before him; finding help in the admirable common sense and efficiency of his aunt's secretary. And because of a night after young Mr. Foster had told the family that he was going to marry Sally Wicklow, the new estate agent's sister, a night, to borrow from a graceful and moving elegy, of memories and of sighs, for many years now deeply buried in deliberate oblivion, Miss Merriman whose whole life had been devoted to the care of one or another Pomfret, said it would be very nice if Ludovic would keep her company. Lady Pomfret looked her gratitude and took Lydia away to the nursery quarters.

The Honourable Giles Foster was now in his last year at his prep school, where his engaging manner, his cheerful insouciance about his work or his punishments, and his intense pleasure in all forms of athletics had made him extremely popular, as indeed these habits would probably do all through his life. During the holidays he was allowed to dine with his parents if they were alone. When there was company he had supper in the nursery and played card games with Nannie, in which pursuit he had all old Lord Pomfret's skill and also what his Uncle Roddy called the devil's own luck.

During the Christmas holidays he had rapidly acquired Canasta and was teaching Nannie, who was on principle scandalized but had so far held her own pretty well against her ex-nursling, having been well brought up in her home village, where the one permanent rule in the whist drives was to play all your trumps first.

"Nannie, I don't think you know Mrs. Merton," said Lady Pomfret.

"How do you do, madam," said Nannie, rising to shake hands with appalling graciousness.

The old Lydia would have said Hullo. The Q.C.'s wife exchanged a friendly handshake with Nannie and said something very suitable.

"Where is Giles?" said Lady Pomfret.

"We were just going to play Canasta, my lady," said
Nannie, "but I told Giles his hands were a disgrace. Young
gentlemen don't play cards with hands like that in *my* nursery, I said, so just go and wash them properly at once and
not just under the tap and a wipe on the towel. Let me see
your hands, Giles," she continued, as the Honourable Giles
Foster entered the room in his shirt-sleeves, as sturdy and
cheerful as his elder brother was overgrown and self-
conscious.

Giles showed his hands, which were faintly fringed with a
half-hearted attempt at cleanliness.

"Pull your sleeves up," said Nannie. "Just what I thought,"
she continued. "Go back to the bathroom and roll those sleeves
right up. I'm coming in to see you wash properly."

Giles, no whit abashed, retreated towards the bathroom,
followed by Nannie. Lady Pomfret and Lydia looked at each
other. It was not safe to laugh, which would only have encouraged Giles in evil-doing and impertinence, so Lady Pomfret showed Lydia one of the family photograph albums, now
relegated to the nursery, with photographs of her wedding.
Old Lord Pomfret looking like Highland Cattle at Bay, Lady
Pomfret as Edwardian elegance in a good state of preservation,
Lord Pomfret's one remaining sister, Lady Emily Leslie, with
her dark eyes and her delicate aquiline features, and many
county people unknown to Lydia.

"They were all extraordinarily nice to me," said Lady
Pomfret. "Of course if it had been old Lord Pomfret's son, the
Lord Mellings who was killed on the Indian Frontier, it
wouldn't have done, but being Gillie, it was all right."

Lydia looked puzzled.

"I only mean," said Lady Pomfret, smiling, "that I don't
think old Lord Pomfret would have liked his son to marry
the young agent's sister. As Gillie was only a distant cousin,

it didn't matter. The Earl and Gillie's father hated each other like poison, I believe. I can't think how Gillie turned out so nice in that peculiar family."

Lydia said perhaps it was just himself that made him like that, and Lady Pomfret's opinion of that handsome Mrs. Merton rose.

"Now we're more like a young gentleman," said Nannie, coming back with a well-washed Giles in tow. "Say How do you do to Mrs. Merton."

"How do you do to Mrs. Merton," said Giles, in perfect imitation of Nannie's manner and with an engaging grin.

"How do you do to Giles," said Lydia, who had not been brought up with brothers for nothing, and she grasped his hand firmly.

"I say," said Giles respectfully, "you *can* grip, Mrs. Merton. Would you like to see us dig a badger out on Monday?"

Flattered as Lydia was by this proof of confidence, she had to tell Giles that she would be too busy, as there was a meeting in Northbridge she must attend.

"It's Monday morning, not afternoon, because of going back to school," said Giles, with a most winning leer.

"Even worse," said Lydia. "I'm driving my husband into Barchester and then I've got to do some shopping and see about having the boathouse cleaned and millions of things. But thank you all the same."

"Have you got a boat, then?" said Giles incredulously.

"Of course I've got a boat," said Lydia. "That's why I have a boathouse. And I've got a punt and a collapsible boat. Would you like to come over in the holidays?—if you will let him," she said with a slight deference to Lady Pomfret which amused and pleased that lady.

"*Really?*" said Giles, hopping from one foot to the other in excitement.

"Now, that's not the way to talk, Giles," said Nannie. "Say thank you to Mrs. Merton. You'll have to behave yourself. And ask your mother if you can go," which seemed to Lydia an odd sequence of commands, but no business of hers.

"Oh, mother, I can go, can't I?" said Giles, embracing his mother with fervour. "I'll take my bathing things and just *wallop* up and down the river. Have you any boys or girls, Mrs. Merton?"

Lydia said she had Lavinia, who was ten, and—

"I'm older than that, I'm eleven and I'm a boy," said Giles.

Nannie said Now then, and that wasn't the way to talk.

"And," Lydia continued, quite unmoved by this interruption, "Harry is seven and Jessica is five. They can all swim, but none of you are to swim unless a grown-up is there."

"I can dive off the top of the diving-board in the Barchester Baths," said Giles, "and swim under water right to the other end."

His mother looked anxious.

"That's enough showing-off," said Nannie. "And I don't want to trouble you, my lady, but Giles's knickers aren't fit to be seen. He's been right through the seats of two pairs since Friday."

Lady Pomfret asked, with admirable calm, what he had been doing.

"I was only trying to climb the obelisk," said Giles in an aggrieved voice, "and I couldn't, so I came back down the hill where the logs are. I came much faster that way because I thought you wouldn't like me to be late for lunch."

"Slid, my lady, that's what he did," said Nannie. "Right down that track where the men that were cutting the trees last year used to drag the logs and things. A nice way for a young gentleman to behave."

"Well, don't try to slide again, Giles," said her ladyship,

apparently unmoved. "And what about the other pair?"
Nannie silently held up a pair of grey flannel knickerbockers whose seat was in holes and apparently charred.

"What *were* you doing?" said Lady Pomfret.

"Well, mother," said Giles in an aggrieved voice, "Nannie
said to take my knickers off only just because I'd slidden
down the hill in them and have a bath and put on the other
ones, and the other ones got splashed somehow and I couldn't
find my school ones, so I ironed them with the nursery iron
and the iron was too hot. Electric irons are *always* too hot,
mother. They need a thermostat."

It was obvious to Lydia's motherly mind that her hostess
was divided between a strong desire to laugh and a sense
that duty bade her speak to Giles for his good, but before
Lady Pomfret had decided the unequal conflict Nannie said
it was as bad as the way Master John Graham went on the
time she was with Lady Graham as temporary nurserymaid,
riding one of Sir Robert Graham's prize pigs round the farm-
yard, at which moment it was possible to laugh without losing
prestige. So Lady Pomfret said Giles's knickers could be
patched and he must *always* wear them the minute he got back
from school and he must wear his Sunday knickers to go back
to school with and she would get two more pairs in Barchester
on Monday and post them to Matron.

"Oh, joy, joy!" said Giles, hugging his mother with great
violence. "Mother, when I go over to Holdings can I ride on
Aunt Agnes's pigs too? Oh, mother, can I?"

Lady Pomfret, in a rather cowardly way, said he must ask
Aunt Agnes about that. Giles hugged his mother again and
seizing Lydia's hand, kissed it with a clumsy grace that considerably affected her. Lydia then bade a respectful farewell
to Nannie and went away with her hostess.

"*What* a nice boy," she said as soon as the nursery door was shut.

"Pure Pomfret," said his mother, with an air of resignation. "He does exactly as he likes and can ride anything."

"But surely you are a very good horsewoman, Lady Pomfret," said Lydia. "I remember my father telling me that old Lord Pomfret, I mean Lord Pomfret's uncle, said his nephew's wife had the best hands in the county," at which Lady Pomfret flushed with pleasure and Lydia suddenly saw in her the Sally Wicklow who had won the shy young heir's confidence and his heart.

"I am always glad I got to know Gillie's uncle better towards the end," said Lady Pomfret. "He was very lonely after his wife died. My brother Roddy used to ride with him till his last illness and I think he got almost fond of Gillie and me. I was very sorry when he died," which last words were like a soliloquy and Lydia wondered if she was meant to hear them.

"You must have missed him," said Lydia, not quite knowing what to say.

"We did," said Lady Pomfret. "And we do more and more in a way. My husband is so conscientious, and when I look at Ludo—" and she fell silent.

The difference in age between Lydia and her hostess could not have been more than a few years, but Lady Pomfret had been forced by her marriage to take a leading part in county affairs and had not shirked any duty. Lydia, who also had never turned back from anything that had to be done, had led a comparatively quiet life since her marriage, very busy with her children and the place, and, except for her visits to their London flat, mostly moving in a small Barsetshire circle. She had admired and even a little envied Lady Pomfret's capable handling of husband, far too large home, children, committees, and the many calls that press upon the great landowner's wife, sharer of an old name, and to find that her hostess felt the burden of responsibility for her husband and the elder son, so like his father, made her compassionate heart rather sad.

"If I could be of any use in the holidays," she said, with a diffidence unusual in her. "I mean if you wanted to get rid of any of the children for a bit, do let them come to North-bridge. My nurse loves having more children about the place and no one ever disobeys her. She was nurse to the Deans over at Winter Overcotes and boasts frightfully about Jessica Dean."

"The actress?" said Lady Pomfret, opening the drawing-room door. "Do you know her, then?"

She did not exactly say Do *you* know her then, but her voice, though not in the least unkind, almost said it for her. Luckily Lydia was not over-sensitive to undertones and took the question at its proper value.

"Oh yes, we know them all," she said, "only there are so many of them, especially now they are nearly all married with families, that one loses count a bit. Jessica is our special one. She is so nice and so is Aubrey. The children adore him."

Lady Pomfret had not the best hands in the county for nothing and took the whole situation in her stride. Mrs. Merton, whom she already liked and respected, knew at least the sea-coast of Bohemia, a country which Lady Pomfret would dearly love to have visited if only as a tourist.

"I quite truly envy you," she said, shutting the drawing-room door. "What a long time the men are. Roddy promised he wouldn't let Gillie stay too long, but I suppose they are doing politics. I hope our nursery visit hasn't bored you."

"Of *course* not," said Lydia, and then in came the men, including Emily, whom her mother then very kindly and quite firmly sent to bed.

"Oh, mother, need I?" said Emily, a question which every mother is heartily tired of hearing, but her Uncle Roddy kissed her good-night and pushed her out of the room.

"Thanks, Roddy," said Lord Pomfret. "I sometimes think of selling Emily to the first bidder. If she isn't careful, she will be as bullying as Emmy Grantly, who makes the Rushwater prize bulls eat out of her hand. It's that dreadful Pomfret blood."

"Well, cheer up, old fellow," said Roddy. "You and Ludo aren't like that and you're the pick of the lot," and Lydia saw young Lord Mellings go pink in the face, but whether with pleasure or embarrassment she was not sure. "And what have you been up to, Sally?"

Lady Pomfret said she had taken Mrs. Merton to see Giles and Nannie. Lydia gave a spirited and pretty accurate description of Giles and his massacre of the knickerbockers, which made his lordship laugh.

"I can't tell you," said Lady Pomfret to Noel, "how grateful I am to your wife. She stood up to Giles quite admirably and she has made a most kind suggestion about the children."

"May I ask, as probably a party concerned, what it is?" said Noel.

"I am afraid you *will* be rather concerned," said Lady Pomfret. "It is that she has most kindly asked Giles and the others to come over to Northbridge in the holidays and mess about with boats in your river."

"Have you *really* got a river, Mr. Merton?" said Lord Mellings, looking more alive than Noel had yet seen him.

"A bit of one," said Noel. "That is to say, we own one bank for about half a mile and the children are in it, or on it, a good deal in summer. But they have to be able to swim first. Lavinia, the eldest, is quite a good swimmer. Harry and Jessica are getting on."

"Oh, Gillie," said Lady Pomfret to her husband, "what do you think? Mrs. Merton knows Jessica Dean. I mean *really* knows. Did you know the Deans were Barsetshire? I didn't."

Lord Pomfret said if it was Mr. Dean the wealthy engineering expert who lived near Winter Overcotes, he had often met him on boards and at the Club, but never knew his daughter was the actress.

"No one knows why she can act," said Noel, rather enjoying presenting the famous actress in absentia, as it were. "She insisted on going on the stage quite young, made a bit of a name for herself, and met Aubrey Clover, who found she could put over anything he wrote. So they got married and go on being a great success here and in America. They have one daughter called Sarah Siddons."

"*How* interesting," said Lord Pomfret, considerably impressed by his guest's information. "And what is she like in private?"

"She hasn't got a private," said Noel, "or if she has, no one has ever seen it. She simply is The Stage. So is he. A fascinating study."

Lord Pomfret said, perhaps rather wistfully, that he knew nothing at all about that kind of life and Lydia felt she would like to give him a week in London and a theatre every night, except that her common sense told her he could not stand it.

"I don't know if you would like to see them," said Lydia to Lady Pomfret, rather tentatively, for she was not sure if an overworked earl would really want an excursion into stage-land, "but I am going to ask Jessica if she and Aubrey would do a little turn at the Northbridge Coronation Festival, and I'll have to ask soon or they will be too busy. If I get them to dinner next time they are with her people, would you both come, quite quietly; no one else if you don't like."

Lady Pomfret looked at her husband, always on the alert to protect him if he needed protection, and had no doubt at all what his feelings were.

"How very kind, and I can't think of anything we would like more," she said.

Young Lord Mellings, who had sat in rather gawky silence while the grown-ups talked, suddenly and with what was apparently considerable effort said: "I saw her in the Christmas holidays, father, when I was in London the time the Luftons asked me to their flat. They took me to the Cockspur. It was *Fly Away My Heart*. It was—" but here words failed his lordship, who went red in the face and said no more.

"Perhaps you could come too if we have our dinner in the Easter holidays," said Lydia, with her usual generosity. "It would be so nice to be a man too many for once," which, though not put with perfect tact, made Ludo feel that he was really wanted, and he said if father and mother didn't mind he would love to, and then relapsed into embarrassment.

"I can't thank you enough," said Lady Pomfret to Lydia, "for making my husband talk so much at dinner. It is so good for him and he has so few treats. He loves good talk and playing piquet. I haven't got any head for cards. Giles has, but he has to go to bed early. Do you or your husband play?"

"Noel does play bridge at his club," said Lydia, "and I believe he's very good. I can't play at all. I am so sorry," she added, feeling real sympathy for Lady Pomfret, who wanted to have a treat for her husband. "But our agent, Mr. Wickham, can play. He is frightfully good at cards and I know he plays piquet with that nice Canon Fewling over at Greshamsbury. I'll ask him, if you like."

Lady Pomfret said it was most kind of Mrs. Merton and she knew Gillie would adore it, and asked if he was one of those

Wickhams over Chaldicotes way. One of them had died last year, she thought, and left an amount of money that surprised everyone to a nephew.

"That's Mr. Wickham," said Lydia. "I mean it was his old uncle, who had always been horrid to Mr. Wickham's mother, who was his sister—I mean the uncle's sister—and Mr. Wickham has inherited quite a lot of money even with death duties."

"Are you talking about Wickham?" said Roddy Wicklow, who as a fellow estate agent had often come across him at the Club and at various meetings. "You're lucky to have him, Mrs. Merton. There isn't a better man in Barsetshire. We must pick his brains about Starveacres Hatches, Sally. I want to know if there's really a spring in the river bed. Old Wheeler, whose family have lived at the Hatches rent-free for the last eight hundred years or so, swears that there is, and he's probably right, but since they deepened the drain at Pomfret Madrigal in '37 everything has been at sixes and sevens and the Monday country absolutely ruined," which was Greek to the Mertons, but Lady Pomfret evidently understood and said she wouldn't forget.

"I did enjoy it," said Lydia as they drove home. "Only I wish that nice elder boy didn't look so delicate. He is dreadfully like his father," to which Noel replied that it wasn't at all unknown for sons to be like their fathers and he often recognized in Harry traits both physical and mental that reminded him most depressingly of himself. Then they both agreed that it had been a very pleasant evening, and Lydia began planning in her mind for the amusement of the young Fosters when the weather became warm enough for the river, and woke up with a start to find that they were home again.

CHAPTER 3

THE DAYS were now getting visibly longer at both ends and also colder, or at any rate hardly less chill, for which people blamed whatever or whomever they fancied. Mr. Wickham, who knew everyone from the Duke of Omnium to old Bodger, the West Barsetshire rat-catcher, brought out a Barsetshire saying, extracted at the expense of half a crown and three beers at the Hop Pole at Marling from Mr. Nandy, a very old gentleman who still affected the Newgate frill of an older generation, his wicked face seamed with the dirt and wrinkles of a long disgraceful life.

"As far as I could get it, for old Nandy smokes and spits all the time he's talking," said Mr. Wickham to Mr. and Mrs. Merton, while they were inspecting the boat-shed on the Sunday after its spring cleaning, "it went like this:

"Twoscore year and add thirteen,
Then a Crowning will be seen,
Crowning of a Queen so good,
Mountain, steed, frost, fire, and flood."

"If I were your brother Robert," said Noel to Lydia, "I should at once get Counsel's Opinion on that statement. But being Counsel myself, I don't know what it is driving at. Twoscore year and thirteen makes 1953 all right and we are certainly having a Crowning of a Queen so good. The last line is obscure, but that is the whole point of prophecy. It always hedges abominably."

"We've certainly had plenty of cold weather, if that will do for Frost," said Mr. Wickham, "and the floods in East Anglia have come up to the mark. Steed and Fire have got me beat. And Mountain."

"But there's quite a lot of the year left," said Lydia. "I dare-say the others will happen."

"Might be anagrams," said Mr. Wickham. "I can't do them myself, but old Peters—you wouldn't know him, man in County Down who runs six illegal stills and always sends me a couple of snorters when the stuff's nicely matured—does the *Times* one every day before breakfast."

Noel idly asked what time he had breakfast.

"Whenever he's finished the crossword," said Mr. Wickham. "I've often had breakfast with him at three in the afternoon when I was over there. Nothing like method to get things done."

"What about the diving-board, Noel?" said Lydia.

Noel said Oh yes, he had quite forgotten and did Wickham think it would be a good thing to have a place the children could dive from. Lavinia could dive quite well at the Bar-chester Baths and Harry wasn't shaping badly. Jessica of course hadn't begun yet. Mr. Wickham said he didn't see why not, and probably some of their grown-up guests would like it in the summer. A real diving-stage would, he thought, be too expensive and look rather showing-off, but a good stout plank, well fastened to an emplacement on the bank, sticking out over the river, would be quite practicable. Above the boathouse, of course, said Noel, so that anyone who felt nervous and fell off it would be carried downstream to the boathouse steps. Mr. Wickham said he couldn't walk to the end of a bounding plank to jump off it: he would fall the minute he was over the water, from sheer fright.

"But you were a sailor, Wicks," said Lydia.

"Only a Temporary," said Mr. Wickham, "and precious little I saw of the sea. We didn't spend our time spittin' over the rail on board of the *Crocodile*—that's a quotation, and from a damn good poet too. Below deck as often as not, hearing complaints or making a fourth at bridge. The Commander couldn't do without his rubber. Of course in action it was different and there's a lot of my bridge winnings I never collected. Poor chaps," said Mr. Wickham, reflecting—and quite without any mercenary feelings—on the various shipmates who had been killed before they had settled their bridge debts. "Are you going to use the diving-board, Mrs. Merton?"

"I don't think so," said Lydia. "It is more for the children and their friends. I used to adore swimming, but now—oh well."

"I've heard doctors say that child-bearing makes people lose their nerve," said Mr. Wickham reflectively. "I don't mean that personally, of course," he added.

"Dear Wicks, don't be so silly," said Lydia, who had during a long acquaintance with Mr. Wickham become a fast friend and trusted him implicitly. "It's just that I feel a bit old. I mean when I was a schoolgirl, the first time you came to Northbridge, Noel, I wasn't frightened of anything in the world. Not even Miss Pettinger, though I loathed her. But— I don't know—something wears out in one perhaps. And I am very happy on dry land and don't in the least want to have to undress and then get wet and then dry myself and then get dressed again," which Noel said were exactly his sentiments, and they were vastly encouraged by the English climate.

"Well, I'm with you every time," said Mr. Wickham, "so I'll see about a nice springy plank for the young people and I'll poke about and see where that bit of gravelly bottom is. You don't want a lot of stinking mud when you dive. It's about six feet deep here and that ought to be enough for your youngsters, or any friends of theirs."

Lydia said that Lady Pomfret's children wanted to come over for a day when it was warmer and the two younger ones were very anxious to dive.

"But Mellings isn't," said Mr. Wickham. "I get you. Every time I see that boy I begin to worry. He's like his father. Nice, hard-working, conscientious, will be a good country gentleman and do all the right things and always be sure he is doing them wrong," which character-sketch of young Lord Mellings was so like his father that Lydia felt almost a pang of distressed sympathy for Lord Pomfret. "And that boy will be six foot two before he's done growing. It's in the family. Old Lord Pomfret was a bit over six foot; but he had the breadth to carry it, and the weight. He used to ride about twelve stone, I remember, between the wars, and more like thirteen when he got older. Well, it takes all sorts, and ever since I grew up I've been ten and a half to eleven, year in year out."

Noel, who always enjoyed his agent's divagations, said he never had the faintest idea how much he weighed.

"In fact," he added, "I don't think I've weighed myself since penny-in-the-slot machines at railway stations died. There is a weighing machine at my club, but it is rather silly. You have to sit in a chair and put weights on a bar sticking out. One looks such a fool. At least the members who weigh themselves do."

"Why not have one of those little gadgets you stand on in the bathroom?" said Mr. Wickham. "Then you can weigh yourself in the buff. And a depressing sight it is, if there's a looking-glass anywhere about," he added, at which Lydia laughed.

"I'll give myself sixpence for making you laugh, Mrs.

Merton," said Mr. Wickham, who in spite of long association which had become real friendship, steadfastly refused to address his employer's wife in any other way; and we think he was right.

"I'll give you another," said Noel. "That laugh is a noise I particularly like," and Lydia looked at him gratefully.

"No one ought to see themselves or anyone else with nothing on," said Mrs. Noel Merton, just as determinedly as Miss Lydia Keith would have said it. "Not after they are quite young. We always went barefoot in the summer when we were small, and one day when Colin was about fourteen we were messing about in the water-meadows and Colin looked down and said: 'Good gracious! I've got grown-up feet,' and he wouldn't ever go barefoot again. One does get older, you know."

"One does, but one likes you all the better for it, my love," said Noel, who had been looking at his pocket diary. "Well, Wicks, Easter Sunday is on the fifth of April. A bit early for bathing, but one never knows, and the Pomfret children will be having holidays. Could we be ready by then? If not, we'll have to put it off till Whitsun."

"Make it fifth of April," said Mr. Wickham. "Come Whitsun we won't be able to do a thing, with the Coronation ten days off, and Mrs. Merton will be up to her eyes in the Northbridge do."

"It would be very nice if you could come on the Committee," said Lydia. "I'm terrified of it."

"Not on your sweet life," said Mr. Wickham with sad want of gallantry; nay even of respect to his employer's wife. "I'm giving old Tubby Fewling a hand at Greshamsbury. We're going to put on a naval show that will knock spots off anything in the county. We've got Captain Fairweather and Captain Gresham and his boy, and Mrs. Gresham's father,

old Admiral Palliser from Hallbury, and one or two of my
old naval pals, and it will be worth seeing. Rose Fairweather
is going to be Britannia, sitting on a shield like a penny."

Lydia said Britannia wasn't *on* a shield, she was *by* a shield.

"By, with, and from take the ablative case," said Mr. Wickham, "if I remember my Latin grammar. But you are wrong,
Mrs. Merton. At least you're right, but it's one of those silly
changes people will make, just to show how clever they are.
When I was a lad we still had a lot of proper pennies with
the young Queen Victoria on them and her back hair like an
elephant—" at which point Lydia interrupted, which she very
seldom did, to ask Mr. Wickham what on earth he meant.

"Sorry. I keep on thinking you're as old as I am," said Mr.
Wickham very unchivalrously. "In the old coins, the proper
coins, her back hair was remarkably like an elephant's trunk
coiled up, with the end hanging down. What was I saying?
Oh yes, our Rose is going to be Britannia. One of my pals,
fellow in Southsea, you wouldn't know him, has made a collection of old helmets and he's going to lend us a fireman's
brass helmet. Our Rose will look like Boadicea, bless her.
Tubby and I wanted to do the cockpit in the *Victory,* but it's
a bit too complicated and Tubby isn't a bit like Nelson. I
don't mean his eye or his arm, we could fake that, but his
figure. So we are going to put on Queen Elizabeth receiving
her great admirals and Tubby is going to be Hawkins because
his people came from Devon originally and Hawkins seems
to have been a thickset kind of chap. Tubby wants a spot of
dialogue so that he can talk Devon, but I put my foot down.
Once we allowed anyone to talk, Rose Fairweather would be
saying her helmet was too foully dispiriting. And how's *your*
Do getting on, Mrs. Merton?"

Lydia, rightly interpreting his words as an inquiry after
the progress of the Northbridge Coronation festivities, said

there had only been one meeting so far, and to her great relief it had been run entirely by Mrs. Paxon and Miss Hopgood's Aunt.

"That's the stuff," said Mr. Wickham approvingly. "Never do anything yourself if other people like to do it for you. And don't overdo it," he said, with a sudden earnestness unusual in him. "I don't get a good employer's wife every day of the week and I don't want you to get run down again."

"But I wasn't run down," said Lydia indignantly.

"Not just lately," said Mr. Wickham. "That hot summer when you and one of the children had measles. I worried like anything."

"How *very* nice of you, Wicks," said Lydia, most grateful for the agent's kind interest. Noel did not say anything, for he remembered that summer and his own part in making it a difficult one for Lydia and did not like the remembrance. But we must do him the justice to say that his chief thought was for her; that she should not remember one of the reasons for her being so low and depressed that the measles found her an easy prey.

"I do wish I could see your show," Lydia went on. "It's really very sad that no one will be able to see anyone else's show. Not even Her Majesty, because she will be in *her* show, just like us."

Then Mr. Wickham went away to his next job, whatever it was, and the Mertons went back to the house.

The Coronation Committee was now meeting once a fort-night and would, as far as Lydia could see, soon be meeting once a week. For two reasons. Firstly that all the Committee, with the exception of Mrs. Villars and Lydia, found Com-mittees as good a deed as drink and would willingly have had one every day, or if possible more; secondly that in spite

of Lydia's willingness and the support given to her by Mrs.
Villars, who had accepted the position of deputy chairman,
practically nothing had yet been decided. Not that helpers
were backward with ideas, but so far it had been extremely
difficult to correlate them. Lydia, feeling that she would be
safer in her own home, had asked Mrs. Villars—to whom as
an elder and a more experienced woman she deferred very
prettily—whether she would mind the next meeting being
held at Northbridge Manor, as she would feel more sure of
herself in her own home. This feeling Mrs. Villars quite
understood and undertook to round up the rest of the Committee for half past two on the following Friday in Lydia's
drawing-room, Mrs. Villars to come to lunch first and decide
with her hostess what line to take.

"Now, what can I best do for you today?" said Mrs. Villars.
And if she did not add anything to her sentence, it was because she and Lydia were at the awkward stage when Christian names are looming but not as yet articulate; which is
about as near as we can get to what we mean.

"Do you think we could make a time limit for people talking?" said Lydia. "If only we could all be a bit shorter, the
meeting wouldn't be so long."

Mrs. Villars said she quite agreed and would suggest a two-
minute limit. Anything really worth saying could, in her
opinion, be said in two minutes. And the same for any argu-
ments for or against; and any question not settled to be
deferred to the following meeting, and to stop at four o'clock
punctually unless the Committee had already exhausted itself
earlier. And she was quite willing, as vice-chairman, to make
the announcement herself if Mrs. Merton wished.

"And as we haven't got a proper secretary yet, I might
suggest Miss Pemberton," said Mrs. Villars. "I did ask her if
she would and I think she rather liked the idea. She has a

very clear, orderly mind and is quite as good as a man for committee work. Better than most, in fact, because she knows her own limitations."

Lydia said that would be a great help.

"And if we elect Minnie Paxon as treasurer, it will be a good thing," said Mrs. Villars. "She has a very clear head for figures and her husband is a bank-manager. I believe he is just retiring, so he may be able to give us a little of his time."

Lydia thanked Mrs. Villars. "And when I see the amount of work one committee for one small town makes," said Lydia, "I can't think how the people on real committees ever have any time at all. Like Lady Pomfret. She is on hundreds of county committees and always seems to have time."

"She is admirable," said Mrs. Villars. "And you must remember, my dear, that a good deal of her way is cleared for her. In her position she is not asked to be on a committee, or take the chair, till everything is organized. Her work, which I must say she does admirably, is to keep the length of the members' remarks under control and conclude the meeting at a given time, settled beforehand by her and the secretary of whatever it is. Also she has that invaluable Miss Merriman at the Towers, a most remarkable woman. Ever since she married Lord Pomfret, before he succeeded to the title, she has given her whole energy—apart from her public life—to helping him. And you must know, as I do, how very happy it is to be able to help a hard-working husband."

"But I don't—not quite," said Lydia, not sadly, nor complainingly, but as a fact. "You see, Noel's work is all in London, but we don't live there. I would have lived in London if he had wanted it, of course, but he loves Northbridge almost as much as I do. I do go up in the week quite often and we have dinner-parties or go to dinner-parties, but my real life is here, especially with the children."

"And so is your husband's, I think," said Mrs. Villars. "This is his shelter from the stormy blast, so to speak, and an insurance for the future. If and when he retires from the bar, or from the bench it may be, this will be a harbour of refuge for him and a perpetual employment. And you can have people down here for him; make him do the travelling, not you. It will be fun for Barsetshire too, to come to your week-end parties."

There was a silence and Mrs. Villars wondered if she had said too much, even as a much older woman to a younger woman whom she liked and admired.

"I do see what you mean," said Lydia, "and thank you very much indeed. I think I hear the front door" (which phenomenon will readily be grasped by our reader) "so shall we go into the drawing-room?"

Accordingly they went into the drawing-room, where a fire had been lighted before lunch. As the central heating was still on, the room was quite bearable. Lydia had arranged the sofa and some comfortable chairs in a kind of semi-circle and proposed to entrench Mrs. Villars and herself behind her writing-table, which she had moved into a strategic position deeply disapproved by Palmer.

The first arrival was Miss Hopgood's Aunt, who had as usual walked out from Northbridge and came through the garden. Then Palmer frigidly announced Mrs. Paxon, who had bicycled, full of apologies for wearing trousers but the Civil Defence were having an anti-incendiary-bomb practice at five thirty; and if she felt this reason was sufficient, Lydia supposed it was.

"It is so nice to see the evenings getting quite light," said Mrs. Paxon. "I'm not one of the nervous sort, but really when you read the sort of things that are happening everywhere and people keeping women's bodies in a cupboard for months without anyone asking where they were, one really begins to wonder."

Mrs. Villars, who knew from the last war that Mrs. Paxon suspected everyone of having the fellest designs upon the honour of England's womanhood, said she didn't think there were any murderers in Northbridge and any outsider who came to murder people would be extremely conspicuous in a place where one knew everyone. Mrs. Paxon appeared to be comforted by these words, but added darkly that there were ways and ways. She then unhitched a khaki knapsack from her shoulder, sat down, and began to look through a mass of papers.

"I always say," she said, looking round for approval, "that it's *method* that counts. Where I put my jottings for this meeting I simply cannot think. I know I did put them in my bag, because I looked again just before I started and they were there. But there was a man in a car who stopped me to ask the way to Hatch End and I thought his manner *most* peculiar, so I simply bicycled on and said nothing. Oh, here they are," and she pulled out some papers covered with her large, rather childish writing.

"Mrs. Dunsford. Miss Pemberton," said Palmer, who had been lying in wait for the later guests and expressed in her voice the scorn she felt for (*a*) Miss Hopgood's Aunt, who had short-circuited her by coming round by the terrace, and (*b*) Mrs. Paxon, who had left her bicycle in the front porch. Lydia welcomed everyone, secretly wishing that they weren't there or, alternatively, that she wasn't.

Lydia then took her place at the writing-table, supported by Mrs. Villars, and said she supposed they had better begin.

"I must apologize for my daughter's absence," said Mrs. Dunsford. "She said to me this morning: 'Mother, I am not feeling quite the thing,' well, to anyone else I would have said, Pull yourself together, but she is so sensitive that I just said: 'Well, dear, I wouldn't try to come if I were you.'"

As neither Mrs. Villars nor Lydia had expected Miss Dunsford, who indeed had not been invited, they bore up very well.

"But I had ordered the taxi," said Mrs. Dunsford, "and as Miss Pemberton was coming with me I did not like to cancel it. I think that is all," she added with a business-like air.

Lydia knew that she must not look at Mrs. Villars or she would have the giggles, and we believe that Mrs. Villars felt much the same.

The proceedings were then opened by Lydia, who briefly stated the business in hand, namely to choose a secretary and a treasurer for the Committee and decide who was going to run the various Coronation things. She would have preferred to specify these, but suddenly realized that she didn't know what they were.

Mrs. Paxon, who had been previously briefed to that effect, said she would like to propose Miss Pemberton as secretary.

"Anyone against that?" said Lydia.

As so often happens in amateur committees, anyone who might have wished to oppose Miss Pemberton (though we do not think anyone did) was too shy to say so and the motion was carried.

"Thank you. I'll do my best," said Miss Pemberton not very graciously; though secretly, we think, both pleased and flattered.

"And I should like to propose Mrs. Paxon as treasurer," said Mrs. Dunsford. "We all know her splendid work in the war."

There was a ladylike murmur of approval from the meeting.

"Then I think that's all right," said Lydia. "Will you do it, Mrs. Paxon?"

"Of course," said that good-natured creature, "and really I was saying to Mr. Paxon only last night, 'Wouldn't it be a good thing if the Committee asked me to be treasurer? It would be something for you to do,' I said to him, because he's just retired from the bank, you know, and I was wondering about it, for they do say when anyone who has been in a position of trust for a long time retires they often go mental. The reaction, you know. So I'll just say I accept with pleasure."

"Perhaps, at this point, if you will excuse my interrupting," said Miss Pemberton, "it would be as well for me to begin my duties at once. I have heard the two appointments just made and shall take notes in writing of all future proceedings," to which end she took a large note-book out of a large shabby bag and began to write.

"Perhaps it would be easier for you at the table, Miss Pemberton," said Lydia, and she put a chair for that lady, who accepted it with thanks and resumed her notes. Lydia's housewife ear heard the front-door bell and she wondered who would come at this hour.

"Miss Talbot and Miss Dolly Talbot," said Palmer, showing clearly by her manner that she neither approved of the newcomers nor took any responsibility for them.

"My fault," said Mrs. Villars in a hurried aside to Lydia. "They were in all the war work here and I suppose they took it for granted they would be wanted."

"That's all right," said Lydia, at once, like a good chairman, coming to the support of her vice-chairman, and she stood up to welcome the newcomers, Miss Talbot in her wine-coloured tailor-made and her stitched beret, Miss Dolly

Talbot in her nice blue coat frock and her blue felt that went
with it; as they had been as far back as the memory of woman
went.

"I am sorry we are late," said Miss Talbot. "Ever since
Dear Father died, we have been a bit upset. It does make a
difference."

As Professor Talbot, who had died in the previous summer
at the age of ninety-five, had been nothing but a very selfish,
cross, complaining old gentleman and bedridden and senile
for the last five years of his life, everyone had felt And a Good
Riddance. His daughters, who had served him with uncom-
plaining energy and devotion, found themselves, to their own
great surprise, quite comfortably off, and being very nice
kind women, they had at once set to work and built up for
themselves and for the world an image called Dear Father.
No one wished to contradict such nice, good women.

"Do sit down," said Lydia. "We were just starting business."

"We would have been here earlier," said Miss Talbot, "but
the taxi was already booked, when most luckily we saw Mr.
Scatcherd at the Stores and he was just going over to Southbridge on business, so we made our humble little plea for help,
and now I am afraid we have interrupted you."

Murmurs of Not at all, How lucky Scatcherd was there
and, from Mrs. Villars to Lydia: "My fault. I had forgotten
all about them. How awful. I would have brought them. I'll
take them back."

"I'm very glad you didn't bring them," said Lydia, also
sotto voce. "There was plenty for lunch, but we couldn't have
talked."

Room was made for the Misses Talbot, and business—if
one can call it that—was resumed, everyone talking at once
in a most friendly way, till Mrs. Dunsford said she was sorry
but she *must* go as there was a meeting of the Children's

Entertainment Sub-Committee and could she give Miss Talbot and her sister a lift and she wouldn't wait for tea, Mrs. Merton, though many thanks all the same. The Misses Talbot, who had remained silent spectators of the scene, thanked Mrs. Dunsford, thanked Lydia for the delightful afternoon, thanked everyone for nothing in particular, and so went away.

"Now I think we'd better have tea," said Lydia. "I said in the dining-room because it's so much easier at a table."

"Then may I move that this meeting should adjourn," said Miss Pemberton. Mrs. Paxon said Seconded, and the Coronation Committee's meeting was over.

"We didn't get much done, did we?" said Lydia to Mrs. Villars, who replied that she had never yet been at any meeting in Northbridge that did anything at all, but with Mrs. Paxon and Miss Pemberton it was perfectly safe and Lydia need not worry.

The tea was very good, for Palmer, though she despised nearly all today's guests as being people who did not usually come to the house, was fully aware that tea at Northbridge Manor would be discussed in Northbridge during the next few days and had spoken to Cook to that effect. Cook had of course taken offence and the atmosphere had been so chilly that Lydia wisely ignored it altogether.

Mrs. Villars got deep into conversation with Mrs. Paxon and Miss Pemberton about the provision of cardboard cups and plates for the children's party. Lydia, after pouring out tea for everyone, found herself the prey of Miss Hopgood's Aunt.

"I have had such an interesting communication this morning," said that lady. "From my late husband's old friend Mr. Walden Concord Porter, in whose Observatory at Porterville my late husband worked. He is coming over for the Coronation."

Lydia said quite a lot of Americans seemed to be coming for the Coronation, and even as she spoke the words she felt how silly they were.

"Something *they* can't do," said Miss Hopgood's Aunt with fine insular pride. "He particularly wants to meet Mr. Downing. I must tell Miss Pemberton."

Miss Pemberton, hearing her name—as we are all apt to hear the sounds, otherwise meaningless, which somehow represent our personality to the world—looked at Miss Hopgood's Aunt.

"I was just saying to Mrs. Merton," said Miss Hopgood's Aunt, "that I had heard from Mr. Porter this morning. He said he was writing to Mr. Downing."

"There was a letter with an American stamp by this morning's post," said Miss Pemberton, "but as it was addressed to Mr. Downing I am unable to say what its contents were."

"Of *course* not," said Miss Hopgood's Aunt, trying to express by the tone of her voice not only that she would never suspect Miss Pemberton of opening her lodger's letters, but that no one could possibly suspect her of suspecting it. "I only mentioned it because Mr. Porter said in his letter to me that he hoped Mr. Downing would come over this fall—autumn we say here, but I was so long at the Observatory in Porterville with my late husband that I still fall quite naturally into the locution of the country—and give some lectures on Provençal poetry. The Lincoln Fish Doppelgänger Lectures, founded by an old alumnus of the Porter University at Porterville who made a large fortune during the war in I really can't remember what. They can only offer five thousand dollars, but of course hospitality would be given and all out-of-pocket expenses paid. They will, I know, be very much honoured if Mr. Downing will accept."

Mrs. Villars, who knew Miss Pemberton very well and

knew Mr. Downing as well as his hostess would permit, was
rather alarmed. For though Miss Pemberton had devoted her
life to Mr. Downing's well-being, having had him as a guest
for many years, nourished him with her excellent cooking and
seen that he was never disturbed while working, and even encouraged him to go to London from time to time and meet
other scholars at his club or at learned societies, she had very
strong feelings about keeping him to herself. Not that she
was in any way jealous of outsiders for Mr. Downing as a
man, but as a scholar she was zealous for his name and knew
that late hours and rich food were death to him; even more,
mixed drinks.

So Miss Pemberton's brow was sad, Miss Pemberton's
speech was low. And darkly looked she at Miss Hopgood's
Aunt and more darkly would she probably look at Mr. Downing when she got home. Even Miss Hopgood's Aunt, who
could look through a telescope without shutting or covering
the eye that wasn't being used, felt that she had this day
lighted a fire that might have any consequences one liked to
imagine.

"That is interesting news," said Miss Pemberton, with
studied moderation. "I daresay Mr. Downing will tell me more
about it when I go home. How does one get to Porterville?"

"Fly to New York, take one plane to Zenith and another
to Porterville," said Miss Hopgood's Aunt. "About thirty-six
hours, allowing for delays or a bad connection at Zenith. Less
if you are lucky. I came back that way last time I visited the
Observatory. Of course you lose several hours one way, but
you get it back the other."

"What I can never understand—but then I have not the
mathematician's or the astronomer's mind," said Miss Pemberton, who appeared to take a masochistic pleasure in be-
littling herself, "is that though one loses several hours or

alternatively gains several hours by flying, one is exactly where one was at the end."

"But you would be," said Miss Hopgood's Aunt. "To put it in simpler terms, x — y, as we might say for the sake of argument, is, as it were, cancelled out by x + y."

"Well, it may be," said Miss Pemberton, "but I don't believe in figures. It's what I feel that matters," to which statement, appallingly subversive of scientific fact, Miss Hopgood's Aunt had no answer at all, though many of us would agree with Miss Pemberton.

"Oh!" said Lydia," there's something I meant to say, but I quite forgot. Which day is the Entertainment at the Town Hall to be? I said I'd ask Jessica Dean if she and Aubrey could come and do a turn for us and I must give her the exact date."

Miss Hopgood's Aunt opened her bag, took out a small engagement book, and turned the pages rapidly.

"Here we are," she said. "It's the day after the Coronation. We thought if we had it on the day itself everyone would be looking at the television. We are having the children's tea and Packer's Universal Royal Derby that afternoon and the Tableaux and Entertainment in the evening."

"You'll find it difficult to get people to the Entertainment if the roundabout is there," said Miss Pemberton.

"That's all right," said Mrs. Paxon. "Packer has to shut up at six as he is going on to Southbridge for the evening. That gives the mothers time to give the kiddies their tea before the Entertainment. We're doing quite well with tickets. Nearly all the shillings are sold and we've only a few two-shillings left. We are getting on nicely with the program. Opening by Mr. Villars, recitations, dancing, piano solo and violin solo by the schoolchildren, and then an interval. It's a nuisance, but with so many children coming, we have somehow to manage two intervals or they'd be in and out all the time. One of the *real*

differences between the Classes, if you see what I mean," said
Mrs. Paxon.

Mrs. Villars said, gravely, that no one who had taken the
schoolchildren for an outing or even had them to tea in the
Rectory garden could mistake Mrs. Paxon's meaning.

"In fact," she added, "I sometimes think it is the only thing
that *does* interest them."

Every lady present would have liked to pursue this fascinating subject, but Mrs. Paxon was not to be deflected from
her course.

"After the first interval we have Miss Pemberton's Tableaux
of Northbridge in the Olden Time," she continued, "and then
another interval, and it would be lovely if Mr. Clover and
Miss Dean really could put on an act for us to end up with."

"Far be it from me to suggest any change in your admirable
program, Mrs. Paxon," said Miss Pemberton, "but don't you
think it would be better to have Mr. Clover and Miss Dean
directly after the interval—supposing they are good enough
to come? Then they can get away. If we have the Tableaux
first, we shan't ever get on to the acting. And I do think our
Grand Finale of 'Saxon and Norman and Dane are We' will
make a good finish. Will you be good enough to let us know
as soon as you hear from your stage friends, Mrs. Merton?"
she added, in a way that made Lydia feel that Miss Pemberton
thought but poorly of the stage.

Lydia said she would ring up Winter Overcotes that evening and find out when the Clovers would be there.

"Oh, but I have just thought!" she said. "Suppose they are
acting all through Coronation week. Jessica did *say* they meant
to have a few days' rest, but you never know."

"You never know anything," said Miss Hopgood's Aunt
majestically. "Not now. One used to, but that is past and
gone. Only the stars remain constant."

"Do they?" said Lydia, interested. "But what about things like meteors and comets. Or aren't they really there?" she added hopefully. "I mean *anything* might happen in the sky, with atom bombs and things. How I HATE science."

The company assembled, who knew that Miss Hopgood's Aunt was skilled in the heavens and that her late husband had discovered a star, were a little alarmed by this challenge, but to their relief she took it in quite good part, with scientific detachment.

"I think what you really hate, Mrs. Merton, is the lack of science," she said. "Or rather, science prostituted," at which word Mrs. Paxon looked alarmed and would have liked not to be there. "The increasing production of senseless weapons of destruction, for instance. My late husband often spoke to me of that. 'Florrie,' he used to say to me, 'we have gone too far. We have trespassed beyond our allotted limits and I have little doubt that the Book of the Revelation will shortly be fulfilled.' He was a highly religious man."

The company, as one woman, were stunned by this speech. Lydia, as usual, was the most courageous; also as hostess and president she felt she ought not to have spoken her mind so freely. But which of us can play our part consistently?

"I think that was wonderful of your husband," she said, "and I'll let you know the moment I hear from Aubrey Clover," and though she did not mean it, her words were almost a royal congé to the party.

"It *is* nice to see it lighter," said Mrs. Paxon. "I never like riding at night. I didn't mind in the war when we were all so happy in the blackout, but now I don't seem to like it. Getting older, I expect. Thank you for a lovely afternoon, Mrs. Merton, and I'll let you know about the next meeting," and she went away on her bicycle.

Mrs. Villars said she would drive Miss Pemberton and Miss

Hopgood's Aunt home, and in a few minutes Lydia was alone, wondering if the afternoon had been any use at all.

"Can I clear away now, madam?" said Palmer, appearing in the door like Retribution, only, far from limping, she stood erect and implacable.

"Yes, please, Palmer," said Lydia.

"And I've cleared up all that mess in the drawing-room, madam," continued the virtuous parlourmaid, "and Nurse happened to be in the kitchen and as she passed my pantry she did pass the remark that Miss Jessica was just going to have her bath."

"Thank you, Palmer," said Lydia and went upstairs to her lovely happy nursery, where there were no committees and no feelings to be considered and over whose young heads the Coronation would pass, hardly comprehended except perhaps by Lavinia. It was enough to make one go on having babies for ever, she thought. And being Friday, Noel would be here by dinner-time, first rescuing his car (for they had two cars now) from the garage where it had been having something adjusted. And after dinner she would ring up the Deans and find when Jessica would be down. Or perhaps ring Jessica up now, at her flat before she went to the theatre; which she did.

It was always with a sense of adventure that Lydia rang up the Clovers's flat. Jessica herself was still to her the baby sister of Susan Dean, who had married that nice sailor Captain Belton over at Harefield, but Aubrey Clover was all the excitement and mystery of Stageland.

As usual the telephone was answered by Miss M., whose full name of Mowbray had become entirely merged in her initial, the perfect watch-dog and guardian of her employers, asking nothing better than to slave for them early and late and never have a holiday except when they went to America, and we think it very probable that she will soon insist on going to America as well.

Miss M.'s voice gave the Clovers's telephone number.

"Oh, Miss M., it's Mrs. Merton speaking. Can I speak to Jessica?" said Lydia and waited.

"Good evening," said Aubrey Clover's voice. "Jessica is having a bath and I won't let her have an extension in the bathroom. People get electrocuted. Is that my Lydia?"

Lydia said it was and how was Sarah Siddons.

"Splendid," said Aubrey. "Teeth sprouting all over her. We have taken the flat above ours and are making what the Americans call a Duplex, so that she can have plenty of nursery room."

"I didn't know one could do that with flats," said Lydia, rather impressed. "Didn't the landlord object?"

"Can a duck swim?" said Aubrey. "Gold, my girl, gold did it."

"Well, what I really rang up about," said Lydia, "was to ask if you and Jessica were acting in Coronation week, or if you would be at Winter Overcotes."

Aubrey said he smelt a rat in the arras.

"Because," said Lydia, ignoring the rat, "I am the president of the Coronation festivities and they want me to ask you if you and Jessica could possibly spare time to do us a sketch at our Entertainment. It will be the day after the Coronation, at the Town Hall, in the evening, and we'd love to give you some food here at any time you like. If it's No, please say it at *once*."

"I adore you," said Aubrey Clover's voice. "I always did. You are the one woman I couldn't possibly have invented, great genius though I am. Wait a minute while I ask Jessica," so Lydia waited by the telephone and occupied her time, as we all do, in what is called doodling on the telephone pad.

"But my *lamb*," said the enchanting voice of the famous actress, "of course we will. I'd do anything for you. That delicate austerity, those candid eyes which show everything the beautiful steadfast lines of your mouth try to conceal, the perfectly *glorious* way you don't always see my jokes. Aubrey and I are shutting the theatre for three days and coming down to rest. Aubrey always goes mad when he rests, so this is the answer to prayer. Which day, what time? Only you'd better tell Aubrey, then if we get it wrong he can't blame me. Bless you, my pet. Over to Aubrey."

Lydia, still like a schoolgirl in her excitement over the theatre, did not have to wait long.

"Sorry, my sweet," said Aubrey. "I was just checking dates with Miss M. She always knows what I'm doing better than I do. We might do the little twenty-minute cameo, as my publicity man will call it, though I in my Victorian way would call it a sketch, *Two-Step for Three*. The only trouble is we do want another man. Any amateur would do, as he only has to be on the stage for a few minutes and be gawky and uncertain. I'll pick up someone all right. Come over to Winter Overcotes one week-end and we'll talk about it. Jessica sends a thousand kisses to Noel. Bless you, Miss Languish, though a *most* unsuitable name for you. Here's Jessica," and almost at once Jessica's voice said: "Heaps of love to your divine husband, darling, who will soon be too great to know us at all. See you at the Dower House on Saturday," and the telephone clicked.

Well, that was something done, thought Lydia. Something that no one else on the Committee could have done, and she hoped, being quite humble inside, that they would feel she was worth her salt. And there was the pleasant prospect of a visit to Winter Overcotes. When Noel came down he was no less pleased. It had taken him some time to get over the rebuke

Jessica had so lightly and skillfully administered to him in the summer when he had found the pretty widow Mrs. Arbuthnot too attractive. It is very difficult to pardon the rebuker when one has been entirely in the wrong, but Noel had a mind trained to clarity of thinking and he had a not inactive conscience that told him, in words far more bitter than Jessica's, how foolish and how unkind he had been. Since that summer he had met Jessica more than once, but always in a crowd. Now he would be seeing her in her parents' house, where he would be at her mercy. But one cannot turn one's back on facts for ever, and we think he was secretly glad that he would be able to face the worst so soon—if worst it was to be. It was early spring now, if one could call it that, and every now and then the sun so far forgot itself as to appear. Perhaps everything would be all right.

On the Saturday he and Lydia drove to Winter Overcotes. The sun was shining. All sorts of trees were showing signs of life, some with sticky shining leaf-holders (or whatever their real name is); some with lamb's tails or catkins, according to taste; the pussy willows with nice silver-grey furry buds. The birds, in classic phrase, were a-hollering and a-bellering. All was gas and gaiters. But anyone accustomed to the English spring would know that it was only a case of reculer pour mieux sauter, as our unpredictable neighbours the Gauls so neatly put it, and that at any moment every bird might be frozen to death, every young shoot blackened, and pipes bursting all over the place. As they drove they speculated on the amount of Deans that might be about, for the large Dean family were now all married and treated their parents' house as a pleasant family hotel, from Laurence, the eldest, who had married Margaret Tebben, to Jessica, and visitors never knew which of the well-brought-up, handsome grandchildren belonged to whom. The front door, in pleasant country fashion, was not locked during the day, and the Mertons went in. There was no sound of voices, so they went through the hall and down the passage into the garden. Here just outside the house, in an angle screened from north and east, was a wide stone terrace, and on a kind of garden chaise longue in the sunniest corner Mrs. Dean was visible, reclining, wrapped in soft shawls. Jessica, who was sitting near her mother, got up and came to them.

"My *sweets*," she said, carelessly giving each her well-known kiss, which we can only describe as cheek to cheek but never touching, for to touch does not do one's make-up any good. "Too, too lovely to see you. Aubrey is somewhere in the garden getting local colour. He wants to write a play about country life and is taking it too passionately seriously. Mamma won't wake up, and even if she did she wouldn't know who you are. Come along," and she led them over the lawn, past the old mulberry tree with some of its branches supported by great wooden crutches, through an arch in a clipped hedge, and so across the grass to where the ground fell away towards the River Woolram. Here an aged gentleman in clothes that looked as if they had been taken off a corpse who had been drowned for several weeks, the bottoms of his disgraceful trousers tied round his boots with string, was cutting the reeds that had too far encroached on the bank where Aubrey Clover, his back to the newcomers, was sitting. Jessica put her finger on her lip and both the Mertons saw her as an exquisite portrait, say a Romney, of someone in the character of Silence, only Jessica was more suitably dressed for an English spring out of doors.

"And what did he say next?" said Aubrey, taking a pipe out of his mouth.

"I never knew Aubrey smoked a pipe before," said Lydia softly.

"He didn't," said Jessica. "And what's more, he doesn't. Lots of smokers go about with their pipes out. It's just the make-up, like his suit," which the Mertons then observed to be a shooting-jacket with poacher's pockets, shabby grey flannel trousers, and heavy shoes. "Don't make a noise. He's got his bird sitting."

"What did he say?" said the old gentleman. "Ar, that's what many a one wants to know. A nasty foul-mouthed fellow he was. But old Margett, he knows. And those as knows don't tell."

Jessica said in a low clear voice that he was the uncle of Margett the builder at Worsted and, as far as anyone knew, never changed his clothes summer or winter. When anything quite fell to pieces he would beg from the local gentry. His cottage belonged to him, and Aubrey had once gone in to get the feeling of the place, but had been obliged to come out almost at once owing to the dirt and the stuffiness.

"There's those as doesn't tell and gets nothing for it," said Aubrey, who had rapidly become another dirty, lazy old man with disgraceful clothes and a filthy old pipe.

"Ar," said old Margett. "All depends, doesn't it? There's some as'll say anything."

"That's right," said Aubrey. "There's some as'll say anything and there's some as'll say nothing. And when I say nothing, I *mean* nothing."

"That's right," said Mr. Margett, chuckling malevolently. "Nothing for nothing's my motter."

"Something for nothing's my motter," said Aubrey, absently clinking the loose coins in his pocket. "If a man was to know a good bawdy song and that man was to sing it to me, well it wouldn't but be fair if I gave him the price of a drink, leastways that's the way I see it."

"Old Margett he knows more bawdy songs than anyone

this side of the county," said the old man. "Old Margett he knows one about a squire's son and the milkmaid in the cowshed that he wouldn't sing not for half a crownd."

"They say," said Aubrey, "that hearing's believing," and he absently clinked his money again. "It might be worth a man's while to give five shillings to hear that fine ditty."

"He's overdoing it," said Jessica in what we can only call a silent whisper, but perfectly audible.

"Old Margett he knows a man not a mile away from here as would sing that song for five shilling," said that gentleman.

"A man as asked five shilling would be asking too much," said Aubrey Clover, looking into the distance.

"Well," said old Margett, "I don't know rightly where that man is, but I'll tell you a line of that song. It goes this away," and uplifting his cracked and tuneless voice, he croaked:

> "An 'e said, I'd like to be doing to yow
> What you are a-doin' to that there cow."

"Catch," said Aubrey Clover, throwing two half-crowns into the air. The old man caught them, spat on them, put them into a hole in his tattered clothes which was probably a pocket, picked up his weapon, and said he was off to have his tea.

"Pubs aren't open yet," said Aubrey Clover, but the old man, with more revolting chuckles, went away at the slow, plodding pace of the labourer.

"Marvellous old fellow," said Aubrey, getting up and addressing Noel.

"Did you know we were here?" said Noel.

"Of course he did, my sweet," said Jessica. "An actor-manager has eyes all over his head. Just wash your hands, Aubrey, and we'll wake mother up for tea. Lydia wants to ask you something."

"Any request of Mrs. Merton's," Aubrey began sententiously.

"I think, though I am not a policeman, that I ought to tell you that anything you say will be faithfully remembered and if necessary used in evidence," said Noel.

"It's about the Coronation Entertainment at Northbridge," said Lydia.

"No, darling, I will *not* be Julius Cæsar, or Becket, or even George the Fourth," said Aubrey. "Crowd off, yes."

"It's not that," said Lydia. "The first half will be quite ghastly, all the schoolchildren showing off with singing, and a horrid little girl doing the Highland fling, and a chorus of pixies. And at the end there will be scenes from Ancient Northbridge. But if you could possibly do *Two-Step for Three,* it would be wonderful. And you wouldn't be expected to see the first half, which will be awful, and you needn't stay for the Northbridge Pageant of History afterwards. Could you?"

Aubrey was silent, and for once, Lydia thought, she was seeing the real face of the man that Aubrey was. Divers et ondoyant on the surface, but granite underneath, at any rate where his work was concerned.

"For you, my pretty, it shall be done," said Aubrey and everyone laughed; partly from pleasure and partly because pretty was the last word that could be used of Lydia. Almost any other word would do. Handsome, good-looking, perhaps noble, full of character, a face with shadows and reticences, a face in which enduring love might make its mark: but pretty, no.

"Oh, *thank* you, Aubrey," said Lydia, going pink in a becoming way quite unusual for her. Noel added his thanks while Jessica fell into a Lady Hamilton attitude, expressive of Approval.

"There's only one thing," said Aubrey. "It is a three-person play. We need someone to be a young man who is in love with Jessica in a most simple-hearted way. He is shy and clumsy and can't say what he wants to say, and yet people must like him. He is only on the stage for two or three minutes, but he has to look like a gentleman."

"I don't know anything about acting," said Lydia," but—"

"Thank God you don't, my darling," said Jessica. "You wouldn't do the part so well if you did."

"What part?" said Noel, amused.

"Herself, of course," said Jessica. "She is a star turn, Noel," and for a moment Noel felt uneasy. But it was obvious that Jessica was not thinking of his lapse and the setting-down she had given him, and he dismissed the thought from his mind.

By the time they got to the house the sky had clouded again. A trail of cushions, newspaper, and scarves showed them that Mrs. Dean had gone indoors, where they found her in a somnolent condition in front of the fire.

"Mother," said Jessica. "Here are Mr. and Mrs. Merton. She used to be Lydia Keith. Over at Northbridge."

Mrs. Dean opened her beautiful eyes and greeted the guests very kindly; particularly as it was obvious that she had not the faintest idea who they were. Then luckily Mr. Dean came in.

"Here is my father," said Jessica. "Father, Mr. and Mrs. Merton. You must know them."

"I am glad to," said Mr. Dean. "I think your brother has spoken of you, Mrs. Merton. He does a good deal of legal work for me. A first-class man on Company Law," which pleased Lydia.

"I've got another brother who is a lawyer, only he's a barrister," said Lydia, "and lives mostly in London. He is Colin."

"Not the Keith who does railway work?" said Mr. Dean. "Jessica, when and where are we going to have tea?"

Jessica said here and at once and she would ring, which she

did with a courage that impressed Noel, for few people dare to ring for anyone now. But Mrs. Dean had always had servants and always would. Some people are like that.

"Your brother used to come here a good deal before he was married," said Mr. Dean. "Would it be asking too much, as I know you are a kind friend to Jessica, to let me meet him again down here some time, quite unprofessionally? I don't deal in railways myself except in South America, but one of my subsidiary companies here is having difficulty with the Crumlinwallinwer branch line that serves the Mewlinwillinwodd collieries, and I want a good opinion."

"I'm sure he would love it," said Lydia, pleased at this recognition of her dear Colin. "He often comes down to Edgewood to his wife's people, the Grantlys. Perhaps you and your wife would come to dinner and meet him?"

"That would be delightful," said Mr. Dean. "But I must tell you that my wife is incurably lazy and hardly ever goes out."

"I suppose I could ask you alone," said Lydia, and added: "How very beautiful she is, if you don't mind my saying that."

"She is," said Mr. Dean and looked at Mrs. Dean with a kind of amused tenderness. "She used to go everywhere with me when I was a young engineer building railways in South America, and the doctors think she got some queer germ there that makes her sleepy so often. But she is quite well," and he looked again with affectionate admiration at his wife's beautiful unlined face and her shining silver-grey hair that had never been cut, brushed back from her noble face and coiled in a knot behind in a way very few women can stand.

"I shall ask you both," said Lydia firmly. "I do know Susan a bit and Jessica."

"A queer outburst from a respectable middle-class family," said Mr. Dean. "But a very good girl. She is fond of you."

"So am I of her and so is Noel," said Lydia.

Then conversation was disrupted by tea, and presently the Mertons had to say good-bye and drove back through the spring evening with a pale-green sky in the west and no warmth in the air. When they got home the younger children were going to bed. Lavinia came down to the drawing-room to do her practising, which she did very nicely and luckily enjoyed. Noel promised to take her to Barchester one Saturday morning to buy Coronation flags and other decorations for the nursery, and peace reigned.

Mr. Wickham was dining with them that evening, as he did about once a week, always bringing a bottle of something with him. Both Lydia and Noel from time to time protested against this, but Mr. Wickham said he was one of those that never drank when he was alone and such a lot of chaps sent him bottles of one thing and another that they were eating him out of house and home—the bottles, he meant—so it was Christian charity for the Mertons to help him with the good work. This evening he had brought some Burgundy, which Lydia always liked.

As they sat at dinner Noel and Lydia told Mr. Wickham about their visit to the Deans and how Jessica and Aubrey Clover had promised to do a short one-act play for the Coronation performance in the Town Hall, only they needed someone local who could do a very short part; a young man who is having calf-love for the heroine.

"He has got to look like a gentleman and behave like one," said Noel, "and be able to learn his lines and not have stage fright, but where to find him I don't know. Theatricals aren't in my line."

Mr. Wickham also ran over his list of acquaintance, all of whom were quite unsuitable, and said probably it would be all right on the night and perhaps Aubrey would find someone.

Then Lydia kindly left the men to talk estate shop and went
to the small sitting-room that they mostly used when they were
alone. There was some telephoning to be done and this was a
good moment. Mr. Wickham had now promised the diving-
board by Easter and if it were at all warm the children would
be using it in the holidays and it would be nice to ask some
young friends. Those two younger Pomfret children, who
were older than her three but not too old. And she wanted to
ask the Pomfrets to dinner before the Coronation had swal-
lowed everything. And then she thought of young Lord Mellings, rather like the bat between the birds and the animals, at
the gawky stage (only one could not call him gawky), not
grown up, not a child, uncomfortably between the ages. Then,
as she considered the matter in her kind heart, a thought
struck her. She rang up the Towers and was answered by a
pleasant voice which only gave its number but was recogniza-
ble as Miss Merriman.

"It is Mrs. Merton speaking—from Northbridge," said
Lydia, in case the Pomfrets knew several other people of the
same name. "It is Miss Merriman, isn't it?"

The telephone said it was and would Mrs. Merton like to
speak to Lady Pomfret, and in a few seconds Lady Pomfret's
voice said: "Good evening. I am so glad you rang up. Emily
and Giles have been pestering me about going to see your
river. I told them it was much too cold for rivers, but they don't
believe me. One forgets how warm one was when one was a
child."

Lydia said it was rather about the river that she was ringing
Lady Pomfret up.

"We have got a diving-board fixed now," she said, "and all
the boats are being cleaned. I feel one can't trust the weather
at Easter, but I wonder if you would let the children come
over a bit later in the holidays and go on the river with mine.

I shall be with them myself or Noel will be, so they will be absolutely safe."

Lady Pomfret said she was sure they would adore it and a date was fixed, subject to alteration if it was snowing or the river was frozen.

"I can send them over with Miss Merriman," she added, "if your Nurse won't mind," but Lydia said there was nothing Nurse liked so much as condescending to other peoples' employees, and both ladies laughed.

"And could we fix a date soon when you and your husband will dine with us?" said Lydia. "And do bring your Ludovic. We liked him so much. I shall try to get Aubrey Clover and Jessica Dean, if it would amuse you. Her family are old friends and both of them are delightful. Only then it must be a Saturday or a Sunday. Saturday is best, as they sometimes go back to town on Sunday night."

"How very kind of you," said Lady Pomfret's voice. "It will be so good for Gillie to meet people outside his world, and he will love it. Otherwise he always meets the same people. And I am sure Ludovic will be immensely flattered. He is so tall, poor darling, that everyone thinks he is about twenty, and he is only fifteen. At least he will be sixteen on the 23rd of April —St. George's Day—bless him."

After some consultation, both ladies being a good deal occupied in their respective spheres, the two dates were fixed, one for the dinner-party and one rather later, in the hopes of getting a warm day for the river and the water-party.

After she had put the dates in her engagement book Lydia rang up her elder sister, Kate Carter, whose husband was headmaster of Southbridge School, for a family gossip. Kate and Everard were taking their three children to London to see the Coronation procession from Everard's club and spending a few nights in Colin Keith's house, Lydia's specially loved brother. Colin and wife and family were going to flee from London and spend the Coronation days at Edgewood with his wife's parents, the Grantleys. Mr. Adams, who lived in the Old Bank House at Edgewood, said Kate, had got the best television money could hire and they were all going to look at the Coronation on it. Lydia said How ghastly and as she wasn't going to London she would wait till the coloured film came to the Barchester Odeon and take the children, and Kate said How sensible, because all television did was to give one a headache the only time she saw one. And then they exchanged news of their respective children, planned to meet in Barchester on Friday morning, and said good-bye.

Then Lydia rang Mrs. Villars up to tell her that Aubrey Clover and Jessica would do a short sketch for them, directly after the first interval, and did Mrs. Villars know any young man with a turn for theatricals who could learn a very short part in Aubrey Clover's sketch and act in it with practically no rehearsal. Mrs. Villars said there was certainly no one like that in Northbridge and wouldn't a girl dressed in boy's clothes do, but no, she supposed it wouldn't; which is the way most of us so often think and feel. Miss Pemberton, said Mrs. Villars, was having rehearsals of the historical pageant scenes almost every night at Punshions, because she said there would be no getting hold of the girls as the evenings got longer, and it was now certain that not only Effie Bunce would be in a highly unpresentable condition by the beginning of June, but Doris Hibberd, that nice good-tempered girl who used to work for Mrs. Turner at the Hollies, would also be much the same.

"Still, Doris's young man is going to marry her, at last," said Mrs. Villars, "but no one ever marries any of the Bunce girls. One sometimes wonders if marriage will die out altogether," but Lydia said she didn't think so as long as there was money and settlements, which practical though un-Christian view made the Rector's wife laugh. Then Lydia said she could hear the men coming and said good-bye.

"You girls," said Mr. Wickham. "At the telephone all the evening!"

"You men, Wicks," said Lydia, "at the bottle all the time," and Mr. Wickham laughed and said Kamarad and he must be off. So when he had gone Lydia told her Noel what plans she had made and he approved them all and said ought they to get another woman if young Lord Mellings was coming? But Lydia said she thought another woman might frighten him to death and perhaps it would be better to leave things as they were unless she could find exactly the right person. For she had come to feel in one evening what Sally Wicklow had realized when she first met young Mr. Foster, the Pomfrets' heir, that he would never have the energy to make friends unless the friends were kindly thrust upon him; with which Noel, with secret admiration for his wife's quickness of perception, agreed.

The days passed by, mostly cold and unpleasant, but there was plenty to be done and Lydia was fully occupied with the Coronation plans, complicated at the moment with an outbreak of measles in Northbridge so that the rehearsals for the Pageant of Northbridge were sparsely attended.

"Not that it really matters," said Miss Pemberton to Lydia whom she met in Scatcherd's Stores one morning, "because they never all turn up together and when Mr. Downing is there they all giggle. Curious how village girls still giggle about gentlemen. Come and see our rehearsal one evening. Saturdays at seven o'clock."

Lydia did not particularly want to go, but in a small community one must be friendly and she had a sincere respect for Miss Pemberton, which was about as far as anybody ever got with that lady. Once Lydia had said to Mrs. Villars that she felt sure Miss Pemberton would never let anyone know if she was ill, so determined was her independence. Mrs. Villars said she quite agreed, adding that if Miss Pemberton did die she hoped it would be some time before, or after, the birth of Effie Bunce's child of shame, because if Effie weren't there Mr. Downing wouldn't know what to do and as he would probably be too frightened to tell anyone and had no idea of cooking for himself, he would die too. Lydia said that was rather awful, and what could they do?

"Not much," said Mrs. Villars cheerfully. "But my cook, Mrs. Chapman, knows Effie Bunce—she is a kind of cousin of hers, though she doesn't like it known—and if Effie's confined she will let me know at once."

Lydia, much impressed by the use of the word confined, said what would happen to the baby?

"Oh, it will be all right," said Mrs. Villars. "Those Bunce girls never have any trouble. They are up and back at work within a fortnight, as a rule. Effie can bring the baby with her and if the weather is too bad she will leave it with her mother and just run back to feed it. It is all very well organized. And don't think I am condoning sin, my dear," she added, very kindly, seeing that Lydia looked anxious. "It isn't sin with old Bunce's family. All the women are like that and have really thoroughly good dispositions. Effie and Ruby are splendid mothers and so was Mrs. Bunce."

"But she was married," said Lydia.

"Never in her life," said Mrs. Villars. "They kept on putting it off, and matters remained like that. And that is why Mrs. Bunce bullies old Bunce. If she were his wife he would beat her. He does beat the girls—not that it does them any good and they laugh at him—but the few times he has beaten Mrs.

Bunce she has given him as good as she got. You don't know village life, my dear. I can assure you that it has never altered since they were real ancient Britons. Effie's children and her sister's may be caught in the mill, with things as they are, but I rather hope they won't. We need some rebels in this age of petty regulations."

"I don't think I would like to have illegitimate children," said Lydia thoughtfully. "Nor would Noel."

"And quite right too," said Mrs. Villars. "The middle classes still keep themselves respectable on the whole, and just as well. I shall have to put Effie and her sister into the final tableau of England in All Ages as Queen Elizabeth's attendants, in farthingales or whatever they called those large skirts, and hope for the best. My cook has an illegitimate son, you know."

"Mrs. Chapman?" said Lydia. "I thought she was a widow."

"So she is. An unmarried widow," said Mrs. Villars placidly. "Her Bert is a poor piece of work and is probably responsible for several fatherless children. He came here once during the war and I was glad when he went. He was reported missing presumed dead later, somewhere in the Far East."

"Did Mrs. Chapman mind?" said Lydia.

"Not in the least," said Mrs. Villars. "He sends her a card every Christmas."

"But I thought you said he was dead," said Lydia.

"Only presumed," said Mrs. Villars. "He didn't like the army life in the Far East, so he went off with a native girl and they hadn't time to hunt for him. He is probably the father of several large families now and I don't suppose we shall ever hear about him again. The cards are probably given to some passing traveller to post, as they all have different stamps. But to talk of something more interesting, what do you want me to do about the Clovers? I mean will they need a special room for making up? It's rather difficult in our little Town Hall. We need the Town Clerk's office for the performers in the pageant and I don't think there is another room we can use."

But Lydia said she was sure Jessica and Aubrey would love the communal green room because they enjoyed everything.

"Lucky they," said Mrs. Villars, not enviously, but a little wistfully; and Lydia in her heart agreed.

CHAPTER 4

AFTER a good deal of telephoning and counter-telephoning, the Clovers were pinned down to a Saturday evening. The Pomfrets were delighted and Lydia, zealous for young Lord Mellings's welfare, ransacked her brain to find a suitable playmate for a quiet anxious overgrown schoolboy born out of his time. Her Noel said being a woman short didn't matter, but she was not at all convinced and rang up her sister Kate to inquire about a suitable sub-deb, or whatever the catchword of the year was; for Kate, as the headmaster's wife, saw a great many sisters of past and present Southbridgians. After a long talk about their respective husbands and children, she asked Kate if she knew any nice girl for a nice and very shy schoolboy, the Pomfrets' elder boy.

Kate, who loved to help everyone and her younger sister in particular, said there weren't any very good sisters on tap at present. Some years there was a good crop, some years there wasn't, and this was a bad year.

"Oh, wait," she said. "I have an idea. Do you remember those nice boys of the John Leslies' that were here? We always called them Major and Minor and Minimus. No one ever remembered their real names."

"But I don't want young men," said Lydia.

"It has just come to me," said Kate, "that they have a very nice cousin, Lady Graham's youngest girl, called Edith. The eldest sister married Tom Grantly and they live at Rushwater and help Emmy's cousin Martin Leslie with the pedigree herd, and the second one, Clarissa, married Charles Belton, a very nice person. Edith must be about sixteen now. Would that do?"

Lydia said it sounded very nice, but her elder sister must have detected a flavour of doubt in her voice, for she asked if anything was wrong.

"Well, only that I hardly know the Grahams," said Lydia. "If it was a man I wanted, I could always ring up and say you said he was so nice and could he come to a dinner-party. But I don't see quite how I can do that with a girl I don't know. Her mother mightn't like it," and Kate said perhaps Lydia was right, and then they talked about Kate's family and how Bobbie said he wanted to go into the Navy and Angela's front teeth needed straightening and Philip had gone mad about Canasta because he was so good at mathematics, and gradually the talk came to an end, with the question of the odd girl unsolved. But Fate occasionally forgets herself and is kind. On the very next day Lady Pomfret rang Lydia up and said their cousin, Lady Graham's youngest girl, was staying with them, and might they bring her?

"Ludovic has been telling Edith about your having a river at the end of your garden," said Lady Pomfret, "and she is longing to meet you because it sounds so romantic." Lydia said of course she would love to have her and felt how nice it was when things went right.

The weather, gradually working itself up towards the Coronation, was as unpleasant as anyone could not wish and Lydia had to have the central heating started again, so that Palmer took offence and said to Lydia that she was never a one to complain but how was she to get the drawing-room properly turned out for the spring cleaning with all the pipes hot?

"Well, you'll have to do the spring cleaning later, Palmer,

that's all," said Lydia. Palmer, who knew when she was beaten, said she would get Effie Bunce's sister to come in and give a hand. Lydia wondered whether it was her duty as one of those set in authority to point out Effie Bunce's sister's present condition to Palmer, but decided it wasn't and that so long as the girl liked to come it was nobody's business. The younger Miss Bunce was accordingly summoned and worked with hearty goodwill, breaking an old glass paperweight in her zeal and managing to cut her hand and bleed all over a good Persian rug, by which means Palmer had a double victory in that most of her work was done for her and she could blame the worker.

The day of the dinner-party dawned bright and fair and, having shown what it could do, proceeded to show what it was jolly well going to do, which was a return to Arctic conditions accompanied by tropical rain. Palmer, seeing a good opportunity to persecute her inferiors, between whom and herself a gulf far wider than that between the Duke of Omnium and an old labourer at Winter Overcotes was set, put Effie Bunce's sister Ruby to clean all the silver, which was shiningly clean; which task Effie Bunce's sister undertook with the greatest good-nature, saying she'd make the brights shine a treat: an expression at which Palmer shuddered and drew in her breath.

"Have a nice cuppa and some bi-carb in it," said Ruby Bunce. "You find it'll act a treat," which remark Palmer coldly ignored. And if Palmer thought that her hireling noticed the ignoring, she was mistaken.

"And when you've done the silver," said Palmer, "you can give the drawing-room fender a rub up with the leather, and the fire-irons too."

"Sounds to me as if a nice polish with the blacklead would be the thing," said Ruby, "but have it your own way," and went on with the silver.

Palmer said icily that fire-irons weren't iron, they were brass.

"Seems funny to me calling them iron then," said Ruby, "but it takes all sorts to make a world," to which Palmer, in Juno-like wrath and indignation, could not find any adequate reply.

Half an hour or so later she came back to the pantry. The silver was beautifully clean and shining, and she noted with approval that her slave had screwed the cap of the silver polish on again firmly. She then went to the drawing-room in pursuance of a general system of harrying her social inferiors and found Effie Bunce's sister on her knees, applying her not inconsiderable strength to rubbing the fender. The bottle of Brassishine, which preparation she considered more highly than Brassiglow or Brassglitter (all of which were made by the same firm and contained the same ingredients), was standing on a newspaper on the hearth rug.

"What are you up to?" said Palmer suspiciously.

"Just doing the brights, the same as you said," said Ruby, shaking onto a rag a liberal application of polish. "I've done the tongs and shovel and things."

"You can't do that," said Palmer, horrified. "They're lacquered."

"New one on me," said Ruby. "Foreign, I s'pose."

"Never mind that," said Palmer. "There's things you can't understand. Just get a pail and some hot water and the soap, quick, and wash that stuff off again. Ruining madam's things, that's what you're doing. You girls don't have sense."

Ruby, a most good-humoured creature (too much so indeed for her own good), rose from her knees, upsetting the tin of brass polish as she did so.

"There now, that's two silly things," said she cheerfully, and at the same time skilfully mopping up the brass polish before it had soaked through the newspaper onto the carpet. "They say where's two there's bound to be three," and she went off to the kitchen quarters.

Palmer, whose dignity did not allow her to bandy words with her social inferiors (unless with the proviso that the bandying, if it broke out, should be unilateral), altered slightly the position of everything on the hearth, just to show. Ruby came back carrying a pail of hot water, which she put down with hearty goodwill, splashing the carpet. Palmer drew in her breath in a marked manner.

"It'll all dry off," said Ruby with the easy optimism of one whose own property is not at stake, and then she wiped and dried the fire-irons and the fender.

"I'll just give them a rub with the leather and we'll be okey-doke," she said.

Palmer asked suspiciously where she got the leather.

"Out of the drawer where the silver is," said Ruby. "If I was Mrs. Merton, I wouldn't have all that silver. You can get lovely stainless steel at Sheepskins's in Barchester."

A hundred retorts rose to Palmer's lips, but she felt it below her to give her thoughts a tongue, especially as the Bunce family were celebrated for their own, so she contented herself by saying with icy detachment that she would trouble her to put that leather back where it belonged and if she would look in the cupboard where the cleaning things were she would find the leather for the brasses. Why anyone should make so much fuss about one bit of wash-leather when it was just as good as another was beyond the hireling's powers of comprehension, but being a kind girl, she did as she was asked and then everyone had elevenses in the kitchen.

"I don't like the look of the tea-leaves," said cook, gloomily contemplating the dregs in her cup. "Seems to me they say my soufflé will be spoilt and that's a thing I can't abide."

"Spit in the cup, ducks, and then throw it all away," said Ruby. "They say it turns the luck."

Cook and Palmer felt in duty bound to be shocked and gave a visible demonstration of the same in their speaking countenances, but Ruby, being unversed in the finer shades, took no notice at all.

The first to arrive for dinner were the party from the Towers, who were evidently looking forward to their evening. Even Lord Pomfret looked we cannot exactly say happy, but hopeful, and Lydia felt how nice it was of him to accept as a treat what was quite an ordinary occurrence. Then she remembered that the Clovers were to be the real attraction and laughed at herself. Young Lord Mellings was wearing his dinner-jacket suit with a kind of shabby grace and Lydia suddenly felt, with rueful amusement, that he would probably be like that all his life and never would a new suit on him look as if it were new.

"And Edith you haven't met," said Lady Pomfret, presenting that young person. "She isn't exactly out, but there isn't much of that now."

Edith shook hands very nicely.

"Thank you so much for asking me," she said. "I simply love parties. I'm not really out, but I did go to a lovely dance at Harefield and I danced the galop with a doctor called Bob Perry and he said Tally-ho at the top of his voice. He had a stuck-up wife, but she Tally-ho'd too."

The composure and aplomb of this young person amused Noel very much, and he asked her if that was the Dr. Perry who was a well-known consultant.

"I expect he is," said Edith Graham, "because his wife is like the wife of one. I mean she looks as if she didn't know other doctors' wives very much. And I think she will make Dr.

Perry be a Sir," which piece of precocious wordly wisdom made her Cousin Pomfret hope she was going to behave herself.

Then, having waited till all the cast were on the stage, in came Mr. and Mrs. Aubrey Clover, announced by Palmer as Miss Jessica, madam, and Mr. Clover. With kind consideration for Palmer's feelings Jessica waited till the door was shut and then embraced her hostess with a fervour that left at least half an inch between their faces.

"I do love the way Palmer called me Miss Jessica," said that lady. "It sounds so funny to be called Mrs. Clover, especially as it isn't really Aubrey's name. Darling Lydia, you are looking madly handsome. Why can't I have dark shining hair like yours?"

"Too many perms," said her husband aside to Noel, with a sotto voce of considerable carrying power.

"Lady Pomfret," said Lydia, "this is a great friend of ours, Jessica Dean in public, and this is Aubrey Clover," which gentleman bowed over Lady Pomfret's hand. Lady Pomfret said quite the right things to Aubrey and looking, as she ceaselessly did, to see if her husband was going to enjoy himself, was pleased to observe him being captivated by Jessica at once. Noel then kissed Jessica's hand, which, being observed by Lord Mellings, caused that young nobleman to wish he had a sword.

"And this is Lord Mellings, Jessica," said Lydia, "a great admirer of yours," and then thought the words sounded silly, but no matter. Poor Lord Mellings, overcome by seeing the stage at close quarters, began to stammer. His parents, who had suffered under this and hoped Ludo had got over it, felt acutely conscious that Ludo was not doing himself justice.

"Do you know," said Jessica, looking up at the tall gawky schoolboy, "I used to stammer dreadfully and my nurse made me say Peter Piper picked a peck of pickled pepper ten times running every morning and I was cured almost at once. Do try it."

There were few people who could resist Miss Jessica Dean, and Lord Mellings, already dazzled and conquered, was certainly not going to be one. Looking down from his gawky height at Jessica's lovely eyes, he repeated the silly jingle after her.

"Lovely," said Jessica. "Say it once a day and think of me."

"If I think of you, I shall say it all day long," said Lord Mellings in a hoarse voice, but Jessica had already gone like Alexander to spread her conquests further and was talking to Lord Pomfret. Really good Spanish sherry was drunk, except by Edith.

"One thing, Lady Pomfret," said Lydia, getting her guest to herself for a moment. "Do your young people have wine? We are having some quite good Burgundy and there will be port for the men afterwards. I don't want your son to feel uncomfortable. And what about Edith? There is ginger beer and orangeade too."

"How kind of you," said Lady Pomfret, meaning what she said. "Edith doesn't have wine yet, but she can deal with soft drinks to an alarming extent. Ludo always has sherry when we do and some wine if he wants it, which he often doesn't. I must leave the question of port to your husband. It is so kind of you to think of Ludo."

"But of course I thought of him," said Lydia. "I do like him so much.

Palmer then announced dinner.

"Shall we take the sherry in with us?" said Noel, seeing that Jessica had not finished hers.

"A heel-tap, a heel-tap, I never could bear it," said Jessica, throwing her charming head back and emptying a thimbleful of sherry down her throat.

"There is a bit of poetry, but I can't remember who wrote it or what the words are, about someone having such delicate skin that one could see her throat glowing when the red wine went down," said Noel as they went into the dining-room, delighted to find Jessica as friendly as if she had never spoken to him for his good. "Here, if you please," and he remained standing till Jessica had taken her seat.

"Poets never think," said Jessica. "One's skin could be as thin as gold-beaters' skin, but there are all the muscles and Adam's apples and odds and ends under it. I don't believe your poet. When Laurence—my eldest brother—was a little boy he used to get his words muddled and he called gold-beaters' skin Peter Goatskin, so the whole family called it that."

"Lydia and I were not quite sure how to arrange the table," said Noel. "With four guests who are all relations of each other—I mean the Pomfrets and their boy and Edith Graham, who is their cousin—it was very difficult to separate relations. It was Lydia who suggested your neighbour. He is so tall and so uncertain of himself. We put his cousin Edith on the other side of him so that he could feel safe. She has never been shy in her life, and she and young Mellings are much the same age."

"And you felt that Aunt Jessica was a suitable companion?" said Jessica.

"I felt that we would not appeal in vain to Aunt Jessica's kindness," said Noel sententiously, at which Jessica winked the wink with which she had brought the house down as Mrs. Carvel in one of Aubrey Clover's plays, and Noel laughed.

"I am so glad," said Lady Pomfret to Aubrey Clover, "that your wife is next to Ludo. He is so dreadfully shy and he will be doing his military service before long."

Aubrey said gravely that he did not see the connection.

"You know perfectly well what I mean," said Lady Pomfret.

"He will be in the Guards, we hope, and he is still so very young. Inside, I mean. He is so shy of people, just as my husband is. What *can* one do about it?"

"I find it peculiar, though flattering," said Aubrey Clover, "that mothers always ask me about their sons. All I have at the moment is a daughter called Sarah Siddons. We haven't decided whether we will call the next one Henry Irving or Henry Kemble. If it is a girl, we have decided nothing at all. A girl's fate is too terribly decided by her Christian name, don't you think?"

Lady Pomfret asked why.

"I wish you had not asked me that," said Aubrey. "I said it because it came into my head. Gagging, as we strollers say. I should like, if I may, to invent a reason," and he paused while Lady Pomfret, entertained by this excursion into Bohemia, waited.

"Not only does a girl's Christian name matter at school," said Aubrey, "but it is most important when she marries. A girl whose Christian name ends in a, and many of the loveliest names in our language end with that vowel, is exposed to great danger. My wife was one."

Lady Pomfret said Jessica was a charming name.

"Aye, charming, your ladyship," said Aubrey Clover in an eighteenth-century manner, "but let the wench marry a man whose name begins with a vowel and the poor wretch is doomed."

Lady Pomfret asked why.

"How often in conversation, or in talks on the wireless," said Aubrey, "does one hear people say Jessicar is, or for example Agathar is. It is but an extension of that popular phrase the idear of. Doubtless it will, under the firm and competent handling of the B.B.C., become standard English."

Lady Pomfret said there was an announcer who said Pardon when he coughed.

"He would," said Aubrey, "whoever he is. But what on earth were we talking about? Ah, I have it. Our sons."

"Have you a son too?" said Lady Pomfret.

"I really don't know," said Aubrey, looking across the table at Jessica. "One doesn't, you know, and the doctors don't know either."

"Then, do I gather—" said Lady Pomfret and she stopped.

"You do," said Aubrey. "But not till October. Then we shall take them both to America for a winter season. Jessica is very good at arranging things," a remark which was so vague that Lady Pomfret said Indeed she must be, and then she was claimed by Noel while Aubrey turned to Lydia.

"You are so clever, Aubrey, that you must have guessed why we asked you here tonight," said Lydia.

Aubrey said rather sententiously that he supposed it was to make himself a motley to the view, but he was here strictly incog.

"You know quite well what I mean," said Lydia. "The Pomfrets don't see many amusing people because they work so hard. That boy of theirs is so tall and so like his father."

Aubrey said he had noticed the likeness, but so much better to be like one's father than to turn out black, or with a harelip like one's mother's uncle, at which Lydia couldn't help smiling, but with bulldog perseverance returned to the charge. "He is so tall and so unsure of himself," she said. "The other children are quite different. They are very cocksure and Emily is a bit of a bully. You understand Life, Aubrey. How could one help? Do think about it," and then, in case she were becoming a bore, she said: "What plays are you taking to America?"

"I wish I could write a play about you," said Aubrey, "but I'm not old enough yet. In another five years or so. It would be a masterpiece."

"Me?" said Lydia, honestly surprised. "Why?"

"Because, dear lady," said Aubrey, which form of address nearly made Lydia have the giggles, as indeed he had intended, "no one knows you properly but myself; the strolling player, the rogue and vagabond."

"What about Noel?" said Lydia stoutly.

Aubrey did not answer, but gave her a quick fleeting glance, and her colour rose, most becomingly.

"That was nothing," she said.

"Very well," said Aubrey, "it was nothing. But out of nothing I could write a play that would make London and New York fill packed houses with tears for months—and my audiences do *love* crying so long as it all comes right in the end. And it did come right in the end," and Lydia remembered again the summer when Noel had for a few weeks been attracted by Peggy Brandon, the pretty widow Arbuthnot as she was then, and how Jessica had saved the situation.

"I suppose I owe you and Jessica something," she said, looking at Aubrey.

"The debt is cancelled," said Aubrey, "by one glance of that eye so bright and black," and Lydia said indignantly that her eyes were brown and always had been.

"Poet's licence," said Aubrey. "That very nice brother-in-law of yours, Everard Carter, told me you were a tremendous Browning addict in your youth. But you women forget your early loves," and then Lydia asked him to tell her more about their plans for the duplex flat and how on earth they had persuaded the landlord of the block of flats where they lived to consent to putting in a staircase from their floor to the new nurseries. Aubrey said one could bribe more effectively and at less expense in his profession than in any other. A box for the Cockspur Theatre, he said, supper in their flat with a few other chosen theatrical stars and plenty of champagne, the sight of Sarah Siddons asleep (by special arrangement with Nurse, who had been given a crocodile-skin bag and a large bottle of scent), and a vivid picture by Jessica, acting every word she spoke, of the peril that Sarah Siddons and her unborn companion would run in having their precious sleep disturbed by the irregularities of an actor's life, and the thing was as good as done. Mr. Appleyard had rung up his secretary at two in the morning and given instructions for Mr. Clover to get everything in the way of licences that was required, and that was that. How much of what he said was true, we do not know, but we may say that the conversion of the upper flat and the making of a staircase between the two was started that autumn, the very day after the Clovers and their family went to America.

"I sometimes wish," said Lydia, turning to Lord Pomfret, "that one could play musical chairs at dinner, especially when people are the same family," which statement Lord Pomfret, with his usual tired courtesy, asked her to explain.

"You know how difficult it is to arrange one's table sometimes," said Lydia. "I mean putting the right people together. You are sitting by me because I am the hostess and this is the first time you have dined here. I ought to have a delightful woman on your other side, I mean Jessica, but every way I tried to arrange the table it got worse and worse."

Lord Pomfret said he always found his young cousin Edith extremely good company.

"She is very much of a Foster," he said, "and my uncle would have liked her immensely and taken her riding about the estate. She gets it through her grandmother, Lady Emily Leslie, Uncle Giles's sister. An impertinent forward minx and no doubts about herself or anything. She will walk straight over people all her life, just as Uncle Giles did. If only my elder boy," he said, lowering his voice, "had some of that in him. That charming Miss Dean—or do I say Mrs. Clover?—is being so kind to him."

Lydia said it didn't really matter by which name one called Jessica, as she answered to both, and the funny thing was, she added, that Aubrey's real name wasn't Clover at all. Lord Pomfret, in whose hard-working life the theatre had played little or no part, asked if his family were ashamed of having an actor with their name.

"Oh, not a bit," said Lydia. "His mother, whom I did meet once at Southbridge at Miss Hampton's cottage—you know Miss Hampton and her friend Miss Bent?"

Lord Pomfret said he was sorry he had not that pleasure.

"Well, you must meet them some time," said Lydia. "Miss Hampton writes very successful novels."

Lord Pomfret said he would very much like to meet a real novelist. He had, he said, once met Mrs. Morland at Lord Stokes's, and liked her very much because she understood boys, but he couldn't read her books.

"That is what is so *very* nice about her," said Lydia, which statement perplexed Lord Pomfret. "I mean," said Lydia, "that she has been writing books for years because she had to educate four sons and now she can't stop and the more she writes the more people read them—like snowballs," at which vivid if not very clear definition Lord Pomfret laughed aloud. He did not easily laugh and it must have been the first time that Lydia had seen him really amused. She found it somehow very touching and hoped something might happen to make him laugh again.

"But about the real name of our fellow guest," said Lord Pomfret.

"Oh, his mother is a Mrs. Lover and his real name is Caleb Lover and he always signed his name C. Lover when he wrote to music publishers and people, when he was starting. But his handwriting was so bad that the C. Lover part all ran together and looked like Clover and he had one or two contracts and they wanted to know his Christian name and he chose Aubrey, though no one knows why. But it suits him very well."

Lord Pomfret was touchingly interested by this sidelight on a celebrity and asked if Jessica Dean's name was imaginary too.

"Oh, no," said Lydia. "The Jessica part is perfectly true and I think Jessica Dean makes a very good stage name. She is the youngest. One of her sisters married Captain Belton over at Harefield, and her mother is Mr. Palmer's sister, the one that runs the prize herd over at Worsted."

Lord Pomfret said he was really ashamed to know so little about families, but he hadn't come to Barsetshire till after he was grown up.

Lydia said she wasn't specially good at families either, because her parents had died a long time ago and the war had made things so difficult.

"If we had roots, as you have," she said. "But Noel's people and mine weren't the old lot, though they were angels, at least my father and mother were. Noel's people were always in the law and somehow the law doesn't count so much in Barsetshire. I mean he had to go to London to be a barrister and become a Q.C. And my brother Colin really lives in London too. I sometimes wish Colin had gone into my elder brother's office in Barchester and solicited there. Tell me, Lord Pomfret, what will your Ludo do?"

"I wish I knew," said Lord Pomfret. "The eldest son usually goes into the Army. Ludo will do his military service, of course, and as far as we know go into the Guards—if they will take him. But I can't see him as a soldier. Now, Giles will adore it. So would Emily if she had the chance. Lucky, lucky children. Yours are quite young, I believe, Mrs. Merton."

Lydia said Yes, a good stage younger than Lord Pomfret's, as her eldest was about Giles's age, and then, inevitably, their talk went to Coronation preparations.

"It will be a heavy time for Sally," said Lord Pomfret. "She has to organize all the treats for the estate and then go to London with me for the Coronation. Luckily my late uncle's and aunt's robes and coronets are in quite good condition. Sally will look magnificent in Aunt Edith's coronet. As for me, my Uncle Giles's white breeches are a world too wide for my shrunk shanks, not to speak of being yellow with age."

Lydia took his meaning and his quotation and couldn't help laughing, which made Lord Pomfret laugh too, and Lady Pomfret looked quickly at them and thought what a very nice woman Mrs. Merton was. Noel also was pleased to hear Lydia's laughter, a rare thing; not that she was without humour, but she had a way of enjoying fun in quietness. The old Lydia, the sixteen-year-old hoyden whom he had first known, was far more boisterous in her amusement; but he loved this Lydia who laughed with her eyes, or a smile which he found continually enchanting.

By this time Edith Graham was slightly intoxicated by company and a great deal of ginger beer, and her cousin Ludo, incited we are afraid by Jessica Dean, was also beginning to thaw, and that side of the table was becoming almost rowdy.

Contrary to Cook's hopefully gloomy prognostications, the soufflé was borne in by Palmer gloriously high and swelling with a perfect light-brown top, and so deftly did Palmer do her work that everyone was quickly served.

"Excuse me, madam," said Palmer, behind her mistress.

Lydia asked what it was, already resigned to some kitchen calamity.

"Cook asked me to say, madam," said Palmer, "that seeing there was his young lordship and the other young lady, there is another soufflé."

"Please thank Cook," said Lydia, and before the first soufflé was quite finished, in came another just as good.

> "Oh my lovely soufflé
> You are so very toothly,"

said Edith Graham, by now quite above herself with good company and ginger beer.

"I didn't know we had a poetess here," said Aubrey Clover.

> "Dear Mr. Clover
> My heart is a rover
> But to you it will come over,"

said Edith, now well away in Pythonic vein.

"I didn't know you had a poet in the family, Lady Pomfret," said Noel.

"Edith has a habit of dropping into verse," said Lady Pomfret. "Sometimes her poetry is rather good, but I don't think much of that effort," and she looked in an auntly way at her husband's young cousin but might have saved herself the trouble, as Edith was now quite above herself.

> "Darling old Mellings
> Is covered with swellings
> Because he did eat
> Too much of the sweet,"

said Edith.

Young Lord Mellings's pale face became pink with shame. He said nothing, but Lydia saw, with compassion, that he was having difficulty in controlling himself. Lady Pomfret gave

Edith one look which silenced that young person, and there was a distinct feeling of uncomfortableness.

"Palmer," said Lydia. "The gentlemen will have their coffee here and we will have ours in the drawing-room. Will your Ludo come with us?" she said to Lady Pomfret as they went to the door together. "He won't want port and I should love to talk with him."

"That is a very kind thought," said Lady Pomfret. "Ludo, darling, will you come and amuse us, while those men talk about dull things?"

"Oh, do," said Jessica Dean, taking the young Lord's arm and, as it were, squiring him from the room.

"I'm sorry, Merton," said Lord Pomfret, when the ladies with Ludovic were safely out of hearing. "Edith needs beating. A spoilt youngest child. Her sister Clarissa was just as bad in another way, but she has settled down as a very good wife to that young Belton. I daresay Edith will improve, but she is a handful."

He looked so wretched that Noel and Aubrey Clover plunged into conversation about a very unpleasant divorce case in which the stage and the peerage were implicated and by great good luck the lady was a very distant connection of Lord Pomfret, which at once gave him status, and while they were all thus a-merry-making Palmer came in and said Mr. Wickham was there but wouldn't come in if Mr. Merton was busy.

"Ask him to join us, please, Palmer," said Noel. "My agent," he explained to Lord Pomfret. "Clover knows him. He drinks harder than anyone I've ever met and is never the worse for it."

"Wickham," said Lord Pomfret. "That's not a local name. They are over Chaldicotes way," and Noel said his Wickham was one of that lot and had inherited a modest fortune from an old uncle who owned property there, and then Palmer said:

"Mr. Wickham, sir," and stood stiffly aside to let the new-comer pass.

"I'll chuck that woman under the chin one day," said Mr. Wickham when Palmer had retired. "Lord Pomfret, I'm glad to see you. And Clover, as I'm a living man," and he sat down between them.

"Help yourself to port, Wicks," said Noel Merton.

"If I had known you had company I'd have brought a bottle of Vanderhum over," said Mr. Wickham. "It isn't like me to come empty-handed, but I've been down in the cowsheds with the men. As nice a little heifer calf as you'd wish to see, Merton. Mother and child doing nicely. I did have some rum, but I left it with Bunce. He deserved it."

"Bunce is our cowman," said Noel to Lord Pomfret. "His sisters are delightful women with quantities of illegitimate children. One of them works here sometimes."

Aubrey Clover said he must meet Bunce.

"It's no good, Clover, you couldn't put Bunce on the stage," said Noel. "You'd never get him past the censor, nor his old father and mother that aren't married," to which Aubrey replied: "Oh, wouldn't I, my boy?"

"I wish I had someone like that over at the Towers," said Lord Pomfret with frank envy. "All my people are so respectable. When Uncle Giles was alive we had a footman called Finch and his old uncle was the worst poacher in the county, and there was old Mrs. Dixon at Starveacres, who was a witch. If she didn't get five shillings on Michaelmas Day she could magic the fox away. And she could charm warts."

"All you newcomers!" said Mr. Wickham. "You only turned up in the twelfth century. We were at Chaldicotes before the Romans came. Remains of Ancient Britons, whoever they were, under the ruins of the Roman villa on our land when the Barsetshire Archæological were excavating before the '14 war," which was perhaps hardly the way for the host's agent to speak to a belted earl, but even Lord Pomfret, though not cow-minded, realized that this was an important occasion when the rank was but the guinea stamp.

"But we can't touch you with pheasants, my lord," said Mr. Wickham, who liked to keep up the old forms from time to time. "Your late uncle understood pheasants and so does your agent. There's not much I could teach Wicklow about game birds," after which words Lord Pomfret naturally said he hoped Mr. Wickham would come over for some shooting as they weren't doing much in the way of parties and could do with a good gun.

Of course Aubrey Clover at once became the keen amateur sportsman and so deluded Lord Pomfret that his lordship said he hoped he would come over one day too, from which pre-dicament Aubrey Clover was able to extricate himself by tell-ing the truth, namely that he and his wife were going to America in the autumn. But the talk continued to be about game, both furred and feathered, and Noel for once felt a little out of things, for his family were Barchester, not of the land, and his work lay in London.

Meanwhile in the drawing-room Edith had, of her own accord, told her cousin Sally that she was sorry, had been for-given, and was looking at some old *Punches* while Lady Pom-fret and Lydia talked Coronation. Both were involved in local celebrations and compared notes about their committees. Lydia listened with real interest and even went so far as to get pencil and paper and make some rapid notes, which she subsequently could not make head or tail of.

Meanwhile Jessica Dean, who as one of a large family had seen boys growing up in every stage of spots, sprouting mous-taches, arms too long for their jackets, legs too long for their trousers, necks too small for their collars, had got young Lord Mellings onto a comfortable little sofa near the fire. Here his young lordship became mute and perspiring, but Jessica, hardened to every kind of stage fright, so gentled her companion that within ten minutes he had stopped twisting his long, elegant, and we must say damp if we are to be truthful hands and was talking to her quite easily about school (which he accepted as a necessary though uninteresting duty), the Pomfret lands, for which he had an inherited and strong feeling, the kind of books and music he liked, and how he never really enjoyed riding.

"I stick on all right," he said, "and Uncle Roddy says my seat's not bad, but I don't think horses like me."

Jessica was ready at once with the suggestion that the horses wanted to be sure that he liked them before they decided to like him. A few lumps of sugar, or a good scrunchy carrot, she said, might be as good as leaving cards on people—if, she added, anyone left cards now.

"Mother has visiting cards and so has father," said Ludovic, "but they are mostly used for giving to shops and things to say where to send parcels to, not for paying calls," and then Jessica told him how great ladies, when the London season began, used to send cards to announce to their friends that they were back in London, and how the cards were left at the house in the morning with a terrific rat-tat-tat at the knocker by a footman in undress who jumped down from the box beside the coachman (who was also in undress) to deliver them, while the horses were being exercised.

"Did you really see it, Miss Dean—I mean Mrs. Clover?" said Ludovic and then went red in the face.

"Whichever you like," said Jessica. "But why not call me Jessica? Everyone does."

"But I couldn't," said Ludovic, if possible redder than ever and twisting his long fingers. "I mean you're much older than I am—I mean you are very famous."

"Not so very much older really," said Jessica. "Actresses never get old. It's hard work, but they don't. And as for fame, our kind doesn't last very long, you know. When we stop being popular we fade out. No one can really make anyone else understand or even imagine what the great actors were like. My father saw Irving when he was a boy and lots of the other big names, but when he described them we used to say 'Father's off again,' and as we were a very large family he laughed and didn't talk about it any more. We are like Roman Candles on Guy Fawkes' Day. A lovely uprush of light, a skyful of glittering coloured stars, and then—pouff!" which last remark Jessica delivered as if it were a first night at the Cockspur, in the lovely muted voice that she kept for her most moving effects. "Your people will last and be remembered because they have roots. We haven't."

To this Ludovic made no answer, unless blushing furiously and becoming uncomfortably damp under the collar constitute an answer. Not only in her step, but in her voice, her charm, her understanding, was the goddess now truly manifest. But it is not given to us all to be able to unpack our heart with words, and all the young Lord Mellings could utter was "Oh, I say."

"I would send you a box for the Cockspur if it weren't for your school," said Jessica. "Perhaps at the end of the term you will be in London," for which crumb Ludovic was so grateful that he overlooked the solecism.

"I did act at my prep school," said Ludovic.

"My lamb, how divine!" said Jessica. "Of course schoolboys are the best actors in the world for tragedy, comedy, and all the rest of that speech. What were you?"

His lordship, rather shyly, ran through the list of his roles, mostly female, adding that since he went to Eton he had grown so fast that he couldn't be a girl any longer, besides not having the right voice.

"But you would be *absolutely* right as Romeo," said Jessica, at once seeing in her player's eye the tall adolescent fulfilling all his dreams of romance and love on the school stage. "Can you still say your lines?"

"I could to *you*," said Ludovic, who was by now head over ears in love.

"Dear boy, you shall some day," said Jessica. "You must come to Winter Overcotes in Coronation week when Aubrey and I are having a holiday and we will say some Shakespeare together," which opening of the doors of Paradise so completely overcame Ludovic that he slipped his hand under Jessica's, raised her fingers to his lips, and gently restored her hand to her; all of which was observed by Aubrey Clover, coming in with the men.

"And where did you learn to kiss a lady's hand so beautifully?" said Jessica.

"Oh, that was Mr. Yardley," said Ludovic. "He was the maths master at my prep school and produced our plays, and he said that was the courtly way to kiss a lady's hand. I do hope it was all right."

"Perfect," said Aubrey Clover, who had come over to them, "and I'd like to send one or two young actors of my acquaintance to your Mr. Yardley. When they have to kiss a lady's hand on the stage they grab it and mumble it like this," and he gave a spirited rendering, with the aid of Jessica's hand, of Prendergast Major doing homage to a Shakespeare Queen, at which Ludovic, his melancholy face transfigured, laughed outright.

"Ludovic is coming to Winter Overcotes in Coronation week," said Jessica. "We might do a little pretence acting,

Aubrey. It would be so good for him. He has acted in school plays."

"The best beginning for anyone," said Aubrey, "now that people aren't allowed to be born in a barn and learn it all the hard way. Of course you must come over, Ludovic. I might even have a little job for you."

"Do you mean—" said Ludovic, scarlet, damp with emotion, and unable to proceed.

"I do," said Aubrey. "A small part, with Jessica and myself, just to amuse the groundlings. With your permission, I shall speak to your father about it," at which Ludovic could only look his gratitude. The Peri had 'come into his life, the doors of Paradise were open.

" 'Twill be but some dozen or sixteen lines which I would set down for you," said Aubrey, to which Ludovic replied: "Ay, my lord."

"Gad! your lordship knows his Shakespeare," said Aubrey, who was amused and even touched—so far as this last was in his nature—by Ludovic's enthusiasm and his acquaintance with the Bard.

Lord Pomfret and Mr. Wickham were now well away about the iniquity of the proposed draining at Starveacres Hatches, with Noel holding a watching brief, and would obviously be happy for the rest of the evening. As it was rather a children's party, Lydia proposed a card game. A table was cleared and she introduced the Towers party to that now neglected game called PIT. Ludovic and his cousin Edith, with the quick facility of the young for games, at once picked it up. Aubrey said he had no card sense, but might he play very quietly on the piano, which he did to his own satisfaction, undisturbed by the frightful noise that Edith Graham and, most surprisingly, Lydia were making, shouting their opponents down and trying to corner Wheat, Rye, or other cereals. Ludovic was at first shy, but as the gambling fever seized him he shouted almost as loudly as the others and, we may add, played much more quickly and skilfully, and before anyone knew where they were he had yelled "Corner in Rye" and slammed down his cards.

"Sorry, mother," he said, observing his mother's doubtful expression of face when a child of hers out-yelled anyone. "I just couldn't help it. I had to back my luck."

"It is so like Gillie's uncle," said Lady Pomfret. "He had an extraordinary card sense and extraordinary luck as well. He nearly always held good cards and even when he didn't he played them so that everyone thought he had. Cards and riding, he was better than anyone."

"Let's have another round," said Ludovic, flushed with excitement and almost handsome, Lydia thought; his melancholy eyes, so like his father's, now alight with the excitement of the chase. So another round they had, and several more, Jessica with her nimble wits and ready to take up any card not doing so badly, but Ludovic winning quite an unfair share of them, partly by the luck of the cards but also by his concentrated and skilful tactics; though everyone had to admit that Edith's peacock shriek was the loudest. Lady Pomfret felt she would have to do something about Edith if she took her out to dinner again.

During all this noise and excitement Aubrey Clover had been strumming and humming, and when the clamour of PIT had died down and Edith and Lydia were building houses of cards, Aubrey began to sing gently in his own peculiar way, which was not quite music yet saturated with it. And if any of our readers know what we mean, it is more than we do ourselves; we did have a faint glimmering of an underlying truth, but it has got so far down the well that we cannot fish it out. He now took the cigarette out of his mouth, played a

few bars, and turning to the room, sang in the voice which had
made thousands of people laugh or cry, though it was really
hardly a voice at all:

> "Though I am not twenty, sweet,
>   Here is my heart.
> You are sweet and twenty, sweet,
>   Where is your heart?
> I'd die for you this very hour,
>   (Quiet, my heart,)
> But let me live, just for this hour,
>   Deep in your heart."

When he had finished Aubrey was pleased to observe that
Lydia was quickly patting her eyes with her handkerchief,
that Edith was staring with her mouth open, and that there
was complete silence from the other end of the room where
Noel and Lord Pomfret and Mr. Wickham had been talking
estate shop.

"And that," said Aubrey, "is specially for you, Lydia my
sweet. Not that it expresses my personal feelings towards you,
which are affectionate but respectful. It is a little song for the
unlucky lover to sing in the sketch Jessica and I are going to
do for your Coronation Entertainment. All we want is someone to sing it."

"But can't you sing it?" said Lydia.

"You have just had proof to the contrary, my admired
Lydia," said Aubrey. "As it is written for the Tertium Quid,
the unlucky lover, and I am the happy lover, I don't quite
see my way to doubling the parts, especially as we are all
three on the stage together. Do you sing, Mellings?"

Ludovic, overcome by this form of address, by emotion, and
by a kind of ecstasy hitherto unknown to him, went very pink
and said he used to sing in the choir at Eton till his voice
broke and once sang "Let the Bright Cherubim" in chapel.

"Then you're the man we want," said Aubrey, now the

brisk impresario, ready to catch young talent and get it cheap with a five-year contract. "Come along, my lady."

Ludovic looked wildly at his mother for help, but she was still dabbing at her eyes and even sniffing and no use to him at all.

"All right, sir," he said, and came over to the piano.

"None of that, or I'll call you My Lord," said Aubrey. "We are all rogues and vagabonds on the stage. I'm going to sing that again for you. I want you to listen."

"Now, fire away," he said, when he had sung.

"Me, sir? I don't know it," said Ludovic, just as he might have said it to his form master when he had forgotten to prepare his French.

"Then you better had," said Aubrey. "Come on. Nobody's listening," and such was Aubrey's power of creating a stage where no stage was that Ludovic had almost an illusion that he and Aubrey were alone together. With some prompting, Ludovic sang the little song.

"What a charming voice," said Noel to Lord Pomfret, who was sitting almost with a dropped jaw (if that ever happens outside books, for we have never seen it) in his surprise.

"I don't know. I never heard him at Eton and I've certainly never heard him at home," said Lord Pomfret.

"Quiet, there," said Aubrey, who was now on the Cockspur stage, ordering everyone about for their own good and the good of the play. Lord Pomfret obeyed.

"Now we'll do it again," said Aubrey. "A semi-tone higher, I think. A nice high baritone you've got. A most useful voice. Come on."

Ludovic, by now entirely under Aubrey's spell, sang it again with increased confidence.

"Fine," said Aubrey. "And for an encore we'll both sing it. I shall join you, like Mr. Frank Churchill, with a second,

slightly but correctly taken. And for the second encore
Jessica can come in too as a counter-tenor or something. She
can do that on her head. And for the rest of the encores the
audience can join us."

"But what are you talking about?" said Ludovic, entirely
at sea.

"What have I been doing for this last half-hour but com-
posing the words and the music for this song?" said Aubrey,
patiently explaining simple facts to an idiot. "The day after
Coronation Day, at Northbridge Town Hall. I want a young
man hopelessly in love with Jessica—with song, of course—
and I've done the song, words and music, and you can sing it.
Everything is fine."

Had Ludovic been a little younger he would have said
"Mother, mother" and rushed to her for protection, but he
was now enough of a grown-up to be treated as such, and
must behave as such.

"Do you mean me to pretend to be in love with Miss, I
mean Mrs.—"

"You mean just Jessica, my lamb," said that lady, looking
up at him with an engaging air of candid innocence. "Let's
do it once more, Aubrey. I'll fadge a part for myself," and
Aubrey played the waltz tune, which was to go round the
world before the year was out. "Up Guards, and at 'em!"

Whether it was the allusion to what he hoped would be
his future career, or the marvel of being allowed to perform,
even in a drawing-room, with Aubrey and Jessica, we do not
know. Probably a mixture of both. But whatever spurred him,
Ludovic made a complete success of his part, all self-consciousness lost, and the trio was sung without a mistake.

"That's fine," said Aubrey, disregarding the rest of the
company, who, as far as he was concerned, were either not
there, or sitting in the front row of dust-sheeted stalls in the

dark theatre waiting for their turn to be heard. "We will fix
a day for you to come to Winter Overcotes and go through it
again before the show, and I'll send you your script. You can
learn it very easily. You are only on the stage for ten minutes
including the song. You tell him roughly what he has to do,
Jessica," and he went over to Lady Pomfret and sat down
by her.

"I *do* like that boy of yours, Lady Pomfret," he said. "He
has just the right voice for an amateur. I know. I'm an
amateur myself. Will you allow him to help Jessica and me
in a very short one-act play at Northbridge? It is part of
the Coronation festivities and won't be till the day after the
Coronation, as everyone will be glued to the television on the
day itself. His part is a very short one and I gather that he
already has school experience of acting. If you say No, I shall
bow to your decision. But pray say Yes. For Queen and
Country," he added, suddenly becoming Colonel Blimp.

"I never knew Ludo could put it over—if that is the expression—so well," said Lady Pomfret. "I really don't see why he
shouldn't. We have got a seat for him to see the Coronation
in a friend's house, but he can easily come down afterwards.
Unless, of course, he wanted to see the illuminations. I must
ask my husband. Or will you?"

"As your ladyship pleases," said Aubrey, and then as she
got up he said: "Nay, come, let's go together," and offered her
his arm, which Lady Pomfret, whose presence of mind rarely
failed, took with a smile.

"Gillie, a most unusual happening," said Lady Pomfret.
"What did you think of the song Mr. Clover was doing?"

"I nearly cried," said Lord Pomfret. "I couldn't help thinking of that day in the estate office when I asked you to marry
me and how awful it would have been if you had turned me
down."

"In that case," said Lady Pomfret, with peculiarly unfair feminine logic, "would you let Ludo help Mr. Clover with a play of his that he is doing for the Coronation festival in Northbridge?"

Lord Pomfret said this was so sudden, and what was it all about?

"If I might put it to you shortly," said Aubrey, "Jessica and I are doing a little one-act play of mine in the second half of the program. It is about a very enchanting lady with two lovers—in the purer sense of the word, of course. One is successful and the other is turned down. I, as actor-manager and the star's husband, am going to be the successful one. If you and Lady Pomfret will allow it, I should like to ask your son to be the other one. The part must be played by someone who can look very young, or who really is very young and a gentleman. Your boy is very young and he picked up the words and the tune as fast as any professional. It's a very short part and I shall coach him in it."

Lord Pomfret said it all seemed very peculiar and he would like to know what his wife thought.

"I'm all for it," said Lady Pomfret. "Ludo is so *dreadfully* shy," she said to Aubrey, lowering her voice, which was really not necessary considering the noise that Edith was making with Mr. Wickham, to which gentleman she had for the moment transferred her unmaidenly affection, "and I am sure this would do him all the good in the world. Don't you think so, Gillie?"

"I must say it is rather short notice," said Lord Pomfret.

Aubrey said there were still nearly eight weeks before the Coronation.

"I meant if I have to make up my mind now," said Lord Pomfret. "What do you think, Sally."

"It will be quite simple," said Lady Pomfret, rather meanly

avoiding a direct answer. "Ludo can go down to Barchester after the Coronation. It's a nuisance that he isn't old enough to drive himself. Licensing laws are so stupid. But I can send one of the men to meet him and he can get over to Winter Overcotes by bus next day. Someone is sure to be driving back in our direction after the entertainment."

Lord Pomfret said as it all seemed to be arranged he supposed it would be all right.

"But if you really disapprove," said Jessica, who had come over to listen, "you have only to say so. It will break my heart, but what of that? Your Ludo, Lord Pomfret, is a very remarkable boy. He must be just like you when you were that age," at which bare-faced flattery Lady Pomfret would have laughed had she not been afraid of spoiling her elder son's chances.

"Well, it can't do him any harm," said Lord Pomfret, which being interpreted as Yes, caused Jessica to kiss her finger-tips and then touch the shoulder of Lord Pomfret's coat.

"Jenny kissed me," said Noel, who had been an amused and slightly sardonic spectator of this scene, and then he took Lord and Lady Pomfret to his study, where he had an old map of their part of Barsetshire before Starveacres Hatches were put across the river in the early part of the eighteenth century.

"Good fellow, that," said Mr. Wickham to Lydia, who came to earth with a start.

"Who?" she said.

Mr. Wickham said Lord Pomfret. Funny, he said, how things turned out. Pomfret was as good a fellow as you make them, but his father, Major Foster, to whom the title would have come but for his premature death, was a very poor piece of work. Difficult, touchy man, liked to live in Italy. Florence too, said Mr. Wickham, as if that made it worse; which perhaps it did. "But Pomfret is just what the county wanted, only he *will* overwork himself."

Lydia said one couldn't help people overworking themselves. She had done it herself. And her eyes darkened as she thought of that hope, never to be realized, while Noel was away in France and she was working in England. But of this Mr. Wickham knew nothing, and she came out of her memories and went back to the table, where Aubrey Clover was most obligingly telling young Lord Mellings and Edith about Miss Sarah Siddons Clover and how she was going to be an even better actress than her mother and marry a Duke and have six sons and six daughters.

"I'd like to make a poem for you about your little girl," said Edith, "but I can't think of a rhyme for Siddons, except middens, which is not poetry."

"Try Sarah, then," said Aubrey, already a little bored by Edith, though increasingly impressed by her cousin Ludovic, but the gifted poetess was not in her best vein, and then the exploring party came back and Lady Pomfret said they must be going and how much they had enjoyed the evening.

"And thank you for your kindness to Ludo," she said to Lydia. "It will do him all the good in the world to act with your charming friends. And Gillie and I have enjoyed meeting them too. Emily and Giles sent you their love and want to know when they may come to your river."

Lydia said the diving-board was now ready and she would telephone on the first fine day and when did they go back to school. In about ten days, said Lady Pomfret.

The farewells were slightly impeded by Edith, who wanted to recite a valedictory poem to the Clovers, but Lady Pomfret said No Nonsense and to go and put her coat on and followed her to see that she did it. Young Lord Mellings kissed Lydia's hand with touching gallantry and thanked her very nicely for a happy evening. Noel and Mr. Wickham went out with them to help with coats and speed the parting guests.

Lord Pomfret, who had been looking at a book with some old engravings of Seats of Landed Gentry in Barsetshire, suddenly realized that the party was over and put the book back in its place.

"I don't know how to thank you, Mrs. Merton," he said, "for what you have done for Ludo, for I am sure you meant it to happen."

Lydia felt herself colouring as she said, quite truthfully, that all she had done was to ask the Clovers because she knew Lord and Lady Pomfret would like them.

"It isn't only that," said Lord Pomfret. "Of course I like them. I am almost dazzled by them. But my poor Ludo is such a worry to us. He is born out of his time, I sometimes think. Not like Emily and Giles, who will trample on everyone like proper Fosters."

"The only thing I wasn't sure of," said Lydia, "was if you and your wife would approve. If you do, it is all perfect."

"Approve?" said Lord Pomfret. "I have seldom approved anything so much. Thank you with all my heart."

"Then thank you for thanking, Lord Pomfret," said Lydia, holding out her hand. "Good-bye."

Lord Pomfret held her hand for a moment and stood looking down at her with his melancholy eyes.

"You have been a guardian angel," he said.

Lydia could not pull her hand away, nor, curiously, did she want to, and her eyes looked up into his.

"Gillie! we're going," his Countess called from the hall.

Lord Pomfret pressed her hand and went out of the room, closing the door after him. There was a tumult of Pomfrets and Clovers, a sound of cars starting, then the bang of the front door being shut, and Noel came back with Mr. Wickham.

"I've only come back to say I'm going," said Mr. Wickham. "What a rum evening it has been. But I like that song of

Clover's. By Jove, he's a clever fellow. So's little Jessica. By the way, Mrs. Merton, we've got to name that new heifer calf. Have you any special wish?"

Lydia, pulling herself back into daily life, said what about Sarah, after the Clovers' baby. Mr. Wickham said it wouldn't do; he didn't know why, but it just wouldn't.

"Then Clover?" said Lydia. Mr. Wickham slapped his right fist into his open left hand. "Northbridge Clover," he said. "I knew you'd get it in one—well anyway in two, Mrs. Merton. Well, I must be off and thank you for asking me to the party. Pomfret's not much to look at, but he's a good plucked 'un. So's that lanky boy of his. I wish I'd had his luck when I was a boy. Acting with little Jessica at his age. No wonder Pomfret looked a bit dazed when he was going."

"You know, I didn't ask you to the party, Wicks," said Lydia, who felt she must say something and come back into the everyday world, "but you're always welcome," to which Mr. Wickham said Kamarad and Lydia laughed and he took himself off.

"And a very nice party too," said Noel when he had shut the front door on Mr. Wickham. "Aubrey was really extraordinary with that boy. It will do him all the good in the world to feel he is someone and get a bit of importance. He is terribly like his father. I know it is no business of mine, but one can't help feeling sorry for Pomfret. His wife is a very nice person and must have some difficult times."

"Well, one does have difficult times," said Lydia, and it speaks well for Noel's affection and trust that he did not for a moment suspect her of alluding to the silly episode of Mrs. Arbuthnot. Nor was she alluding to it. But whatever it was that had been in her mind had vanished—or been ordered to vanish—and after a little desultory talk about what fun Aubrey and Jessica had been, they went to bed.

CHAPTER 5

FATE, while determinedly saving up her strength for the worst
weather possible in Coronation week, thought it would be
amusing to have a week of warm, nay, in the middle of the
day, hot spring weather. Summer Time had come cranking in
as usual and everyone said as usual (*a*) did one put the clocks
on or back, (*b*) how on earth did they arrange about the trains,
and (*c*) anyone but a fool would know the cows don't like it
and how could you start mowing before the sun had dried the
dew from the grass, and (*d*) that they didn't seem to have seen
the piece in the paper about it and couldn't think why the
trains were so funny.

So Lydia telephoned to Lady Pomfret and suggested the
Saturday of that week for the river-party as Noel would be
there and also her brother Colin with his wife, Eleanor. Lady
Pomfret's voice said the children would be delighted and if
Mrs. Merton didn't mind, she would send them over with
Miss Merriman as she and her husband had to go to the
Omniums that day. Mr. Clover had mostly kindly sent Ludo
his part, nicely typed, and Ludo was learning it all over the
house. And when would the Mertons come over and do the
tour of Pomfret Towers by daylight? A possible Sunday was
settled for Noel and Lydia to come to lunch. Lady Pomfret
said again how much they had enjoyed the party and with
expressions of goodwill the conversation closed. Ten minutes
later Lady Pomfret rang Lydia up to say she found that one
of her husband's young Leslie cousins was coming to the

Towers that day, and would Mrs. Merton mind if he came too. Lydia said of course she would love to have him and what was his name. Lady Pomfret said that ever since they were small the Leslie boys had been called Major, Minor, and Minimus, and this one was Minor and very good at climbing anything, older than Ludo, and just going to do his military service.

When Noel telephoned from London, Lydia told him about the contingent from the Towers. "As far as I can make out," she said, "we shall be rather a large party. Four from the Towers and Miss Merriman, who is coming with them, you and Colin and Eleanor and I, and Lavinia and Harry. Nurse might give the younger ones tea in the nursery. Or if it is still really warm we could all have it in the garden room."

Noel said the garden room would be rather nice. This room had been added to the house in about 1820 and was approached through the room that was now Noel's study. Its walls were white, with columns painted on them, and it was lighted by an immense French window opening onto the terrace and an equally large sash window (which always stuck) which looked towards the pond and the gardener's cottage. Its only drawback was that Palmer resented it, feeling that a room onto the garden was not a parlourmaid's legitimate province, so Lydia's mother had put a service hatch from the kitchen passage. We need not say that Palmer had always refused to use the hatch, preferring to carry her trays through the house with a sense of injury. An excellent tea-trolley with rubber-tired wheels and ball bearings had also been provided and this Palmer occasionally consented to push before her as if it were a dust-cart that she unfortunately found herself obliged to drive.

The weather, doubtless owing to its concentration upon being as cold and wet as possible during the Coronation week, still remained warm and fine. Tea on a sumptuous scale was prepared and everything was ready for the guests.

On Thursday Noel came down as usual by train. Lydia's dearly loved brother Colin and his wife, formerly Eleanor Grantly, elder sister of the Grace Grantly who had married Lord Lufton, came by car. Their children had been sent to Eleanor's parents and on Saturday Eleanor and Colin were going on to join them at Edgewood for the week-end.

With Summer Time it was now light enough to go out after dinner, and Lydia with Colin walked down to look at the boat-shed and the new diving board.

Between Lydia and Colin there had always been a strong bond of affection and though each was devoted to her and his respective husband and wife, they had a very special happiness in being together. They walked by the garden, through the little gate, down the water-meadows, talking nineteen to the dozen about the days before the war and how they used every year to have a Grand Opening of the boating season and with equal ceremony have a Grand Closing and as they spoke about the past Lydia was overcome, as one so often is, by a sense of unreality in the present.

"I say, Colin," she said. "What is real; Now, or Then?"

Colin said philosophers and all kinds of other people had been trying to answer that question for millions of years and no one seemed to get anywhere. As a lawyer, he said, he must plump for Now, but when he got down to Northbridge he felt very Then-ish.

"Hullo," he said, as they reached the river's edge. "That's something new. I wish we'd had a diving-board when I was at home. It's too late now to try it, but tomorrow I'll have a go," and then Lydia told him about the Saturday party and how it had all come about by a chance meeting with the Pomfrets at Barchester Central.

"An excellent thing," said Colin, to whom Lydia would always be his young sister to be cared for and if necessary spoken to for her own good, "Pomfret is a good fellow," which words Lydia found a little patronizing but did not say so, and then she showed him the various improvements she and Noel had made for the children, including the damming of a very small stream which here flowed into the river, so making a safe place for the younger children to splash and paddle and sail toy boats. From the upper end the water ran over a low concrete wall, thus affording to the young a foretaste of Niagara, and at the lower end ran away through a grating in another concrete barrier. Colin expressed warm approval of these arrangements and said the one defect of his in-laws' garden at Edgewood was that there was no running water immediately available.

"But did Kate tell you what we are doing?" he asked. "You two are always chattering on the telephone."

Lydia said nothing special as far as she knew, and what was it?

"You know that place in Devonshire where Kate takes the children most summers," said Colin. "Everard and I together are buying a house there with a garden, right on the sea. At least it is on the cliffs, but they aren't very high and a local man is putting in some concrete steps down to the beach. I daresay the next winter storm will wash them away, but we'll wait and see. Next summer you must bring the children, old Lyddy-Widdy," which name of affection from their childhood made Lydia rub her cheek against Colin's shoulder in a very comfortable way.

"Would you like to walk along the diving-board?" said Lydia, but Colin said Not in his London clothes and shoes, and then they went a little way along the bank. From the opposite side the Bunces' cottage looked incredibly Morlandesque, a curl of blue smoke rising from the chimney, the thatch with enough grass and weeds on it to feed a cow, old Bunce sitting on an upturned wheelbarrow smoking a pipe, while from time to time one of his daughters would come out and empty a pail or a tin into the vegetables, exchange a few words in the language of Alfred and Ethelred with her father —words, as far as Lydia and Colin could judge, of an opprobrious nature—and go back into the house with shrieks of unrefined laughter.

"Do my eyes deceive me," said Colin, "or are those girls in trouble *again?* I've practically never known them when they weren't."

Lydia said that was just the trouble, to which Colin replied that anyway it was their trouble and nothing new.

"But it's the Coronation," said Lydia.

"Look here, Lydia," said Colin, "don't tell me that Effie and Ruby are going to London," adding rather coarsely that if they did they would be bound to get into double trouble; in for a penny, in for a pound.

"Shut up," said the sixteen-year-old Lydia Keith to her brother who was trying schoolmastering and not really liking it, then adding, in the character of the distinguished Q.C.'s wife: "The real bother is the Coronation pageant at Northbridge. Miss Pemberton, who is organizing it, says they can come on in the Elizabethan scene with farthingales or whatever they were, but not in the other scenes," at which Colin fell into very coarse laughter and said they would just look at the boat-shed and then go back. The boat-shed was inspected and approved and Colin promised to act as resident waterman for the party if Lydia would manage the children on dry land.

When they got back to the house Lydia sent Colin up to the nursery to see his nieces and nephew. The most gratifying shrieks of joy greeted him from all three children, who clung to any part of their uncle they could reach. Colin, disembarrassing himself of these human limpets, said he felt rather like Andrew Fairservice when Rob Roy's men picked him up and stripped him in one breath. Nurse cast a disapproving eye on him and was ostentatiously silent.

"That's enough now," said Colin, disentangling himself from Lavinia and Harry, but Jessica's limpet attachment had to be forcibly dealt with by Nurse. Jessica began to cry and was removed by Nurse to have her bath.

"She's only a baby," said Lavinia contemptuously, "and goes to bed now. I have my supper before I go to bed. I'm doing decimals, Uncle Colin. They're awfully silly, but you must know decimals to pass your exams. Harry can't do decimals, he isn't old enough."

Harry, goaded by his elder sister's remark, said he was going to do Latin next term and girls couldn't do Latin.

Nurse, who after the Mede and Persian code of the nursery, quite rightly held all education to be superfluous, having always got on very well without it, said Not to go on like that or Uncle Colin would tell his little girls what naughty cousins they had, which put Colin into an awkward predicament, unwilling to let Lavinia and Harry think so ill of their young cousins, but equally unwilling to incur Nurse's disapproval and contempt, both of which regrettable passions Nurse could show by silence and a tightening of the mouth capable of overawing the boldest and most insensitive.

"Look here, Lavinia and Harry, just do what Nurse tells you," said Uncle Colin, "and say good-night. And tomorrow if you are good I'll take you on the river."

"I can swim," said Lavinia. "Harry can't swim as well as I can. Boys are always stupider than girls."

"Only while they are small," said Colin, with the rather

mean but intelligible wish to deflate his elder niece's over-powering personality. "When they get bigger they get cleverer and cleverer, like your father."

"But he's not clever," said Lavinia. "He tried to help me with my geometry prep and got all muddled. He said it was different when he was a little boy. Oh, Uncle Colin, do stay here for *ever*."

"That's only because she wants Uncle Colin to take her on the river," said Nurse. "Say good-night nicely."

So Lavinia, being really of a generous disposition, stood on tiptoe and warmly embraced Colin as high up as she could reach. Colin lifted Harry, gave him a hearty avuncular kiss, and put him down.

"Kiss *me* like that, Uncle Colin," said Lavinia, jiggling up and down with excitement, to which Nurse said that was Quite Enough and they'd see Uncle Colin tomorrow after breakfast if they were good, and then Colin, not forgetting to inquire after Nurse's invalid aunt at Southend, went away, quite glad, much as he liked his young relations, to exchange the super-charged atmosphere of the nursery for the simpler life of intelligent grown-up people.

Meanwhile Lydia had been having a very nice comfortable talk downstairs with her sister-in-law Eleanor, of whom we have seen and heard little since her marriage, because she and Colin live in London. After going through the family news Lydia told Eleanor about the plans for a water-party on Saturday, provided the weather held. "Our three and Lady Pomfret's three and a cousin," said Lydia. "Do stay for it, you and Colin, and stay to supper. Or if you must get over to Edgewood, you can go after tea," which Eleanor thought a very good plan.

"Colin has always told me," she said, "what heavenly times

he used to have here when he was at home. I wish we had a river at Edgewood. But the children will learn to swim very soon in Devonshire. Did Colin tell you about it?"

Lydia said he had, and what a delightful plan.

"There's another house next to ours on the cliff," said Eleanor, "that the owners want to let this summer. You wouldn't think of it?" and Lydia said she certainly would and what fun if all the young cousins could be together, and Kate's children, who were a good bit older, could be trusted to keep an eye on the younger ones paddling.

Eleanor asked whether Lord and Lady Pomfret were coming to the water-party.

"They can't," said Lydia, "they are going to the Omniums. That nice Miss Merriman will bring the young people. Do you know her?"

"Quite well," said Eleanor. "I was at the Towers two or three times when I was Lady Pomfret's secretary at the Red Cross. What very nice children they are. And I liked poor Lord Pomfret immensely," to all of which Lydia heartily agreed, though she was at the same time conscious of a small dull ache of resentment inside herself; the constriction that the less explored windings of our strange minds send to our equally peculiar bodies long before we know why we suddenly feel hollow and knotted inside. And if our Reader is so dull, or so unsympathetic that she does not understand this feeling, we envy her most heartily. Hope deferred maketh the heart sick, as the Book of Proverbs tells us, but so do other feelings or emotions and there would appear to be no way of short-circuiting the horrid connection, swifter than lightning or super-sonic something-or-other, between head and whatever that bit of our insides is that takes the fatal electric shock, the knockout blow.

"I helped him a bit with his papers," said Eleanor, "and told the children some new fairy stories. I couldn't help feeling sorry for him, he was always so tired and so polite. The eldest boy was just like him. What is he like now?"

Lydia said very much the same, she thought, but by a great piece of luck Aubrey Clover had taken a fancy to him and had invited him to act in one of his short plays at the Northbridge Coronation Festival.

"*What* luck," said Eleanor. "It will be so good for him." Eleanor, looking at her sister-in-law, admired her with the generosity that so many good-looking women have for other good-looking women; for jealousy of another woman's looks is, we believe, not one half as common as people say or think. A handsome woman who has any sense realizes that her looks are far better set off by other beauties than by plain or ugly people.

"You are looking very nice, Lydia," she said. "Have you been having a new hair-do or anything?"

Lydia said she was very glad she looked nice and could only think it was in comparison with the faithful Palmer, who had never been a beauty and certainly didn't improve. Eleanor said she must keep Palmer in the house on purpose. Lydia laughed and Eleanor asked what she was laughing at. Had Lydia spoken the truth she would have said: "Just look at the maze-in-the-house; jever see such maze," but she felt it would need too much explaining, so she said: "Oh, just laughing," and went on to ask about Eleanor's children, but this conversation we shall not report, for at the moment we neither know nor care how many and what kind there were. Colin and Eleanor are Londoners now and though we still think of them as friends, their lives concern us very little save as they sometimes touch Barsetshire.

On Friday morning we need hardly say that Colin, after

putting up a most unconvincing show of not having brought the right clothes, changed into a very old pair of old flannel trousers, stuffed an old bathing suit of Noel's into his pocket, and spent the whole morning down at the boathouse. By twelve o'clock it was getting really hot. Lydia and Eleanor came down to watch.

"Try the diving-board, Colin," said his sister.

Nothing loath, Colin changed into the bathing suit and went very nimbly up the ladder to the diving-board, which was a little platform built out on legs over the river and also had a plank sticking out for people who were brave enough to use it. He walked along the quivering plank, stood on the end of it making it go up and down, and then did a clean dive into the river, disappeared, and came up unexpectedly on the far side.

"Look out for mud," Lydia called, as loudly as Miss Lydia Keith would have called—except that the old Lydia would not have thought of warning her brother, nor indeed anyone else.

Colin swam back across the river and came up dripping to where they sat. "Did you think I'd forgotten the mud?" he said. "Do you remember when old Bunce came home drunker than usual and walked into the river head-first and we had to get the boat out and rescue him? Lord! how one does see life in the country."

"And we aren't the only ones," said Eleanor, looking across the river to where Effie and Ruby Bunce, having observed from afar that something was going on in Mrs. Merton's boathouse, had come to look, some of their offspring draggling after them. Loud unrefined laughter, echoed by the innocent voices of the children of shame, floated across the water.

"I'd love to go over and talk to them," said Colin. "It is so nostalgic and like one's happy past—sorry, Eleanor darling, that doesn't mean anything—but I know it would only mean 'Ow, Mr. Colin, you are a one!' and giggling flight."

Eleanor said she wondered if all the people in Greek stories that were pursued by people giggled before they were turned into trees or fountains. Colin said he was sure they did, only they giggled in Greek and probably said something like Hopopitoipopapikos, which, though neither Lydia nor Eleanor knew any Greek, made them laugh. Colin said it was most flattering.

"Look here, Colin, as you are here," said Lydia, "could you just go across again and ask Effie or Ruby what time Miss Pemberton is having the Pageant meeting tomorrow? I promised to go, but I don't know when it starts."

"Not as I am," said Colin. "They will have me up before the beak for a maintenance order. Let me get some clothes on."

He went back into the boathouse and in a few moments came out, fully dressed, standing in the coracle, a small, almost circular collapsible canvas boat with no particular bow or stern and one narrow seat across it, a great favourite of Miss Lydia Keith's some sixteen or seventeen years ago.

"One can paddle it," Colin said to his wife, bringing it alongside the bank, "or punt it. I have always found punting more amusing," and with deliberately fantastic bends and swoops of his long body he shot slantingly across the river to the bottom of old Bunce's garden.

"I'm sorry to trouble you, but Mrs. Merton wants to know what time the Pageant Meeting is tomorrow," said Colin to the Misses Bunce, who at the sight of the gentry standing up in that funny little boat fell into high-pitched giggles. Two very healthy-looking, extremely dirty children who were skinning a dead mouse also began to giggle and to address Colin in the fine uncouth Saxon or Middle English to which his ear had for long been unaccustomed. He poled his coracle into the rushy bank and held it there with the pole.

"Give us a ride, mister," said one of the children, who was at once cuffed by its mother and told not to talk to the gentleman like that.

"Look here, Effie, you're Effie, aren't you," said Colin, "Mrs. Merton wants to know what time you are rehearsing at Miss Pemberton's tomorrow."

"Fancy you remembering me, Mr. Colin," said Effie Bunce. "I'm ever so pleased to see you. I was saying to father only last Tuesday it was, we don't see you the way we used."

"You couldn't," said Colin, "I live in London. That's my wife over there with Mrs. Merton and I've got two children. How many have you girls got?" which caused the Misses Bunce to laugh so loudly that their father yelled to them in unintelligible words.

"Don't you listen to father, Mr. Colin," said Effie. "Seems to think he's old Staylin, he does. You tell Miss Lydia the rehearsal begins at seven, but Ruby and me don't come on in the first bit, so she needn't hurry."

"Thanks awfully. Good-bye," said Colin and sped back upon the water to the other bank to give Lydia the information.

"I rather wish I hadn't got to go, but as I'm chairman of the Committee I'll have to," said Lydia. "Oh well."

Then Colin put the coracle back in the boat-shed and they walked back through the water-meadow, already deep in grass, watered by the little irrigation canals. Later there would be yellow iris and forget-me-nots and in the hedges dog roses, but the year was still too young. The dinner was good, the wine was good. By way of a change from professional life Noel and Colin talked legal shop while Lydia and Eleanor talked about children and summer plans till everyone began to yawn very comfortably and they all went to bed early.

By some serious oversight on the part of Providence the weather on Saturday was still fine and warm and got warmer as the day went on. Uncle Colin was graciously allowed by Nurse to take the three children out in the punt so long as they got back in time for Jessica to have a rest before lunch or she'd be as cross as two sticks by tea-time.

"If Jessica didn't come," said Harry, "we wouldn't need to come back," but this very sensible remark was ignored by the grown-ups.

"I wish," said Jessica, whose choice of words and articulation of the same were extremely advanced, "to catch a frog in the pond, Nurse."

Nurse said that was enough and frogs were nasty things.

"I like nasty things better than nice things," said Jessica, with such a Prunes and Prism of diction that all the grown-ups (except Nurse) had to laugh.

"Look here," said Eleanor good-naturedly, "I don't particularly want to go on the river. I'll look after Jessica, Nurse. How does she catch frogs?"

"Well, Mrs. Colin," said Nurse, a mode of expression which we think she dimly felt to be suitable to an old retainer who had been in the family longer than Eleanor Keith had, "I'll get the old shrimping net we had at the sea last year and she'll be no trouble. If she fishes those nasty green weeds up, she must put them back again, not on the grass or Twicker will complain. There's no pleasing some people," for a slight coldness existed between Nurse and the Mertons' old gardener, the feud being entirely, we think, Nurse's unfounded jealousy of Mrs. Twicker, the gardener's wife, who gave the children such glorious teas in her cottage that they had all, at various times, expressed a wish to live there for ever.

"Are you coming, Lydia?" said Colin.

Lydia was going to say no, for she had various things to do about the house, but suddenly she felt that her beloved Colin would like her company, so with the two children they went down to the river, joined by Noel, who said he was damned if he was going to spend the one fine morning of the year indoors, which words, unsuitable for the young, were of course treasured by Lavinia and Harry. When they got down to the boat-shed Colin brought out the punt, gave each child a paddle, ostensibly to row with but really to keep it quiet, saw that Lydia and Noel were safely on board, and pushed out into the river.

"Up or down?" he said.

"Let's go up to Parsley Island," said Lydia, "where we had that picnic the Whitsun that Noel and Everard came down and Everard fell in love with Kate."

Noel said, feelingly, that indeed Everard did, and it would have blighted the whole holiday if he and Colin hadn't been there.

"But you didn't fall in love with *me* then, Noel," said Lydia.

"Not a bit," said Noel cheerfully. "What a sight you were, my love. You had no stockings and were dressed in a kind of sack that was far too tight for your figure and you were bright red about the face, neck, arms, and legs."

Lydia said she remembered. A horrid dress, she said, that she had always hated, so she wore it on the river just to finish it off. "But you weren't in love with me then, Noel," she said. "You thought I was a forward flapper."

Noel said he had completely forgotten what he thought then, but he thought now, and always would think, that she was the nicest girl and woman he had ever known. And with such complete satisfaction did he say this that Lydia felt a surge of gratitude. Not that she had brooded upon anything that was past, but her affection for Noel made her glad to know that he did not think of it either; for that might have made him unhappy.

At Parsley Island Colin ran the punt into the bank and tied up. Lower downstream, on the opposite bank, the Rectory exhibited its Gothic Revival windows and the garden that Mrs. Villars kept so beautifully, embanked with a red brick wall.

"What happened to the ferry in the end?" said Colin, who had not seen his old home for some time.

Noel said since old Bunce got past work—or more probably because he was too lazy to work—the ferry had died. And in any case hardly anyone had used it for years now, as everyone had a car or a motor-bicycle. The punt had lain among the rushes till it fell to bits or was used by the Bunce family for kindling, and another small piece of civilization had died.

"Can I fish, mother?" said Harry. "I've brought a safety pin and some string," so his Uncle Colin most obligingly cut a tall bulrush for him and tied the safety pin onto it. Harry lowered his line into the water.

"You ought to have some bait," said Lavinia. "People always have bait."

"I don't," said Harry and went on fishing. Lavinia said could she sit on the end of the punt if she promised not to fall off. Her mother said yes, so long as she didn't talk all the time, and then Noel and Colin re-argued, very comfortably, one or two points of law that they had been talking about the night before and earlier in the same morning, in connection with the theft of two empty packing-cases from the parcels office at Winter Overcotes Junction, which reminded Lydia of the

silver cup, won three years running for the best-kept stretch of
line, whose rape and subsequent restitution had been the talk
of the county. This had happened during the war when Noel
had been at the local Hush-Hush camp which was really the
Dower House at Worsted, and he and Lydia had been very
happy as paying guests at Beliers Priory with Sir Harry and
Lady Waring. And now—not so very many years afterwards,
but it felt like centuries—those kind Warings were dead, their
nephew and heir, Captain Sir Cecil Waring, R.N., had married Lady Cora Palliser, and Lydia with Noel was living in her
parents' old home. All most confusing, she felt, with the water
shimmering and the sun warm upon her. She may even have
slept for a moment. But of course Lavinia leant over too far
and fell into about nine inches of water and was very crossly
rescued by her father, who said Straight home and go up to
Nurse at once. Colin took them back very quickly and Lavinia
was dismissed to Nurse.

Noel brought drinks out onto the terrace, where the heat
was quite delightful except for those people who do not like
heat. But what they have to grumble about in our beloved
England we really do not know. Then they had lunch and
were comfortably lazy till the party from the Towers arrived,
personally conducted by Miss Merriman, competent and self-
contained as always. Young Lord Mellings appeared to the
Mertons to have grown since they last saw him. Lady Emily
and the Honourable Giles were bursting with health and good
looks, and with them was Leslie Minor, a very nice-faced boy
of about Ludovic's age but not so tall and very neatly made.
Ludovic, with the talent for nursery-maiding that many boys
have, at once became the adored friend of Jessica Merton, who
was showing off quite disgracefully. Giles very good-naturedly
allowed Harry to do a kind of all-in wrestling with him on the
lawn, while Emily glued herself to Noel with the complete

unselfconsciousness of the young schoolgirl when overcome
by the tender passion. Leslie Minor, looking rather contemptuously upon such weakness, at once attached himself to Lydia.

"I say, Mrs. Merton," he said, "have you anything I could
climb?"

Lydia said she was afraid there wasn't much in the garden,
but there were some quite good willows down by the river
and some beeches on the far side of the house.

"You haven't got a cedar, have you?" said Leslie Minor.
"I've done the big tulip-tree at Rushwater and the one in the
Palace garden in Barchester. I want to do the one at Wool-
beding, which is the biggest of all, at least Mr. Wickham said
so. I suppose one could write to people and ask if one could
climb their tree. Do you know Mr. Wickham? He came to
Greshamsbury, that's where my people live, the day we all
went up the church tower to see the mippet's nest in the gar-
goyle. I'm going to be someone's agent when I've done my
military service. Seriously, I mean. If there isn't a land-
agenting school at Oxford, I shall go to Redbrick University.
It's modern and frightfully good."

"If you have finished talking for a moment," said Lydia,
who had at once taken Leslie Minor's measure, "it is my turn.
I know Mr. Wickham quite well because he's our agent. He
didn't go to a college or anything, but he's about the best agent
in the county. We haven't got a cedar, but we've got a monkey
puzzle down by the gardener's cottage."

"Oh, golly, golly, golly," said Leslie Minor. "I've got one
or two monkey puzzles in my eye, but the people that own
them think I might hurt the trees, silly idiots. Could you very
kindly let me climb yours, Mrs. Merton?"

Lydia, rather apprehensive of the effect of a monkey puzzle
on her guest's skin and clothes, said he had better ask Noel.

"Can I watch you climb the monkey puzzle?" said Lavinia,

who, too young for the older children and not wishing to be considered as of the nursery party, was feeling a little out of it.

"Of course," said Leslie Minor, "and I'll wave a handkerchief when I get to the top. All for you," he added kindly, from which moment Lavinia of course was his slave.

"What do you like best?" said Lydia to Emily, seeing that she was a little bit out of it.

"Riding at home and games at school," said Emily. "And swimming. When are we going to swim, Mrs. Merton? Oh, and father and mother said they sent their love and I wasn't to forget it, so I haven't."

Lydia thanked her and then said to Miss Merriman that it would perhaps be as well to go down to the river now so that all the children could have a large tea afterwards and she had said they wouldn't have tea till five.

"A very good plan," said Miss Merriman. "Then I shall take them home directly afterwards before they get out of hand. Children never know how boring they can be."

"I wish I'd thought of that," said Lydia with unfeigned envy. "They are even more boring than some grown-ups. Ludo isn't. He is so civilized."

"Yes, he is," said Miss Merriman. "Like Lord Pomfret," and so dispassionately did Miss Merriman speak, as always, that Lydia was left to wonder whether this was meant as praise, or dispraise, or a mere statement of fact.

Twicker, the gardener, had been giving the punt a rub-up, or so he said, though we think he really came to see what mischief unknown boys might be up to.

"I've not cleaned up the row-boat, Miss Lydia," he said confidentially. "Those young ladies and gentlemen are bound to be up to their mischief. And I've put the oars away. I'm going back to the garden."

"Well, just keep an eye on the pond," said Lydia. "Jessica wants to fish for frogs there again and Nurse may be helping Palmer with tea."

Twicker said leave it to him and if Nurse was helping Palmer it would be like crossing a lemon with a cooking apple, and went away chuckling at his own wit.

It had been arranged that the girls, which meant Emily and any other lady who wished to bathe, were to use the boat-house for their tiring-room and the boys could change in the little coppice beside it under Colin's eye, who was going to do duty as general life-saver. Lydia with Miss Merriman and Eleanor sat on the bank, where there was a stone seat in the sun, and talked about the Coronation, a subject which it was, indeed, increasingly difficult to avoid. Colin was seen going up the ladder. He ran along the diving-board and went head-first into the water most neatly, with hardly a splash, and swam about on his back, waiting for the others. Then came Ludovic and Giles, neither of them very good, followed by Emily, who was quite tolerable. Noel came down with a huge india-rubber ball. He tossed it into the river, which raised a cheer.

"Where is Minor?" said Miss Merriman.

Lydia said he was prospecting for trees to climb and she had told the gardener to keep an eye on him. She thought Lavinia was with him.

Miss Merriman asked how the Coronation fête was getting on. "Lady Pomfret asked me to say," she added, "that she has some very good sham jewellery if it would be useful for your Tableaux and would be delighted to lend it. She found it when she was clearing out some of the empty rooms and thinks it was used for a pageant in 1909—one of the first pageants. I brought it over for you to look at and she says she hopes you will keep it as long as you like."

"Oh, do let's go and look at it," said Lydia. "Will you come,

Eleanor?" but her sister-in-law said it amused her to watch Colin in the water, so they left her and went back to the house. Miss Merriman took a suitcase out of the car and they went into the drawing-room, which was flooded with sun, and on a table near the window she unpacked three crowns, rings, brooches, bracelets, an orb, a sceptre, a sword, a golden flagon, and six golden goblets.

"My goodness!" said Lydia. "Where did they come from?"

Miss Merriman said she thought they used to have amateur theatricals in the sixth Lord Pomfret's time when they were immensely rich from coal-mines in the north and rents in the prosperous days of English farming, and these had been specially made for a kind of pageant in the Great Drawing-Room. Lydia said the Committee would go quite mad when they saw them and how good of Lady Pomfret and she would write to her.

"Lady Pomfret wanted me to say that it is partly in gratitude for the party to which you kindly invited Lord Mellings," said Miss Merriman. "The idea of acting with Aubrey Clover and Jessica Dean has done him so much good. He needed some self-confidence and this was exactly right."

Lydia said it was pure luck that she could get the Clovers that evening and what a charming voice Ludo had.

"I believe Lady Pomfret, I mean the wife of Lord Pomfret's uncle," said Miss Merriman, speaking of the former Countess to whom she had been a faithful friend and help, "used to sing very well as a younger woman. But of course Lord Pomfret is no relation of hers, nor is Ludo. How stupid of me."

"Music is a rum thing," said Lydia. "It suddenly bursts out. And hardly ever where you expect it. Please thank Lady Pomfret. I will take the jewels and things to the Coronation Committee tonight—unless you think that would be a risk," to which Miss Merriman replied that they were insured against third-party risks—if that was what she thought she meant—and no thief would be silly enough to take things of that sort, as they would either be in a strong-box or else had no value.

"And if you do not mind, Mrs. Merton," she said, "I would like to see what Minor is doing. He is such a nice boy, but one never knows where he will turn up next. He climbed out of one of the attic windows at the Towers the day before yesterday and came down one of the big chimneys on the other side of the roof into the ante-chapel where they used to have a fire. He was filthy, and had enjoyed it immensely."

Lydia said how could there be an ante-chapel in the house, and Miss Merriman explained that the sixth Earl when he built the Towers made a large chapel with a pavement of marble and lapis lazuli for his very High Church countess. But Mrs. Merton must see it all when she and Mr. Merton came to lunch on Sunday fortnight, wasn't it. And now, she said, might they look for Minor, as she felt responsible to his parents, Mr. and Mrs. John Leslie over at Greshamsbury?

So they went across the lawn, where Jessica was happily fishing for frogs with some of the reeds from the little stream that fed the pond as fishing rods, but had not so far caught any. Her mother asked her where Nurse was.

"Getting tea ready with Palmer," said Jessica. "And I'm catching frogs. I've caught twenty hundred. Lavinia said not to say about the monkey puzzle," and with the quiet obstinacy of the angler she returned to her fishing.

"Oh dear!" said Lydia, and Miss Merriman begged her not to worry, as Minor had never yet fallen off or out of anything. Lydia said she was thinking more of his clothes. A short walk by the grass path among the rhododendrons brought them to the monkey puzzle.

Below it a slavishly adoring Lavinia was looking up towards the tree, from which came occasional yells.

"Are you all right, Minor?" said Lydia, calling up to where she thought he must be, but evidently she did not make herself heard. Then, amid a shower of the horrid, brittle, dead leaves that are part of that revolting tree's equipage, Minor came down and emerged from the spiky branches, his hair full of bits of foliage (if one can call it that), a long scratch on one arm, an abraded knee, and a large tear in his shirt.

"It's just as well mother isn't here," said Minor, looking at the damage, not without pride. "She always thinks people fall out of trees. I say, Mrs. Merton, that's a marvellous tree. May I come here again?"

Lydia, who, if only for Colin's sake, liked young boys, said he could come whenever he liked and she would tell the gardener.

"Thanks awfully," said Minor.

"That young gentleman, he's got himself in a fine mess," said Twicker, who had come up and was listening. "No one's ever got up that tree. I'd cut it down if it was mine, great useless fellow."

"Oh, I say, please don't," said Minor. "Next time I come I'll bring a hatchet. I think if one could knock off some of the leaves on the trunk and cut a few places for one's hands and feet, one might manage. It would be rather fun to get up that way; rather like the Alps, or Mount Everest, when they have to cut steps. And then I'd put a Union Jack on the top."

"Oh, Minor, would you *really?*" said Lavinia, almost on her knees with hero-worship.

"Of course I would," said Minor, who had pulled some spikes out of his arms and was licking his wounds. "Lick's the best thing for scratches."

Lydia could see in Lavinia's face that she was going to express her adoration by offering to do the licking herself, when Mrs. Twicker, the gardener's wife and former Nanny to Lydia, her elder sister, and her two brothers, came up from her cottage.

"Dear me," said Mrs. Twicker, "the young gentleman *is* in a state. You shouldn't have let him, Twicker."

Her husband said it wasn't no business of his nor of hers neither and he hoped the young gentleman had enjoyed himself.

"He is one of Mr. Leslie's boys over at Greshamsbury, Nanny," said Lydia. "They call him Minor."

"Well, now," said Nanny, evidently accepting the name as one of the eccentricities of the class whom she had always served and who had to be humoured. "Like the cigarettes. You'd better come along to Nanny's cottage, Master Minor, and wash some of that dirt off and Nanny'll put some stuff on those scratches, or you'll be getting blood-poisoning. And I'll just put a stitch in your trousers, sir. They aren't hardly decent. I've got a lovely fruit cake just out of the oven."

Lydia, who knew that once boy-lust shone in Nanny's eyes there was nothing for it but to submit, told Minor not to eat too much cake as they would be having tea in half an hour.

"That's all right, Miss Lydia," said Nanny, who had never officially recognized Lydia's married status. "Hollow legs they have at their age."

Minor said he liked peroxide best for cuts because it fizzled.

"Oh, mother, can I go and see it fizzle?" said Lavinia.

"Certainly not. The idea!" said Nanny. "She's just like you, Miss Lydia. Do you remember the Whitsun when Mr. Tony and Mr. Eric and their friend were in the cottage and you were all going to clean out the pond before breakfast, and you wanted to go up to their room and wake them? Nice goings-on!"

Lydia did not answer at once. Tony Morland was long since married and several times a happy father made; Eric Swan had married Lord Lufton's younger sister. Hacker was a very learned classical scholar. And she was the mother of three rapidly growing-up children and going to be Lady Merton by Her Majesty's pleasure. By one of the twirls of that extraordinary creature compounded of memory and association that lives inside us, a line from a song whose long popularity lies, we think, in its nostalgia came to her mind: "Gone, alas, like our youth, too soon." Some lower-school boy had sung it, years ago, at one of the Southbridge School concerts, in a pure, soul-less soprano, and now it re-echoed from past time.

"Come along, Lavinia," she said, "and wash your hands for tea. And will you come along, Minor, as soon as Nanny has tidied you," and she took her daughter away.

"I am going to marry Minor when I'm grown-up," said Lavinia.

"Very well, darling," said her mother, remembering how as a schoolgirl she had artlessly decided to marry Bulldog Drummond, Richard Hannay, Hamlet, Everard Carter, and several of Browning's male characters as well as the Northbridge butcher who had a large black moustache. And then Noel, whom she had known since she was an overgrown schoolgirl and treated as an equal, had become apparent to her eyes, to her mind, to her heart, and was still to her not only the most loved but the nicest and most understanding person she knew. She shook herself back into the present, took Lavinia up to the house and handed her over to Nurse to be cleaned.

Palmer now grudgingly rang the bell for tea and they all went into the garden room, where noise was unconfined. The party from the river were full of their own exploits and young Lord Mellings was being as loud and almost rowdy as any of them; so much so that Miss Merriman said quietly to Noel that she hoped the young people would meet often during the summer. Jessica, who was having tea downstairs for a treat while Nurse in a mood of condescension helped to hand cake, made eyes in a most unblushing way at his young lordship, who most good-naturedly treated her as an equal. Noel and Colin, by way of a complete change, criticized Mr. Justice Stareleigh's ruling in *Regina* v. *Stickleback*. Emily with true Pomfret frankness told her cousin Leslie Minor her opinion of people who tried to climb monkey puzzles, and everyone was very happy and noisy.

"Tell me, Ludo," said Lydia, when there was a slight lull —owing mostly to repletion among the younger members of the company, we think—in the talk, "how are you getting on with the play?"

Ludovic said, rather shyly, that he thought he was word-perfect now, but he was afraid he would forget the words on the night.

"You couldn't," said Lydia, confidently. "Aubrey wouldn't let you."

"Oh, do you really think so?" said Ludovic. "I did remember my words when I was Titania in the *Midsummer Night's Dream* at my prep school. Only I wasn't so tall then," he added, as a kind of apology, looking at his hostess with eyes so like his father's. And then Lydia told him how a great actress, dead now for many years, used to have her words pinned up on the stage, behind a chair, or on a screen where the audience couldn't see them, and refresh her memory. Ludovic said gravely that he didn't think he would be as bad as that.

"I'm pretty slow," he said, "but I remember things I enjoy. I say poetry aloud to myself quite often when I'm alone, or in the woods at home. I wish you could see our woods, Mrs. Merton. There is a very lovely valley between wooded hills and a long avenue up one side with an obelisk at the end of it.

It makes me think of things like Keats or the *Pilgrim's Progress*. I hope you will see it when you come to the Towers."

Lydia said she would love to and Ludovic described the estate and its beauties with an enthusiasm that surprised and also touched her.

"Do you ride?" he asked.

Lydia said she didn't and felt that she had failed to come up to his picture of her.

"I only asked because riding is the best way to see it all," said Ludovic. "I don't hunt, because I don't ride well enough and it frightens me, but in the holidays I get about the place on a pony and talk with the people. Giles is the rider. He could ride anything. And Emily is pretty good. I am a kind of outsize. But when you come to the Towers, make it a fine day to see the obelisk," and Lydia said she would certainly make it a fine day.

A considerable noise at the other end of the table then resolved itself into Leslie Minor and Giles and Lavinia, who were seeing who could put most little biscuits into their mouths and were by now unable to articulate distinctly. Leslie Minor began to choke and was ignominiously led away by Nurse.

Colin said it reminded him of the summer he was a master at Southbridge School and had a tea-party on Sports Day with those delightful alphabet biscuits that one couldn't get now and two boys called Swan and Morland tried to get the whole alphabet into their mouths and choked.

Miss Merriman asked if that was any relation of the Mrs. Morland who wrote novels.

Colin said her youngest son, only he was married with three or four children now.

Miss Merriman said she supposed Swan was that very nice good-looking master at Harefield House School who had married the Dowager Lady Lufton's younger daughter, for one could not say Old Lady Lufton, and did Mrs. Merton know them.

Not really, said Lydia, because it was so long since she had seen Swan, when he and Tony Morland spent the Whitsun Holidays with her parents, years ago, but she would like to see him again and his wife.

"We might write and ask them to supper one Sunday," she said to Noel, who agreed and said what about Tony Morland. But Miss Merriman, who always knew everything, said that Tony lived in London now, so everyone lost interest and we shall know no more about him.

"And now," said Miss Merriman to Lydia, "I must take the children back, Mrs. Merton. We have enjoyed the party so much and I hope Minor hasn't done any damage." Lydia said only to his own arms and legs, but the gardener's wife had seen that the cuts and abrasions were clean and had put peroxide on them. Miss Merriman collected her young, who all said good-bye with very nice manners, thanking their hostess for the river, the punt, the diving-board, and the tea. Then all the Merton and Keith family went to the front door to see the guests go.

Ludovic and Emily said good-bye again to everyone with very polite and genuine thanks. Jessica, who had fallen in love with Giles, showed her passion very openly and it was lucky that Nurse was not there or she would have been publicly rebuked. Giles took it as a man of the world, having found the riper charms of Eleanor Keith much more to his schoolboy taste. Jessica, not content with Giles, then embraced everyone's legs with fervour. Minor drew Lavinia aside.

"Next time you want anything climbed, just let me know," he said. "And if your mother will let me I'll come again with my old corduroy trousers and some hedging gloves and have another go at that monkey puzzle. You can watch me," at which condescension Lavinia's heart swelled with pride.

Everyone was at last in the car and Miss Merriman drove them away.

"A most successful party," said Noel, "but exhausting in the extreme. Come on the terrace and we'll have some sherry," but Eleanor said they simply must fly as her mother was expecting them at Edgewood for dinner and their suitcases were packed, so they too got into their car and drove away.

"How delightful it is," said Noel as he and Lydia went out onto the terrace, "when one's guests go."

"So the silence was, So was the hush," said Lydia thoughtfully and then, at a questioning look from Noel, said it was a couple of lines from a poem of Matthew Arnold. Noel said he didn't know his Matthew Arnold at all well and always hoped to have time to read as he got older, but all that happened was that he had less time.

"Good gracious, so have I," said Lydia. "I'm sorry, Noel, but it's the rehearsal at Miss Pemberton's at seven. You will have to dine alone, darling. I'll take the little car."

Noel said his evening and his wife's digestion were going to be ruined, but he supposed it was in a good cause.

"Of course it is," said Lydia. "It is for Her Majesty."

"When will you be back?" said Noel.

Lydia said it might be any time and not to bother about her, but he might go up and see Lavinia in bed and would he put the suitcase with Lady Pomfret's stage properties into the car for her, which he did.

"Don't kill yourself, my love," he said. "I do need you. What about you?"

"Oh, me? Always," said Lydia, and Noel wondered, as he had often wondered, how such luck as marrying Lydia had ever been granted to him.

CHAPTER 6

Such of our readers as knew Northbridge in the happy days of the war may remember that Miss Pemberton lived just beyond the Mitre in a picturesque stone cottage called Punshions, about whose name a controversy (or as the wireless so often prefers to say, contròversy) had long been raging among members of the Barchester Archæological, some saying it had originally been a small brewery, others that it was the name of the family who built it, now long extinct. But whatever its beginnings, it was as uncomfortable as only an old stone cottage can be. The ground floor was stone-flagged and exuded damp on the slightest provocation. The living-room, two rooms on slightly different levels which some previous occupier had thrown into one so that all newcomers fell up or down the step, had a large open fireplace and a wide chimney down which rain, snow, and wind hurled themselves with enthusiasm. The stairs were solid oak beams, uncarpeted, and the ceilings so thin that every noise from above could be distinctly heard.

Miss Pemberton had in earlier days made a name for herself by a life of Edward IV's queen, Elizabeth Rivers, written with great accuracy, an exhausting number of footnotes, and complete dullness. She was also a considerable authority on the Langue d'Oc and, as we know, she and her lodger, Mr. Downing, had for some twelve years past been working on a Biographical Dictionary of Provence, financed by Mr. Walden Concord Porter, who owned the Observatory at Porterville,

Texas, where Miss Hopgood's Aunt's husband had worked. A rival authority, Professor Gawky, had lately made disparaging remarks about it at a meeting of the Friends of the Félibristes. These strictures having been seen in the Félibriste Journal of Studies by Mr. Porter, that gentleman had at once put through a transatlantic call to Punshions and told Miss Pemberton to keep right on and take no notice of Old Woman Gawky and had then told his secretary to put through a personal call to his wine-merchant in London, England, and tell him to send a dozen bottles of real good English port wine to Punshions every month. Californian port, he added, though a wine that did credit to the Golden West, had not yet attained the matoority of those bottles that had been stored for a hundred years in the vineyards of France, but his secretary, who was not only Miss Texas in the Stenographers' Olympic Beauty Contest but a very intelligent young woman, considered his last words as off the record. So why we know them, we cannot imagine.

But do not let anyone think that the last twelve years had been wasted, for from Falh-Féau the dictionary had made progress as far as the volume Mas-Moult and if the compilers lived and kept possession of their wits it was possible that it might reach its completion about nineteen hundred and sixty-two, by which time it was also probable that both the editors would be dead, or past work, even if we leave out W and, on the whole, discount X. At the moment their work was held up while they waited for the comments of an ardent Félibriste, maire of a small commune near Lille and better known in literary circles as Numa Garagou, himself the editor of the *Andalhou,* a very dull and prolix poem on the twenty-five different qualities of Amitié par Amour as opposed to Amour par Amitié, by one Guibert le Biau.

Domestic life at Punshions was on the simple side, as neither Miss Pemberton nor her lodger had much money. The

rough work and most of the washing were done by Effie
Bunce, who had come to Miss Pemberton when she left school
and with a kind of Saxon tribal loyalty had stuck to her off and
on ever since. The offs had become more frequent during the
war, but Effie's mother didn't mind having children about the
place, so Effie was now at Miss Pemberton's at least five days a
week, moved thereto, we think, less by loyalty to Miss Pemberton than by her womanly compassion for Mr. Downing, who,
as she said, didn't rightly know if his boots went on the right
foot or the wrong one unless you were at him all the time.

From the very first the Coronation Pageant of Northbridge
had been strongly supported by Effie Bunce, chiefly, we think,
because Miss Pemberton had offered the living-room for rehearsals and Effie said she was always a one for a good bit of
fun and so was her sister Ruby and she'd be pleased to come
along too. This offer Miss Pemberton ungracefully accepted,
for to do anything with grace was not in her and, as Mr. Villars
said to his wife, one had to remember that the willingness
was all.

If, said Mrs. Villars, it came to willingness, the whole village
was far too willing. There had already been one or two quite
awkward clashes between rival claimants for Boadicea and
Queen Elizabeth—she supposed one would have to say Queen
Elizabeth the First now. To which her husband replied that it
would be correct, but he did not like to think of the language
that Gloriana would use at the thought of being deposed from
her unique position. This, however, he said, was a purely
academic proposition.

The meeting this evening was to settle, finally (allowing, of
course, for Mrs. Paxon being called away to nurse her husband's old aunt, Mrs. Dunsford taking offence, Miss Hopgood's Aunt wanting her telescope to figure among the properties, Miss Hopgood and her friend Miss Crowder giving way

to each other all over the place, and a round dozen other con-
tingencies), the casts for the Historical Tableaux. These had
been chosen by Miss Pemberton and Mrs. Villars, chiefly, we
must say, with a view to giving everyone their turn, though
anything they or anyone else arranged was bound to give offence to someone. As she left the Rectory Mrs. Villars said to
her husband that she hoped they would get through the evening without a major coldness between any of the ladies concerned, and how they would miss Tubby. For Canon Fewling
over at Greshamsbury, when priest-in-charge at St. Sycorax
during and for some time after the war, had by his pugnacious
good-nature and endless patience made it impossible for people
to quarrel while he was there, and though Mr. Highmore was
a good fellow he wasn't so far the sort that people paid much
attention to.

When she got to Punshions the front door was wide open,
which she took as an invitation to walk in.

"Nice you've come, Mrs. Villars," said Effie Bunce, as she
came down the steep stairs carrying a large unwieldy bundle.
"Dust sheets, these are," she added, "to wear in the acts. You'll
laugh when you see Ruby and me. We don't half look funny
in fancy dress. You go on in. She's waiting, and Mrs. Merton's
there, too," and she continued her way into the kitchen, which
was evidently to be the wardrobe room.

Miss Pemberton, dressed in her usual shapeless greeny-
brown sacking, though we believe its real name was home-
spun, was sorting the properties into neat piles for the various
episodes. When she saw Mrs. Villars she came forward to
greet her. "Mr. Downing is over there," she added.

Mr. Downing, already wearing a kind of robe or mantle in
which Mrs. Villars recognized the grey emergency blankets
left over from the evacuation, was sitting on a three-legged
wooden stool by the great fireplace. A fire, as Mrs. Villars ob-

served to her great relief, was burning, though not very well. A gust came down the chimney and sprinkled Mr. Downing's smooth silver-grey hair with wood-ash.

"It's the draught," he said apologetically, which remark Miss Pemberton ignored in a way which showed quite clearly her determination that everyone should enjoy the evening. Effie Bunce, looking in from the kitchen, saw his misery and her kind heart felt compassion for him, as did her sister Ruby's.

The rest of the performers then came pouring in, all well known to those who have known Northbridge, but not so well known to Lydia, whose life, as we know, turned to London when she was not in her own home.

"No good waiting for people," said Miss Pemberton. "Will you read the list of episodes, Mrs. Merton, as our president?"

Lydia said should they wait a moment for Mrs. Paxon and even as she spoke the door opened and Mrs. Paxon, wearing her old A.F.S. trousers and a zip lumber jacket, came in, half closing the door behind her.

"Good evening, all," she said. "Guess who I've brought."

There was, of course, a dead silence. Mrs. Villars, used to championing lost causes, said was it Mr. Churchill, which went down very well. Miss Pemberton represented Impatience and Contempt struggling with Self-Control in a most lively manner.

"Well, we've no time to waste," said Mrs. Paxon, "so here she is," and in came Mrs. Turner, who used to live at The Hollies with her two nieces. The nieces had married and Mrs. Turner had gone to Norfolk to be near one of them, so her appearance was a complete surprise and gave everyone great pleasure, for her kind heart and warm hospitality had made her many friends and she had been much missed. A kind of general round of acclamation greeted her as with her pretty silver hair curling wildly into tendrils, her neat ankle, and her trim waist (expressions which rose involuntarily to Mrs. Villars's mind) she stood smiling in the doorway, taking the applause.

"Poppy!" said Mrs. Villars. "How *very* nice this is. Where have you come from? I think we are all old friends here," and there was a great noise and shaking of hands, which Mrs. Villars interrupted to say she didn't think Mrs. Turner and Mrs. Merton had met.

"Not for ages. It was at the Communal Kitchen at the beginning of the war," said Mrs. Turner, "but it's a pleasure to meet her again," and Lydia said she had been away from Northbridge nearly all through the war but had heard so much about Mrs. Turner. As indeed she had and always much to that kind and hospitable lady's credit.

"It's all Minnie Paxon's doing," said Mrs. Turner. "I was up in London for a few days and if we didn't run into each other outside Luke and Huxley's. Talk of coincidences!"

"I had just run up with a cheap day ticket to do Oxford Street," said Mrs. Paxon, "and I had noticed one of those men that sell stockings on the pavement looking at me in quite a nasty sort of way, I mean you know at once from the way a man looks at you what he's thinking, and I got pushed up against someone and I said 'Sorry, I'm sure,' and if it wasn't Poppy! Well, that's life."

A kind of hum of approval rose from the company, most of whom had never known Mrs. Turner's Christian name and were fascinated.

"So I'm spending a couple of nights on Minnie's divan bed in the back dining-room," said Mrs. Turner, "and isn't it lovely that you are rehearsing and I see such a lot of old faces. And there's Mr. Downing. *Isn't* that nice!"

Mr. Downing had seen her as she came in, and his mind had flown back to the evening when both Mrs. Turner's nieces who lived with her had got engaged. Mrs. Turner had shown him a photograph of her late husband, who had been a complete cad and bounder and died of drink within a year of the marriage, and then, in the kindest way, had managed to convey to him that her heart was buried in her husband's grave. Mr. Downing's heart had not broken, nor had his sleep been haunted by dreams, but when he saw Mrs. Turner his old wounds bled, very nostalgically and comfortably, anew. Rather encumbered by his grey blanket robes, he got up to shake hands and was glad to find that she was just as pretty as ever and just as pleasantly kind.

"I'm Merlin," he said, in explanation of his blanket robes.

Mrs. Turner, to whom the name conveyed, if it conveyed anything at all, a writer on Form and Betting Odds in a popular newspaper, said Now she was going to see a real bit of the Olden Times and they mustn't interrupt Miss Pemberton.

"You are not in the least interrupting me, Mrs. Turner," said Miss Pemberton, with a slight though ominous stress on the word me. "It is merely that we are having a general meeting about the Northbridge Coronation Pageant arrangements. Nothing of importance," at which words Mr. Downing did not blench, but appeared to Mrs. Villars to fold himself up in his blankets and, though this her husband refused to believe when she told him about it afterwards, become visibly smaller.

Mrs. Villars, anxious to get on with the meeting before anything worse occurred, said a word to Lydia, who got up and said they all welcomed Mrs. Turner, and now Miss Pemberton, as Pageant Mistress, would run through the episodes, distribute some of the roles, and as far as possible suit the properties to the right wearers. The talk died down.

"I have to express my regrets that my small house does not have many chairs," said Miss Pemberton, which made Mr. Downing rise hastily from his stool, to which he had retired again, and try to look as if he didn't recognize it, but as no one paid any attention to this gesture, he sat down again.

Mrs. Turner, beaming with happiness among her old friends, said she would sit on the floor, like Puss-in-the-Ring, a comparison which Miss Pemberton, if one was to judge by her speaking countenance, found far too apt. Lydia, prompted thereto by Mrs. Villars, got up and took the notes that Mrs. Villars handed her.

"The entertainment will be at the Town Hall, the day after Coronation Day, at half past seven. All tickets are now sold," she said. "It will begin with the Children's Performance. Miss Hopgood and Miss Crowder, who are organizing it together with the schoolmistress, Miss Hart, will tell us about it later. Then there is a short interval. At eight o'clock sharp there will be a one-act play by Aubrey Clover. Mr. Clover has very kindly consented to act in it himself and so has his wife, who is Miss Jessica Dean," at which applause burst out. "And there will be a young performer for the third character in the play whose name will be a secret till the evening," at which a buzz of speculation ran round the room, under cover of which Lydia said to Mrs. Villars: "I thought I'd better put it that way, because if they know it's Lord Mellings they won't pay any attention to the play," and Mrs. Villars nodded approval.

"Then there will be another short interval with tea and coffee in the Town Clerk's room, tickets sixpence each," said Lydia. "And at a quarter to nine we have the Northbridge Pageant of History in five episodes, written, organized, and directed by Miss Pemberton, who is now going to tell us roughly what the scenes are and what everyone is to wear. Miss Pemberton."

To the accompaniment of hearty clapping, Miss Pemberton stood up. Mr. Downing pulled his stool a little further back so that the majestic figure of Miss Hopgood's Aunt might better shield him.

"The first episode in the Pageant of Northbridge," Miss Pemberton began, "is in the days of King Arthur. Northbridge is then only a few huts on the bank of the river. The scouts are kindly lending a couple of small tents for huts. Ancient Britons are seen. Some are dressed in skins, for which a generous offer of hearth rugs has been made. Others bring back game they have killed. Miss Talbot and Miss Dolly Talbot are kindly lending some stuffed animals shot by their uncle, the late Sir Alwyn Talbot, K.C.M.G., on a holiday in Africa. Women go down to the river to fetch water and the Cosie Tea-Room is kindly lending us some earthenware jugs, which I hope everyone will treat very carefully. The men lament, in dumb show of course, the forays of the fierce Danes. Merlin appears and prophesies that where the huts are there will be houses built of stone and where the ford is there will be a bridge. Mr. Downing will be Merlin. Will you stand up, Harold, so that everyone can look at you," said Miss Pemberton. "He is wearing his magic robe, as you see."

Ruby Bunce said she thought it was his mack and was suppressed.

"The second episode," said Miss Pemberton, "—you may sit down again, Harold—is the coming of the Normans. The villagers are alarmed. Their chief, Mr. Clifford, the headmaster of the infants' school, is killed. The Normans show them how to build a church and a bridge. The scouts will make the bridge. They are very good at it. Mrs. Dunsford's gardener, who runs the Wolf Cubs, will be responsible for this."

Mrs. Dunsford said she was sure Bunce would do his best.

Effie and Ruby Bunce said they'd have a good laugh seeing Sid make a bridge, seeing as he was their cousin.

"The third episode," said Miss Pemberton, quite unmoved by public or private opinion, "is the Wars of the Roses. Richard Crookback, known by Shakespeare's play of Richard the Third, destroys the bridge after a fierce battle. For this bridge we shall have some of the banisters from that cottage that is condemned at Faraway Corner. Mr. Hopper will play Richard III with a false hump. Harold! let everyone see the hump."

Mr. Downing, who had been dreaming we know not what Provençal dreams, started.

"Where is it, Ianthe?" he said, looking miserably round.

"Here, I'll get it," said Effie Bunce and extricated from behind Mr. Downing's stool a shapeless cushion with loops at two of the corners. With great good-nature she helped Mr. Downing to get his arms through the loops and hung the cloak over his shoulders. Everyone said it was lovely.

"You can take it off now, Harold," said Miss Pemberton, which Effie Bunce most kindly helped him to do, and he sat down in his corner again.

"Who is Mr. Hopper?" said Lydia aside to Mrs. Villars, who replied in another aside: "The cobbler. The nasty one, not the nice one."

When the tumult had died down Miss Pemberton continued. "We now come to the next episode, in which Good Queen Bess comes to Northbridge to see the villagers dance."

"Did she ever?" said Mrs. Villars to Lydia.

Lydia said she shouldn't think so.

"Miss Crowder has kindly consented to take the part of the Virgin Queen," said Miss Pemberton, "as she has an old crinoline dress which can easily be altered to a farthingale. Two more crinoline dresses are being lent by kind permission of the Barchester City Council for the maids of honour, whose parts will be taken by Effie and Ruby Bunce. Mr. Scatcherd, the artist, brother of Mr. Scatcherd at The Shop, will do a quick portrait of the Queen in real crayons, which will be auctioned afterwards. The Queen will dance a pavane with Sir Walter Raleigh, Commander Beasley, who says though he is rather old for the part he can still shake a leg. I believe I report his words correctly."

Mrs. Villars said aside to Lydia that he had retired from the Navy after the 'fourteen war, but was a keen dancer, and had a pair of tights, no one quite knew why.

"The last episode is Northbridge in the War, and then the whole cast will sing *God Save the Queen*," said Miss Pemberton. "All three verses," she added in a rather threatening way. "If we *don't* want our Lord God to arise and Scatter our Enemies, we ought to. And now you will find some of the dresses laid out, and for the rest we must do as well as we can," and she sat down amid loud applause which was presently quelled by Mrs. Villars, who said she would like to ask for a hearty vote of thanks to Mrs. Merton for taking the chair, to Miss Pemberton for her delightful description of the pageant and all the work she had done, and to everyone present for the splendid help they were giving. There was loud applause and everyone felt that the entertainment was indeed making progress.

Effie and Ruby then each brought in a tray full of cups of hot, very good soup, and all the people who saw each other every day had a nice gossip. Mr. Downing, greatly daring, came over to talk with Mrs. Turner.

"I can't tell you, Mr. Downing, how nice it is to see so many old friends again," said Mrs. Turner, whose pretty silver hair was now almost in corkscrew ringlets with excitement. "You remember my niece Betty? She married that nice Captain Topham who was billeted with Mrs. Villars in the war and they live at his place in Norfolk and I've got a dear little cottage in the village with an ingle-nook and central heating.

Betty has a wonderful time. She and Topsy—that's our pet name for her husband—spend absolutely hours in a punt bird-watching and never mind the weather a bit. And now I want to hear *all* about the Troubadours playing their guitars and coming back from the Crusades."

Mr. Downing, already again under the spell of Mrs. Turner's cosy (for we cannot think of any other word) friendliness, asked after her other niece.

"Oh, she married that nice Mr. Greaves who was at the Rectory too," said Mrs. Turner. "He's a stockbroker and they've got a quite marvellous flat, frightfully expensive and very small rooms and there's a restaurant downstairs so my other niece doesn't have to bother about cooking. They take me to a lot of lovely shows when I go to stay with them. There's only one thing that makes me wonder," and she paused.

Mr. Downing asked what it was. Unless, he said, it was something she did not want to discuss.

"Well, to be perfectly frank and truthful, though very often one finds that truth is much better left alone," said Mrs. Turner, "I'll tell you."

Mr. Downing, who felt rather alarmed, wondering what sinister shadow lurked behind her words, said of course she must not dream of telling him anything that she would rather not tell.

"Well, it's nothing I couldn't repeat on the housetops as it happens quite often," said Mrs. Turner, "and when I remember the lovely times we had in the war, Mr. Downing, and how you used to come in and tell us about the Troubadours, I'm sure my other niece wouldn't mind my mentioning it, for even if they have been married for nearly ten years, while there's life there's hope, as they say. I was only married for one year because of poor Cecil dying and I daresay if he had lived we might have had some chicks. I showed you his photo once."

Mr. Downing said he remembered it quite well, and how good-looking her husband was. He also remembered that Mr. Turner had died within a year of his marriage in a home for inebriates and how often he had pictured to himself so charming and kind a woman as Mrs. Turner being at the mercy of such a man and had inwardly groaned; though never outwardly, for if Miss Pemberton had heard him she would undoubtedly have examined him with the remorseless patience of an Inquisitor and made the atmosphere of Punshions blacker and its living conditions even more cheerless than they at present were.

"Well, it's no good crying over spilt milk," Mrs. Turner continued, "and she and Bing, that's her husband's name—he's really Crosby after an uncle who left him some money, so we call him Bing jokingly—get along splendidly and I always say what you haven't got you don't miss. And I can't tell you how like old times it is to be here again. Now tell me about the Troubadours," and Mr. Downing, nothing loath, told her how he had been invited to give some lectures on Provençal poetry in America. Mrs. Turner said How lovely and she wished she could hear them and it was funny how lectures always seemed to make her go to sleep.

A great buzz of talk then broke out of people telling one another exactly what his and in the majority of cases her war work had been. Mrs. Paxon was quite obviously already distracted at the choice of one among the many uniforms which her activities had entailed. Mrs. Dunsford said that she was afraid she had had her W.V.S. uniform dyed black, as green was never her colour, but would do her best, though neither she nor anyone else could grapple with this statement. Lydia was silent, for she hoped as president to be let out of the epi-

sode and had the very valid excuse that she had done all her
war work elsewhere.

"It does seem a shame," said Mrs. Paxon, "Mrs. Turner not
being here for the festival. She did the Communal Kitchen
like anything. You'll remember that, Mrs. Merton. You were
working there too, the year the war began."

Lydia said she remembered it very well and how splendid
Mrs. Turner was and her nieces.

"Look here, Poppy, be a sport," said Mrs. Paxon to Mrs.
Turner. "Come down for the Fête and help me with the War
in Northbridge Scenes. You could come in with some of those
dinners we used to send out from the Communal Kitchen to
the old people in those tin containers."

Mrs. Turner, blushing in a most becoming way, said she
would simply love to if her niece didn't want her.

"Surely she can do without you for a few days, Poppy," said
Mrs. Paxon.

Mrs. Turner, visibly weakening, said it was an idea, as Betty
and her husband would be abroad then at a Congress or something about bird-watching in Mixo-Lydia and even if it meant
missing the Coronation they would have to go, because Topsy
was chosen as delegate from the East Anglian bird-watchers
and couldn't very well let the side down. The only thing was,
she said, she would be house-hunting, as the lease of her cottage was up in June.

Everyone, with the easy optimism we all have for other
people's difficulties, said they were sure she would find a cottage. One always did. From every side came pressing entreaties
that Mrs. Turner would stay.

"Well, Minnie," she said to Mrs. Paxon. "Here's a fair offer.
If I come down and do the Dinners for Old People, you must
be a hysteria case. You remember," she said, appealing to the
whole company, "how wonderfully Minnie did it."

Nearly every voice was raised in approval.

"Well, I really can't say no, as you're all so kind," said Mrs. Paxon. "I'll have to practise a bit beforehand. It was when I was with the South Wembley Dramatic I learnt how to have hysterics. You mustn't breathe in. You must empty your lungs as much as possible and then begin to laugh. It's quite surprising how long you can go on and what a noise it makes. Quite a realistic noise. You'll remember it, Commander Beasley; you were being a gas case."

Commander Beasley, R.N. (ret.), who always described himself as a man of few words, said he remembered hearing about it, but as he was being a gas case and no one appeared to take any interest in anti-gas technique, he had gone home. And if, he said, people would join the British-Needlers Society and realize that everything that had happened before and after 1914 was foretold in so many words by a triangle with Cleopatra's Needle as its base, the world would be a better place. Mrs. Villars said everyone was most grateful to him and she was sure there was a great deal in it. Commander Beasley, taking instant offence, said that Everything was in it. Every Thing, he added, with a perceptible hiatus between the two words which led the more sceptical of those present to feel that only in deference to Mrs. Villars had he omitted a pejorative adjective between Every and Thing.

This matter having been settled, everyone began to talk with everyone else more loudly than ever. Mrs. Villars said to Miss Pemberton that if there was any more business to be done, perhaps they had better go on with it, as some of the company had to get home. So Miss Pemberton spoke to Effie Bunce, who immediately brought in a large tin tray and clattered onto it all the soup cups and spoons, while her sister Ruby replenished the fire with such hearty goodwill that it was temporarily suffocated. Mrs. Villars asked Lydia, in her capacity as president, to ask Miss Pemberton about the dresses and properties, which she did.

Miss Pemberton said the response to an appeal for anything that could be used for dressing-up was most generous and she had put some of the properties for the various episodes on view, so that everyone could make suggestions and perhaps supply some deficiencies.

"There is just one question I should like to ask," said Miss Hopgood.

Lydia said Please do.

"About what Miss Pemberton said about that first episode," said Miss Hopgood, "I was just wondering about it being in King Arthur's time. Couldn't we have Sir Lancelot or someone? Chère amie and I," said Miss Hopgood, looking tenderly towards Miss Crowder, otherwise known as My-Friend-That-I-Live-With, "feel it would be rather wonderful. And Mr. Highmore would make a wonderful knight. One can make a splendid helmet out of an old cloche hat painted silver and if we can't manage armour—which is perhaps rather difficult—he could have a surcoat. Just two bits of an old sheet sewn together at the shoulders and a big Red Cross that I could easily cut out of half a yard of red flannel and machine on. I know he'd love to do it and he would look like a real Paladin."

There was a brief but noticeable silence.

Mrs. Villars, feeling that she more or less represented her husband, who was Mr. Highmore's superior, said that was a most interesting suggestion and she felt the Committee would like to find out Mr. Highmore's view before making a decision. A slight movement at the back of the room attracted her attention for a second, but she could not see what was happening and paid no further attention.

"And just one more thing," said Miss Hopgood. "Wouldn't it be rather effective in the Norman scene to have some French spoken? Chère amie and I would willingly be female Normans, if there were any. It would just introduce that French touch," and she sat down, rather red in the face with excitement.

As the whole company at once began to talk to each other, Lydia and Mrs. Villars were able to hold a swift consultation.

"You see," said Mrs. Villars to Lydia in a brief aside, "they used to go to an English pension somewhere on the Riviera every winter before the war and feel very French. They call their house Glycerine Cottage because they saw a house somewhere near Mentone with wisteria on it called Les Glycines," at which Lydia nearly had the giggles.

"I think," said Miss Pemberton to Mrs. Villars, "that Mr. Highmore is trying to speak," and indeed the slight commotion now made itself manifest as Mr. Highmore, who had been trying valiantly to overcome his constitutional shyness and apparently had something to say.

"Yes, Mr. Highmore," said Mrs. Villars, who always felt sorry for the young priest-in-charge at St. Sycorax; as indeed she would have felt sorry for almost anyone who followed the much loved and respected Tubby Fewling, now Rector of Greshamsbury and an honorary Canon of Barchester, whether she liked what the cottages called his "goings-on" in the church or not.

Poor Mr. Highmore, unnerved by these words from his Rector's wife, was struck dumb.

"Perhaps you had a suggestion to make. If so, we should be so glad to hear it," said Mrs. Villars, who had learnt a good deal about the male young while her husband was headmaster of Coppins School.

"I'm awfully sorry, but I couldn't do it," said Mr. Highmore desperately, "I mean Sir Lancelot was rather wonderful and I don't think I could undertake the part. One couldn't ackcherly live up to it."

Commander Beasley was overheard to say aloud to himself that a young milksop like that wouldn't have looked at Queen Guinevere, let alone what's-her-name, that other one, adding, to the great joy of his hearers: "Bah!"

Mrs. Villars, who had heard Commander Beasley's comment and would have liked to laugh at it, said she was quite sure everyone would understand and respect Mr. Highmore's point of view and perhaps the matter might be considered closed, while thanking Miss Hopgood for her very good idea. She also thanked Miss Hopgood warmly for her suggestion of speaking French, no one, she said, being better qualified than Miss Hopgood, but she believed that the Normans talked a quite different kind of French.

Miss Crowder said, archly, that perhaps Mr. Downing could coach them, with all his Troubadours and things.

"May I answer that contribution?" said Miss Pemberton, rising majestically to address the Chair.

Lydia, by now peacefully resigned to letting Mrs. Villars do all the work, did not answer.

"You!" said Mrs. Villars in an undertone. "Say yes."

Lydia said they would all like to hear what Miss Pemberton, well known as a French scholar, had to say.

"Merely this," said Miss Pemberton, her shapeless draperies assuming the effect of a toga, which, added to her large powerful face, reminded several people of one of the less agreeable Roman emperors. "The Langue d'Oc is not the Langue d'Oil, nor was the Norman tongue. Or so I believe," and she sat down with the air of having nailed her thesis to the cathedral door at Wittenberg.

As most of her hearers did not quite understand what she said, the effect was excellent.

"There is just one thing I would like to say, if I may," said Mrs. Dunsford. "About the Richard the Third episode. I do

think, considering that the pageant is in honour of our Young
Queen, that a Monarch who though not her ancester was in a
manner of speaking one of her Predecessors, should not be
held up, in any way, to ridicule. I do not know how many of
you have read a most interesting book, which can also be got in
a cheap edition, by a very distinguished and prolific writer
who, alas, is no more among us, but anyone who has read that
book will feel that the character of Richard of Gloucester has
been till now grossly misrepresented. The so-called hump
was, I understand, little more than a slight malformation
and *not*," she added severely "a cross between Quasimodo
in Victor Yugo's great novel of mediæval Paris and Quilp,"
at which point Miss Hopgood and Miss Crowder were heard
to say, the one How she wished she had seen Paris before
the Revolution, and the other that Just one breath of Paris
and you seemed to understand the whole of the Middle
Ages.

"Richard the Third was, in fact," Mrs. Dunsford continued,
"a great King and a great Englishman and that is all I have
to say."

Mrs. Villars said she was sure everyone was most grateful to
Mrs. Dunsford for her interesting and original contribution
and she was sure the hump was not intended as any slur on
Richard the Third, but simply as a token, as it were. Just, she
said, as King Alfred might be associated with burnt cakes, or
King George the Third with fits of insanity, without any
thought of disloyalty, which apologia Mrs. Dunsford graciously accepted.

A good deal of giggling which had been going on in the
background now resolved itself into Effie and Ruby Bunce,
who both began to speak at once.

"Now, one at a time, you girls," said Miss Pemberton.
"What is it, Effie?"

Effie Bunce said it was only her and Ruby laughing about what father said.

"I think perhaps, Miss Pemberton," said Mrs. Villars, leaning across to that lady and speaking in a low voice, "it might be as well if we heard what old Bunce was laughing about *afterwards*. One never knows."

Miss Pemberton said one knew only too well and she would speak to the girls.

"Thank you very much, Effie," said Mrs. Villars. "Come and tell me afterwards, please. Are there more questions?"

It was quite obvious that the room was seething with questions suitable and unsuitable. Miss Pemberton said to Mrs. Villars she thought that was enough, which message was passed on to Lydia, who stood up and said what a delightful meeting it had been and she would like to thank everyone for coming and thank all those who had spoken so helpfully and now she believed some of the dresses for the pageant would be on view and if they would stay in their seats Mrs. Paxon and Mrs. Turner would show them. Accordingly she and the other members of the Committee went and sat with the audience while Mrs. Paxon, with incredible quickness, hustled some of the performers into and out of the more or less historical costumes, and everyone was pleased. Partly because a Dress Show is always a draw and partly because every member of the audience was pleased to recognize and point out her own contribution.

Miss Hopgood's Aunt then got up and said Might she ask one question. So commanding were both her voice and her figure that quite a number of people stopped talking.

"This is," said Miss Hopgood's Aunt, apparently addressing some unseen power in the far corner of the ceiling, "merely a formal question, Mrs. Merton. Miss Pemberton told us there were five episodes. I may be in error, but I have only heard of four. You will forgive me, but my experience with my late husband trained me in habits of accuracy."

"Perhaps, Miss Pemberton," said Mrs. Villars, coming to Lydia's rescue, "you would deal with that question?"

"You are perfectly correct in your statement," said Miss Pemberton. "When I said five episodes it would perhaps have been more correct to say four episodes and a tableau."

Effie Bunce was heard to say "Tabloid, more likely" and both the Bunce girls giggled.

"The Tableau—and when you girls say Tabloid you are simply being silly," said Miss Pemberton, not in the least discomposed, "is really the performers out of the four episodes grouped together. We cannot of course show all the characters, as so many of our actors are playing more than one part, but as many as possible will be on the stage at once, with Mr. Scatcherd's portrait of the stage Queen Elizabeth and a large photograph of Her Present Majesty. God save the Queen will be sung by everyone and I should like to remind anyone who is bringing children that one of the steps is higher than the others as you go downstairs. It always has been and I suppose it always will be. So don't let any of the children fall down. We will now have some coffee. Harold! if you wish to spend the whole evening as Merlin you are welcome. It is no concern of mine."

Thus suddenly attacked, Mr. Downing became a prey to despair and did not know whether it would be wiser to take off his Merlin robes or remain as he was, but luckily for him Mrs. Turner saw his perplexity and came over to him.

"Let me fold it up for you, Mr. Downing," she said, helping him to free his other arm. "I *have* enjoyed the evening so much. It reminded me of the Good Old Days in 1941, wasn't it, when you used to come to The Hollies and how well you played rummy."

"I have often thought of those evenings and how pleasant they were," said Mr. Downing. "Do you remember how that nice young officer who was billeted at the Rectory made a Queen of Clubs for us when she was missing from the pack, and made her exactly like Hitler? I can't remember his name."

"Oh, that was Tommy Greaves," said Mrs. Turner. "The one that married my other niece. You know, Mr. Downing, it is a real treat to be here tonight and see so many old faces. I feel quite like the Auld Folk at Hame," which interesting variant on a respectable theme might have revolted Mr. Downing's hyper-critical mind in anyone else, but somehow from Mrs. Turner seemed rather touching, and they continued to relive the happy days when England, encompassed by enemies above, by land, on the water, and under the water, almost forgot in the common cause that an Englishman's—and even more an Englishwoman's—house is his or her own castle and doors were opened to every kind of refugee, whether the extremely selfish and irritating Mixo-Lydians or the free natives of our free land, who were in some ways even less easy to deal with than the foreigners.

"Really!" said Mrs. Turner, "the de-lousing! Every day and all day it was, and as soon as you'd done one lot another lot was sent down from London and by the time we'd been right through their heads the first lot were as bad as ever. Still, they say it takes all sorts to make a world. Now, I want to hear *all* about the Troubadours, Mr. Downing."

Mr. Downing, not at all insensible to this request from an old friend, who looked as young and pretty as ever, said it wasn't exactly Troubadours that he and Miss Pemberton were working on, but rather the language in which their songs, or poems, were written.

"It is a Biographical Dictionary of Provence," he said, "and we have got more than halfway through."

"Then it will take you a long time," said Mrs. Turner, "because I remember you and Miss Pemberton were writing it the year after the war began."

Mr. Downing said that luckily the second half would not be so long as the first. Mrs. Turner said that was funny, because a half was usually the same size as another half—so long as they were both halves of the same thing, she meant.

"I am afraid I have not expressed myself well," said Mr. Downing. "In Provençal there are a few letters that are seldom if ever used. W is one and—"

Mrs. Turner said she and her nieces had once stayed for a week at Wimereux, but perhaps that was different.

Mr. Downing toyed for a moment with the idea of explaining the incidence of Scandinavian languages upon the north coast of France, but somehow did not feel equal to it. So he went on: "X is, of course, another, thus already eliminating two letters. And as for Z, it is practically negligible. There are of course scholars, or they pass as such, who use Z for S in the interior of some words, but to my mind the Z is not really a Z. It may, or—for one must keep an open mind—perhaps it may not represent a sound between S and Z which we have entirely lost," and then wondered if he had said what he meant.

"I know," said Mrs. Turner, her pretty eyes alight with interest. "Like when people tell you their name and when you write it down it is all wrong. Like Pool Carey."

Mr. Downing said he was sure it was his own fault but he didn't quite understand.

"Well, sometimes it's Pole Caroo," said Mrs. Turner. "So it all shows," and she smiled.

"Dulce ridentem, dulce loquentem Lalagen," said Mr. Downing half aloud to himself, but left the verse unfinished. Mrs. Turner said Now she knew what Provençal sounded like and not a bit like French, but of course in the Olden Times things were different and if one said Summer is a-coming in to Mr. Scatcherd at The Shop, she expected he would be quite at a loss.

Mr. Downing said he could not tell Mrs. Turner what pleasure it gave him to hear her speak those lovely words in plain English and each century, or generation, must pronounce in its own way.

"May I join this discussion?" said Mr. Highmore, who had got wedged up against them by the crowd.

"By all means, sir," said Mr. Downing courteously, "though at the moment I am far from clear as to what Mrs. Turner and I were talking about. I think we were both out of our depth. Do you know Mr. Highmore, Mrs. Turner? He has only been here since Canon Fewling left us."

Mrs. Turner extended the hand of friendship to Mr. Highmore.

That unfortunate young cleric, who looked upon himself as a celibate—in which indeed he was correct, seeing that he was neither married nor even engaged—was immediately bowled over by Mrs. Turner's ripe charms and became incapable of speech.

"I'm sure only someone very nice could come after Tubby," said Mrs. Turner, turning her kind beautiful eyes upon Mr. Highmore. "I used to live here, you know, and then both my nieces got married and I've been living in East Anglia."

Mr. Highmore said he didn't know East Anglia at all.

"Oh, but you ought to," said Mrs. Turner. "There are such a lot of churches. Great big ones, really like the Olden Times, and practically empty."

Mr. Highmore could not think of any suitable comment and remained dumb. Mrs. Paxon and other ardent festival workers called Mrs. Turner to help with getting Ruby Bunce into her farthingale and the two gentlemen were left alone.

"Excuse me, sir," said Mr. Highmore, who had only been in

this, his first situation or cure of souls, for a short time, "but who is Mrs. Turner? I am trying to call on everyone, but they are so hospitable that it is difficult to get in more than one in an afternoon."

Mr. Downing explained that Mrs. Turner used to live at The Hollies, but was now living in Norfolk, and congratulated Mr. Highmore on his courage in refusing to be Sir Lancelot.

Mr. Highmore, who was obviously longing to talk about himself, then did so. Mr. Downing, politely uninterested by the newcomer's post, had fallen into a dream of King René's court from which he was roused by hearing Mr. Highmore saying how splendid it had been to hear King Richard the Third defended. He had always liked that monarch immensely, he said, and had taken part in an O.U.D.S. performance.

"The hour has come and the man!" said Mr. Downing, with unusual vehemence. "Ianthe!" he called to Miss Pemberton, who was talking to Lydia near at hand, "Mr. Highmore has acted in Richard the Third. Why not ask him to take the part here?"

Miss Pemberton, who had a deep respect for the clergy as a historical survival, said graciously that she saw no objection except that Hopper the cobbler was cast for it, but as he had not yet been approached and was often very difficult and cantankerous she thought it an excellent idea. As Lydia was near at hand she asked her opinion as chairman and Lydia, who had no wish to go against any plan of Miss Pemberton's, said How nice and shook hands with Mr. Highmore, who felt she was like Joan of Arc, though on no grounds at all.

"And then I can wear the hump," said Mr. Highmore. "We had a rotten hump at Lazarus, rather like Punch. This one looks splendid. Could I just try it on, sir?"

The hump was slung over his shoulders. Mr. Downing put

the Merlin cloak over it and Mr. Highmore stood enraptured, a dark scowl on his very young face.

"I couldn't say a bit of it, I suppose?" he said hopefully, "just that bit about

> Fight, gentlemen of England! fight, bold yeomen!
> Draw, archers, draw your arrows to the head!
> Spur your proud horses hard, and ride in blood!"

"*Well*, Mr. Highmore, you *are* a dark horse," said Mrs. Paxon, who had joined them. "I've not heard an amateur like that for a long time. I was in the South Wembley Amateur Dramatic years ago and we had some real talent."

"My mother was in that," said Mr. Highmore, who in his struggles to get out of his hump had now got it hanging round his neck in front. "She did Helena in *All's Well That Ends Well*."

"Not Florence Peel!" said Mrs. Paxon.

Mr. Highmore, now freed by the kind exertions of Mr. Downing, said that was the one and he was called Henry Peel Highmore after her maiden name.

"Not a word more!" said Mrs. Paxon, though Mr. Highmore had quite finished what he wanted to say. "We need some new blood here. I'll see that you are elected to our little Drama Club at once—an honorary member, of course—and I hope you will be able to come to some of our evenings," an invitation which Mr. Highmore, who was living alone in the lodgings formerly occupied by Canon Fewling and found them very dull, accepted with joy.

"My mother," said Mr. Highmore, "still keeps a lot of her theatrical properties in a chest. We used to be allowed to dress up in them. I am sure she would lend them if there is anything you specially want."

"Well, we could do with a few ruffs for the Queen Elizabeth scene," said Mrs. Paxon thoughtfully, "and I seem to remember Florence had a pair of green tights when she did Rosalind in *As You Like It*. I was Audrey. It was a lovely part to do."

Mr. Highmore said the green tights were in the chest as far as he knew and he would write to his mother about them. He was afraid they were a bit spoilt where the moth had got at them during the war, but his mother had darned them beautifully. He sent his socks back to his mother to be darned once a fortnight, he said.

By this time several people, interested to see Mr. Highmore coming out of his shell, had gathered round them, including Effie and Ruby Bunce, who had expressed the opinion, far too loudly everyone thought, that Mr. Highmore was a lovely man; which artless tribute only meant that they considered him one of the gentry and as such to be helped and protected. Nor were they the only people to have that feeling.

"You must come to Glycerine Cottage, Mr. Highmore," said Miss Crowder, "and have a nice Continental supper with us one Sunday. Just let us know what time you are likely to be free and the pottofur will be sitting in the oven on a low gas. My Friend and I love French cooking."

To this Miss Hopgood added her entreaties. Mr. Highmore looked round desperately for help, but none came, so he said it would be very nice and was then emboldened to ask what a pottofur was.

"Oh, *so* simple," said Miss Crowder. "You just have a casserole and put everything into it and leave it to itself."

Miss Hopgood said one didn't expect gentlemen to know all about La Kweeseen, though she had always found that when a man was a good cook, he *was* a good cook. One simply, she said, put all sorts of things into the casserole; anything left over from lunch and supper and some more potatoes and a good teaspoonful of Beefine—or Oxone would do just as well, but *not* Gravylene because she had heard it was made in the Argentine, and goodness knows what went into it—then you fried a few onions and let the whole thing sit in the oven on a low gas as long as you liked.

"But you must not like *too* long," said Miss Crowder. "I shall never forget when we went over to spend the day with some friends at—now where was it?—well, never mind where, but when we got back we found the girl who came in the mornings to help had turned on the gas just a wee bit too high and the whole thing was burnt. Quite uneatable."

While this conversation was going on, the rest of the company had been looking through the properties. They were rather a job lot, lent with an enthusiasm that hardly made up for their deficiencies, but no one was inclined to cavil. Several of the audience said they had given literally everything away, first to the London refugees, then to the foreign refugees, and of late years to Flood Relief or Earthquake Relief pretty well everywhere from East Anglia to the Antipodes. Mrs. Paxon said she would have a Whist Drive in aid of the funds. Those ladies who were comfortably off promised cheques. Commander Beasley said he was willing to speak on the British-Needlers Society if everyone would pay a shilling or bring something for the dressing-up, and Mrs. Paxon said she would go into Barchester and do the shopping. There was some really lovely jewellery at Sheepshanks, she said.

"Oh! I'd quite forgotten," said Lydia. "I'll be back in a minute, Mrs. Paxon," and she went out to her car and returned with Lady Pomfret's suitcase. In the general hubbub about clothes no one had paid much attention to her and it was not till she had put the lovely gauds on the chairman's table that anyone turned round.

"One moment, please," said Lydia. "Lady Pomfret has been kind enough to lend us these beautiful things. She said they

were used for amateur theatricals years ago at the Towers.
Miss Pemberton, would you and Mrs. Paxon come and decide
which episodes will need them? We will label them and then
I'll take them home till the day. I ought to have thought of
labels, but I didn't. Has anyone got any?"

Miss Pemberton said she hadn't any tie-on labels, but she
had a lot of those sticky labels one was supposed to use during
the war to economize envelopes.

Miss Hopgood's Aunt said anyone with a scientific mind
would have realized at once that, allowing for the expenditure
on cutting, printing, and gumming the labels, the amount of
tongue-power required to lick them all over because if you
didn't the unlicked bits rose up into bubbles, and the extra
sticky paper needed to make them secure if you had, as most
people did, just torn the envelope open anyhow, and the time
consumed in all these operations, the labels were no economy
and merely an added strain on the civil population.

Miss Dolly Talbot said after all we were told to economize.

"Well," said Miss Dunsford, "I'm sure Mr. Churchill never
uses the same envelope twice. Besides, we were asked to give
all our paper to salvage and if the Government wanted paper
salvage what was the use of saving paper?" which comment
seemed to many of her hearers a reasonable one.

Lydia, with great courage, rang the little bell which was on
the table. Its feeble tinkle so surprised the meeting that the
talk died down.

"I put the bell there on purpose," said Miss Pemberton,
who had rallied to the Committee table. "Mr. Downing and I
bought it in the Pays du Grand Gargou when we were ex-
amining some of the documents connected with the Puys des
Stryges."

Lydia thanked Miss Pemberton and asked if that was in
Provence.

"Mr. Downing and I hold that it was there or thereabouts that Ghismon Beauxcilsz, who had deserted the Dame d'Aiguesdouces, sought the favours of Madon lou Cabrou. He was later found dead on the Puy des Stryges with the mark of a cloven hoof on his chest," said Miss Pemberton, as one might say that one had been to Barchester and bought some stockings. "If Professor Gawky thinks otherwise, everyone to her own taste and her own lights. Mr. Downing contributed a very scholarly article on the subject to the *Journal of Provençal Studies.*"

Lydia, to whom the *Journal of Provençal Studies* meant as little as it means to us—nomen et præterea nihil—said how very interesting and now, if the meeting had a few moments to spare, she would like them to decide in which episode, or episodes, the beautiful things that Lady Pomfret had lent them should be used.

All were (for a moment) silent and not only kept their gaze fixed with interest on the glittering spoil, but in some cases—or so Mrs. Paxon said—held their breath till they nearly burst.

Mrs. Villars suggested that Mrs. Merton should apportion the jewellery and perhaps Mr. Highmore would be kind enough to act as umpire in the case of any friendly disagreement. Mr. Highmore looked alarmed, but his Rector's wife must be obeyed, so he said Certainly.

"Crowns first," said Lydia, who—as Mrs. Villars noticed with pleasure—was warming to her chairmanship and evidently enjoying it. "Ancient Britons wouldn't have any, so that leaves one crown for each of the other scenes. What about Richard the Third?"

Mrs. Paxon said he must have his crown on so that he could leave it at Bosworth Field, and this was carried without discussion.

"Then," said Lydia, "we come to Queen Elizabeth—I mean Queen Elizabeth the First."

Miss Dolly Talbot said she had often thought how wonderful it must be for Queen Elizabeth—she meant the old one—to think that there was now another Queen Elizabeth.

"Oh, I hardly think so," said Mrs. Dunsford. "I mean one can hardly feel that in the Better Life people think about such things; do they, Mr. Highmore?" which very mean appeal to his professional knowledge took Mr. Highmore so much aback that he could not answer.

"Perhaps, Mrs. Merton, we could discuss that question later," said Mrs. Villars. "Our time is nearly up," which words made Mr. Highmore feel a respectful kind of adoration for the Rector's wife.

"The orb and sceptre will be useful for the Queen Elizabeth scene too," said Lydia firmly. "And perhaps, Mrs. Paxon, some of her attendants could pour pretence wine out of the flagons into the goblets," to which Mrs. Paxon cheerfully agreed, saying that she would get a bottle of that nice Vinitono that you got at the grocer's because it was a nice colour and non-alcoholic.

"If I may speak, Madam Chairman," said Mrs. Dunsford, "there is still the third crown to dispose of. May I suggest that Queen Elizabeth the First should lay it before the picture of Her Present Majesty? I think that would be a very fine gesture."

By this time nearly everyone was anxious to get home and the suggestion was carried without any trouble.

"I think we can easily deal with the small ornaments," said Lydia. "Queen Elizabeth's—I mean Queen Elizabeth the First's maids of honour could wear some of them."

"Just one word," said Miss Dolly Talbot. "Hadn't we better try the crowns on? Old Lady Norton once told me that when she married she had to have her mother-in-law's rings altered as they were too large for her."

Mrs. Villars, seeing that Lydia was not prepared to deal with this, got up and said the Committee were all very grateful for Miss Dolly Talbot's suggestion and she would ask Mrs. Paxon to move a vote of thanks to Mrs. Merton—a very busy woman, she added, whose duties lay in London as well as in Northbridge—for so kindly taking the chair.

"Well, I'm sure," said Mrs. Paxon, who was always ready to help, "we are all very grateful to Mrs. Merton for so kindly taking the chair and Mrs. Villars for supporting her and Miss Pemberton for being the secretary of the Committee and to all friends who have helped us and Miss Pemberton for lending her room and the wonderful refreshments she gave us, and would like to give them a big Thank You in the usual way," and that everyone might feel at ease she clapped her hands. The audience all joined her and then there was a great saying of good-nights and the room emptied.

Lydia thanked everyone within reach. Mrs. Paxon and Mrs. Turner went off, deep in theatrical shop. The Misses Talbot left in company with Mrs. Dunsford and her daughter because, as they said, You never knew in these days who was about, and the really shocking things that were happening everywhere made one feel really quite uncomfortable. The room was now almost empty. Effie and Ruby were washing up in the kitchen with loud laughter.

Mr. Highmore, who had been nerving himself for this moment ever since the beginning of the meeting, came up to Mrs. Villars and asked if he might escort her home. Mrs. Villars thanked him and said it was such a short way to the Rectory and she knew he lived in the other direction and it was so kind of him but she really was quite all right.

Mr. Highmore said he liked walking and really, if one went

by the Rectory, he was practically on his way home. He felt, he said, that in the absence of Mr. Villars he ought, though of course he did not for one moment wish to compare himself with the Rector, to act as his locum tenens. Mrs. Villars, torn between her wish not to make Mr. Highmore feel slighted and her far stronger wish not to be seen home by him, as she had in her time been seen most boringly home by various curates, thanked him again and said she really could not trouble him. But Mr. Highmore was not of those who having put their hand to the plough cease in good works and was again urging his plea when Lydia, who had noticed and drawn her own conclusions, came up to Mrs. Villars and said she would drive her home. Mr. Highmore, defeated, his bosom's lord sitting sadly on his throne, said good-bye to Mrs. Villars with the slightly too long handshake which had bored her in assistant masters for the first part of her married life and in curates in later years, and went away to his lodgings.

"You have saved my life, Mrs. Merton," said Mrs. Villars, and they got into the car and Lydia drove up to the Rectory.

Lydia said she liked doing it.

"Thank you, my dear," said Mrs. Villars. "You were an excellent chairman. I will ring you up about the next meeting or if anything special needs attention. And do say Verena unless you feel I am too old."

"You too then," said Lydia, an ellipsis which we need not explain. "Oh my goodness! I've left Lady Pomfret's jewellery at Punshions. Good-bye," and she backed down the narrow Rectory Lane and so down the High Street. As there was still a light in the house she opened the door and went into the living-room. Miss Pemberton was repacking some properties which were to be stored with her. Mr. Downing was nervously getting in the way.

"I'm so sorry," said Lydia. "I forgot Lady Pomfret's crowns

and things. I told Miss Merriman I would look after them till the Pageant was over," and she picked up the suitcase.

"If you wish to stand there idle, Harold, while Mrs. Merton carries that box to her car, it is not for me to interfere," said Miss Pemberton, her utterance slightly impeded by a long piece of drapery one end of which she had gripped between her teeth the better to fold the rest—and we are sure our Reader has also done this more than once.

Mr. Downing, who far from standing was bending over the hearth and sweeping the wood-ash back under the large open grate, turned round with a nervous look.

"I am so sorry," he said courteously to Lydia. "Let me take it for you," and he took hold of the handles.

"Here, that's too much for you," said Lydia. Wresting one handle from him she said good-night to Miss Pemberton and, accompanied by Mr. Downing, went to the car, heaved the suitcase into the back, said good-night, and drove away. Mr. Downing went back to the living-room.

"Did you lock the front door, Harold?" said Miss Pemberton.

"I don't think so, Ianthe," said Mr. Downing. "But I'll make sure."

"I had better make sure myself," said Miss Pemberton, with the resigned impatience of one who knows that her lodger will never do the right thing. "And then, Harold, you had better go to bed."

She went into the hall and Mr. Downing heard the noise of bolts and the usual tussle with the large key.

"I'm sorry, Ianthe," he said when his Egeria returned. "I did mean to oil the lock, but I couldn't find a feather."

"I shall find one for you tomorrow. Good night, Harold," said Miss Pemberton, turning down the lamps, which began that long death of flickering which we so well remember in our nursery days when staying in old houses where the gas was, if it was anywhere, only on the ground floor owing to a rooted belief that the one aim of gas in a bedroom was to Escape. She then went majestically upstairs, leaving Mr. Downing to darkness, but to himself.

He sat down again on the stool in the great hearth, watching the fire die, thinking of the delightful hours he had spent at Mrs. Turner's house during the war; of the life, so alien to his own, of young people and noise and generous food and drink; and of Mrs. Turner's kindness and how she had showed him a snapshot of her husband, who had died in a Home for Inebriates, and told him, without words, where her heart still was.

Owing to the age and—whatever people may say about How wonderful old craftsmen were, my dear, so *thorough* in their work—the warped woodwork and the bad floors of the house, it was impossible to move without being heard. He felt cold and knew he ought to go to bed, but did not go. The staircase creaked loudly two or three times and he knew the worst had happened. Miss Pemberton in a dressing-gown bearing a striking resemblance to Merlin's cloak opened the door, a flat candlestick in her hand.

"Harold!" she said.

It was enough. Her lodger got up, nearly fell down over the little step from the hearth to the floor, and came miserably across the room.

"You can have the candle, Harold," said Miss Pemberton, "I will lock the door. Good night."

Mr. Downing with a mumbled good-night took the candlestick and went up to his room. Miss Pemberton locked the living-room door and stumped slowly up to her room. Darkness and silence reigned in Punshions.

CHAPTER 7

ALTHOUGH it may appear to the reader and certainly did appear to Lydia that the meeting had accomplished practically nothing, that it was much ado about nothing, and full of sound and a certain amount of fury signifying nothing, it had set the busy wheels of Northbridge organizations turning. Mrs. Turner had been as good as her word in response to Mrs. Paxon's appeal and taken up her temporary abode at the Mitre. She and Mrs. Paxon collected anyone who could cut out, or sew, or machine, or paint, or stencil. Mrs Dunsford lent the back drawing-room at Hovis House as a workroom. Commander Beasley kindly lent a large table with folding legs for cutting out and machining, and when the ladies had learnt to brace the legs properly so that the table did not come down on one end with a run, nothing could have been more useful. Commander Beasley also turned out to be expert in cutting metal stencils so that the various garments could be decorated with bold designs, and had a very neat hand with the paint brush as well, and if he had a habit of finding Cleopatra's Needle, like King Charles's head, in the most improbable places, the ladies were usually talking so hard themselves that they paid scant attention. There was a general feeling that Mr. Highmore, who had come out so strong at the last Committee Meeting, ought to be encouraged, and in a discussion about the Arrival of the Normans episode he proved most useful.

"I don't want to intrude," said Mr. Highmore, who had

come into the workroom about half past eleven when all the
working ladies were having cups of tea, "but I wonder if I
might make a suggestion."

As he had not addressed any particular worker, Mrs. Dunsford, who was pinning an old red cotton curtain, the gift of
Miss Hopgood, so that Miss Dolly Talbot could make a military cloak for Richard the Third because she understood the
machine better than anyone else, said, rather indistinctly,
owing to her mouth being used as a temporary pin-cushion,
that they would all be delighted to hear Mr. Highmore's idea.

"Well," said Mr. Highmore, with the mixture of nervousness and defiance that an early Christian might have shown to
a lion, "it's about the Norman episode. You see, the Normans
would probably have had a priest with them. I think they had
one at Hastings, some kind of illegitimate relation of William
the Conqueror's, a bishop or something. I was thinking, if the
Rector doesn't mind, that I could be one."

Mrs. Dunsford said it seemed quite a good idea, and if he
was a fighting man he would probably have a cassock over his
armour, just to show, and there was that sheet that had been
sides-to-middled and had all gone again (a statement which
our female reader will at once understand) that she could use,
and machine a Red Cross on it with a bit of that red flannel.

"It *is* a pity we haven't any armour," said Miss Dunsford.

Her mother said Barbara was so thoughtful.

"But," said Miss Dunsford, who but rarely made her presence felt, owing to her mother's kind but overbearing personality, "we haven't."

"There is just one thing," said Mr. Highmore, his Adam's
apple surging with emotion, "if I can't have a helmet I could
have a tonsure."

Miss Dolly Talbot voiced, we think, the feelings of the party
when she said she didn't suppose there was anyone left who

could tonsure people now. A very interesting discussion then took place as to how often one had to have one's tonsure re-cut, but as the premises were entirely non-existent no one got very far.

"I wouldn't need that," said Mr. Highmore. "I thought of that and I've got it."

"Do you mean you got a barber to shave your head?" said Commander Beasley. "Stout fellow. I only wish I had some hair to shave."

As Mr. Highmore had, not unnaturally, left his hat in the hall, it was really obvious to everyone that his thick reddish-brown hair was in full possession of his head.

"Oh, no, I made it," said Mr. Highmore, pulling a parcel out of his pocket. "I used to make quite a lot of the props for my prep-school plays," and unwrapping the parcel, he took out a small cap, not unlike a surgeon's, which he fitted neatly to his head. Its material was more or less flesh-coloured and round its edge was a rim of quite sufficiently convincing hair.

"There," he said, not without pride, "I got the hair from a friend who has a red setter," at which moment the Rector came in.

Everyone waited in the pleasurable anticipation of ex-communication or at least an interdict, but Mr. Villars, who as a schoolmaster and a priest had found private theatricals an excellent soother of the savage breast, whether of boys or men, merely said: "That's a neat piece of work, Highmore," and went over to ask Mrs. Dunsford whether she could do the flowers for next Sunday as his wife would be in London for the week-end, and after admiring the historical costumes that the ladies were making out of all sorts of scraps and hoardings and borrowings, went away again, resisting Mrs. Dunsford's offer of tea which, she said, was a bit stewed now, but with China it never seemed to matter so much. Mr. Highmore took off his tonsure, put it in his pocket, and said he must be off. Having made this sacrifice on the social altar, he then stayed for a quarter of an hour or so, making himself very pleasant to everyone in a quiet way.

"There was just one other thing I had thought of," he said to his hostess, "but I don't know if Mr. Villars would approve. I was thinking yesterday evening what fun it would be if I could be martyred. After all, the Northbridge people must have been pretty furious when the Normans came and if they could kill me it would be so realistic. I mean the Normans could make them build the church in revenge. At least I don't exactly mean that, but you will see what I mean."

Mrs. Dunsford, who had no sense of humour at all but was very kind, said it was a splendid idea, but she was afraid the other actors might be too excited and certainly the Scouts who were putting up the bridge would get out of hand. So obvious was Mr. Highmore's dejection that the whole working party united to comfort him. Then he went away to his duties and the ladies continued their talk and their work, their talk being largely, as nearly always happens at a party, about the guest who had just left them. Miss Dolly Talbot said one could not help feeling that Mr. Highmore was a *real* Christian. No one felt equal to dealing with this, as to disagree would have been a slur on Mr. Highmore, whom everyone liked, and to agree would be encouraging Miss Dolly Talbot, who, so Mrs. Dunsford and one or two other friends considered, was too apt to look upon the clergy as her peculiar property and had always adopted a kind of religious archness with Canon Fewling for which they could willingly have smacked her. Miss Hopgood's Aunt, who had been very friendly with Canon Fewling on the subject of astronomy, said she quite missed her astronomical talks with him and did Commander Beasley know where that roll of white plastic had got to as she thought she could make a petticoat out of it to go under Queen Elizabeth's farthingale because it would make it stand out so well.

Commander Beasley said he had put it on the table by the window.

"Oh, dear!" said Mrs. Dunsford. "I'm afraid I used it for the Ancient Britons episode for a Druid. Trowel the builder is to be the Druid because he knows all about old Northbridge. His grandfather told him that the drain under Hooper's Platt, where we had the Air Raid Wardens' Shelter in the war, used to be called Hallbrook and Mr. Downing looked it up in some old book in London and found the land used to belong to a thane or someone, like Ivanhoe you know, called Haella. So all the rainwater runs away just as it did in the Olden Times."

Several workers said: It was wonderful the way those old customs survived, Just fancy, What would a Thane think if he saw Northbridge now.

Commander Beasley said that to British-Needlers the Past and the Present were one.

"But people do *dress* differently now from the way they did in the Olden Times," said Miss Dunsford. "If they hadn't, we couldn't really have a pageant, because half the fun is dressing up," and then she looked round, hoping that she had not offended anyone. Far from being offended, the company in general were surprised and interested, for Miss Dunsford had very little existence apart from being her mother's daughter and, so far as anyone knew, had never wished to.

"A very good point," said Miss Hopgood's Aunt. "We had a fancy-dress ball one winter when my husband and I were at the Observatory at Porterville and there were astronomical tableaux after supper. I went as Cassiopeia."

There was an interested silence. Commander Beasley, who was stencilling white roses on Richard III's cloak (those old red curtains we put away and found they were a bit mothy but it won't show on the stage, from the Aloes, contributed by Miss Talbot and her sister), looked up suspiciously and asked how she did it. Miss Hopgood's Aunt, who as, roughly speaking, a believer in the starry heavens and man's moral law, had no opinion at all of other people's beliefs, said it was quite simple. She was in white—she was a good deal younger then, she said—with gold stars on her dress and her hair—which was then very long and thick, she said—down her back, seated like a doubleyou.

Mrs. Dunsford asked what she meant, thus earning the gratitude of the other workers who did not like to ask.

"I can best explain it," said Miss Hopgood's Aunt, "by saying it was what used to be called a pose plastique. You know the appearance of Cassiopeia. I endeavoured, as far as is possible, to follow that shape. I was reclining on a couch, very cleverly made by one of our students, with my knees bent, if you take me, and everyone admitted that it would have been impossible to present the final up-stroke of the W unless one had feet at least eighteen inches long. But with an intelligent audience there was no difficulty."

Great interest was expressed by the workers. Commander Beasley said *all* the constellations were symbolized on Cleopatra's Needle and he must be going as it was a quarter to one, at which the ladies exclaimed. The work was left tidily for next day and the party dispersed.

Lydia Merton, wishing to do all that a president should do, had wondered if she ought to volunteer for the Working Party, but Mrs. Villars, who had a kindly protective feeling for her, spoke with authority as an older woman and one who had experience of good works, saying that she would only make herself tired and Northbridge was boiling over with women who had never enjoyed themselves so much since the war;

which advice Lydia gladly followed, for a life divided between London and the country is tiring in itself and apart from the pleasure of being with Noel for two or three evenings, she had a thousand things to occupy her in her house, her children, and the estate; and now the Coronation festivities.

The Sunday for Noel and herself to lunch with the Pomfrets was fixed, and from the Towers they would take young Lord Mellings over to the Deans for the promised talk with Aubrey Clover and Jessica. The weather—by a serious oversight on its own part—was again fairly warm and by the time Noel and Lydia got to the Towers it might almost have been called hot. They were received by Miss Merriman, who said Lord Pomfret would be with them shortly and Lady Pomfret was somewhere about outside and took them along a passage and out onto the wide terrace that was raised on an arcade above the level of the Italian garden. Here there were chairs, and Miss Merriman left the guests in the sun while she went in search of their hostess. The formal Italian garden had been laid out by the old Earl's wife in the usual jig-saw puzzle of little box-edged flower beds, which in more prosperous days were bedded out with flowers perpetually renewed from the large conservatories. The hothouses had long since been given over to tomatoes for the market in summer and chrysanthemums in winter and the present Lady Pomfret had compromised on a lavish use of sixpenny packets of seed from Sheepshanks, which made a brilliant and extremely pretty effect. On the far side of the Italian garden, walks of green grass, which were still scythe-mown by an old labourer, meandered among beech trees towards the kitchen gardens, the grounds on that side being bordered by a little stream, edged by rushes and tall grasses, yellow with wild iris in early summer, blue with forget-me-nots, much loved by children of every generation.

"Isn't it *wicked*," said Lydia. "I mean people as nice as the Pomfrets having to live in a corner of the house and have nasturtiums instead of begonias or whatever they did have."

"Well, there it is," said Noel, "and short of Ludo marrying an heiress with millions of dollars I don't see what can be done. What seems even more remarkable to me is what the present owners *have* done. Making this great white elephant of a place—only it's red and a hideous red at that—into a home and doing their duty uncommonly well in the station to which it has pleased the present state of things to call them. There's no doubt about it; blood does tell."

Lydia said it was mostly Lady Pomfret who had done it and she wasn't exactly blood. Noel, always amused by his Lydia's reflections on life, said the Wicklows were as old a name in Barsetshire as any and had lived in Nutfield for a very long time off and on. Good yeoman stock, he said, like Wickham's, and exactly what the Pomfret side needed. Those two younger children were going to bully and laugh their way through life and enjoy all the ups and downs. But Ludo, said Lydia; and fell silent.

"Well, my love," said Noel, "you can't do anything about it, so don't take it too seriously. After all, you have done more for him than anyone else."

"I?" said Lydia, lifting her eyes in wonder at Noel's stupidity; just as Lydia Keith had looked at Noel Merton once, long ago.

"My delightful goose," said Noel, "you introduced that boy to Aubrey and Jessica."

"Oh, *that*," said Lydia, for one's own deeds, as a rule unrecognized by oneself, never seem so impressive, or so real, as other peoples'. Doubtless the other people feel the same about ours; one does not know. "Well, I thought it would be nice for him."

" 'And the goose, Was a goose, In Lord Pomfret's garden,' "
said Noel, misquoting from an excellent rhymed story, and
then Lady Pomfret came out of a shrubbery and up the steps
to the terrace and apologized for having neglected them.

"As we are going to look over the Towers," she said, "and
you are so kindly taking Ludo to the Clovers, I thought we
would have more time if we didn't have a party. You won't
mind it just being family?" which was of course exactly what
the Mertons liked. "After lunch we will show you the house
and then if there is time Gillie wants you to see the Long
Valley and the Obelisk. And," she added, seeing with her
professional chairman's committee eye that Lydia was thinking of the visit to the Deans, "I will see that you get away in
plenty of time. Are you sure that it won't be a bother to bring
Ludo back? It is rather out of your way and if you drop Ludo
in Barchester he can get a bus back to the lodge gates," but
Lydia, thanking her hostess, said they had plenty of time.

"I can't tell you," said Lady Pomfret, "how much Ludo is
looking forward to the play. He looks so much less harassed,
poor darling."

Lydia asked if he was unhappy at school, or found his work
a strain. Lady Pomfret said that luckily he accepted Eton and
its life, had made some friends and did quite well enough in
his work.

"It is just," she said, almost talking aloud to herself, "that
Ludo is so like Gillie. They are both angels and as good as
they can be, but they don't know where to stop. I sometimes
think it's a disease. They are never happy unless they are
doing more than they really can. It's a horrid kind of conscientiousness. I hope none of your children are conscientious,
Mrs. Merton," which words were spoken with a sort of earnest
kindness that Lydia felt to be very friendly.

"I think they are quite ordinary," she said, hoping not to

sound smug. "I mean I think they are very nice and I adore
them, but they aren't much trouble. I daresay they will get
troublesome as they get older," she added hopefully, and
thought to herself that as far as conscientiousness went there
was hardly a pin to choose between the Earl and his Countess,
except that she had perfect health.

Lunch was short, pleasant, and rather noisy, owing to the
high spirits of Giles and Emily, who were going to a Pony
Club meeting. Lord Mellings was polite but quiet. Miss Merriman was as pleasant and impersonal as ever. The talk was
mostly about Coronation festivities, in which Lady Pomfret,
as the Lord Lieutenant's wife, was of course deeply involved,
and Lydia felt rather ashamed of herself for taking the Northbridge doings as seriously as she did, but comforted herself by
reflecting that Lady Pomfret had Miss Merriman in the background.

"Now," said Lady Pomfret when they got up from table (at
what age exactly does one stop saying "May I get down,
please?" or has that formula vanished with the decay of
Nanny-dom?), "we will see the big rooms downstairs and if
you do not feel tired, you might care to see some of the bedrooms. I wish you could have seen the kitchens, with hundreds
of copper saucepans that had to be re-tinned every year, but
all that had to be done away with," but evidently she did not
expect a reply and led the way, followed by the Mertons and
her husband. A stone passage led them to a door which opened
on to the entrance hall, a large stone-floored room with doors
separating it on one side from the inner hall, on the other
from the front steps and the draught. It was furnished with
what looked to Lydia like hundreds of hooks for hats and coats,
an outsize umbrella rack, and a hideous china vase like a
chimney pot about five feet high with a pair of skis and a
hockey stick in it. On the walls were some very bad sporting

pictures, two crossed hunting crops, a mouldering fox's brush,
and a view of Assisi, of no value at all, painted by an Italian
artist whose name no one knew. In a corner stood a real weighing chair, with the notched brass beam sticking out like a railway signal and below it a pile of brass weights.

"This *is* remarkable," said Noel reverently.

"My uncle got it from Blacks'," said Lord Pomfret, naming
an old and respected club, "hundreds of years ago. They were
getting a more modern machine and Uncle Giles, who believed in getting his own way, said he would resign if they
did, so the secretary—they always choose a secretary who has
tact—said he would put it up to the committee that Lord
Pomfret would like to have it as a Historic Monument. I
believe Uncle Giles gave ten pounds to the Club Servants'
Christmas Fund. And now," he said, opening one half of a
huge and hideous wooden door with what was obviously imitation graining on it, "this is the hall. It's pretty good, isn't it?"

To the Mertons this appeared to be an understatement.
The hall was—or so they felt—about the size and height of
Westminster Hall. A hideous carved wainscot rose about six
feet all round it, above which the walls were stone, hung with
very unconvincing tapestry, rising to a high pitched roof supported by equally hideous struts and corbels or whatever that
part of roof architecture is called. An enormous stone fireplace
surmounted by heraldic carvings allowed the air to circulate
far too freely. A wide pitchpine staircase went up to the first
floor, round which was a corridor with Gothic windows onto
the hall.

"Gosh!" said Lydia, reverently.

"I know," said Lord Pomfret, evidently gratified by this
remark. "It took four years to build the Towers and cost about
four hundred thousand pounds first and last. The money
people had then!" to which Noel replied that to have that

amount of money now would be simply asking for trouble unless one were both fraudulent and successful in concealing fraud. They then went on to the Large Yellow Drawing-Room, the Library, the Billiard Room, the Green Drawing-Room, and the Small Green Drawing-Room, which last was particularly admired by the visitors. The walls were hung with olive-green brocade, on which large patches of darker colour showed where pictures had been. The ceiling was, incredibly, covered with pleated green silk, coming out in rays (if we make ourselves clear) from a gilded sunflower. The furniture, some of which Lord Pomfret obligingly unsheeted, was in the highest style of Pre-Raphaelite discomfort; sofas apparently hewn from solid blocks of wood and armchairs suited to no known human frame, all with stamped green velvet cushions of extreme hardness.

"You ought to see these," said Lady Pomfret, lifting a dust-sheet from a pile of curtains. "Olive-green velvet like the cushions and it will never wear out and no one wants it."

"Why don't you give it to the Friends of Barchester Cathedral?" said Lydia. "They could use it for choir-stall cushions and things, or to hang over the North Door, where that awful draught always comes in," by which idea Lady Pomfret was much impressed and said she would certainly speak to the Dean about it. Lord Pomfret said all the pictures were ghastly too, as his Aunt Edith had bought largely from second-rate contemporary artists.

"The only decent pictures," he said "were some water-colour drawings by Uncle Giles's mother. Elegant water-colours of Italy, with some real style. We kept those. Shall we go upstairs? I don't want to make you late."

So up they went and looked into one or two of the huge bedrooms, again all sheeted and cold, saw the multiple bath-room that had been made out of a bedroom, and admired the fine period bath of which mention had previously been made, on its platform in one of the best bedrooms.

"Would you care to see some of the nursery floor?" said Lady Pomfret. "We still have time," so with great willingness they followed her up a steep wooden stair to the top floor.

"Maids' rooms on one side and nurseries on the other," said Lady Pomfret. "You must see the old day nursery," and she opened the door. "Gillie, do show Mrs. Merton the fire-escape. I want to show Mr. Merton the under housemaids' rooms and then we must go down. Four in one room with no fireplace and one small dormer window," she added proudly as she led Noel away.

"You see," said Lord Pomfret to Lydia, in his kind, tired voice, "the only way to this floor is by that narrow wooden staircase we have just come up, so they had a very modern fire-escape—at least it was modern then—put in," and he showed her, in the window, the remains of a complicated apparatus of rope and canvas on an iron framework.

"If the house was on fire, you were supposed to let it down and slide down a kind of canvas chute to the bottom," he said, "but old Cousin Emily—Lady Emily Leslie—told me that their nurse said the children would catch their deaths of cold going down that thing, and luckily it was never needed. Well, what do you think of it all, Mrs. Merton?"

"I think you and Lady Pomfret are marvellous," said Lydia. "I suppose if one is born to a big house it's a bit easier. I'd burn it all down if it were mine. But," she added, feeling that she had gone too far, "perhaps you like it in a way."

"I dislike it in every way," said Lord Pomfret. "But there it is. I have thought of pulling some of it down, as you suggest, but it would cost so much that it wouldn't be worth it. I always live in hopes that it may be bought for a County Asylum."

Lydia said that Ludo must marry an American heiress.

"I don't suppose he'll ever meet one," said Lord Pomfret. "He is too shy."

"Not really," said Lydia. "He is perfectly un-shy with the right people, like Jessica and Aubrey."

"He gets it from me," said Lord Pomfret, still absorbed in thoughts of his tall diffident son.

"But you aren't shy," said Lydia. "At least I daresay you are shy about meetings and committees and things. I would be. But you aren't shy with people. I mean it was such fun the evening we dined here and when you dined with us— and then today."

"I have never felt shy with you," said Lord Pomfret, look-ing down at her with his melancholy eyes. "You have been so extraordinarily kind to my poor Ludo."

"But I couldn't help it," said Lydia. "He is a dear boy— and so like you."

"Unfortunately, yes," said Lord Pomfret, to which Lydia, with almost the violence of the young Lydia Keith she had been, said: *"Fortunately.* You don't think enough of yourself, Lord Pomfret. Honestly you don't."

"That is what Sally says," said Lord Pomfret, "but thank you all the same," and for a moment there was a silence. Into Lydia's mind there came, unsought, a few lines from Brown-ing, at one time the favourite poet of Miss Lydia Keith:

> The silence grows
> To that degree, you half believe
> It must get rid of what it knows,
> Its bosom does so heave.

"I think I ought to go down, if you don't mind," said Lydia, looking at her wrist watch. "We must be getting on to Winter

Overcotes. I do want your Ludo to have a good innings with Aubrey and Jessica."

Lord Pomfret moved aside to let her pass and then locked the old nursery door and followed her downstairs.

In the hall Lady Pomfret was waiting with Lord Mellings.

"I am afraid," she said, "we have kept you too long looking at the house. You must come another day and see the Long Valley and the Obelisk. But you must just see the chapel before you go. It won't take a minute," and she led them into the big hall, opened one half of a richly carved door, and took them through a kind of ante-room into what looked to Lydia far less like a chapel than Abroad.

"The Lord Pomfret who built the house had this made specially for his wife," said Lady Pomfret. "She had been in Italy a lot and was very High Church. It cost about twenty thousand pounds first and last, with bringing workmen specially from Italy to do the floor. It is in squares of real lapis lazuli and marble. The baroque altar with those lovely twisted golden pillars came from some castle in Austria. The windows are revolting. The fireplace in the ante-chapel came from some French château. I don't know why they troubled to have a fire there, as the chapel itself had no heating. I believe Lord Pomfret was going to have hot pipes under those gratings, but he died before he did it and no one else bothered. We have used it occasionally in summer, but otherwise we go to the village church," and she took her guests away again. Very friendly good-byes were said and the Mertons with young Lord Mellings drove away.

"*What* a nice woman Mrs. Merton is," said Lady Pomfret as she and her husband went back to their wing.

Lord Pomfret said she was. So was Merton, he added. Nice, he meant. And how kind they were being to Ludo.

"Nice people," said Lady Pomfret. "I can't tell you, Gillie, how grateful I am to Mrs. Merton," and her husband agreed.

During the drive to Winter Overcotes young Lord Mellings was very pleasant and even talkative, confiding to Lydia that he really wanted to be a farmer and wear a kind of flat-topped brown bowler like old Lord Stoke on market-days and have a first-class dairy herd and prize bulls like his cousins the Martin Leslies over at Rushwater, and how another cousin, Emmy Graham, who had married young Lady Lufton's brother, knew more about contagious abortion than anyone in the county, to all of which Noel, who was in the back seat, gave an amused and intermittent attention, though at times he had to confess that he was out of his depth and his mind wandered to easier and more frivolous subjects such as *The Mixo-Lydian Smelting and Refining Corporation and Others* v. *Thompson, Thompson and Thompson and Sons, Ltd.*

Knowing the habits of the Deans, Lydia took Lord Mellings round the house to the terrace, where Mrs. Dean was surrounded by various members of her large family, who were all married and were always coming and going with their young and growing broods. Rather to Lydia's relief, Mrs. Dean was not in her usual somnolent condition and appeared pleased to see them.

"I don't think we have ever met, have we?" she said when Lord Mellings was introduced to her. "I remember your grandfather *perfectly* well. He used to terrify me when I was a young married woman because he had such a huge moustache and was almost bald and didn't listen to what one said except when he contradicted one."

"It wasn't exactly my grandfather," said Lord Mellings. "It was father's Uncle Giles. I never saw him, at least not to remember, because I was quite small when he died."

"You poor boy," said Mrs. Dean with genuine pity for

what did not in the least need pitying. Jessica Dean, coming out through one of the French windows, heard and was amused.

"It's only mother's way of talking," she said, holding out her hand to Lord Mellings, who rose and gravely bowed over it. "How lovely to see you, my lamb. I don't suppose anyone has done any introducing, but all these people are my brothers and sisters and brothers-in-law and sisters-in-law and nephews and nieces. Too, too confusing, as Clarissa Belton, whose brother-in-law, Freddy Belton, married my elder sister Susan, would say. That is my sister Betty van Dryven and that's her husband Woolcot van Dryven. They live in New York and have come over for the summer to see the Coronation. But I won't tell you any more or you will go mad. Are you word-perfect?"

"If you mean have I remembered about all your relations, I haven't," said Lord Mellings, an answer for whose readiness Jessica gave him full marks, "but if you mean my part in *Two-Step for Three,* I know it. Only I'm sure I'll forget when I am with you and Mr. Clover."

"If you say Mr. Clover I shall call the whole thing off," said Jessica. "Aubrey to you—and to everyone except his accompanist, who always calls him Mr. Clover, I really don't know why."

"Then," said Lord Mellings, his courage rising in his atmosphere to undreamed of heights, "do I call you Jessica?"

"What else, my sweet?" said Jessica. "The whole world calls me Jessica," at which Lord Mellings looked a little dashed. "No one says Mrs. Clover. It is always Jessica except Aubrey's accompanist, who always calls me Miss Dean. He plays quite divinely and is devoted to his mother. He always goes straight back to her after a show. If we did the provinces I really don't know what would happen to him."

"Then what happens when you go to New York?" said Lord Mellings.

"His mother just has to do without him," said Jessica, "and he telephones to her every day at three in the morning."

Lord Mellings said what an extraordinary time, or was it because people in America went to bed so late.

"Some of them do, in New York," said Jessica, "but Aubrey and I can't afford to. We always go home by midnight like Cinderella. His mother has breakfast at eight and he likes to talk to Mums. That's all. New York is five hours behind us. Would you like to run through the song with him before we start our rehearsal? I thought we would do it in the drawing-room so that the others can see it if they like."

"I didn't know we were going to *act* it," said Lord Mellings, visibly jibbing.

"Well, I daresay it won't get quite as far as acting, my pet," said Jessica. "Aubrey and I are only reading our script, which means we have to read with one hand and speak with the other. You can do the same. If you don't like anything, just say so. It would be so good for Aubrey," and she favoured him with Mrs. Carvel's famous wink from Aubrey Clover's *Attitude to Life*, which made him feel very man-of-the-world.

" 'They go into the house by the French window,' " said Jessica. "That is the stage direction for us," she added, seeing him a little puzzled, and they went from the sunny terrace to the large drawing-room, where a man with a completely expressionless face was seated at Mrs. Dean's very good piano, contemptuously throwing off a kind of Brock's Benefit of arpeggios, trills, chromatic scales, crashing chords, and a final glissando to the note that is so high that it has no tune to ordinary ears. Aubrey Clover, obviously in his rooms in the Albany waiting for the arrival of the second Mrs. Tanqueray, got up and shook hands with Lord Mellings.

"This is my one and only accompanist," said Aubrey Clover. "Lord Mellings, who is going to do the third part in *Two-Step for Three*," he added to his accompanist, who got up, shook hands with complete want of interest, and returned to the piano.

"Quite nicely tuned," he said to Aubrey Clover. "Feels to me like Gadson."

"I say, Susan," said Aubrey Clover, calling from the French window to Jessica's sister Susan Belton, "who tunes this piano?"

"A man from Beechwood, I think," said Susan, naming an old and honourable firm of piano-makers. "He comes once a quarter and goes to several houses. He says this is a very good piano. Mr. Godson or something like it."

"I knew it was Gadson," said Aubrey Clover's accompanist, not puffed up, but as one stating an ineluctable law of nature. "He is usually about an eighth of a tone too high on the C in alt. Trade mark, as you might say. What key do you want the song in, Mr. Clover?"

"Can you transpose?" said Lord Mellings, dazzled. "I wish I could."

For answer Aubrey Clover's accompanist played the opening bars of Mendelssohn's *Spring Song* in its own key, in C Major, and in a flat key.

"God!" said Aubrey Clover. "I've thought of something. Look here!" and he went over to the piano and said a few words to his accompanist, who after a moment's reflection said there was certainly something in it and they might try.

"What are you two sphinx-ing about?" said Jessica, but her husband said Never mind and they would know on the night.

"Now," he said to Lord Mellings, "this is the stage. If I know platforms at local town halls, there will be two horrible wicker-work chairs painted a sickly blue-green, a table with one gammy leg, and possibly some pot plants along the front, which you mustn't knock over. And you mustn't step backwards without looking or you will probably fall down six very steep steps into the Mayor's lap. Well, all right, there isn't a Mayor of Northbridge, I was thinking of Casterbridge. Anyway you will fall into someone's lap. Now, Miss Dean," and he stood aside to allow the brilliant star of the Cockspur Theatre to make her entrance. The story was so slight as to be negligible and really a pretext for the gifted writer-actor-manager and his leading lady to show off as many as possible of their various gifts. Suffice it to say that Lord Mellings, though at first so overcome by stage-fright and emotion that his voice sounded as if it were going to crack all over again, got through his little scene with Jessica quite well till the moment for the song came, when his courage sank to his boots (or rather shoes). He began nervously, faltered, and stopped.

"I think my voice is going to break again," he said, red in the face and damp with nervousness.

"My lamb, it can't," said Jessica. "Take it from me, it won't break any more than your beard will stop growing," at which Lord Mellings, who shaved twice a week with a kind of secret pride, went red in the face again. "Listen, dear boy. Look at me and *think* about me. Not this me, but the one I'm acting. And SING."

The accompanist played the opening bars. Lord Mellings obediently followed Jessica's instructions and to his everlasting surprise found he was singing.

"Now," said Jessica, "the audience will clap like anything. Then what do you do?"

There was what we can only call a perspiring silence from Lord Mellings.

"Time!" said Aubrey, but quite kindly.

"I think," said Lord Mellings, "I make a sort of bow to you, to show that you really did it all."

"Faith, my lord, we'll make a player of your lordship yet," said Aubrey Clover. "You've hit it in one, Ludo. Then Jessica shows off to the audience and you sing it again and she sings too. Only of course she alters the words a bit for her part and says 'you' where you say 'I' and so on. Carry on," he said to his accompanist, who played the little prelude with variations.

"Look here," said Aubrey Clover, "that's not in the script."

His accompanist said people liked a bit of a change.

"Well, if they do, *I'll* make the changes," said Aubrey Clover.

His accompanist with an unmoved expression played through the prelude in ragtime.

"Oh, all right, damn you," said Aubrey Clover. "Have it your own way."

"He always does," said Jessica to Lord Mellings. "Aubrey gets the credit and everyone is happy."

"Now, for God's sake let's *start*," said Aubrey Clover, "and not waste time fooling."

His accompanist, still unmoved, played the prelude again, Lord Mellings sang his part with more confidence, and Aubrey joined with variations of his own.

"I say," said Lord Mellings when they had finished, "you *do* sing well."

"All illusion, alles Wahn, as that old bore says in one of those eternal things of Wagner's," said Aubrey. "I can make a noise like a good singer. The quickness of the 'and deceives the heye," but Ludovic was too young to take this quotation, echo of a past age.

"And now Altogether, Boys," said Aubrey Clover, "and a long pull and a strong pull. Just let yourself relax, my boy. Let her rip."

Partly the mounting excitement of the rehearsal, partly the extreme grown-upness of being called My boy, so raised Lord Mellings's heart that, following Aubrey Clover's advice, he let himself go. Aubrey supported him while Jessica improvised what is, we believe, called a descant, which is singing a quite different tune only it fits in with the one other people are singing and distracts the audience's attention from the original, so that they don't really hear either tune properly.

When they had finished, Aubrey Clover clapped Ludovic on the shoulder.

"You'll do, my boy," he said, to which Lord Mellings, already overcome by the excitement, the music, the new atmosphere, and the extreme grown-upness of being so treated by a real actor, lost his nerve, went red in the face, and gobbled incoherently. "If we have time we'll run through it once more. What about the day before the show?"

Lord Mellings, loath to lose a treat but feeling that truth must prevail, said diffidently that the day before was the Coronation and he would be in London.

"I'd forgotten that," said Aubrey Clover. "Why must they have the Coronation on that particular day when I want to rehearse you?" which fine example of the hold that the stage has upon its true devotees impressed Lord Mellings very much.

"Well, then," said Aubrey Clover, resigned to make the best of a bad job, "we'll have to rehearse on the day itself. When are you coming back from London?"

Lord Mellings said the same evening, after the Coronation.

"Then, look here," said Aubrey Clover, "I'll send to meet you at Barchester if you tell me what train you're coming by and you can spend the night here; we'll rehearse next day and I'll send you back after the show. Is that all right?"

Lord Mellings, with a mixture of the grand air and a schoolboy's gaucherie, thanked Aubrey Clover and Jessica and said what clothes had he better wear for the play.

"How clever you are, Ludo my sweet, to think of that," said Jessica. "Aubrey! Ludo wants to know what he ought to wear, morning, afternoon, or night?"

"Night, of course," said Aubrey Clover. "All love scenes have to be at night—except Shakespeare, of course. The way that man got away with things! Absolutely unprofessional."

"I was only wondering," said Lord Mellings and became dumb.

"Dinner jacket will be just right," said Jessica, giving her husband a look which somehow conveyed to him, like Lord Burleigh's nod, that probably the young lord had not got a tail coat yet. In which she was right, for when people are growing at the rate of six or seven inches in a twelvemonth it is hardly worth having new and very expensive clothes which are to last them for as many years as possible. And Lord Mellings's look of relief was so marked as to leave Jessica no doubt of the correctness of her guess.

"Excuse me," said Aubrey Clover's accompanist, addressing Lord Mellings. "Would you mind just singing the first line once more. I've got an idea in my head."

Though Lord Mellings did not quite see the connection, he kindly obliged with the first lines:

"Though I am not twenty, sweet,
Here is my heart,"

adding: "Is that all right?"

"I knew he had absolute pitch," said Aubrey Clover's accompanist, rather smugly. "Well, I'm off. Mums is expecting me for supper. Good-bye, all," and he went away. And if anyone is interfering or untrustful enough to wonder how he got to Barchester Central, the answer is that he didn't. For Winter

Overcotes is on the Worsted line and one of Mr. Dean's cars was ready to take him to the Junction, where he would pick up the London express.

"And now I expect tea is ready," said Jessica, by which Lord Mellings felt confused, for so many things had happened that afternoon that he felt it might be any time at all. But the drive to Winter Overcotes and the rehearsal had not taken more than an hour and a half or so and tea-time it was, as was made abundantly clear by the ringing of a large bell to get the family in from the garden and the stream. Tea was at a large table in the dining-room, which was rapidly filled with Deans of all sizes and ages.

"You must be sick of me by now," said Jessica. "I am going to put you by Laurence's wife, who is very gentle and kind. Margaret," she said to her sister-in-law, "this is Ludo, otherwise Lord Mellings, who is helping Aubrey and me with *Two-Step for Three*. Take care of him, my lamb."

Lord Mellings sat down, and shyness fell upon him like the ashes upon Pompeii. He looked round wildly for help, but the seat on the other side of him was empty. Then his good manners came to his rescue and told him he must talk to this Mrs. Laurence Dean and he was at once rewarded by finding that she was very kind and easy to get on with and, what was more, appeared to be impressed by what Jessica had said.

"It is so kind of you to act in Aubrey's play," said Margaret Dean. "He says you are frightfully good. I wish I could see you, but we are having our own celebrations at Worsted, where we live. Mr. Birkett, who was the headmaster of South-bridge School, and his wife live at the Dower House and are helping us to arrange a Worsted Pageant. There used to be an old abbey called Beliers near Worsted and my brother Richard has invented a lot of things that might have happened there and we are going to act them in Mr. Palmer's big tithe barn. He is Laurence's uncle. My father is going to do the scene about the English driving the Danes out because he knows all about the Sagas."

Lord Mellings, enveloped by this pleasant voice telling him all about people to whom he had little or no clue, felt rather like a fly in a treacle-pot, but Mrs. Laurence Dean was so gentle and kind that he could not mind and presently, with great courage, he began to tell her about the Towers and how awful the house was and how his people lived in a bit of it, because they couldn't afford to keep it open, to all of which she listened attentively and said How dreadful it was, in just the right places.

Presently a large man in good tweeds came in, accompanied by a handsome woman with a rather weather-beaten face. A clamour of welcome greeted the newcomers. Lord Mellings asked Mrs. Laurence Dean who they were.

"Oh, don't you know them?" said she. "I thought everyone did. It's Mr. and Mrs. Adams. She was Lucy Marling. Mr. Adams has the big works at Hogglestock, and Laurence's father is on the Board. They do a lot of engineering things together."

Lord Mellings said his people knew the Marlings but not very well, and then Mrs. Adams found a place on the other side of the table while Mr. Adams, after looking round to see where there was an empty place, came round and took the seat beside him.

"Mr. Adams," said Mrs. Laurence Dean, leaning across her young neighbour, "how are you? This is Lord Mellings, Lord Pomfret's son. He is going to act in one of Aubrey's plays with Aubrey and Jessica for the Northbridge Coronation Festival."

"Well, young man," said Mr. Adams, good-naturedly, "I don't know you, but I come across your father on county work and if we'd a few more like him, we could do nicely with them. And what do *you* do?" and though the question was rather abrupt it was so obviously asked from real interest that Lord Mellings did not feel any embarrassment.

"Well, sir, I'm still at Eton," he said. "And then I do my military service."

"Guards, I suppose," said Mr. Adams and Lord Mellings said modestly If they would have him.

"Rum thing about the Guards," said Mr. Adams reflectively, "that all the men are so big and some of the officers so little. How tall are you, my boy? Six foot?"

Lord Mellings said not quite and he did hope he wouldn't be, because it made one's clothes so expensive, especially if one was on an allowance.

"That's a queer house of yours, Pomfret Towers," said Mr. Adams. "I went over it once when it was open for the Friends of Barchester Cathedral. I've seen some rum places in my time, but this one beats the band. It must have cost a pretty penny to build."

"About four hundred thousand pounds, sir," said Lord Mellings, who found the wealthy ironmaster very easy to talk to. "My people can't afford to live there, but we live in what was the servants' wing. Father often says he wishes he could pull the rest of the Towers down, but it would cost too much."

"If it were mine," said Mr. Adams reflectively, "I'd take that top floor off. There's quite a lot you could do with it then. Put in central heating and there you'd be."

"We have got some central heating in our part, sir," said Lord Mellings, surprised at the ease with which he was talking, "but it would cost too much to do the other part. Father says they used to burn about a hundred tons a year in his uncle's time, before the last war. The coal came by the truck-load. It was all open fires, of course, and huge kitchen ranges. There wasn't any hot water except in two bedrooms. One of them was turned into a bathroom later with four baths partitioned off, and the other has a huge bath up two steps. Everyone else still had hip baths."

Mr. Adams said reflectively that English country life took a lot of beating and he would like to see how that system worked. Lord Mellings, flown with the stage and absolute pitch and the Deans' very good tea, said he was sure his people would like it if Mr. Adams could come over one day—and Mrs. Adams too, he added.

"Now, that's an idea," said Mr. Adams, "and it's a very good idea. I'll tell you what, Mellings. You talk to my wife after tea. She runs the family, and I think your people know her old father. Fine old gentleman he is. Can be as deaf as a post when it suits him," which Mr. Adams appeared to find a praiseworthy and enviable characteristic. "And if you'd like to go over my works any day, just ring up my sekertary, Miss Pickthorn. I'll tell her to see that they show you everything. We've just got a big new contract for about half a million. Hyper-annealed-ferro-magnesium conturbators for the Middle East. And the money to be paid before delivery, with a good big deposit in an English bank to show they mean business. I'd like to see any of those foreigners doing Sam Adams in the eye and I'm taking steps about it. They know that Sam Adams's word is as good as—well, never mind," and Lord Mellings was vaguely conscious that Mrs. Adams, at the opposite side of the table, was casting not sheep's eyes but what we can only describe as wife's eyes at her husband.

"Thank you awfully, sir," said Lord Mellings, and then the wealthy ironmaster turned to Mr. Woolcot van Dryven to talk about the American exchange. Mrs. Laurence Dean was talking to her other neighbour, so Lord Mellings went on with his tea and rather enjoyed being a spectator and listener. Gradually the party went out into the garden, where Lord

Mellings was seized by Mr. Woolcot van Dryven, who said he had always wanted to know exactly what a haff was. By luck Lord Mellings was able to guess that Mr. Woolcot van Dryven meant a harf and was probably alluding to Eton.

"I don't quite know why it is a half instead of a term, sir," he said, "but I think they used to have one term from after Christmas till summer and another from the end of summer till Christmas. I don't know when schools began to have three terms."

Mr. Woolcot van Dryven said those old customs were very, very interesting: and if we do not write vurry, that is because we do not wish to disparage the intelligence of our reader who has just got this book from the libery, having been told by the nice girl who does customers from F to L that it was a Nice Book. The Campus at Eton, Mr. Woolcot van Dryven added, was, so he understood, steeped in history.

"Now, Pomfret Towers," said Mr. Woolcot van Dryven. "I have seen photographs of it. It is grandiose."

"We all think it is ghastly, sir," said Lord Mellings, feeling, we imagine, that having lost control of the conversation, he might as well speak the truth. "Father would like to pull it down, but he can't afford to."

Mr. Woolcot van Dryven said if Lord Pomfret did pull any of it down he would like to know. He would, he said, get his architect and his attorney onto it and re-erect part of it on his ranch in Texas, for his Long Island place was not spacious enough.

"Hullo," said a very handsome dark-haired woman advancing upon them. "Jessica says you are wonderful."

Lord Mellings, suddenly self-conscious again of his height and his responsibilities, almost stammered a reply.

"I hope Woolcot hasn't been preaching at you," said the dark handsome woman. "I'm Jessica's sister Betty van Dryven.

How are you?" and she took Lord Mellings's hand in a painful grip.

"No, it wasn't preaching a *bit*," said Lord Mellings. "I was telling him how ghastly the Towers is and how we wished we could afford to pull it down, but we can't."

Mr. Woolcot van Dryven said to his wife if Lord Pomfret did decide to pull it down it would be a fine civic contribution to have the stones numbered and shipped to the States and to re-erect part of it on his ranch in Texas, where a cultural centre was desiderated.

Lord Mellings, amused and with a curious feeling hitherto unknown to him of being master of the situation, said he would tell his father and perhaps Mr. and Mrs. van Dryven would come and see the Towers one day; that was, he added, appealing to a fellow countrywoman, if Mrs. van Dryven would like it.

"The trouble with Woolcot is," said his wife, with kindly detachment, "that he is an idealist. But we'd love to see the Towers if your people will let us," and then up came Mr. Adams with his wife, to whom he presented Lord Mellings.

"Hullo," said Mrs. Adams, crushing Lord Mellings's long hand in her powerful grasp. "Sam says you've asked us to come and see Pomfret Towers. We'd simply love to. I do know your mother a bit on committees and things. Only we don't want to gate-crash."

It was pretty clear to Lord Mellings, with an inherited sixth sense about people and social matters under his rather gawky appearance and shy manner, that Mrs. Adams was being, in her own downright way, kind and tactful. In his own rather diffident way (which we think many people were going to find very attractive as he became better known) he said that if Mrs. Adams didn't think he was interfering he would ask his mother to ring her up, and after that we need hardly say that Mr. Adams and Mr. Woolcot van Dryven got together again on the fascinating subject of dollar *v.* sterling, where we will leave them, as no amount of camouflage would conceal our entire ignorance of and want of interest in that subject except in so far as it prevents us from visiting the most hospitable country in the world.

Lord Mellings, after being a kind of social success, now found himself suddenly stranded and felt rather like a new boy left alone in his school. There are some happy (or lucky) people who are never left high and dry, but the other ninety and nine have, at one time or another, had the depressing experience of being quite alone in the middle of a large crowd who are all on intimate terms and have jokes and passwords to which one has no clue. We do not say that he was unhappy, for he found considerable entertainment in watching people, but his over-sensitive sense of other people's feelings made him wonder if his hostess thought he was bored or too stand-offish. If he had known her better he need have had no such qualms, for Mrs. Dean was celebrated for never being ruffled by anything that her large brood with their husbands and wives and growing families did; nor had she much reason to be ruffled, for the Dean family were all good-looking, healthy, and gifted in their different ways. All were what one would call comfortably off and the Woolcot van Dryvens almost millionaires—in dollars, at any rate.

A slight stirring of the people on the terrace made Lord Mellings look round. Through one of the French windows came a clerical gentleman in gaiters with an extremely pretty woman, not young but none the less attractive. They were warmly greeted by as many people as were near them, who all pressed round as if they were asking questions. Lord

Mellings, looking round for help, caught Mrs. Adams's eye.

"Please, who are they?" he said. "I ought to know, but I'm awfully bad at people."

"Oh, that's Canon Joram and Mrs. Joram. He's the one with the gaiters," said Lucy, which suddenly made Lord Mellings laugh. We do not think that Mrs. Adams, of whom we have been very fond for the last dozen years or so, saw what there was to laugh at, but she was pleased to see his young melancholy face crumple into amusement. "His wife was Mrs. Brandon. Isn't she pretty?" as indeed she was with her lovely eyes and her hair that wreathed itself into silver-grey tendrils. "Come and talk to her," and she clove a way through the crowd, Lord Mellings following in her wake.

"Hullo, Mrs. Joram," she said. "This is Ludovic Mellings, the one that Lord Pomfret's his father," and then stood back, as one who has exhibited a prize selection of vegetables and would like everyone to see it.

Mrs. Joram welcomed Lord Mellings as if he were an old friend. More chairs were brought out and most of the party settled on the terrace. Everyone liked the Jorams, who were justly popular, and most of those present were hoping for some gossip from the Close.

"Now, Joram," said Mr. Dean. "What's all this about a Mystery Play in the crypt for the Coronation? I never hear anything and my young people are too lazy to tell me."

"Well," said Canon Joram, "it is not for me to criticize," but he was interrupted, though very prettily, by Jessica, who said he must tell the truth and shame the devil.

Aubrey Clover said that was not the way to talk about the Bishop.

"I only said the *Devil*," said Jessica. "Darling Dr. Joram, *is* it true that the play is about Lust?"

"That, I understand, *is* one of the characters," said Canon Joram, "but as everyone is modern he is called Mr. Lusty. It is partly in verse—at least the author calls it verse. I think there is also a Mrs. O'Gonnoreagh, an Irish woman. They are all in modern dress, of course, and at the end someone has their face clawed off by a bear, who typifies something-or-other."

"Pinching things from Kipling!" said Jessica indignantly.

"And the hero, if you can call him that," Canon Joram continued, "is a full-blooded African whose mother was a crocodile."

Owing to the Progress of Poesy, no one appeared to find this unreasonable.

"I say, Dr. Joram," said Mrs. Adams, "how does one pronounce Mow-Mow? You've lived in Africa. Is it Mor-mor, or Mo-Mo, or what?"

Dr. Joram said that luckily Mngangaland was, in his time, not yet affected by that appalling cult.

"The Head Chief," he said, "did show some leanings towards it, but I put a stop to that."

"Angel!" said Jessica. "How *did* you do it?"

"It was quite simple," said Canon Joram. "He had a first-rate wireless and I used to go to the Palace—as we called his hut, which was larger than the others—every evening and make him listen to the whole of the Third Program. Then I told him that unless he changed his way of thinking the whole of his Future existence would be like that, instead of spending eternity in over-eating and over-drinking and beating his wives and slaughtering his enemies. I had no trouble after that."

Mr. Woolcot van Dryven said the American Protestant Episcopal Church would not stand for any performance within

her walls of dramatic scenes dealing with the Grosser Forms
of Sin, at which one of the elder Dean grandchildren had the
giggles and was suppressed.

Lydia, who would willingly have giggled too, took advantage of the slight uproar to get up and say good-bye to as
many Deans as possible.

Lord Mellings was rather overwhelmed by all the people
who said good-bye to him in a very friendly way. He promised
Mr. Adams and Mr. Woolcot van Dryven that he would ask
his mother to arrange a day when they could come to the
Towers and of course Mrs. Adams and Mrs. Woolcot van
Dryven too.

"Come again, dear boy," said Mrs. Dean, looking up from
her chaise longue with beautiful dark eyes. "I never go anywhere because it is so much more comfortable at home, as I
am *sure* you feel too," to which there appeared to be no answer.

"Farewell," said Jessica, "thou art too tall for my possessing,
but you are a perfect lamb. Our scene will go like forked
lightning," and Aubrey said much the same thing in rather
different words. Then Lord Mellings and the Mertons got into
the car and Noel drove back to Pomfret Towers, where he
decanted Lord Mellings, at his own request, at the lodge
gates, and then sped back to Northbridge. They drove in
silence for some miles, though a very comfortable, compan-
ionable silence.

"Do you remember those Japanese toys one used to have?"
said Lydia presently. "Like little bits of hard paper and when
you put them into a bowl of water they gradually unfolded
and turned into flowers and things?"

Noel said he did and when he was little he ate some and his
nurse told him they would all swell inside his stomach and
kill him. And what, he added, made Lydia think of them?

"That nice Ludo," said Lydia. "He is all coming uncurled and opening. What luck it was that Aubrey took a liking to him."

"What Machiavellian management it was, my love," said Noel, "that you asked him to dinner when his people first came to us and you knew Aubrey and Jessica were coming."

Young Lord Mellings walked slowly down the long avenue reflecting in a rather addled way upon the experiences of the afternoon. Never before, he felt, had so much happened to someone who so little expected it, in so short a time. That he had managed to please Aubrey Clover, that Jessica Dean had sung with him, that Aubrey Clover's accompanist had said he had absolute pitch (whatever that was), that his voice had not broken again (which had been a perpetually recurring nightmare ever since the party at the Mertons'), that Mr. Adams and that American who had married Jessica Dean's sister should both take an interest in Pomfret Towers, that so many good-looking, well-mannered people had, as it seemed to him, gone out of their way to be nice to him: it was all rather confusing.

Then he began to wonder how much he ought to tell his father of the suggestions made by Mr. Adams and Mr. Woolcot van Dryven, the plans of which latter reminded him of a very good film called *The Ghost Goes West,* so that he had to stop and laugh aloud to himself. Miss Merriman, coming into the drive from a side avenue, heard him laugh and her mind went back to another tall, anxious young man who had walked in those same avenues while old Lord Pomfret was still alive.

"Oh, hullo, Merry," said Lord Mellings, waiting for her to join him. "I *must* tell you about this afternoon, because I don't know if I ought to tell father or not," which proof of confidence touched Miss Merriman not a little.

"Tell me," she said. "Only don't walk too fast. Your legs are twice as long as mine."

"Sorry, Merry," said Lord Mellings. "I think I was walking quickly because I was thinking of such a lot of things. Listen," and he poured out, eagerly, his account of all the things that had happened between after lunch and the present moment. Miss Merriman listened in silence till his excited story had come to an end with the words, "And I thought you could tell me what to do next. What I thought was not to tell father all the things they said, because it would sound silly, but to say they were awfully keen to see the place. Then, you see, if they didn't really mean anything they said, father wouldn't be disappointed. Is that right?"

Miss Merriman said Perfectly right. Mr. Adams was, she said, absolutely straight and reliable as far as she knew. Of Mr. Woolcot van Dryven she only knew that he was extremely rich by English standards. It would do no harm to ask them to the Towers if his father and mother liked the idea, as she was pretty sure they would.

"I say, Merry," said Lord Mellings, as they came round to their end of the Towers, "will you come to Northbridge and see the play? Father and mother can't come because they've got to be at the Coronation Concert at Nutfield. Do."

That the son of the family to whom, in one way and another, so many of her years had been given should want her company, touched her more deeply than she could have suspected, but she did not make any promise, for her duties would come first and as yet she did not quite know what they might be.

CHAPTER 8

SOME of the old Barsetshire stock, if they ever troubled to reflect on their own thoughts, which we are glad to say they mostly didn't, occasionally took a serious if puzzled interest in the way some families gently came up while others as gently declined. Undoubtedly the Noel Mertons had come up, from good provincial legal stock on Noel's side and quiet undistinguished small landowners on Lydia's. That Noel was a Q.C. in London and becoming a wealthy man hardly explained it, for Barsetshire neither knew nor cared about his income. Partly because he had a good dairy herd, partly because he was willing to take on responsibility in the county so far as his London work permitted, he was now considered not only as a man who on the whole did credit to the county, but as one who could be called upon to work for the county and would do the work well. Lydia had quietly done whatever she was asked to do with untiring efficiency and also with the right manner and, we may add, the right clothes. For the really old Barsetshire stock, Wickhams, Sowerbys (though the last of that family had some years ago sold her house at Edgewood to Mr. Adams and gone to live with her widowed sister at Worthing), Grantlys, Thornes (for Mrs. Belton had been a Thorne), and others, they could live as they wished and wear what they liked, without criticism, as could Mrs. Sam Adams in virtue of being a Marling though her husband was a self-made man. But for people like Victoria, Lady Norton, relic of the first creation and generally known as the Dreadful

Dowager, and even for Lord Bond at Staple Park, though his mother was sister to Lord Stoke, there was a slight almost imperceptible barrier. Canon Joram's wife, formerly Mrs. Brandon, held honorary Barsetshire rank owing to her own charm and her husband's position in the Close, but her well-to-do son Francis and his pretty wife, who had been Mrs. Captain Arbuthnot, would never quite attain it. And so one could go on for ever, noting those who were county (whether high or low), those who would become county, and those who somehow never would. These are things that no Gotha Almanack can fathom, and go partly by centuries of unwritten custom and partly, we believe, by what the English cottages feel. For though old Bunce and his family at Northbridge, or the large Thatcher family at Pomfret Madrigal, had not a moral among them as far as legalized marriage went, their instinct, rooted in the soil on and by which they had lived from the days of woad and wolfskins, told them unerringly who were gentry and who were not. Theirs the right to serve the gentry, but in their own way, and if the Pucken family quietly bullied and cheated the Luftons over at Framley; if the Wheelers (including old Wheeler, cousin of the landlord of the Nabob at Harefield, and known to be the only man who understood the chimneys at Pomfret Towers) picked and stole at the Pomfrets' kitchen door; if Jasper, the half-gypsy keeper at Beliers Priory, sold what he considered a fair percentage of Sir Cecil Waring's rabbits to the Barchester black market, it was as much their rooted privilege as infang and outfang (if we have it correctly) was the right of the overlord; though we strongly suspect that Cedric the Saxon's thralls did him down and he knew it, but suffered the custom of the country.

The present Lord Pomfret, as we know, had come in sideways as it were, because the late Earl's only son had been killed in India many years ago. He had had honour thrust upon him and taken up with quiet courage a position that he had never coveted but had to accept. In everything his Countess, of good Barsetshire stock herself, had loyally helped and supported him and he had been accepted as overlord by the descendants of Alured de Pomfret's yeomanry and peasantry, who cheated him up to the limits of their conventions but would have tarred and feathered any outsider who tried to impose on their lord. If Lord Pomfret was shooting, a certain number of birds who had been seen to fall were usually reported missing; but should foreigners from Barchester come poaching, they were as soundly beaten off as were the louts from the city who had tried to spoil the skating on the lake at Harefield during the war. All this Lord Pomfret had come to recognize and though he did not often speak of it, it gave him pleasure, and when he renewed the lease of old Finch's cottage, knowing that Finch, who was supposed to look after the inside of it, had kept a pig in the wash house and bees in the back room upstairs for fifty years or so, he also knew that he was doing his duty in the station to which it had pleased God to call him. Duties are often troublesome and even to one's own disadvantage, but there they are.

Though Lord Pomfret's tenants were ready to impose on him up to the limit of his tolerance, knowing that from Roddy Wicklow they would get full justice but no more, they resented the changes at the Towers deeply, for in the status of the Lord Lieutenant's great hideous house they shared a reflected glory. There was a general feeling that They—not in the pejorative sense in which we used that word from 1945 onwards, but just persons unknown—ought to do something about it, They ought. But as no one knew who They were, nor what They could do if found, the argument was apt to lapse, or to go on in a beery way without getting anywhere. No less did Lord Pomfret grieve, for resentment was not in his nature, over the unwieldy, hideous mansion that was his heritage, but what is, is; and he set himself to deal with it as best he could, always with his Countess to support him. Nothing, of course, was said to the children about these difficulties, but as they got older they would begin to feel it. Especially the tall anxious heir (so like his tall anxious father), who, as we know, was beginning to share his father's troubles. Emily and Giles were pure Pomfret and would bang their way heartily through life, but what would Ludovic do? Lord and Lady Pomfret had often discussed this question and come to absolutely no conclusion at all.

"There is one thing you did do," said Lord Pomfret to his wife. "You asked the Mertons to dinner."

"And there is one thing the Mertons did," said Lady Pomfret. "They asked the Clovers to dinner. It was the luckiest thing in the world that they asked Ludo too."

Not so much luck as kindness, said Lord Pomfret, and his Countess thought what a good thing it was for Gillie to make friends with such a nice woman as Mrs. Merton, who had the wits to see what a darling Ludo really was, at which moment their elder son with Miss Merriman came into the room.

"Well, darling, how did it go?" said Lady Pomfret, and it speaks volumes for Lord Mellings's kind disposition that he did not go straight out of the room and bang the door or, though not quite so unsatisfactory a response, say "Oh, all right," and then have the Sulks.

"Oh, it was rather fun," said Lord Mellings. "Jessica sang in parts with Aubrey and me. She *is* clever," which were perhaps the most dashing words his lordship had yet spoken to his family. "And then we had tea at a huge dining-room table and I was next to Mrs. Laurence Dean. She is awfully nice and kind. And then I had Mr. Adams on the other side. He was awfully nice too. I say, mother, could we ask them here some time? They'd awfully like to see the house, and Mr. Adams said you knew Mrs. Adams's people, the Marlings."

Both Lord and Lady Pomfret had met Mrs. Marling on various county committees and Lord Pomfret had talked to Mr. Adams at the Club more than once. Lord Pomfret said the Marlings were a much older family in the county than the de Pomfrets, as they used to be.

"And there was a sister of Jessica's," said Lord Mellings. "She's rather handsome in a dark sort of way and her husband is American. Woolcot van Dryven he's called. They were awfully nice to me and I wondered if you could ask them too. The same day as the Adamses, perhaps."

To this his parents saw no objection and his mother said she would see about it.

"I'm sorry you won't be here, darling," she said to Lord Mellings, "but as you can't, that's that."

Lord Mellings said Eton did cut into a man's life a bit and looked at his mother to see how she would take it. Ever since the dinner with the Mertons Lady Pomfret had been wondering what on earth her ugly duckling was going to turn into, for on that evening she had realized, as we all have to sooner or later, that the tall schoolboy was nearly grown-up. As far as height went, she hoped he was quite grown-up, for it would take time to fill out that rather lanky frame and her husband's side of the Foster family had not the robust health of the late Earl; that had gone in this generation to Emily and Giles. But all this passed through her mind with the swiftness that no one has yet been able to explain or record, and she said at once that the Army would cut into it a good deal more and he must not sin his mercies, as old Mr. Macpherson, the Scotch agent to the Leslie family, used to say. So Lady Pomfret rang up the Deans' house and asked Betty van Dryven if she and her husband would come to lunch next

Saturday, which they would, and then rang up Mrs. Samuel Adams with the same request. Mrs. Adams said they would love to and how lucky it was a Saturday because her husband would be free, and Lady Pomfret wondered at Mrs. Adams's simplicity and then blamed herself for being a prig.

Then the Easter holidays were at an end and the Pomfrets continued their ceaseless round of unrequited toil. But not altogether unrequiting, for very often one's duty, though one may dread it in advance, loathe it while being performed, feel a hypocrite while one smiles and says the right things, does turn out to be all for the best. It is very annoying that we do not always enjoy doing what is right, but the fault is probably in ourselves, not in our stars.

The appointed Saturday came. To make even numbers Lady Pomfret asked her brother, Roddy Wicklow, to join them. Not that she did not want Roddy's pretty wife, of whom she saw a good deal, but it had gradually come to be a tacit agreement that if the Towers were a man short, the agent would oblige, and Alice Wicklow was perfectly agreeable to this arrangement. There was also, as we know, an alternative friendly arrangement by which Miss Merriman sometimes went to the Vicarage, where she was always welcome, when there was a woman too many; but today Lady Pomfret needed her help in showing the house. The first to come, very punctually, were the Adamses. Lucy had occasionally been at the Towers for county meetings of various sorts, but this was Mr. Adams's first visit.

The weather had relapsed into the sulks, in which state it proposed to remain for the rest of the year sooner than miss the Coronation. It was difficult to say whether the Towers looked more depressing in grey sky and squalls of rain, or flaunting its hideous red bulk under a sunny sky, but the

Pomfrets were on the whole glad that it cleared up, a little before lunch, so that the visitors could see in comfort the whole horror of the scene, to which end Lady Pomfret walked the Adamses to a distance of a hundred yards or so into the park, where they turned and stood in reverent silence.

"Gosh!" said Mrs. Adams, "I remembered it was awful, but I'd forgotten it was as awful as that. I mean it isn't even. I mean the two ends don't match. Was that on purpose, or did the money run out?"

Mr. Adams had always prided himself on being a plain-spoken man, but his plainness was as nought compared with the interested and uninhibited comments of his wife, and he looked at her uneasily—a very rare occurrence.

Lord Pomfret, amused by Mrs. Adams's frankness, said he believed the Earl who built it had wanted two towers, but for some reason only one was built. The architect had been ordered to take St. Pancras station as his model and not spare expense and if, he said, Mrs. Adams remembered the outside of St. Pancras, she would see that one tower was really more correct, but somehow the name Towers had stuck. At this point a car about forty feet long and ten feet wide, or so it appeared to the party, drew up at the bottom of the ramp which led up to the front door.

"That must be the van Dryvens," said Lady Pomfret. "No wonder one can't get about in London now. Will you go and fetch them, Gillie?" but even as his lordship turned to go, Miss Merriman materialized beside the car. They saw the van Dryvens get out, and after a few words Miss Merriman brought them across the grass to meet her employers. We do not know what Betty may have said to her husband, but Mr. van Dryven was obviously making a great effort not to launch into a set speech.

"I *say*," said Betty, when the proper greetings had been

exchanged, "isn't it *ghastly*. I don't mean ghastly ghastly but really *smashingly* ghastly," which artless comment made her hosts feel that the treat was being a success.

"Now, what style would that be?" said Mr. van Dryven. "Would you call it rococo?"

"I brought the old Guide to Pomfret Towers," said Miss Merriman, opening a book bound in maroon crushed morocco with rounded corners which, together with red china ribbon bookmarkers, made it look uncommonly like a prayer book that had gone mad. "Shall I just read the description of the outside, Lady Pomfret?"

"Yes, do, Merry," said her ladyship in as serious a voice as she could manage.

" 'Pomfret Towers has a frontage of about three hundred feet,' " Miss Merriman began, " 'and stands without a rival for palatial beauty and comfort. It is constructed of red brick with dressings of Bath Stone. The style of architecture is a happy combination of various mediæval features, the inspection of which recall to mind the Lombardic and Venetian brick Gothic or Gothic-Italian type, while the critical eye of the student will observe touches of Milan and other Italian terracotta buildings interlaced with good reproductions of details from Winchester and Salisbury cathedrals, Westminster Abbey, etc.; while there may also be seen the ornaments of Laon, Amiens, and other French edifices, which, though conglomerate, must have required great pains and skill to properly harmonize in order to produce so attractive a result. At the northwest corner is a clock-tower one hundred and fifty feet high, more than half the height of the Monument at London Bridge.' Shall I go on Lady Pomfret?"

"Now, the Monument, what exactly is that?" said Mr. van Dryven. "Is that the Cleopatra's Needle on your Embankment?"

Miss Merriman said Not exactly, and looked at Lady Pomfret for instructions.

"I think that has given us a general idea," said Lady Pomfret with great presence of mind. "Shall we walk round to the
other side, Mrs. van Dryven? I would like to show you the
Italian garden that my husband's aunt, the late Lady Pomfret,
laid out. She had lived a great deal in Italy and was a very keen
gardener. Do you garden?"

Betty, who was by now feeling much more Dean than van
Dryven, said they had trees in tubs and flowering climbers
outside their penthouse apartment in New York and a formal
garden in their Long Island place, but did not say anything
about the ranch in Texas, and then they came round the corner of the house to the long terrace, below which the formal
beds of brilliant cheap flowers were looking their best and the
clipped beech hedges shining in their brightest early summer
green.

"I think," said Lady Pomfret to her husband, who had followed with the men, "we have time to go up the green river
and see the kitchen gardens and the grotto."

Mrs. Adams asked why the river was green. For answer
Lady Pomfret pointed towards the wide path of closely mown
grass, winding among shrubs and high beech trees. Lucy
Adams and Betty van Dryven, the one Barsetshire by birth
and long inheritance, the other of a family which though not
true Barsetshire had now struck its roots there, were both overcome by the gentle beauty of the place. It was to Betty for a
moment as if New York and Long Island and the ranch in
Texas were the baseless fabric of a vision and she again was
eighteen years old and had just won a classical scholarship at
Oxford and was taking the part of Phædra in a performance
in her Uncle Palmer's large barn at Worsted on the day when
her brother Laurence sprained his ankle. And, as if in a dream,

she followed Lady Pomfret and Lucy Adams beside the little stream to where, below a rough stone grotto, was a sandy, shallow-bottomed pool from whose depths the spring came stirring through the sand. Presently the men, loitering behind, as men do, to talk of uninteresting things, came up with them.

"My old mother, and when I say old she was a good deal less than my age when she died," said Mr. Adams, "was always a one for running water. When I was a little lad I made a grotto out of old bits of stone I'd picked up and some oyster shells off the Council refuse dump and one thing and another, and I borrowed a bit of rubber tubing off the man at the motor-repair shop where I'd got a job on Saturday mornings and got the water from the kitchen tap to run round the grotto."

Everyone was touched by this reminiscence of the wealthy ironmaster's past. Lady Pomfret asked what happened to the grotto.

"Went up the spout, like most other things," said Mr. Adams. "My father was as good a tradesman as you'd meet in a month of Sundays, but he thought elbows were made for lifting and most of what he earned went that way and so did my rubber tubing. Well, well. I suppose old Lord Pomfret had the grotto made; I mean the last Earl's father."

"Yes, he did," said Lady Pomfret. "But how did you guess?"

"Well, I couldn't exactly say," said Mr. Adams. "A man that could build a house like the Towers, well, he couldn't do that over again, so it stands to reason he'd have to do something else. And when Lucy and I were in Italy last year, where I may say I didn't do badly by letting my Italian friends talk themselves right out and then saying my bit, we saw a lot of villas and gardens and that's the kind of thing you'd find there. So I put two and two together."

"And they made four," said Lord Pomfret. "I found a lot of old journals—day-books—I don't know what you would call them, about the building of the Towers. They are extraordinarily interesting. The work that was done every day, what the wages were every week, and how many thousand pounds of Consols he sold out every month to pay the contractors. Perhaps they might interest you, Mr. Adams," and Mr. Adams said he would very much like to see them. Then Lady Pomfret said they really must go in because of lunch, so they walked back the other way, among the beech trees, and found Roddy Wicklow talking to Miss Merriman about an otter.

Rather to the Pomfrets' relief the general talk was about the approaching Coronation, a subject on which everyone could agree.

"I must say," said Betty van Dryven, "that I feel a bit of a heel about it," a locution not quite clear to Lady Pomfret, who asked why.

"Well," said Betty, "you've *got* to go, Lady Pomfret, because you and Lord Pomfret are yourselves, but Woolcot and I are only sight-seers that can afford good seats," to which Lady Pomfret was inspired to reply that Mr. and Mrs. van Dryven were, if she could explain what she meant, a kind of ambassadors and would carry back with them their own account of the greatest pageant that the world could show.

"Sally's right," said her brother. "There's not a country in the world that can put on a show like this. And I hope the Russians will see what they did to themselves by murdering their Royal Family. You *can't* do a proper ceremony with nothing but people in frock coats or uniforms. The French might do the decorations better. I was in Paris when King George the Sixth and Queen Elizabeth were there, and what the French couldn't do with a few poles and some flags and bits of velvet or whatnot was not worth talking about. But they could only do it for outsiders. They've no one of their own to do it for. We have. And that makes all the difference."

Mr. Woolcot van Dryven said he must, however unwillingly, agree. Though his feelings for any President of the United States, he said, must necessarily be those of the deepest veneration, representing as the President did the sovereign will of millions of citizens, yet, he said, if that President belonged to a faction, for a party he would not call it, which all right-thinking—he did not mean the opposite of left-thinking but what it would perhaps be more correct to call all truly civic-minded—citizens could but look upon with scorn and abhorrence as prostituters—and he must beg the ladies present to forgive the use of the word when events justified it—of the State, why then, he said, any hundred-per-cent American must contemn such a man.

"I say, Woolcot, you *did* get out of that well," said Mrs. Adams. "I never thought you would. What are you, a Republican or a Democrat?"

"You needn't explain, Woolcot," said his wife, breaking in before her husband could collect himself. "It would take too long," for which words, firmly spoken, the company were extremely grateful. "Lady Pomfret, it is frightfully kind of you to let us come over and see the Towers. There is one more thing, but I hardly like to bother you, only it would be marvellous if you could."

Lady Pomfret asked what it was.

"Only to see your robes and things, if it wouldn't be a bother," said Betty. "It would do Woolcot a lot of good. He needs a bit of pulling up sometimes."

Lady Pomfret looked to Miss Merriman for help. That invaluable woman said the robes were in the Green Bedroom on those two dressmakers' dummies that used to live in the South Attic and Mr. and Mrs. van Dryven could easily see them. Roddy Wicklow, also ready to help or protect his sister and her husband in their dual roles of relations and employers,

said why shouldn't Mr. and Mrs. van Dryven put them on for
a few moments. There was a very short but appreciable pause
before Betty van Dryven spoke and then it was to thank Mr.
Wicklow and say they would love to if Lord and Lady Pomfret
didn't mind. Then Roddy quickly asked Mr. van Dryven
about fox-hunting in U.S.A., and in which states one could
hunt, and was rewarded by so long and detailed an account of
various packs that he was able to think quietly about Six
Corners Covert and whether that vixen had got away and if so
where she was.

"Now," said Lady Pomfret, when lunch was over. "If you
would really like to see the house, we will look at the top floor
first and then work down. The place isn't really quite as big as
it looks, because all the rooms are so large, until one gets to the
top floor. We might go up there first. Shall I show you the
way?" and she took the party along the stone passage and into
the big hall, up the hideously carved staircase to the first floor
with the gallery round the hall, and so up the narrow stairs to
the top floor with its rabbit warren of bedrooms and the old
nurseries. To Betty van Dryven a house of this kind was of
course not unfamiliar and she took it very well, having stayed
in various English houses of varying uncomfortableness before
she married Mr. van Dryven, which gentleman was divided
between genuine horror at the thought of English ladies living
in such conditions and interest in seeing history come true.

"But these were only the maids' and the nursery quarters,"
said Lady Pomfret, with a calm that Mr. van Dryven found
surprising. "The visiting ladies' maids had separate rooms, each
with a bell direct from their mistress's bedroom. I think we
have the Directions to Visitors that the sixth Earl, the father of
Gillie's uncle Giles, had printed for the bedrooms. They would
interest you. The housemaids slept three and four, or more, in
a room. Of course all the menservants slept downstairs in the

kitchen wing. These are the old nurseries. There were two nursery footmen to take the children's meals up and bring up the hot water for their baths and carry the smaller children up and down, as the nurseries were so high up and the stairs so steep. Life must have been very easy then," which last words so completely staggered Mr. van Dryven that he had nothing to say.

Lord Pomfret was also doing his duty by acting as guide to Mrs. Adams and Mrs. van Dryven, both of whom were pleased to recognize a nobleman's house, though fallen upon evil days, and thought how lovely it had been to have so many servants and people to wait on the nurseries, and to ring bells that were answered.

"I wonder where Sam is," said Mrs. Adams. "He was with Mr. Wicklow when we came upstairs," but it was improbable that Mr. Adams would have fallen into an oubliette or been shut into a cupboard with a spring lock, so she thought no more of him.

Then Lady Pomfret took her guests down again to the first floor and showed them some of the bedrooms, including one which she had not had time to show to the Mertons.

"This was old Lady Pomfret's bedroom," she said, opening a door and letting her guests go in. "I'll turn the lights on. It isn't worth while opening the shutters. I want to show you the four-poster. I think," she added, with the unaccountable pride we all have in the failings of our ancestors, "the bed is the most uncomfortable in England—in Barsetshire, at any rate."

"It certainly couldn't be more hideous," said Mrs. Adams reverently. "It beats the state bed at Gatherum Castle hollow."

"I'm glad you feel that," said Lady Pomfret. "When the Duchess was here she said the Gatherum state bed was worse, but it has at least a comfortable mattress. Just look at this one," and she turned back the dust-sheet at one side.

Mrs. Adams felt it.

"I *know* that kind of mattress," she said enthusiastically. "Quite hard and stuffed with marbles and a great ridge in the middle so that whichever side you sleep on, you fall out."

Mr. van Dryven, who had been a deeply interested but silent spectator, now said it was a museum specimen and should be skeduled as a National Monument. He would suggest to Lady Pomfret that one of those mattresses made of a kind of sponge would be the thing to have, as no matter where you lay, the mattress, owing to the resilience of the rubber, kept its spring and resumed its natural shape when you got up.

"I know those mattresses," said Lady Pomfret. "But we simply couldn't afford one, especially for a double bed. Of course we can't use this part at all and it will be even worse for Ludo when he comes into the place. We do open one or two of the big rooms downstairs occasionally for a Conservative Do, or the Barsetshire Agricultural Annual General Meeting. But that's all."

"We must show them the frescoes, Sally," said Lord Pomfret: "I'll open the window. One can't see with these awful lights," and indeed the chandelier with eight very weak electric lights imperfectly disguised as candles was darkness made visible. "Just look at the end wall. They were painted by the wife of the Lord Pomfret who built the Towers. She had a few lessons with an R.A.—I've forgotten his name, but it is somewhere among my papers."

He pulled back the faded green velvet curtains, undid the shutters, and let in the afternoon light. On the end wall were paintings of knights, ladies, minstrels, damsels, and other romantic figures, rather badly drawn and coloured in the most depressing pale greens and dirty blues and watery gamboge.

Mr. van Dryven drew a deep breath and said they should be skeduled as National Monuments. Lord Pomfret said he entirely agreed with him, but the people in London didn't.

"If they were mine," said Mrs. Adams, "I'd put several good coats of whitewash over them. Then if anyone wanted to rediscover them in five hundred years or so, they could clean off the whitewash and guess what they were; like that Professor Tristram, who goes hunting in churches to find frescoes that aren't there," a description which any reader will understand.

"Well, I think we've seen the best horrors," said Lord Pomfret cheerfully, and he closed the shutters and drew the curtains. "Now shall we look at the ground floor?"

"If it won't tire you," said Mrs. Adams, which words, overheard by Lady Pomfret, made her ladyship think very highly of her.

As we have already described the ground floor, we will not do so again. Lady Pomfret, anxious not to spoil the treat by overtiring her guests, took them at a hand gallop through the great reception rooms and then opened the door of the antechapel. After the opulent mid-Victorianism of the house the elegant ornament of the lovely baroque ante-chapel, the marble and lapis and gold, the gilded carving of the chapel itself, were like a cool dawn after a fevered night.

"It is just about the size of the little church we go to in Texas," said Mr. van Dryven, "but rather different. The Reverend Grubacker is a fine preacher and a very fine man and I can just imagine his feelings if he saw this. He would feel as I do, only in a higher degree," and Lady Pomfret was touched to see how truly his feelings were moved.

Miss Merriman, who had not accompanied them on the tour of the house, now materialized to say that if Mr. and Mrs. van Dryven would really like to see the Coronation robes, would they come with her to the Green Bedroom. Lady Pomfret asked Lucy Adams if she would like to go and see them, but her guest said she would really rather not, so Lady Pomfret took her back to their own end of the Towers, where they could be quiet till tea-time.

After talking about one or two committees on which they both sat and the various Coronation festivities in which they were involved, Lady Pomfret said she would show Mrs. Adams some of the old notepaper and the Directions to Visitors and from her writing-table brought a large cardboard box.

"These were still all in use when old Lady Pomfret, Gillie's aunt, was alive," she said. "At least we called her Aunt Edith, just as we called old Lord Pomfret Uncle Giles, though they were really some sort of cousins. When Gillie first came here his father was the heir. He was a cousin of old Lord Pomfret, who loathed him, and Gillie was on approval. We had just got engaged the day the news came that Gillie's father had died. Lady Pomfret died fairly soon after that and Lord Pomfret died the year the war began. That is why Gillie came into the title while he was fairly young. We didn't much want it, either of us, but there it is."

"And very good for everyone," said Mrs. Adams with all the downright vehemence of Miss Lucy Marling. "I can't think what the county would do without you. There isn't anyone who would work as hard as you do."

"Thank you," said Lady Pomfret and touched Lucy's hand. "Now these are what I thought you might care to see. This was the notepaper," and she laid before Lucy a large sheet of paper such as we have not seen in England for years, of finest quality, strong and very smooth. At the head of each sheet was an exquisitely delicate steel engraving of the Towers with a view of the parkland and grazing deer and below this the address in a fine Italian script or type. Lucy expressed the warmest admiration for it and said it was almost too good to write on.

"Not if one wrote well," said Lady Pomfret, taking another

sheet out of the box. "This is a letter from the Lady Pomfret who was Uncle Giles's mother, about a butler's character," and she handed to Lucy a sheet of the fine paper presenting, in an exquisite hand with very fine upstrokes and rather darker downstrokes, The Countess of Pomfret's compliments to Lady Dumbello, begging to know if Roger Hickson was well-trained, trustworthy, understood wine, could manage four footmen, and whether married or single. Lucy almost sighed with delight at the elegance of it all.

"I don't know what happened about Hickson," said Lady Pomfret. "We have got the Servants' Wages book for that time, but his name only occurs once. It was something to do with one of the maids, I expect. It usually was. That Lord Pomfret asked his wife to promise never to lick a stamp because it was so unladylike. This is for wetting stamps," and she showed Lucy a small golden trough across which was fastened a golden rod transfixing a kind of small fat rolling-pin of roughened crystal.

"Every day the butler put fresh water in the bottom," said Lady Pomfret, "and you turned the crystal till it was wetted all over and then moistened your stamp. Uncle Giles said she lived much longer than her husband, but she was faithful to her promise. He remembered her, when she was a very old lady, moistening all her stamps as her husband had asked her."

"What a nice story," said Lucy. "It's rather like a duke in one of Miss Edgeworth's books I read years ago. *Patronage*, I think it was, and there is a very proud duke who refuses to accept a letter with a wafer instead of sealed because he says it is below him to touch a letter fastened with another man's spittle," and Lady Pomfret said they must have known one another, but we think her dates were wrong.

"Oh, and here are the Instructions to Guests, that I told you about," she said, handing Lucy a large card with that same steel engraving of the Towers at the head. On it were the hours for Prayers, Breakfast, Luncheon, and Dinner, and the time of Divine Service on Sunday morning, also the hours at which the post left. Below were the words:

Guests are requested not to ring for their personal attendants between twelve o'clock and one o'clock, as this is the hour of dinner in the Housekeeper's Room.

"I have never been in any other house where the guests were given their orders like that," said Lady Pomfret, not without pride, to which Lucy replied sadly that there was no one now to give orders to.

"The Lady Pomfret that I was telling you about," said the present Countess, "had never put on a pair of shoes or boots in her life. She sat on a chair and her maid put them on for her and buttoned her boots."

"I wouldn't mind my shoes being put on, but not button boots," said Lucy. "I had a pair when I was small and one always got a bit of one's leg caught in the buttonhook."

Lady Pomfret said she had never had button boots, but catching a bit of yourself in the zip fastener of a belt was just as bad.

"I can't see why one says belt now," she added. "Belts don't go from above your waist to halfway down your thighs," to which Lucy replied that girdle was even sillier, but what else was there to call them and her mother *would* say stays when she bought them, which Lady Pomfret said was perhaps better than corsets, and then she put the papers away and discussed with Lucy the next meeting of the Barchester General Hospital Ladies' Association and how best to stop Victoria, Lady Norton (better known as the Dreadful Dowager), from throwing her weight about.

"You can't," said Lucy. "I don't think anyone can, unless it was Rose Fairweather over at Greshamsbury."

Lady Pomfret said she did not know Miss Fairweather and would like to hear more about her.

"Oh, she's Mrs., not Miss," said Lucy, "and her husband is a captain in the Royal Navy. Once you get an idea into her head you can't stop her," which testimonial, though peculiar, sounded to Lady Pomfret as if something might be done about getting the right idea planted in so promising a recruit, and then the rest of the party began to come in from various parts of the house, putting an end to the discussion.

As we noticed, a little earlier in the afternoon Mr. Adams had been lost while the guests were seeing the upstairs rooms, nor had Roddy Wicklow been seen. These two gentlemen, who between them knew most things about the county in its different aspects, had basely deserted the party and were in the room which Lord Pomfret now used as the estate office, looking at various documents of interest.

"When I first came here," said Roddy Wicklow, "I was under the old agent, Mr. Hoare. He knew his job, all right, and I learnt a lot from him, but he didn't like a younger man coming in. Then he retired and old Lord Pomfret gave me the job. Just about the time Gillie and Sally got married, it was. The old estate office was right at the other end of the house looking towards the kennels. But this room isn't bad. That's the big estate map," and he went over to the wall and pulled down the huge map, which was mounted on linen and when not wanted flew up with a click.

"And a very pretty bit of work," said Mr. Adams, admiring the draughtsmanship as he would have admired a blueprint of a new crushing machine. "Now, where's Hamaker's Spinney? Lady Pomfret mentioned it at lunch," and Roddy pointed out the place that Miss Wicklow, before the war, had shown on the map to young Mr. Foster, telling him that those earths ought to be stopped. Mr. Adams then asked one or two very pertinent questions about flooding at Starveacres Hatches and feelingly described the trouble he had had over his big market-gardening venture at Adamsfield, a piece of land on the Marling estate, down by the river, which had a habit of flooding once in every seven or eight years.

"But it's doing finely now," he said. "We get all the vegetables we need for our canteen and that's not a small order, and we sell the rest. My wife did most of it."

"I suppose you called it Adamsfield after yourself," said Roddy.

"One would think that," said Mr. Adams, "but it was one of those coincidences you wouldn't believe if you found it in a book. I was over there one day with my father-in-law, Squire Marling, and we were talking about that field down by the river, the three-acre it was called, and there was an old character called Nandy there, a real old ruffian who spends every penny he has at the pub and hasn't ever washed in his life, and old Nandy said that bit of land was where his grandfather Adam Nandy used to live and the bit of land and the cottage were always called Adamsfield. Lucy looked it up at the Barchester Public Library and the old man was perfectly right. So we kept the name."

As still sometimes happened when Mr. Adams had been speaking, the subject appeared to be so entirely exhausted that there was no possible reply; though since his marriage he had appreciably improved in this respect. Roddy took from a shelf some large books bound in red leather and put them on the big writing-table.

"These are the daily journals that the sixth Lord Pomfret kept while the Towers were building," said Roddy. "The clerk of the works had to enter each day's work and on Saturday the weekly wages, and then the book was brought to Lord Pomfret. I believe he never minded the expense, but if he found a bit of work had been badly done, he made them pull it down and do it again. And as he had a clause in the builders' contract that he would pay so much extra if the work was finished before the term in the contract and the builder was to forfeit so much if he exceeded his limit, you can imagine that things went pretty well."

"Evidently they did," said Mr. Adams, who was going through one of the volumes with a professional eye. "By the way, why is it called the Towers? There's only one tower, as far as I have seen."

"I always wondered that," said Roddy, "till I read the second volume. I had never gone through it properly till quite lately. They had a lot of trouble with the clock-tower. The builder's surveyor hadn't paid enough attention to the ground for the foundations and after there had been one or two nasty subsidences they had to stop building and examine the subsoil and they found a very small trickle coming from the higher ground in the part and flowing into the stream that you saw before lunch. They diverted it and the tower was built and there has never been any trouble. Lord Pomfret wanted to take the affair into the courts, but that wouldn't have done the contractors any good, so they compromised and Lord Pomfret had the pleasure of getting quite a nice sum for the time that had been wasted. So they didn't try to build the other tower, but the Lord Pomfret of that time had determined to call it the Towers, so he did. A stubborn lot they were."

Mr. Adams said it was just as well. One tower like that was quite enough for anybody, and then he asked questions about the clock and who wound it and how often, all of which Roddy was able to answer, and both men enjoyed the intellectual feast.

"Now, look here, Wicklow," said Mr. Adams. "How does

Lord Pomfret stand about the estate and the Towers? Can he do what he likes?"

Pretty well, Roddy said, rather wondering what Mr. Adams had in his mind.

"Now, I want to put something before you," said Mr. Adams. "I'm a director of a pretty large number of concerns, besides my own works at Hogglestock, and I expect to control a good many more. Macfadyen of Amalgamated Vedge is in with me on a good many of them and so is Pilward the big brewer—his boy married my girl and he's almost good enough for her," which Roddy felt to be high praise. "What we need are offices big enough to take a large clerical staff who will be dealing mostly with our overseas business. If we can find the premises we want, which will include a good bit of land for Amalgamated Vedge to use as an experimental station for producing first-class root and green vegetables, we can afford to pay for it. Lord Aberfordbury would like us to rent his place, but he's not a man I'd trust with a crooked sixpence. Am I clear?"

Roddy Wicklow had not been through the last war for nothing.

"Do I understand, sir," he said, as if Mr. Adams were his commanding officer who was issuing some rather important instructions, "that you wish to go into the possibility of taking a part of the Towers and some land on lease?"

"That's right," said Mr. Adams. "I've explored a lot of avenues, as they were always saying in the House when I was a member, but this time I think I'm barking up the right tree. I won't say any more now. Think over what I've said and tell Lord Pomfret if and when you think fit. There's no hurry. The place would suit us if the idea suits him. Lord Pomfret's part of the house would not be touched and any experimental vegetable-growing would be where he wouldn't see it unless he wanted to. We shall need water and from what you have just been telling me, we'll find plenty. Macfadyen and Pilward and I are going into pretty big business unless those damnfools with their atom bombs blow the whole world up. Any more questions?"

Roddy said there were at least a hundred he could think of on the spot, but there wasn't time for the answers.

"Look here, sir," he said. "I take it that no one else will know about your offer, or your suggestion, whichever you prefer."

"Macfadyen and Pilward will have to know," said Mr. Adams. "We've discussed the matter a good deal lately. But I am quite willing not to say a word to them till you let me know if there is a likelihood of our getting what we want. Don't hurry. If you say Lord Pomfret will consider it, then we'll get going. And till then no one but you and myself will know what I've said today. And now I had better find my wife. We ought to be getting home."

So Roddy put the journals away and the two men went to the drawing-room, where the Pomfrets and Lucy were talking. They were soon joined by the van Dryvens and Miss Merriman.

"Thanks most *awfully* for letting us see those Coronation things," said Betty. "Miss Merriman helped me to put on the robe and Woolcot put on yours, Lord Pomfret. But they are frightfully heavy to walk in."

"I am sure you looked very well in them," said Lady Pomfret, admiring Betty's dark, statuesque (and we must confess to our eye rather dull) good looks. "I wish you could have seen the coronets too, but they are at the jeweller's in London. We shall collect them when we go up and put them in the safe overnight."

Mr. van Dryven said the ceremony must be rather tiring.

"But how much more tiring for Her Majesty," said Lord

Pomfret. "No one will look at us. We are just part of the crowd. But when you think that every person in the Abbey will be looking at that one figure and that millions of people all over the world will be looking at her on the television, it is rather frightening," and for a moment the party were silent, rather awed by the thought of one sovereign lady, the target of so many million eyes.

Lady Pomfret broke the silence by asking Lucy if she took milk and sugar, and the talk began to flow again about ordinary things. Then Betty said they must be going and thanked her host and hostess as she said good-bye. Her husband also thanked them warmly.

"If money would buy your chapel, Lady Pomfret," he said, "I would be the first bidder. It is a very beautiful place, which I shall never forget. But if you won't think it presuming on my part, I should like to have the privilege of giving you something for the chapel," at which Lady Pomfret vaguely wondered if he were going to tip her; and if he had we feel sure that she would have accepted the tip with perfect grace and composure.

"It is a pair of silver-gilt candlesticks, about two hundred years old," said Mr. van Dryven. "I meant them for the little church we go to when we are on our ranch in Texas, but I guess that church can wait. I got them in a sale here in London and the people who were selling them gave me their pedigree. Everyone in that world knows them. I didn't. I was just backing my fancy and I happened to be right."

"Really, you are *too* kind, Mr. van Dryven," said Lady Pomfret, a little embarrassed, yet more touched than she would have liked to admit.

Mr. van Dryven, with his rather formal courtesy, said the kindness would be all on Lady Pomfret's side if she would accept them and he would have them sent to her as soon as he

was back in London. And then both he and his wife thanked
the Pomfrets so much for kindly allowing himself and his wife
to express their gratitude in this way that Lady Pomfret felt
she must really have done something worth doing, though
what it was she couldn't quite make out. If guests came to the
Towers, one showed them over the house as a matter of course.
But all the same she and her husband were really touched and
grateful.

Roddy had already told one of the men to bring the van
Dryvens' monster car round to the door of the Pomfrets' present quarters and with renewed expressions of gratitude and an
invitation to all those present to visit them in New York, or at
their place on Long Island, or on the ranch in Texas, Betty and
her husband got into the car and went back to Winter
Overcotes.

Then the Adamses went too. Lucy said they hoped the
Pomfrets would come to lunch with them and see the Old
Bank House and of course Lord Pomfret remembered having
visited it as a young man when old Miss Sowerby still lived
there and he and his wife had also been at the housewarming
party before Lucy had married Mr. Adams, and altogether the
feeling was very friendly. Roddy took them to their car, accepted a general invitation from Lucy to see the market gardening at Adamsfield whenever he liked, and went back to the
office, where he put the journals away and tidied his papers
before going home.

CHAPTER 9

TIME was passing quickly. Far too quickly was the opinion of all the organizers of Coronation celebrations, for it is but human nature to plan far ahead with meticulous care and then, whether consciously or unconsciously, take up the attitude that it will be all right on the day. As indeed it very often is, so nothing makes sense.

All over the country, on a larger or a smaller scale, the little world of Northbridge was being repeated and multiplied, and whether it was a large manufacturing town in the north, or a remote village in Cornwall, the underlying sentiments were much the same. Barchester itself would of course have the Cathedral as the central point of its rejoicings. Instead of an entertainment or pageant, it was having a special service at which every kind of county organization from the Lord Lieutenant and the Chief Constable with attendant satellites down to the Barsetshire Bird Watchers' Association was to be represented. Lord Pomfret, the Lord Lieutenant, could not be present, as duty called him to Westminster Abbey, so the pride of place was to be given, quite rightly we think, to Sir Edmund Pridham, doyen of those who had devoted their lives to the service of their own part of England. And as Sir Edmund was only eighty-six we hope that he will continue in his ways, for apart from a slight and often deliberate deafness he was an extremely going concern, his only fault, and that an increasing one, being that after the fashion of some deaf people he was apt to utter his less favourable thoughts about other people aloud. The country people all adored him with the fawning affection that dogs have for the hand that alternately feeds and beats them, and we can truly say of Sir Edmund that Many a poacher he'd restored To his friends and his relations. But not before he had, in his best orderly-room manner, pointed out to the culprit, far more afraid of Sir Edmund than of any officer of the law, the exact extent of his crime and his folly and where, in this world and the world to come, he was likely to go. And if anyone asks us why Sir Edmund should have as it were represented the Lord Lieutenant, our answer is that we have not yet invented a Deputy Lieutenant. We might of course say that Sir Edmund was the Deputy Lieutenant, which position he would undoubtedly have filled in a most satisfactory way, but if one cannot invent a really convincing lie it is often better to stick to the truth.

The Cathedral was to be flood-lit for a week and, as we know, a kind of religious play was to be acted in the crypt by permission of the Dean, who felt it was but courteous to waive his privileges when the Palace insisted, and made no bones about explaining his position to everyone, nor of voicing his disapproval of the play in question.

It was the custom for the Palace and the Deanery to entertain one another twice a year and it now happened to be the turn of the Deanery, a piece of luck for which we are extremely grateful, as to describe a dinner-party at the Palace, with that beautiful mahogany wine-cooler stuffed with ferns instead of the drink that cheereth the heart of man, would be quite beyond us. The Dean had suggested that they should put one of the extra leafs (or would one say leaves?) into the dining-room table and have twelve guests, but Mrs. Crawley, we think rightly, said it was quite bad enough to have the Palace to dinner and ten would do nicely. Invitations were accordingly issued to the Palace, to Lord and Lady Pomfret, to Canon and Mrs. Joram, and to Mr. and Mrs. Noel Merton, who had known the Crawleys on and off for a long time, Lydia having been, at the Barchester High School, a contemporary of Octavia Needham, eighth child of the Deanery. And though Northbridge was not deeply interested in Barchester matters, looking rather to Southbridge and the School, Lydia and Mrs. Crawley had always been good friends.

On the grounds that it was bound to be a sticky party with the Palace as guests, Mrs. Crawley had decided to offer gin and Dubonnet instead of sherry before dinner. There had also been a slight Scene of Domestic Life between Dr. Crawley and his wife about who should say grace, Dr. Crawley maintaining that it would but be civil to ask the Bishop, who after all was his guest and head of the diocese, to bless the meal, while Mrs. Crawley said that a Deanery in a Cathedral city was, as it were, a city within a city with diplomatic privileges and if anything could put Verger off his stroke it would be having to wait while his lordship said his Mumbo-Jumbo, which, her husband said, was one of those truths better left unspoken and they must give the Bishop a run for his money.

"All I can say is that Verger will not like it," said Mrs. Crawley (for that really was their butler's name, though it is difficult to believe); but like a good and wise wife, she said no more, feeling that her husband must occasionally be allowed to know best and take the results.

At this moment Verger came into the room.

"Yes, Verger?" said Mrs. Crawley. "Is it someone who can't come?"

"Oh no, madam," said Verger, almost shocked at the thought that anyone should basely let the Deanery down. "It was only to inquire who will be saying grace, madam, as I should wish to be in my proper place while this is occurring."

"The Dean is asking the Bishop to say grace before dinner,"

said Mrs. Crawley, "and he will say grace himself before you bring the port."

"Thank you, madam," said Verger and withdrew, to reappear in a very short time with the Pomfrets. The Mertons followed hard upon, and then came Dr. and Mrs. Joram, she who had been the charming widow Mrs. Brandon and was, so most people including her husband thought, prettier than ever, ageless in her charm, her hair most becomingly touched with silver. Everyone present knew everyone else well enough for very little introducing to be needed. Verger came in with glasses on an old silver tray, which he put on a side table.

"Excuse me, madam," he said respectfully to Mrs. Crawley, "but dinner may be slightly delayed. I have just had a message from his lordship's secretary to say he has been unavoidably detained, but will be here as soon as possible."

"Nothing serious, I hope," said Mrs. Crawley, full of delightful apprehension that one of the Bishop's zip gaiters had stuck halfway.

"I gathered from the secretary that his lordship was listening in to an item on the Third Program, madam," said Verger, "about Capital Punishment and did not observe how late it was till the item came to an end, when he was reminded what time it was. I have let Cook know."

By this time the whole party was listening and while Verger handed the drinks he was able to store up for future use in the kitchen and elsewhere the comments of the guests, who were drinking their gin and Dubonnet. It was not long before the Palace guests arrived and it was agreeably obvious to most of those present that there must have been some quite unpleasant words between his lordship and the lady who was known among the Upper Servants in the Close as The Old Cat. The newcomers accepted the gin and Dubonnet, which afforded a good opportunity for everyone else to have another, and then

the party went to the dining-room. Mrs. Crawley had thought
of sending them in couples, after the pleasant formal usage of
proper dinner-parties, but on reflection left people to sort themselves, anticipating, we think on valid grounds, that her husband would have quite enough of the Bishopess at dinner
without having to squire her to the table.

When the guests were seated Dr. Crawley nodded to
Verger, who came quietly to the end of the table where Mrs.
Crawley sat and bending over her neighbour said: "Excuse
me, my lord, but Dr. Crawley says will your lordship say
grace," and stood erect behind the Bishop's chair, apparently
prepared to brain him if he offered any resistance. Spurred on
by these words and by a look from his lawful spouse at the far
corner of the table, the Bishop said one of the short formulas
(or formulae if anyone prefers it) which preface the eating
and drinking of a great many people. As everyone present had
got up and sat down again there was a good deal of scraping
of chairs. The Dean very meanly turned at once to Lydia Merton, and the Bishop's wife had to be content with Lord Pomfret, while the Dean's wife, giving her husband a very
un-Christian look, began to do her best with the Bishop, asking him if he and his wife were going on a winter cruise again.
The Bishop said they hoped to do so, but not to Madeira this
time. Rather, he said, to the Bahamas, or did he mean Ber-
mudas, for it was essential to travel in the sterling area, as the
travel allowance did not go far.

"Why don't you go to the Northern Capitals?" said Mrs.
Crawley. "Josiah and I went on a cruise there some years ago
and as we lived in the ship we could afford the shore expenses."

The Bishop said that to his shame be it said the northern
civilizations did not appeal to him.

Mrs. Crawley said, very sensibly we think, that there was

nothing shameful in not liking some things and liking others, and as far as she was concerned anyone could have Germany and Russia and Japan and China and South America and quite a lot of other places, and why didn't they go on a Hellenic Cruise, where you got everything cheap or free if you lectured.

"I have been tempted—I have been tempted," said the Bishop, "but my dear wife dreads the idea of Greece. These terrible earthquakes!"

Mrs. Crawley said in a serious voice that earthquakes must indeed be terrible, and her mind looked back to the year when the Palace went to Madeira in the motor cruiser *Anubis,* which had encountered very bad weather most of the way and how, when its safe arrival had been reported, Mrs. Joram had said how dreadful it would be to have someone at the Palace whom one couldn't really dislike. Then she pulled herself away from these recollections and asked the Bishop about the old cesspool under the Palace, and in describing his difficulties with Ec-clesiastical Commissioners and Local Authorities and the Con-tractors his lordship became more human than Mrs. Crawley had thought possible.

Lady Pomfret meanwhile had been getting on very well with Canon Joram, as indeed it would have been almost im-possible not to do with that excellent and warm-hearted cleric.

"Gillie and I shall be in the Abbey," she said when, now quite inevitably, the subject of the Coronation came up. "I am rather glad our elder boy won't be a page. It would be a great privilege, but he is so frightfully nervous. Are you seeing any-thing of it, Dr. Joram?"

"As it happens, I shall see a good deal," said Dr. Joram. "You know I was Bishop of Mngangaland and became very friendly with the Head Chief. His eightieth son, who got through Balliol with a quite good second and is now reading law, is an old pupil of mine. He has taken a whole house on the route and has kindly asked me among his other friends to spend the previous night there and see the procession. He is anxious to throw some nail-parings or some hair under Her Majesty's state coach, as this would ensure for him a long life and a hundred male children."

"What can you do about it?" said Lady Pomfret.

"I told him that in England to do such a thing would mean that he would become a Mpongo-mpongo," said Dr. Joram. "The Mpongo-mpongo is a black man with a white face turned back to front and long yellow hair and both his elbows and knees bend the wrong way. Anyone who sees him becomes a Mpongo-mpongo too and the only way of dealing with them is to invite them to a great feast and stupefy them with a native drink and burn the hut with them in it."

"And did he believe it?" said Lady Pomfret.

"Of course," said Canon Joram, mildly surprised. "He was properly brought up. If his father kills the rest of his elder brothers—there are only about a dozen left—a poor lot— Mngangaland will come into line as one of our most loyal over-seas possessions. They make splendid soldiers and take to the air like ducks—I mean like anything. You've only got to un-derstand them and they'll eat out of your hand. And I have promised to take him to Windsor, where he can throw the nail-parings in the Castle grounds, which will do just as well. But I mustn't bore you with my black friends. Tell me about your own family, Lady Pomfret. I have met that very nice elder son of yours once or twice. How very like his father he is. What is he doing now?"

So Lady Pomfret, pleased to hear Ludovic praised, told Dr. Joram how kind the Mertons had been in introducing him to the Aubrey Clovers and how he was going to act with them in a short one-act play of Mr. Clover's for the Northbridge Coronation Festival, on which the Canon's unclerical comment was Lucky Dog.

Lord Pomfret had now got into very pleasant conversation with Mrs. Joram. She, as we have said before, though very much liked by all who had known her as Mrs. Brandon, somehow used not to have any particular standing in Barsetshire society, being happily and innocently employed as she was in her own small circle round Pomfret Madrigal and busy first during the war with resident evacuee children from a very nice Home and later with her son Francis and his pretty wife and his young family. But when she married the delightful Colonial Bishop, now Canon Joram, the county and the Close suddenly sat up and began to take notice and now no party in Barchester was complete without her.

"I once went to Pomfret Towers with the Barsetshire Archæological Society," said Mrs. Joram. "I cannot remember why we went, because it isn't in the least archæological, but it is always delightful to see other people's houses."

Lord Pomfret said he wished he could be National Trust, but from a money point of view it was too difficult, though he hoped it might somehow be arranged.

"It is so awkward," he said, looking down kindly at his pretty neighbour, "to have a house you can't afford to live in and can't sell."

Mrs. Joram said sympathetically that she supposed it was an entail, only she never knew what an entail was. Lord Pomfret said it practically meant that you couldn't do anything with what was your own property. Or if you wanted to, you had to get the consent of the person who would inherit it and he felt it would be a most unfair thing to ask his elder son to agree.

"But why wouldn't he agree?" said Mrs. Joram.

"It's not that Ludo wouldn't," said Lord Pomfret. "He is the kindest of creatures. But I can't feel that it would be fair to ask him to make a renunciation, and in any case he couldn't do it till he is twenty-one. As far as I can see, we are all doomed, and of course we shall never organize ourselves. We remain Individualists."

"But that is what makes you so *nice*," said Mrs. Joram. "It would be quite dreadful if people were all like other people. I mean, in some cases. Suppose we were all like Lady Norton —the old one, I mean."

Lord Pomfret said gravely that in such a case it mightn't be a bad thing if there were a Revolution, except that the lady in question would undoubtedly join the revolutionaries and become a female Commissar. And what a Commissar was, he added, he had not the faintest idea. Probably someone like Cromwell.

"Oh, do you hate Cromwell too?" said Mrs. Joram. "A quite *dreadful* man. One could not *possibly* ask him to dinner."

Lord Pomfret, whose charitable nature made him feel that even regicides ought to have a fair deal, said Cromwell probably did what he felt was his duty.

"It depends what you mean by duty," said Mrs. Joram, putting on her large horn-rimmed spectacles, the better to see what Lord Pomfret was saying (a state of mind which only those whose eyesight never knows from day to day whether it will be able to distinguish one friend from another, and sometimes will read several paragraphs of a book before it suddenly realizes that the reason the type is not very clear is that its owner has left her spectacles in the bathroom because you *cannot* do your face with your spectacles on, will appreciate). "It simply *can't* be your duty to kill kings, whatever you do," at which simple words the scales fell from Lord Pomfret's eyes and he determined to dislike Cromwell for the future.

"But one thing I *will* tell you," she said, as though Lord

Pomfret had been pressing her to divulge important secrets. "I think it is quite *dreadful* about Pomfret Towers," and so seriously did she speak that Lord Pomfret wondered if he had left undone one single thing that he ought to have done and came to the conclusion that, humanly speaking, he hadn't, at which point another shifting of conversation took place and he was forced back upon the Bishopess while Mrs. Joram turned to Noel. As she had known him on and off since before the war and they had flirted deliberately and delicately without anyone's heart being even ruffled, they at once got into the delightful "And do you remember" kind of conversation which can go on indefinitely. And those were indeed Mrs. Joram's first words.

"Do you remember," she said, looking up at Noel with a kind of deliberately artless provocativeness which amused him vastly, "how you used to like me—a little—before the war, so long ago?"

"I have never forgotten it," said Noel. "You were everything that Lydia was not. If I remember correctly, she brought me, captive of her bow and spear, to your Flower Show at Pomfret Madrigal and I had to go on the roundabout in a kind of a canoe with a swan's head and shoulders growing out of the prow, like Lohengrin. I think your son-in-law was with me and we both felt extremely sick," and they fell into reminiscences of that summer and were so amusing to one another that Lydia, at the farthest corner from them; found her attention straying from Dr. Crawley's account of his eldest son's pastoral visits in the mining district where his present cure of souls was situated and how he had a whippet that had beaten all competitors. Not that she felt the faintest curiosity about their conversation, but to see Noel laughing gave her great pleasure.

Whether it was by her own bad management, or a desire to

spare the hard-working Lady Pomfret, Mrs. Crawley had
somehow managed to hold the Bishop in check during the
earlier part of dinner, but at the turn of the tide, as it were,
when the sweet or pudding course (only it was neither, being
large helpings of Messrs. Scatcherd and Tozer's very best ice
cream and meltingly crisp sweet biscuits, which were a spe-
ciality of the Deanery) replaced the saddle of real mutton into
whose provenance no one liked to inquire, Mrs. Crawley
turned to Noel Merton, leaving Lady Pomfret a prey to his
lordship.

"I hear," said Lady Pomfret, "that you are having a kind of
mystery play in the crypt. Is it an old one?"

The Bishop said not in point of time, for it was written by
a young man whose name, Dhoidreagh O'Seianmhe, was
doubtless familiar to her.

Lady Pomfret said that somehow she had not come across it
and blamed herself inwardly for cowardice.

His real name, of course, said the Bishop, was Bert Hobson,
so that when the play was chosen and the judges had to con-
gratulate him, they all called him Mr. Hobson, which had
offended him very much.

Lady Pomfret, seeing an endless boredom in this conversation, did her best to keep her end up by saying it sounded so
like the Germans, who took a masochistic pleasure in being
offended and whose proudest boast was "Ich bin sehr leicht
beleidigt," to which the Bishop replied that German was, alas,
a sealed book to him and he kindly gave a synopsis of the play
to Lady Pomfret; but as we have already heard roughly what it
was about, we do not wish to hear any more. The whole key-
note of the play, the Bishop said, was—with all reverence be it
said—an attitude of reverence to Certain Ideas which were, as
it were, incorporated in various characters, among them a murderer and a prostitute, who typified, as it were, how the Best in

us can become the Worst unless, by an agency Far above our human powers, the Best can be sublimated to the Better.

"I know *exactly* what you mean," said Lady Pomfret. "Like the end of *The Only Way,* when Sydney Carton says he is doing a far, far better thing than he has ever done, and it is really the *best* thing."

The Bishop, who we think had got to that point (well known to us all) when we hear ourselves saying rather importantly things that obviously have no meaning, said That was indeed what he had in his mind. The action of the play, he said, took place in a shebeen, which he took to be the Irish for a cottage, and the characters were Mrs. O'Gonnoreagh the Bad One, Pegeen the Prostitute, Mickeen the Murderer, Father Aloysius the Good One, and a mysterious stranger with a club-foot called Himself from Below.

Lady Pomfret, who had sometimes blamed herself for ingratitude when her heart rather failed at the thought of the long Coronation Day, now felt her heart swell with gratitude that she would be, for two or three days, in a place where she couldn't possibly see the play in the crypt, and she asked the Bishop how often it would be acted.

The Bishop said alas! only twice, for the actors—Them That Does Be After Entertaining of You All, as they described themselves—were due to give the play in Manchester at the end of the week, so that Lady Pomfret was able to say, very untruthfully, how sorry she was that she would not see them, at which point she became aware that she was the only person speaking and her voice trailed away into nothingness. Dr. Crawley said a few words in the Latin tongue, there was a scraping of chairs, and the ladies, shepherded by Mrs. Crawley, went into the large drawing-room, which, though it has no evening light in it, has an exquisite view of the houses on the far side of the Close—Canon Joram's among them—with a sunset glow on their mellow red brick. Having got rid of the men, in some ways such Separators of Companions and Terminators of Delight, the ladies were able to settle down to really comfortable talk. Lady Pomfret, with a mixture of kindness and heroism, got the Bishopess to herself to discuss the gros-point embroidery for the backs and cushions of the choir stalls; a work of love which a number of county ladies were sharing, though to their mortification the Dowager Lady Norton's work was by far the best and most professional. But as she had never been known to do any other kind of work, this was not surprising. Lady Pomfret generously said hers was the worst, which she attributed to having been brought up more or less in the saddle and with the rod or gun.

The Bishopess said her great-grandmother used to do stump-work and became rather boring about it. It had to be admitted —and by no one was it admitted more freely than by the ladies themselves—that although Mrs. Crawley had a workmanlike touch, Mrs. Joram turned everything she did in the needlework line to favour and to prettiness, while Lady Pomfret's, done in her scanty moments of leisure, was good enough for a lady of quality. Lydia felt a little ashamed at not being one of the embroideresses, but her capable hands were almost clumsy with a needle—or even with four needles when she had tried to knit for the forces during the war and could be relied upon to make no two socks alike.

The women being safely out of the way, the men had a very pleasant time, only marred by the presence of the Bishop who, it must in fairness be owned, was much less trying without his wife, whose shadow and reflection he was far too apt to be. Dr. Crawley saw to it that his excellent port was well circulated

and his lordship's glass filled, which refilling the Bishop managed not to observe, with unfailing regularity, until it was too
late.

"Do you know our Chancellor of the Diocese?" said the
Dean to Lord Pomfret.

Lord Pomfret said very likely he did know him, only he
didn't know who he was, but on hearing that he was Sir
Robert Fielding he said they met quite often on committees
and how handsome Lady Fielding was.

"They are old friends of ours," said Dr. Crawley. "I married
their daughter Anne in the Cathedral. Her husband is one of
the Dales, a kind of cousin of Lady Silverbridge, and taught at
Southbridge School. I hope the Fieldings are coming over this
evening. What is it, Verger?"

"It was Sir Robert rang up, sir," said Verger, "and would
you mind if Sir Robert brought some guests as are staying the
night at Number Seventeen" (for it was a peculiarity of the
Close that every house was known by its number and no house
except the Deanery by a name, and that only a courtesy title
as it were). "It was a Miss Harvey, sir and a Mr. Harvey."

The Dean said of course any guests of Lady Fielding's
would be more than welcome, but the expression observed
upon his face by Lord Pomfret was far from hospitable.

"Did you ever come across the Harveys?" said the Dean.
"He was down here during the war for the Red Tape and
Sealing Wax Department and his lot have stayed on, near
Silverbridge. I understand that he did his work, whatever it
may have been, extremely well. He was not liked—he was not
liked," and the Dean beat the tips of his fingers gently together, as one who by long practice could suffer fools with
tolerable equanimity.

Lord Pomfret said he didn't think he knew them, but he had
heard Lady Cora Waring speak of them, quite unlovingly. Her

ladyship, said the Dean, had as sound a judgment of people as anyone he knew.

"And I am willing to bet five shillings," he added, most unclerically, "that the Palace" (which word he spoke low and cautiously) "asked the Fieldings to have them because they didn't want them themselves. Well, perhaps the ladies are ready for us," and he rose with a kind of courteous inclination towards the Bishop, who was too much afraid of his wife to say he would rather spend the rest of the evening in the dining-room if nobody minded.

The men came out of the dining-room just as Verger opened the front door to Sir Robert and Lady Fielding and what were obviously Miss Harvey and her brother. He was a tall, lean man with dark eyes, a saturnine expression, and rather long dark hair very becomingly streaked with grey which was perpetually falling over one eye and as often thrown back by a toss of his head, or put aside by one of his long hands. To those who admired him this trait was very endearing, having a certain air of one so innocent and defenceless that he could not even protect himself against his own hair. To the increasing number who disliked him it was but a reason the more for their (as they considered) well-founded dislike. His sister, who was not young, was as fair as her brother was dark, her rather lank yellow hair streaked with grey, with the expression of an educated woman who is high up in the Civil Service and not particularly liked by those under her.

The Dean greeted the Fieldings warmly, as did the rest of the company to whom they were known, and after shaking hands with the Harveys made a general introduction and led the way upstairs, talking to Miss Harvey.

"We are only a small party," he said, "and I expect you know them all. The Bishop and his wife, the Pomfrets, the Noel Mertons, and the Jorams."

Miss Harvey said she was sure she had met Mr. Merton—the Q.C., wasn't it?—somewhere, but didn't know the Jorams and asked who they were in a way which rather implied that as she did not know them, it really did not matter.

"Here are the Fieldings and their guests, my dear," said the Dean to Mrs. Crawley. "Miss Harvey and her brother."

Miss Crawley came forward to welcome the Fieldings and to make the acquaintance of the Harveys, of whom she had heard something from Mrs. Adams, for the Harveys had spent part of the war at Marling Melicent, had received hospitality from Mrs. Adams's parents, and had been cordially disliked by both Hall and Village.

"Lady Pomfret, I don't think you know Miss Harvey," she said, leaving her husband to deal with Mr. Harvey. "She is with the Ministry of General Interference at Gatherum Castle. Her brother is in the Red Tape and Sealing Wax Department at Silverbridge," an introduction which Lady Pomfret honoured kindly and politely. "And I want you to know Canon Joram and Mrs. Joram, Miss Harvey."

Miss Harvey acknowledged the existence of the guests with the savoir vivre of a woman of the world, but anyone who knew her would have observed that Lord Pomfret was the prey on whom her eyes were fixed. Mr. Harvey was also introduced to everyone present and, in spite of his increasing self-esteem, could not help being bowled over by Mrs. Joram.

"Now I *know* I have heard about you somewhere," said Mrs. Joram, inviting Mr. Harvey to sit beside her. "I know! It was the Mixo-Lydian Ambassadress, whom we met at Gatherum Castle. What a delightful woman she is."

"So amusing to see the impact of civilization on those Central European people," said Mr. Harvey, tossing back what in moments of Wild Parisianism he called his mèche.

"Yes, indeed, she is *most* intelligent and charming," said

Mrs. Joram. "The Omniums are devoted to her and so is Lady Cora."

"Ah, well, de gustibus," said Mr. Harvey, remembering with extreme dislike how the Mixo-Lydian Ambassadress at their last meeting, where Lady Cora Palliser as she was then, now Lady Cora Waring, was also present, had said that Red Tape was all robbish and he was a robbisher and had also compared him with a Schwenk which, as she explained, is a vermin that is died and becomm eaten by maggots.

"Now *do* tell me," said Mrs. Joram, turning her lovely eyes on Mr. Harvey, "what is the *rest* of de gustibus. I have heard people say it and always wondered. Is it the Bible?"

"My dear lady!" said Mr. Harvey.

"Well, the Bible *is* in Latin," said Mrs. Joram. "William has one. And a Greek one too. We will ask Dr. Crawley. Oh! Dr. Crawley. *Can* you tell us where de gustibus comes from?"

The Dean said how pleasant it was to hear anyone pronouncing Latin properly, in the English way. As far as he knew, he said, the full text was De gustibus et coloribus non disputandum, and where it was to be found he had not the faintest idea. He believed it was an academic term in use among the scholiasts of the middle ages. He was sorry he could not be more precise. And how, he said, had this discussion arisen?

"Oh, it was only that Mr. Harvey said it," said Mrs. Joram, "and I wondered if it was in the Bible—the Vulgate," she added, with an air of immense learning, "and Mr. Harvey didn't know, so I thought you would."

"Then my wretched ignorance is the less blamable," said Mr. Harvey, laughing. Dr. Crawley looked at him, his heavy eyebrows bent in a formidable way upon the guest (unwanted) who could speak with such a combination of illiteracy and tactlessness, and passed on.

"May I?" said Mr. Harvey, taking a silver cigarette-case from his pocket.

"Oh, don't ask *me*," said Mrs. Joram. "I don't smoke. At least I don't know if I do or not because I've never tried. I never wanted to try, so I didn't. You had better ask Mrs. Crawley. What a charming case," and indeed it was a very pretty piece of the silversmith's work, old, elegant, probably French.

"It is flattered by your approval," said Mr. Harvey, almost flicking a grain of snuff from his jabot. "It belonged to my old Uncle George. He left a small legacy to Frances and myself and two from his well-known collection of French snuff-boxes. As the elder I had first choice and I flatter myself that this is very chaste."

"Well, not *very*," said Mrs. Joram. "In fact it seems to me unusually plain, which is what makes it so charming."

Mr. Harvey looked perplexed. Then his brow cleared.

"Ah! I have it!" he said.

Mrs. Joram, looking pensively at her still lovely hands and the diamond ring whose strange family history we learnt earlier in these very wandering chronicles, asked what he had.

"When I said chaste, you took me to mean chased," he said with the gay laugh that so many of his acquaintance heartily disliked, Mrs. Joram immediately becoming one of their number.

"But you did, didn't you?" she said, at which point Mr. Harvey rather basely made room for Sir Robert and Lady Fielding on the sofa by Mrs. Joram and moved on towards the Pomfrets. As the Jorams and the Fieldings lived only a few doors apart and saw each other nearly every day, they naturally had plenty of things to talk about and Mrs. Joram asked Lady Fielding if she was going to the religious drama in the crypt.

"Certainly not," said Lady Fielding. "We shall of course go to the Coronation service in the Cathedral and then we are going to stay with my daughter Anne and her husband for a few days. You know Robin came into that house at Allington. The bulk of old Mrs. Dale's money went to her daughter—Lady Silverbridge—but Robin has some of his own and they are seriously thinking of a preparatory school for little boys. It will be quite convenient for their little Robin when he is old enough and they are thinking of having the twins there too, till they are old enough for boarding school. Dora and Roberta are four years old. One can't believe it."

It was extraordinary, Sir Robert said, how as everyone got poorer and schools got more and more expensive, people sent their children to them all the same. "I never feel quite sure if it is noble or silly," he added. "Both probably. Did you know the Harveys, Mrs. Joram?"

Mrs. Joram assumed what her son Francis used to call her mysterious mischief face and said she had just been talking to one and that was more than enough. It was, said Lady Fielding, just like the Palace to wish them onto her and luckily it was only for one night or her husband would undoubtedly have pushed them into that empty cellar and turned the key. But thank goodness they were going tomorrow morning early and had Mrs. Joram read Mrs. Morland's last book, which she had, and then they had a delightful time comparing notes on the various thrillers and shockers they had been reading.

"Well, I suppose I must go and do the polite with the Palace," said Lady Fielding. "By the way, did Mr. Harvey tell you about his silver cigarette-case?"

Mrs. Joram said he did and it was very charming.

"You'll hear more about it before the evening is out," said Lady Fielding ominously and went off to do the polite.

Mrs. Joram, who had the gift of remaining peaceful in one place, sat composedly where she was till Mrs. Crawley brought Miss Harvey up to her and said she knew they would have

much in common. Then, with something uncommonly like a
wink at Mrs. Joram, if the wives of the higher clergy do wink,
she left them together.

"I think you know a charming friend of ours, Mrs. Samuel
Adams," said Miss Harvey. "Geoffrey and I had a house in
their village during the war and I think we helped to brighten
things for them. One felt that Lucy might have done better,
but—" and she shrugged her shoulders, which were, Mrs.
Joram thought, viewing them without prejudice, a bit on the
bony side for shrugging, which accentuates what are known in
female circles as salt-cellars.

"Oh, I don't know," she said. "We are very fond of Mr.
Adams and of her too. You are staying with old Lady Norton,
aren't you?"

Miss Harvey said yes, a *very* old friend, but it was sad to
see old friends going down-hill.

"Your brother," said Mrs. Joram, feeling that this conversation was getting out of hand, "showed me such a lovely
cigarette-case—a family heirloom, I think he said," at which
Miss Harvey's face darkened and she looked all her age and
more.

"Of course to me possessions mean nothing, absolutely
nothing," she said, "but as Uncle George gave explicit instructions in his will that his personal possessions were to be divided
between my brother and myself by mutual agreement, with
the lawyers as umpire if necesary, I cannot help my feelings.
It is not that I grudge Geoffrey *anything*, for he *needs* things,
poor fellow. He has not the vie intérieure that keeps one above
such pettiness. He practically stole it, before I had a chance to
put in my modest claim, and if I did get the little Morland, he
need only have told me he wanted it and of course I should
have said, "Take it, if you feel like that about it." But just to
take offence is *so* foolish. However, we will not speak of it,"

which she proceeded not to do, with a fine flow of words, till the Dean took her away.

"I am so sorry, dear Mrs. Joram," he said, when he had forced his guest upon Lady Pomfret, "that you had that trial. It is all the Palace's fault and the Fieldings are furious, but what can one do?"

"I know it's not your fault a bit, Dr. Crawley," said Mrs. Joram. "But it does seem unnecessary to make such a fuss about a silver case. If it had been money—"

"As you get older," said the Dean, who in point of years was not so very much older than Mrs. Joram, but liked to speak of himself as an octogenarian at least, "you will find that the difficulties over wills are seldom about money. It is always small personal things that people quarrel about. In fact, "Uncle George's silver cigarette-case" is at the root of nearly all family squabbles. And now it has ruined the evening," but Mrs. Joram, exercising all her female wiles and charm, got him into a good humour again. Noel Merton, who had been standing near by, an amused spectator, then slipped himself into the talk, while the Dean went to talk with the Fieldings.

"I remember you on this very sofa," said Noel. "It was at a dinner-party here before the war—no, the first winter of the war. I was longing to talk to Lydia, but there were so many people that I couldn't get at her."

"Yes, I remember your telling me about it," said Mrs. Joram. "And you looked so set up and pleased that I thought you would propose to her at once and I was *furious* when you didn't."

"And Lydia was talking so hard with Tommy Needham that I thought she cared for him," said Noel, "and really she was only telling him to get on with it with Octavia. I was a fool."

"Men are like that," said Mrs. Joram placidly. "I simply cannot think why they are so silly, unless it is to give us something

to do. And now I must take William home. We will all meet
after the Coronation, and she gave her still lovely hand to
Noel, who said he would kiss it for twopence but felt that to do
so in the Deanery would be brawling in church.

Mrs. Crawley was telling Lady Fielding that she had bought
tickets for the Mystery Play—only that sounded like something on the B.B.C.—but was going to be taken seriously
though temporarily ill that day and thought she would send
the tickets to the Palace by Verger with her compliments and
she was so distressed and hoped the Bishopess could use them.

"Why not send them to the Harveys?" said Mrs. Joram. "It
would look as if you were doing a kindness."

Then Lady Pomfret, who had enjoyed Canon Joram's company very much at dinner, wanted to talk to his wife and asked
if they would both come to the Towers one day and see the
chapel that old Lord Pomfret's father had built by Italian
workmen and perhaps Mrs. Joram would show her some embroidery stitches, and Mrs. Crawley, all ears as a good hostess
should be, was pleased that her party had such good results.
Then there were more good-byes and the party came to an end.

"Another of your successes, my dear," said the Dean to Mrs.
Crawley when the last guest had gone.

Mrs. Crawley said No thanks to the Bishopess, who had
made the poor Fieldings bring those quite dreadful Harveys
and she thought a brother and sister quarrelling in public was
even worse than a husband and wife.

As the Pomfrets drove home, Lady Pomfret driving because
her husband looked so tired, they talked about the party and
about married life and how very nice it was to see people like
the Jorams and the Mertons who were really fond of each
other. He had, he said, had some talk with Merton after dinner

and liked him more than ever. Lady Pomfret said, not for the first time, how very nice Mrs. Merton was; the sort of person that could be relied on. Lord Pomfret said there was one person, at present driving the car rather too fast, he thought, with the roundabout ahead, who could be relied upon to the end of the world.

"Never mind, darling," said his wife, slowing down a little to please him. "You ought to have married Cora Waring. That would have cured you of worrying about people who drive fast. And every policeman in the county looks the other way. How does she get away with it?"

Lord Pomfret said that being a Duke's daughter still counted for something, thank goodness.

"And with great respect to everyone concerned, *how* I wish the Coronation were over," he added. "I know that no one will be looking at me or thinking of me, but I can't help feeling nervous," to which Lady Pomfret made no answer beyond putting her hand on his for a moment, but as it was a perfectly straight bit of road and no traffic to speak of, all was well.

"Do you know, Gillie, you haven't fallen in love once since we were married," said Lady Pomfret.

"Why should I?" said Lord Pomfret. "I had never been in love till I met Miss Sally Wicklow and that is the end of my story. Dearest," he added.

"It is rather good for married men with responsibilities," said Lady Pomfret, "to stray, very respectably, now and again. Don't think I wouldn't understand if you ever felt like it."

"If I ever did feel like it, I have told myself not to," said Lord Pomfret. "One must not look into people's eyes," he added, half to himself, echoing unconsciously the words of a Shropshire lad.

"Don't think that I don't know and understand," said Lady

Pomfret. "At least as far as anyone can understand who has not looked into anyone's eyes except her lawful husband's. But you never know."

"A true remark, generally speaking," said Lord Pomfret. "But not always. I know on the whole where I'm going and I know, thank God, who is going with me. But there is always Friendliness."

"So I should hope," said Lady Pomfret, "and an all-round friendliness between all parties concerned. Amitié carrée if you like," to which Lord Pomfret's only answer was "Bless you, darling" and they began to talk about estate matters.

By the time they got back to the Towers everyone was in bed except Miss Merriman, who was playing beggar-my-neighbour with Roddy Wicklow. And if our reader asks why beggar-my-neighbour, we will tell her, here and now, that it is the only game we can play ourself, unless Happy Families may be counted; but alas! the cards for that noble game are now so debased that we blush for our country's shame. Miss Merriman, however, had an old pack from her childish days and all the young Fosters had been blooded, as it were, on the right families with their proper names and callings.

"I was never so pleased to see you, Gillie," said his brother-in-law. "Merry has rooked me of one and threepence. How was the party?"

Lady Pomfret said it had been very pleasant, except that she had to sit next to the Bishop, but she was aware that he was her cross and had borne it.

"But I had that delightful Canon Joram on the other side," she said. "If ever I become a mourning widow," she added to her husband, "I shall poison Mrs. Joram and marry the Canon," to which Lord Pomfret said she couldn't, because she would probably die first owing to working too hard and being too conscientious, and then he would kill Canon Joram and marry Mrs. Joram, and then they all had some mild drinks. By which we do not mean un-alcoholic, for the men had whisky and soda, on an unassuming scale.

"I don't know what is wrong with Mr. Wicklow," said Miss Merriman, who, intimate as she had been for years with the family, never derogated from her own rules of how one addressed one's employers, "but he was not concentrating on the game, else I wouldn't have won."

"Look here, Gillie," said his brother-in-law, "I've something to tell you, that's why I came over. It has been worrying me a bit and I couldn't concentrate on beggar-my-neighbour. Merry would have won in any case. Lucky at cards, unlucky in love is her motto, isn't it Merry?"

Miss Merriman, with her usual calm, said she had never had time to consider love, unless, she added, one could count a very plain architect with no chin, about thirty years older than herself, for whom she had cherished a passion when she was fifteen.

"Good old Merry," said Lord Pomfret and bowed to her over his weak whisky and soda. "And what's worrying you, Roddy? Nothing wrong at home, I hope."

"Oh, *they're* all right, bless them," said Roddy Wicklow. "It's a letter from Mr. Adams. It will keep till tomorrow quite well, though."

"Well, we haven't mortgaged the Towers to him, so he can't be dunning us," said Lord Pomfret, no whit disturbed but slightly curious. "Does he want me to sell our vegetables to Amalgamated Vedge? There are only just enough for the house and the people on the place as it is," for Lord Pomfret was still keeping in potatoes and green vegetables a number of old licensed impostors on the estate; which number was, to his sorrow, decreasing yearly, for though he had never known the place as a boy, some atavistic instinct in him made him feel responsible for a number of people who expected to be helped as their right and more often than not returned it with grumbling instead of thanks.

"No, he doesn't want you to sell vegetables," said Roddy. "He wants—well, I've got his letter here—the Towers."

Lord Pomfret, surprised but unmoved, said that didn't make sense and Adams must be mad.

"Or perhaps we are all mad," said Lady Pomfret, whose quicker mind was guessing at what we already know, and though her guesses were far from the mark they were in the right direction. "Is it the chapel that Mr. van Dryven wanted? I'm afraid that's out of the question."

"Not the chapel," said Roddy, laying a typed letter on the table. "I must tell you, Gillie, that Adams spoke to me on this matter the day he and the van Dryvens came over, but he asked me not to say anything till he could put it in writing. There you are."

Lord Pomfret took the letter up and put it down.

"I'm afraid to read it," he said quite simply.

His Countess was going to say, "I'm not," but she did not utter the words and looked at her brother.

"It is quite simple," said Roddy, quietly taking up the letter. "He and Macfadyen of Amalgamated Vedge and Pilward the brewer are going in for business in a big way together and need large permanent quarters for their clerical staff and some ground for experimental farming. This is an offer to take a long-term lease of the whole of the towers for offices—except your own quarters and the chapel—and a certain number of acres with the stream running through them beyond the little wood, so you wouldn't see it. As far as I can see, the terms he suggests are generous. Of course it will take some time to settle, but that is for the lawyers. He would like it if you will consider his suggestions and says he does not wish you to feel in any

way rushed or hurried. He wrote to me, as your agent, to inquire whether you would consider going into the matter.
There is a good deal to be said for it, but it is not for me to
decide. That's all, I think."

Neither the Earl nor his Countess said anything. Miss
Merriman, we think, was crying, but she had dried her eyes
with a swift movement and sat by (for surely one can do that
as well as stand by) ready to give any help in her power.

"A most unusual happening, said Lord Pomfret, which
words seemed to everyone present an excellent description of
their feelings. "We had better talk about it tomorrow, Roddy.
Lord! how Uncle Giles would have sworn if he had a letter
like that," which true and simple reflection made everyone
laugh and vastly relieved their feelings.

"And how Cousin Emily would have begun arranging
everything and not let Mr. Adams call his soul his own," said
Lady Pomfret, half laughing, half tearful, thinking of the old
Earl's sister, Lady Emily Leslie, with her maddening and delightful intromissions (as Macpherson, the old Scotch agent,
always called them) into everyone's affairs. Now they were all
dead; the old Earl and his Countess, his sister, the old agent;
and Miss Merriman felt in some ways nearer to them than she
did to the persons in the room. But to the Pomfrets she owed
the service that she, without any conceit, knew to be almost
invaluable, and now it looked as if good fortune were at last
casting an auspicious eye upon the family that Miss Merriman
had so long, in one branch or other, served and protected.

"Well, it is time we all went to bed," said Miss Merriman
in a matter-of-fact voice. "Good-night, Mr. Wicklow," and she
went away.

"Damn that woman, I do like her," said Roddy, as soon as
the door was shut behind her. "She'd have broken down if she
tried to say anything to you and Gillie. Well, best of luck,

Sally, and you'll take all your fences. You always did, you know. Old Lord Pomfret said so and *he* knew," and he finished his glass and went away.

"Yes, but I didn't expect this fence," said Lady Pomfret. "Gillie!"

"What is it?" said Lord Pomfret, anxious, for he had come to look upon his wife as an eternal rock of strength and security. "Darling!"

"I want a *very* stiff whisky and soda," said Lady Pomfret, and she drank it in such a hurry that she nearly choked and her husband had to beat her on the back.

"We can't do anything about it tonight, Sally," he said, when she had finished coughing and spluttering. "Nor, if it comes to that, for days and weeks and probably months. But we've got Adams's word on paper—though far be it from me not to remember that his word is as good as his bond," at which Lady Pomfret had to laugh again, but quite sanely and comfortably now.

"What an evening," said Lady Pomfret as they went upstairs.

"And Ludo. How I hope it will mean that things will be a little easier for him than they are for us. He is growing up so quickly," said Lord Pomfret.

"So quickly," said Lady Pomfret. "And we owe a great deal to the Mertons. Especially Mrs. Merton, who has really been an angel to him."

Lord Pomfret agreed. And he also felt, though he did not trouble to examine his feelings closely, or perhaps did not wish to, that the Mertons were a delightful couple. It was so rare to find a husband and wife whom one liked equally.

CHAPTER 10

IT HAD for some time been obvious to the ladies of Northbridge
that Miss Pemberton was not as well as she used to be. No one
wanted to say this aloud, and the various working parties who
were making things for the Coronation Pageant showed great
ingenuity in inventing phrases to express what no one liked to
say. Among them were Not quite, A little piano (which, being
spoken by Miss Crowder in good Franco-British, made the
more highbrow of her hearers think of a spinet), A bit off
colour (Commander Beasley), Going Down Hill (this from
Miss Dolly Talbot, who was frowned at by Miss Talbot), Like
my poor Aunt Agnes (Mrs. Dunsford), Entering into the Sere
(which truncated literary allusion from Miss Dunsford puzzled her audience a good deal), and from Mrs. Paxon, Breaking Up if you ask me; but as she was holding half a dozen pins
in her mouth while arranging some Bolton sheeting for an early
Briton's tunic (it having been considered by the Committee
that if the gentlemen wore hearthrugs only it might be Awkward), no one heard what she said. All the ladies were right,
but no one dared to ask Miss Pemberton, who went on with
her work at the Biographical Dictionary of Provence, while
Mr. Downing noticed very little. For, like a true man, he felt
that so long as women didn't faint or have hysterics and continued to provide food at stated intervals, there was nothing
wrong with them. Mrs. Villars would probably have noticed
more than the others, but she also was so busy in so many ways
that she just felt vaguely that she ought to go and see Miss

Pemberton more often. But "dropping in" was not encouraged at Punshions and there was not a telephone, so she had let things slide. And indeed a rector's hard-working and conscientious wife, not so young as she was, whose own health is not robust, has her hands and her mind about as full as is possible, especially with a Coronation imminent.

The person who kept most in touch with Miss Pemberton was that indefatigable worker Mrs. Paxon, who out of her very busy active life and the excellent breakfast and supper or high tea that she gave her husband and the amount of cooking she did at the week-end, and her activities on every Coronation committee, found time to run down to, or pop into (her words, not ours), Punshions almost every day, undeterred by the absence of any welcome from Miss Pemberton, for whom she somehow felt herself responsible. We cannot exactly say that Miss Pemberton was grateful, but she went so far as not to resent Mrs. Paxon's district visiting.

It was on a most unpleasant morning of late spring when Mrs. Paxon, carrying a basket, went round to the back of the house, where Effie Bunce, having just given the clorths a bit of a rinse (her words, not ours), was pegging them out on the line.

"Nice day for anyone as feels too hot," said Effie. "I lighted the fire in the sitting-room this morning and didn't her ladyship tell me off. That por gentleman doing his writing and all, there in the cold. All that writing and reading makes the blood thin. That's what my granny said and she never had a day's illness in her life. Come in, Mrs. Paxon," and she stood aside for Mrs. Paxon to go into the kitchen, from which came warmth and a very good smell.

"I told her ladyship, I said to her," said Effie Bunce, "if I'm cold, I said, there's plenty of places as I could be warm in. And I got a couple of buckets of coal and the oven's going beautiful. Father got three couple of rabbits last night, so I brought a couple over here. Smell them?" and indeed something in the oven was sending a very appetizing smell through the kitchen. "She's gone to Barchester to the Free Libery. Always at her books, she is, but it takes all sorts to make a world. Have a nice cuppa, Mrs. Paxon, I'm just making one for myself and the por gentleman. Sitting there with his books, he is. Now, I don't fancy books myself."

"Not a nice love story?" said Mrs. Paxon, settling herself in an old rather broken-down wicker easy chair, such as many country kitchens own.

"Never did fancy reading," said Effie Bunce, taking the round iron lid off the stove with a crooked poker and setting a large, blackened kettle over the fiery hole. "They did learn me some at school, but I didn't seem to take to it. I've got the radio in the kitchen, though. Would you like it on?"

"But it is on," said Mrs. Paxon, who had found it rather difficult to hear everything Effie said through its blaring. "Turn it off, Effie, there's a good girl."

"There now, I'd have turned it off when you come in, only I didn't seem to notice it," said Effie. "That's where the radio comes in so handy. You don't hardly know if it's on or off. Miss Pemberton, she goes off a treat if she hears it, but Mr. Downing, you could have it on night and day and he wouldn't notice, with all his books and things. Same he often doesn't see a cup of tea till it's cold."

"Ask him to come into the kitchen, Effie," said Mrs. Paxon.

Effie Bunce said admiringly it was a brain-wave and that reminded her, she said, she needed a new perm.

"Now look here, Effie," said Mrs. Paxon, "you can't have a perm till the Coronation's over, if you want to be one of Queen Elizabeth's ladies. You haven't long to wait now," to which Effie replied good-naturedly that it was O.K. by her and went into the living-room, whence she re-emerged with Mr. Downing, who had the half-witted look of those who live a great deal in their own minds and come up blinking into daily life.

"You sit down and have a nice hot cup of tea, Mr. Downing," said Mrs. Paxon. "However the Troubadours and people got on without tea I can't think; still it takes all sorts to make a world. How's the book getting on?"

Mr. Downing, quite touchingly pleased by this attention from someone to whom the subject obviously meant nothing, told Mrs. Paxon how it was making good progress and how he had been invited to lecture on Provençal Poetry in America next autumn but didn't know if he could manage it.

"Of course you can," said Mrs. Paxon, who had the wonderful faith, which even in the most disillusioned of us dies hard, that men can do anything, except of course the ordinary, sensible things that they expect us to do for them. "Miss Pemberton could go with you and call herself a secretary, couldn't she?"

"I don't know," said Mr. Downing, looking at the kitchen wall, where a row of shining saucepans hung. "I don't know. Miss Pemberton hasn't been well this year. She won't tell me anything, but I know she is in pain often," and then he started nervously as a knock was heard on the scullery door.

Effie opened it, voices were heard, and then in came Mrs. Turner.

"I've got it, Minnie!" she said to Mrs. Paxon. Effie, who had of course followed her into the room, said she'd make a fresh pot and took the teapot away.

"No!" said Mrs. Paxon. "Well, wonders will never cease."

"And from half quarter-day too," said Mrs. Turner, putting her shopping basket on the table and sitting down. "I've got quite a lot of my furniture stored in Barchester and I must say those people have kept everything beautifully clean. And the agent says if I want to move in almost at once he doesn't think the people will mind, as they are going to Hemel Hempsted," and so excited was her audience that it did not occur to anyone that her last remark had been of a highly non-sequiturial character.

"If I might ask, what is it you have got?" said Mr. Downing. "I should very much like to offer my congratulations."

"The Hollies, of course," said Mrs. Turner. "Isn't it wonderful to think I'll be back in my old home again? Of course I'll miss the girls, still they've got their husbands and they can all come and stay with me. It will be just like old times, only we shan't have the siren. Do you remember that evening, Mr. Downing, when Father Fewling had to go because the siren went off and luckily the All Clear came so soon that he was back almost at once?" and though Mr. Downing did not precisely remember that striking and unusual episode, he said very truly that he remembered with gratitude some very happy evenings at The Hollies.

"Good gracious," said Mrs. Paxon, "half past twelve and I've been sitting here while Mr. Downing wanted to be writing his books," and she got up and began collecting her basket and her bag and other light impedimenta, when the noise of the front door being shut was heard. Mr. Downing, hoping by a miracle to escape to the living-room, got up quickly and upset his cup with the sordid remains of milk, tea, and some sugar that had not quite melted. The door from the living-room opened. Miss Pemberton came in, looked at everyone, and sat down heavily.

"We were just having a cup of tea and asking Mr. Downing about you," said Mrs. Paxon, not nervously, for that sentiment did not exist in her, but hoping that there would not be an unpleasant scene.

"Won't you have some, Ianthe?" said Mr. Downing, almost tripping up over his own tongue, so convinced was he that his Egeria's comment on his behaviour would be neither friendly nor short.

"No, thank you, Harold," said Miss Pemberton, not unkindly. "I had one at the hospital."

Mrs. Paxon and Mrs. Turner both said, in a jumbled kind of way, trying to express simultaneously a real and friendly interest and a wish not in any way to appear curious, that they hoped it was all right; though what "it" was they did not quite know.

"'Does truth sound bitter, As one at first believes?'" said Miss Pemberton to no one in particular, and there was a silence.

"Browning," she added.

"Please do tell us, Miss Pemberton," said Mrs. Turner, "and perhaps we could do something for you. I have got The Hollies back and I would like so much to be useful as I'm going to live here again."

"I always knew you weren't a fool," said Miss Pemberton, not unkindly. "Harold!" at which trumpet-call the unfortunate Mr. Downing almost jumped in his seat, "America is off as far as I am concerned, but you must go. I shall be seriously vexed if you do not. I am perfectly safe in Northbridge with friends all round me," at which words Mrs. Turner's pretty eyes began to brim over and even the valiant Mrs. Paxon had to sniff, for Miss Pemberton had been on the whole so stand-offish, though in a ladylike way, that Northbridge had never felt much at ease with her, and now suddenly to find her apparently ready to accept sympathy, though she would never ask for it, almost unmanned her hearers.

"I shall of course carry on with the rehearsals as usual," said Miss Pemberton. "If I simply can't, I shall suggest to Mrs.

Merton that you and Mrs. Turner are more than competent to do so," and she eyed Mrs. Paxon with grim determination.

"Well, of *course* I will," said Mrs. Paxon, "and Poppy will give me a hand, won't you?"

Mrs. Turner, who appeared to have a slight difficulty in articulating clearly, said she would do anything she was asked and it would be like the good old days in the war and she and Mrs. Paxon really must be going.

When they had gone Miss Pemberton sat quite still. Her lodger was too frightened, and also too truly concerned about her, to dare to open his mouth.

"It is all right, Harold," said Miss Pemberton. "If necessary I shall go into the Barsetshire General Hospital."

"Ruby and me was ward maids there for a bit," said Effie Bunce, feeling quite within her rights to converse with her employers if they sat in her kitchen. "Ever so nice it was, and the doctors were lovely men. Sister was a bit of a pain in the neck, but she couldn't help it. Ruby and me had a lovely time and when we was short-handed at Christmas, Sister let us help lay out old Mrs. Wheeler. Wheeler the sweep's great-aunt she was and not a tooth in her head nor a hair on her head, but she'd eat anything. And the Reverend Hooker was a lovely man too. He used to visit on Thursdays."

Miss Pemberton said, calmly, that it all sounded very nice.

"But, Ianthe, you can't," said Mr. Downing.

"First things first," said Miss Pemberton, which phrase, somehow carrying with it the authority of Holy Writ, frightened Mr. Downing so much that he remained silent. "We cannot let the Coronation down. When that is over, we can discuss the matter. How is the rabbit, Effie?"

"Lovely," said Effie. "I browned it nicely first the way you said, and it's a beautiful young one. Father he don't hold with old rabbits. Gives them to the dogs, he does," and then she began to clatter the tea-things into the scullery and Miss Pemberton withdrew to her own room. Mr. Downing, oppressed by a horrid sense of insecurity, sat where he was and seemed to find comfort in watching Effie bustling about the kitchen and listening to her artless talk of poaching and snaring and wife-beating, which, together with daughter-beating, appeared to have been old Bunce's most usual occupations till his daughters turned on him and kept him in some fear of their strong arms.

Meanwhile Mrs. Turner and Mrs. Paxon went to the Mitre, where was usually a quite good lunch and Mrs. Turner would have one or two guests nearly every day, re-knitting all her old friendships.

When they went into the dining-room, the proprietress, Mrs. Vidler, sister-in-law of Vidler the poulterer, was talking with a lady unknown to Mrs. Turner, and even to Mrs. Paxon, who had lived in Northbridge ever since she married Mr. Paxon. Luckily, before they could burst with curiosity, Mrs. Vidler came up to take their orders.

"You saw the lady I was talking to, Mrs. Paxon," said Mrs. Vidler, "thick soup it is today and very nice and then there's fried plaice it's a bit off but not hardly so as you'd notice it and lamb but that lamb was a sheep long before it was killed, well, she's a trained nurse and she wants to find a nice place to retire to and she came to have a look here, which will you have?"

"The soup and the fried plaice, please, Mrs. Vidler," said Mrs. Turner, skilfully disentangling Mrs. Vidler's words. "Same for you, Minnie? What's her name?"

"Miss Heath's what she wrote when she sent me a letter about taking a room here for a few days," said Mrs. Vidler.

"I think I know her," said Mrs. Turner and, getting up, she went across the room to the newcomer.

"Excuse me, but you're Miss Heath, aren't you?" she said. "I used to hear about a Miss Heath from an old school friend of mine, Sister Chiffinch. I think she had a flat with you and a Miss Ward."

"Now *isn't* that nice to run into a friend the first thing," said Miss Heath. "Yes, I had the flat with Chiffy and another friend of ours, Miss Ward, we always called her Wardy. I'm here for a few days while I look out for nice lodgings. What a sweetly pretty old-world place it is."

"Won't you have lunch with me and Mrs. Paxon?" said Mrs. Turner. "I'm sure she can help you. She always can. She did nearly all the billeting in the war," and Miss Heath graciously accepted the invitation. The talk soon went, as all talk did then, to the Coronation and in particular to the Northbridge celebrations and when Miss Heath heard that Aubrey Clover and Jessica Dean were to put on an act (Mrs. Paxon's words, not ours) her excitement was great.

"My pal Chiffy—Sister Chiffinch—was with Mrs. Clover for the first baby," she said, "and I was up in town and had a peep at her—such a sweet wee mite, well, what a coincidence," with which both the others agreed, though neither was quite sure where the coincidence came in.

"Northbridge seems to be rather full," said Miss Heath. "I heard of some quite nice rooms in the Plashington Road. I must go and look at them. Meanwhile I am quite enjoying this quaint old place."

"If it's Mrs. Hicks, she is the mother of the housemaid at the Rectory," said Mrs. Paxon, "and I believe she is rather booked up. I must inquire. By the way, Miss Heath, would you mind being a paying guest? It isn't quite the same as lodgings, but quite a lot of the ladies here like to have a guest. It helps with the weekly bills."

"In a place like Northbridge I'm sure I wouldn't mind a

bit," said Miss Heath. "It's not like some places where really you don't know what's going on. Just a quiet house and if there was an elderly lady I wouldn't mind giving a hand with her."

Mrs. Turner said she wished she were an elderly lady, but if Miss Heath couldn't find suitable rooms she would be glad to take her as a temporary guest, as she was just moving back into her own house, The Hollies, and Miss Heath seemed pleased by the suggestion, though nothing was settled. Miss Heath was quite content to stay on at the Mitre for the present and said she was looking forward to some rambles at this lovely time of year. As it was at the moment raining with a steady, cold drizzle (which was merely Nature keeping her hand in for the Coronation weather), that particular subject of conversation languished. But there were plenty of other things to talk about, and, rather neglecting their guest, Mrs. Turner and Mrs. Paxon fell back into a discussion of the pageant and whether Miss Pemberton would be well enough to carry on. Miss Heath asked with interest what was the matter with her, but neither lady knew. Miss Heath said she knew the type very well. She had a patient just like that in 1948, or was it 1949, who wouldn't admit that she was ill when it was really quite serious, and she pursed up her lips with a great air of she could an if she would. Then, with friendly words on both sides, they parted; Mrs. Turner to look at her furniture that was in store in Barchester, Mrs. Paxon to one of her many civic activities, and Miss Heath to have a nice tramp along a muddy lane, across a soggy field, through a hedge and so back by where the men were repairing the road and the steam roller wouldn't be along till next day.

There are times when everything goes right for a change and Mrs. Turner found it much easier to get into The Hollies

again than she had anticipated. Her tenants had been ex-
emplary, very little redecorating was necessary, and her furniture was in good condition. The only possible difficulty was
help, but Mrs. Turner's ex-maid, or ex-help, or whatever
genteelism one likes, Doris Hibberd, was most willing to oblige
if Mrs. Turner didn't mind having her boy too and she'd see
he wasn't a nuisance, which offer Mrs. Turner at once accepted, for to give free board and lodging to a fatherless (at
any rate in the eyes of the law) child gives one a certain
amount of hold over the mother. Doris was a very nice girl
and her boy was a Wolf Cub and at school every day and
liked gardening and had got the Cubs' Boot Cleaning badge.
Miss Heath moved into the smaller spare room and rapidly
became so popular in the little town (for Northbridge could
hardly be called a village since the war) that she was out a
good deal and no trouble at all.

The Coronation preparations became daily more intense
and complicated. At Hovis House the ladies of the town
worked indefatigably at the pageant costumes. Commander
Beasley, R.N. (Retd.), gave a lecture on British-Needlers at
The Aloes (by kind permission of Miss Talbot and Miss Dolly
Talbot), realizing the sum of £1–17–6 for the Costumes Fund.
Miss Hopgood and Miss Crowder gave a talk on the Riviera
at Glycerine Cottage which brought in £1–16–3 (the near-
silver threepenny piece being subsequently detected by the
bank as a Lydion, one of the Mixo-Lydian small nickel coins
worth .4325 of a farthing at the present rate of exchange).
But the crowning success was a talk by Miss Pemberton at
Punshions on Home Cooking for the Coronation, with a
practical demonstration, which added £4–5–0 to the fund, as
people were allowed to buy the succulent dishes and take them
home, subject to a promise that they would bring the casseroles
and pipkins back afterwards, properly cleaned. This news

coming indirectly to Mr. Holden, he suggested to his chief, Adrian Coates, a quick reprint of Miss Pemberton's cookery book, which, we are glad to say, was to do very well.

Rehearsals of the pageant episodes now took place twice a week. They had begun at Punshions, but when Mrs. Villars had seen Miss Pemberton grey with fatigue, every line in her face so deeply marked that she looked like a bad wood-engraving of herself, she asked Lydia to back her up in moving the final rehearsals to the Town Hall. It was difficult to find the right moment and the right way to do this. Dr. Ford, who was trusted as well as liked in all that part of the county, happened to look in at the Rectory to see the cook's bad leg (a chronic condition which gave that lady considerable standing at the Women's Institute) and stayed to have tea with Mrs. Villars, who asked him what was his opinion of Miss Pemberton.

"Speaking extra-professionally, I'm not pleased with her," said Dr. Ford. "She has been driving herself far too hard for far too long. Just like a woman. I have suggested that she should go into the Barchester General for a good overhaul and a rest. I'd manage a private room for her and get it on the Health Service. When you've got a damned silly nuisance," said Dr. Ford, who held no opinion of the Health Service at all, saying that if he were on it he would have to give up his dining-room for a waiting-room and put all his savings into Jeyes' Fluid or Lysol, and his two faithful maids would certainly give notice, "you might as well use it, seeing that it has come to stay. But it's one thing to take a horse to the water and another to make her drink," which made them both laugh, though quite kindly, for Miss Pemberton's large face and her habit of shying away from any subject she disliked were not unlike the general folly of that noble beast, described in a standard book on the equine species as "a nervous, unintelligent animal." "If Downing would assert himself—" But Mrs. Villars interrupted him to say it was quite impossible and she had thought of several other plans, including getting Effie Bunce to sleep at Punshions, but none of them would work. Mrs. Villars then suggested that when Mr. Downing went to America to give the Lincoln Fish Doppelgänger Lectures, Miss Pemberton could have a real rest, to which Dr. Ford replied that she would either go with Mr. Downing to see that he kept out of mischief, which would mean that both of them would have a nervous breakdown, or if she stayed at home she wouldn't eat anything, for everyone knew that women never cooked for themselves when they were alone and, as a rider, that he was sick of the whole lot of them.

"Canon Fewling was telling us," said Mrs. Villars, "that there was a kind of society of Friends of Admiral and Mrs. Phelps over at Southbridge. Couldn't we have Friends of Miss Pemberton here?"

"You've got it already," said Dr. Ford, "and not a thing can it do. You have to let elderly people kill themselves in their own way. That's one of the few things I've learned in a long life. And talking of the Phelpses, did you know that Rose Fairweather has found a petty-officer's widow who is a very good cook? She likes elderly naval people and finds she can't live on her pension, and she is going to the Phelpses as a working housekeeper. I had a few words with Macfadyen about it and he said he would not say but it might not be a bad thing if he and Margot Phelps got married before the housekeeper changed her mind," which news gave Mrs. Villars great pleasure, for ever since the rich Mr. Macfadyen's proposal to the Admiral's daughter had become public property there had been a growing feeling that unless he married her out of hand she would go on being engaged all her life and probably die an old maid, while her parents survived her.

Mrs. Villars said she had seldom heard better news and why couldn't they get someone to marry Miss Pemberton. Or to marry Mr. Downing, she added, which Dr. Ford said was an idea, only he didn't see Miss Pemberton allowing anyone to marry him, nor did he know anyone who wanted to.

"It certainly is peculiar that he can't find a wife when Northbridge is seething with spinsters," said Mrs. Villars. "There is an extremely nice hospital nurse, a Miss Heath, who seems to be quite comfortably off. I believe she is a paying guest with Mrs. Turner at present. How would that do?" but Dr. Ford did not appear hopeful and the matter dropped.

A few days later, at a rehearsal of the War of the Roses episode, Mr. Downing was invited by Mrs. Turner to go back to tea with her. It was with a strange and not unpleasant feeling of Time Recaptured, with a nostalgia for those happy days of blackout, rations, air-raids, and a closely knit band of rather elderly brothers—which word of course included sisters—that he once again went through the hospitable door of The Hollies. The rooms were but little changed. Mrs. Turner's tenants had put up some fresh wallpaper in the hall and the general tone of the drawing-room was rose pink rather than salmon pink, but Mrs. Turner's comfortable unimaginative furniture had settled down happily again in its home. There was the fire, blazing in May as cosily as it had done in a far-off Christmas during the war. There was the chair in which he had been sitting when Mrs. Turner had showed him her old snap-shots, including her husband, whose brief married life had been followed, through excessive drinking, by his early death in what Mrs. Turner's nieces called the loony bin. There he had sat, his head bowed in silence, when Mrs. Turner had said that her dearest wish was that she could have been more patient with her husband and helped him more.

And there, Mrs. Turner also remembered, she had for the first and only time done what she had for some time wished to do and very gently smoothed his grey hair, which felt just as she had known it would feel, like stroking a grey bird's head and shoulders.

But these were not subjects for conversation, thirteen years later and in quite different surroundings, so they talked about the pageant and Mrs. Turner said she felt Miss Pemberton was doing too much, at least she didn't mean it that way if Mr. Downing saw what she meant.

"I do see," he said. "You always put things so clearly, Mrs. Turner," and as he said the words he remembered from past days that her name was Poppy. "I really don't know what to do. I can't give up the American lectures, when Mr. Walden Concord Porter has done so much for the B.D.P.," which mystic letters Mrs. Turner now knew to mean the Biographical Dictionary of Provence. "It isn't as if I could do much for Miss Pemberton when I'm here, because she won't let me. But at least it is someone in the house. I know she will not cook when I am not there. When I go to London or Oxford she gives Effie Bunce a holiday and eats lettuces and things. Oh, dear!"

Had Mrs. Turner's nieces been there as in old days, they would undoubtedly have said, in no uncertain manner, that Pussy, for such was their artless way of alluding to Mr. Downing, had got it in one. Mrs. Turner, torn between female loyalty to Miss Pemberton and real anxiety about her health, decided to be disloyal; which is nearly always a Good Thing.

"I do so see what you mean, Mr. Downing," she said. "Women are just like that—it can't be helped. When the girls were here I was cooking all the time when I wasn't at A.R.P. or the Communal Kitchen, or delousing those London children. I'd like to take it up again. I've lost my hand a bit,

I expect, but I'd soon get it back with someone to cook for. As soon as I'm settled, I'll start getting my hand in, ready for a nice dinner to welcome you when you come back. I might ask Mr. and Mrs. Villars and Mr. Highmore, only that might be awkward because I expect Mr. Highmore would feel a bit nervous. I mean he does a wonderful imitation of the Bishop preaching, only I don't suppose he could do it in front of the Rector. Not but what Mr. Villars feels quite properly about the Bishop, but you know the way things get about and it wouldn't quite do as Mr. Highmore is so keen on his pro-fession," to which rather muddled argument Mr. Downing replied that he didn't think anyone would give Mr. Highmore away and it took more than that to get a priest unfrocked, in-stancing a clergyman before the war, somewhere in East Anglia, who lived in a barrel like Diogenes and was finally clawed to death by a lion in a travelling menagerie, but—so far as he could remember—was still a priest. Mrs. Turner said What an extraordinary coincidence, it was quite near where one of her married nieces lived and whenever there was a flood the Fire Brigade brought the meat and groceries in a rowing-boat.

"High Tide on the Coast of Lincoln," said Mr. Downing aloud to himself and Mrs. Turner said it wasn't as far north as that, when luckily Miss Heath came in, radiating Love of Nature even in that lady's present disagreeable aspect, and said she had seen a Blue Bird down by the river. It speaks poorly for human nature that both Mrs. Turner and Mr. Downing thought she meant something like the Spirit of Something-or-other in that quite dreadful play by the late M. Mæterlinck which (together with the more mawkish aspects of Peter Pan) still exercises a whimsy influence over literature and—one regrets to say—statuary by the Serpen-tine; and as for saying There are no Dead, why do we also say, with some vague idea of placating the Grim Tyrant Mors, that people have passed over, or joined the majority, which last phrase became, during the war, a perfect pitfall for misunderstanding in cases of promotion, and why people say Majority and not Generality we do not know. But when Miss Heath said she expected it was a woodpecker they at once knew, such is the agility of the human brain, that she had seen a kingfisher.

Miss Heath's hearty appreciation of Mrs. Turner's scones made that lady's silver hair wreathe into wilder tendrils than ever. While Mrs. Turner went out to get a fresh batch, Miss Heath suddenly became professional and said she knew it wasn't her business, but she didn't like Miss Pemberton being alone all autumn with Mr. Downing away, as she was quite certain Miss Pemberton would not feed herself properly while she was alone.

"And that," she said, "is a thing we nurses have to guard against. You must eat well to do justice to your patient—keep your strength up, I mean. Besides, it isn't like before the war when the nurse could still have her meals separately. As often as not I've done the cooking myself if it wasn't a heavy case," and then the front door was heard shutting—a loose construction but we hope intelligible, for that is how we mostly talk—and a man's voice was heard speaking to Mrs. Turner, who came in, flushed by the warm kitchen, with Dr. Ford, who said he had smelt Mrs. Turner's scones halfway down the street and couldn't resist them. Mrs. Turner made fresh tea and everyone began to eat again.

"Well, as we're all friends here, there's something I want to say," said Dr. Ford and in each of the three other very worthy and unsinful people in the room, that horrid sense of general guilt began to surge.

"About Miss Pemberton," said Dr. Ford. "Two lumps if

you can spare them, Mrs. Turner. I never know if it's on the ration or off."

The whole party joined in saying they all felt exactly the same, because even if things were on the ration you could always get as much as you wanted if you could pay for it because everyone didn't take up their full ration and Scatcherds' Stores had been practically *begging* people to buy more bacon and things.

"In the case I have in mind, there would be no difficulty about rations," said Dr. Ford. "It's your pigeon, Downing."

Mr. Downing looked, and indeed felt, quite mad.

"That obstinate woman will *not* trouble to eat when she's alone," said Dr. Ford. "Which means that while you are in America, Downing, she will live on bread and butter, if that. I don't want to have them bring it in felo de se, because then I'd get into trouble."

"But there's Effie Bunce," said Mrs. Turner.

"As nice a girl as I know," said Dr. Ford warmly. "Every good female instinct, even if she overdoes some of them a bit. But if Miss Pemberton won't trouble to buy the food, or let Effie go and buy it, Effie can't cook it," which words Dr. Ford spoke with the mild resignation of the chemist who was called as a juror in the case of *Bardell* v. *Pickwick*; and if there is a reader who does not take the allusion, we can only, taking example by that remarkable woman Miss Fanny Squeers, pity the ignorance of such a one and despise her.

"I'd ask her to lunch or supper every day, if that would help," said Mrs. Turner, "but she wouldn't come."

"I suppose I'd better not go," said Mr. Downing. And we may add that this was said with no pettishness, nor pettiness, but because his duty appeared to lie clear before him.

"But, Pussy, you *couldn't* not go," said Mrs. Turner, and then blushed so violently at having used this name, given affectionately to Mr. Downing by her nieces during the war, that any dispassionate observer would almost have expected her pretty silvery hair to go red in sympathy. "I mean you've promised that American Professor and everyone will be frightfully disappointed." Even in his agony the scholar in Mr. Downing made him utter a mild protest against the word Professor applied to Mr. Walden Concord Porter, who, though full of admiration for that status, was himself an industrialist with very very high ideals; or so at least he described himself and who are we to quibble with him. "Couldn't Miss Pemberton go to a nursing home for a bit, Dr. Ford? I mean a really good one. We'd all love to subscribe and we could tell her it was On The Health."

"You are a thoroughly good woman, Mrs Turner," said Dr. Ford, "but you underestimate Miss Pemberton's powers of getting at facts. She would have the truth out of everyone in three seconds and insist on staying in Punshions, or at the worst going to St. Boscobel's Home."

Mrs. Turner said where was that, she had never heard of it.

"Workhouse Infirmary," said Dr. Ford. "Then they called it The Institution and several other meaningless things and for the moment it is St. Boscobel's, whoever he was. I daresay it will be Buckingham Palace Hostel soon."

"I could ask her to stay here," said Mrs. Turner. "After all, I've plenty of room. The only thing is, I know she wouldn't come. She'd rather go to the Bunce family and pay for dirt and rabbit stew."

"Damn her, I'd certify her for sixpence," said Dr. Ford. "Women! They never know when to give in and all they do know is how to make nuisances of themselves. I could make out a case for sending her to the Barchester General for observation, but no one could force her to go, short of hitting her over the head with a rolling-pin."

All were silent, but it did not occur to anyone to turn his or her countenance towards Miss Heath, who now spoke from the sofa.

"I daresay," said Miss Heath, "you may think what I am going to suggest quite foolish, but I've had a good bit of experience with elderly people. If you couldn't keep me here, Mrs. Turner, I could ask Miss Pemberton if I could come to her as a P.G. while Mr. Downing was away, just the same as with you."

"But I *could* keep you here," said Mrs. Turner. "Oh, I see what you mean. *Pretend* I said I couldn't manage it. I could say my other niece and her husband were coming and I hadn't room. Only of course I have—but Miss Pemberton was never upstairs here, so she doesn't know. I wish Minnie Paxon were here. She's awfully good at amateur theatricals," at which Dr. Ford laughed unrestrainedly.

"Ackcherly," said Miss Heath (almost as if it were Old Times and Mrs. Turner's niece Betty were there, using her favourite expression, now used, together with the frequent interjection of Um, in every rank of society), "there's nothing I'd like better than to live in that old house for a bit. I'm funny about antique architecture. It somehow gets me, if you see what I mean. I could ask her to teach me some of her dishes— you can always get round people that way. We would be quite cosy," and though cosy was the last adjective that anyone could have used of Punshions, it was evident that Miss Heath saw that quality in it: or at any rate saw something to which her being responded. There was a short silence while everyone thought about the plan.

"Well," said Mrs. Turner, "I can't see anything wrong with your idea, Miss Heath, except that it's too good to be true. I should miss you, but one mustn't think of oneself. When are you going to start on it?" But Miss Heath said it was no good rushing one's fences and she must feel her way and really with the Coronation getting so near we must all be thinking of Her Majesty, at which words Mrs. Turner, easily moved to emotion, found tears welling to the surface and had to dab her eyes.

"I know how you feel," said Miss Heath sympathetically, "and sometimes I get quite weepy myself when I think of Her Majesty and all she does for us."

"No self-respecting Trades Unionist would work the hours Her Majesty does," said Dr. Ford, and then he took Mr. Downing away with him, while Mrs. Turner and Miss Heath had a delightful conspiratorial talk, so that they quite forgot to turn off the stew in the oven (a phrase which every housewife will understand) till they smelt something burning.

Whatever Miss Pemberton's aches or ills may have been, nothing had yet deterred her from directing the rehearsals for the pageant with a firm hand, and so popular were they that Effie Bunce and her sister Ruby had to be detailed to keep out anyone not actually in the historical scenes; which they did with a fine mixture of good-humour and firmness, and Effie (having senior status in her employer's house) entertained a large number of the outcasts to tea in the kitchen, whence they could hear and see quite a lot of what was going on, till everyone said it was almost as good as the war. There had been a good deal of discussion as to how often they should rehearse at the Town Hall, but as the Town Hall was not going to lend itself for nothing it was decided that one dress rehearsal of the Historical Scenes would be enough. We need hardly say that the Kiddies' Rehearsal was going to take up most of the morning and part of the afternoon, and most of the wives had to get tea for their husbands, and finally the hour of 6 p.m. was settled, as even if one's husband wasn't home one could always pop something in the oven for him and let's hope to goodness he'll remember to turn the gas off and not let the rissoles burn to cinders the way he did that night I was at the Women's Institute.

The weather, which had never been agreeable, was now lashing itself up to mid-winter fury. We will not say that snow fell, or frost lay on the roofs, but the general effect was the same and the housewives had to resign themselves with sullen rage to wearing that old skirt all through the rest of the year as it's no use putting on your cotton frock once and that's about all. Northbridge Town Hall had an old heating system, but as it had been condemned by the surveyor's last report and in any case only burnt the people sitting near it and left the rest of the room cold, the Committee could only hope that the weather would be mild. But there was no faith in their hope, nor we think would faith have made the slightest difference, for it had decided to be wet and bitterly cold and there was nothing to be done about it. At least, as Mrs. Paxon so truly said, having the kiddies rehearsing there half the day would warm things up a bit, and there are times when even the fugginess of other people is better than being cold.

By the time the performers had arrived for the rehearsal the temperature was not much below 50°, but several of the older ladies came in their winter fleece or fur-lined boots, determined not to wear bare feet or sandals until the night itself. The properties had mostly been sent the day before. Commander Beasley and Mr. Highmore were checking the gifts, or rather loans, as they came in. A certain amount of difficulty had been caused by there being nowhere to put the clothes, but Mrs. Paxon had a Coat-Hanger Drive the day before and Commander Beasley had put up a long metal rail in the Committee room, turning a deliberately and provocatively deaf ear to the Town Hall caretaker, who finally fell into the spirit of the thing and offered to knock a few more tacks into that carpet on the platform as it would be a shame if anyone was to fall down the steps the way Mr. Scatcherd did at the last vestry meeting.

"Is everyone here?" said Miss Pemberton. Those present said Yes and as the people who hadn't yet come couldn't say No, everyone was satisfied.

"The Days of King Arthur," said Miss Pemberton, and all the actors stopped scurrying about.

"All clothes and other properties are arranged on tables and ticketed with the number of the episode and the name of the character represented," said Miss Pemberton. "Principal characters are at the end where the clock is. The crowds are at the other end and you had better be careful about the radiators there, as the caretaker tells me they ought to have been renewed two years ago and if one of them leaks, boiling water will spurt out. Though if I know Hopper, the water will *not* be boiling. Are you there, Hopper?"

The less agreeable of the two cobblers said he *was* there and if there was anyone as said he wasn't, well he was.

"We must have the pipes нот before the pageant begins, Hopper," said Miss Pemberton. "When the hall's full you can let the fire down a bit. All that breath does make a difference."

Mr. Hopper, an avowed Communist and Atheist, though what meaning exactly he attributed to those words we do not think he knew, said it took someone as *did* understand those pipes to keep them going.

"Well, if you hadn't understood them we'd have got someone else to do it," said Miss Pemberton. "All right, Hopper," and to his fury Mr. Hopper found himself saying "Thank you, Miss" instead of Crushing the Tyrant.

"Now, episode one," said Miss Pemberton. "And I'm going to time you," upon which there was a scurry of Early Britons and Danes into the Committee room, where Mrs. Paxon and her helpers, already dressed for their parts, hustled the players into their clothes.

"Just a minute," said Mrs. Paxon, ringing a small bell. "Quiet, please. Every bit of the costumes has a number sewn onto it. As soon as you come off the stage, put your things where you see your number. Some are on the tables and some are on those hooks on the wall. It does seem a pity," she said to Miss Pemberton, "that we can't have any music. I never thought of that."

"Not madrigals," said Miss Pemberton. "This isn't Third Program stuff."

"No, I mean *music*," said Mrs. Paxon. "Like the pianos in the silent films. The Town Hall piano is just about bad enough."

"It's a lovely idea," said Mrs. Turner. "Ad lib till you're ready, you mean, and a nice frightening bit in the bass for the fighting bits; but I don't know anyone that could do it. People don't play the piano now the way they did. Still, I daresay it will be all right on the night," which triumph of hope over not only experience but plain hard fact so stunned Miss Pemberton that she said no more and took her place in the front row of seats.

With unrefined giggles the British women went to the river (only visible to the eye of faith) with their water-jugs; the British men made faces expressive of their dislike of the Danes and some daring spirits took advantage of this opportunity to name the Danes as Churchill or Bevan according to their fancy, thus considerably increasing the noise. Mr. Downing miserably came forward as Merlin, did his best to prophesy in dumb show, and retired, miserably conscious of having failed.

"It'll all be all right on the night," said Mrs. Turner, taking his Merlin robe and putting it back in its place. "All the best actors have stage-fright and you know a good dress rehearsal always brings bad luck," which appeared to reassure Mr. Downing.

"It's shaping quite nicely," said Mrs. Paxon. "Next scene. Are the scouts ready? That's right. Be Prepared, you know."

"That's O.K., miss," said the scout-in-charge. "We'll get the bridge up in no time," and Mrs. Paxon's confidence revived.

The Normans (with some excellent coats of mail made by the Women's Institute of roughly knitted string painted silver) killed the British chief, Mr. Clifford, the headmaster of the infants' school, an ardent pacifist who had never enjoyed anything so much in his life as the sham fighting, and was carried away by the Wolf Cubs, while the scouts made a bridge.

Then followed the Wars of the Roses, in which Mr. Highmore so enjoyed being Richard III with a false hump that his attack on the bridge (constructed by the scouts from some old banisters from the condemned cottage at Faraway Corner) was as good as The War; or so everyone said.

As for the Elizabethan episode, Miss Crowder in her farthingale had never enjoyed herself so much, so much so indeed that her friend Miss Hopgood felt constrained when they got home to remind her that fine feathers did not make fine birds and both ladies burst into tears and had to drink a great deal of tea before they recovered their senses. And even that was not enough, for Miss Hopgood, finding that remorse was preying on her, put on her very special camel-hair dressing-gown and went into Miss Crowder's room to re-apologize, which lady received the apologies with tears and said it was all her fault and Miss Hopgood also was moved to tears and said she would always call that dressing-gown the Dressing-Gown of Reconciliation.

But we must not go too far ahead. Miss Crowder and Commander Beasley performed their pavane, which was only marred by Commander Beasley appearing in ordinary clothes as he said he knew his tights wouldn't stand up to more than one performance, thus agreeably shocking such of the performers as heard him. Mr. Scatcherd, the artist who was to do a quick crayon sketch of the Queen, could not come over till the day itself, but no one felt that it mattered.

"That was all very nice," said Miss Pemberton, "and it will be even better on the day. We aren't to rehearse again. Once is quite enough," and there were those who averred that she had said "quite bad enough," but as we have not yet quite invented that bit, we cannot speak with assurance. "We are not rehearsing the Final Scene of War Work in Northbridge because we haven't time, but Mrs. Paxon assures me that all is going well. Please put everything in the Committee room, and on the day itself don't forget to put all the properties that have been used on the table marked USED. Then we are not so likely to get into a muddle," and she sat down, rather more quickly than was her massive wont.

"Now, Miss Pemberton, you are coming straight back to The Hollies," said Mrs. Turner, "and have a nice cup of tea. I'll ask Mr. Highmore to take us in his little car."

"I had rather walk," said Miss Pemberton. "Mr. Downing can go with me. I am going home. Harold!"

Mr. Downing, now in his ordinary clothes, came up to her.

"We are going home," said Miss Pemberton. "Are you ready?"

Mr. Downing said, miserably, that Mrs. Turner had asked him to tea at The Hollies, to which Miss Pemberton replied "Oh," and shut her eyes.

"Mr. Highmore has his little car here and can take us all,"

said Mrs. Turner with bright determination. "Minnie Paxon is coming too. We can easily cram in."

Her audience, thinking of the size of Mr. Highmore's little car, did not share her opinion, but did not say anything to make the situation more difficult.

"Very well," said Miss Pemberton quietly. "I'll come," and rather ungraciously she added, "thank you." Before she could re-change her mind Mr. Highmore had offered her his arm to help her downstairs. To everyone's surprise she accepted it, but we think it was because he was so young, compared with herself, that she did not like to snub him, as she would undoubtedly have snubbed the old friends who were nearer her own age. Mr. Highmore, somehow feeling that he had a rather sacred charge, took her down (as Mrs. Paxon afterwards said rather disrespectfully to Mrs. Turner) as if she were a basket of eggs and helped her into his car. Mrs. Turner got in behind, in case she was wanted. Mrs. Paxon said she and Mr. Downing would walk, and Mr. Highmore drove to The Hollies with great care. Not that much care was needed, as it was still broad daylight and very few people about, but the willingness is all. In fact with such caution did he drive and so short was the distance that the walking party got to The Hollies almost neck and neck with them. Miss Pemberton was carefully taken out and conducted into the drawing-room, where there was a good fire, highly suitable for the horrible spring weather, and was thankful to sit back in one of Mrs. Turner's super-comfortable chairs. Mr. Highmore said he would stay with her while the ladies got the tea.

"You are a good young man," said Miss Pemberton, surveying him not unkindly.

"Oh, really, do you think so?" said Mr. Highmore. "It is most kind of you. I mean it is a pleasure. I mean everyone is so kind here that there doesn't seem much to do. I don't exactly mean that," and his voice trailed away, as one's voice so often does when it becomes conscious that its owner is making it talk nonsense.

"Are you an only son?" said Miss Pemberton.

Mr. Highmore said he supposed he was.

"Come, come, you must know," said Miss Pemberton with a snappishness that quite cheered the curate.

"You see," he explained, "I didn't know if you wanted me to be an only son or not, so—"

"I don't mind what you are," said Miss Pemberton, which made him wish he were at home. "But it isn't every young man that will trouble to be kind to an ugly, useless old woman."

"Excuse me," said Mr. Highmore, going rather pink as he spoke, "but I can't agree. May I alter your words and say that you are a very courageous and kind person, and one can't help seeing that in your face. The rehearsal went well, I think. If it had been better I should have been anxious, but now I think we shall do quite well on the day. By the way, did you notice in the Norman episode that I had a very good tonsure? Would you like to look at it?" and he took from a pocket his wig-tonsure, at the sight of which Miss Pemberton laughed. Not unkindly but with a kind of admiring amusement.

"You must forgive me," she said. "It is a splendid piece of work. Do you do embroidery?"

Mr. Highmore said he wasn't much good at it, but he could make almost any kind of wig out of anything. His mother was a very good needlewoman, he said, and by the time the rest of the party came back with tea, they had become quite good friends.

"I see you have been making yourself useful, Harold," said Miss Pemberton to her lodger, who was carrying a plate of cakes, at which he nearly dropped them. Just as they had settled down to tea, in came Miss Heath, back from an ever so exciting ramble, she said, and how nice to see Miss Pemberton and there now, how nice to see Mr. Downing and well, there was Mr. Highmore and Mrs. Paxon too. As the talk became more and more animated, with discussion of the pageant and reminiscences of the happy war-days, Miss Pemberton felt more and more tired and thankful not to speak, which indeed was not necessary while everyone else was talking.

Presently Miss Heath touched Mrs. Turner's arm. "I think Miss Pemberton ought to go home," she said. "The rehearsal has been a bit too much for her," and when Mrs. Turner saw Miss Pemberton's face her kind heart smote her for neglecting a guest.

"Don't you worry, Mrs. Turner," said Miss Heath, who was by now Sister Heath again, in charge of a case. "I'll get Mr. Highmore to run us down to Punshions and I'll take my little bag. It's funny, but I always keep my bag handy, just as I did when I was on call. If you can keep Mr. Downing to supper, I'll see to everything and I daresay she will be all right to-morrow. I can ring up Dr. Ford from the post office if he is needed. It's only a step away and they are such nice people. They said I could always come in by their side door if I wanted to make a professional call after hours," and she went quietly out of the room and was soon back with her bag.

"Excuse me interrupting," she said to Miss Pemberton, "but you look a bit tired. Mr. Highmore will drive you home, I'm sure, and I'll come with you just to see everything's all right. Mr. Downing will come on later when I've got everything nice and comfy," and so beaten was Miss Pemberton that she accepted the offer, with distinct signs of gratitude. Mr. Highmore, who was not the son of a distinguished member of the

South Wembley Dramatic for nothing, at once took his cue
and gave Miss Pemberton his arm. Good-byes were said and
Miss Heath followed them out of the room.

"I *am* sorry, Mr. Downing," said Mrs. Turner. "But I'm
sure it's all right. Miss Heath is a splendid nurse and will
make Miss Pemberton very comfortable. You stay to supper
here and then you won't be in the way. It will be just like
old times. I'll tell Doris to run down to Punshions after supper
and see if anything's wanted and then you can take it. Miss
Heath will stay the night and I'm sure Miss Pemberton will
be better in the morning."

Mr. Downing did not quite believe all she said, but the
warm, comfortable, unassuming atmosphere of The Hollies
was very soothing and he allowed his uneasy feelings to sub-
side and retire into the cavern from which those odious creatures are far too apt to burst out and annoy us.

"There are plenty of books," said Mrs. Turner, pointing out
a heap of magazines, "and the wireless, so you just have a nice
quiet rest while I see about supper. And I'll switch the telephone off here so that it won't bother you and take the calls
in the pantry. I have an extension there so that Doris can
take messages when I'm out, and there's another in my bedroom," and when she had opened the door she picked up the
tray with the rest of the tea-things, shut the door behind her
with her foot, and went away.

Left alone, Mr. Downing felt as if, suddenly, he were surrounded by flood-waters, helpless unless a boat came to his
aid. Mrs. Turner was being as kind as kind could be and while
he was at The Hollies he was safe. Outside The Hollies were
darkness (figuratively, as Summer Time was now providing
very long, chill, depressing evenings in a grudging way) and
uncertainties. Inside were light, warmth, safety, and very
pleasant companionship. He began to think of what had hap-

pened, what might happen, and the more he thought about everything the more depressed he became and the more did the feeling of guilt where he was quite guiltless—perhaps the worst heritage that the Serpent in Eden left to us—overwhelm him. So that when Mrs. Turner came back, she found her guest brooding by the fire. The wheel had come full circle. He had not heard her come in and was sitting quite still, his head bowed upon his hands, nor did he notice that she was standing over him. So, as she had done so many years ago, she very gently smoothed his silver-grey hair. It felt just as she remembered it, like stroking a grey bird's head and shoulders. Mr. Downing, without moving, put up his hand and reached for hers. Before she knew what she was doing she was kneeling beside him with her arms round him and he had turned his head and laid it on her shoulder.

Of course Doris had to choose that moment to come in to ask if Mr. Downing was staying to supper, and so enthralled was she by the sight, far more glamorous than anything the Barchester Odeon had yet produced, that she remained silent upon the drawing-room carpet. A coal fell into the red heart of the fire. Mrs. Turner looked up and saw Doris.

"Mr. Downing is staying to supper, Doris," she said. "And don't mention this to anyone. I shall have something interesting to tell you later," and Doris withdrew, with such visions of romance as nearly made her let the soup burn.

"Poppy," said Mr. Downing, and so unperceptive does Love make us that he felt it was the most beautiful sound in the world.

"I just couldn't help it," said Mrs. Turner, "when I thought of poor Miss Pemberton and everything. I felt so *sorry* for you, darling."

Not for many, many years had anyone called Mr. Downing a darling and he liked it very much: almost as much as Poppy.

"I don't know what Miss Pemberton would say," said Mrs. Turner, "but she needn't know," which words made Mr. Downing feel how practical she was.

"Not just at present," he said. "But I'll have to tell her before I go to America. I did dread going. One gets into such a rut here. But with you I shall feel so safe. Dear, dearest."

Mrs. Turner looked at him.

"Oh, do you mean we'll get married?" she said.

"Well, I'm certainly not going to leave you behind," said Mr. Downing. "And I believe one has to meet lots of people in the United States and I am so afraid of people and can't remember their faces and now I shall be quite safe. *Dearest Poppy*," which piece of fine masculine selfishness of course appeared to Mrs. Turner the most beautiful sentiment ever expressed.

"I'm afraid I'm not well off," said Mr. Downing, "and there's Ianthe," by which name Mrs. Turner did not at first recognize Miss Pemberton.

"Never mind, I've got quite enough," said Mrs. Turner. "Poor Cecil hadn't time to spend all his money on drink, so I'm quite well off, and there's heaps of room here. But I don't suppose Miss Pemberton would want to live here. It's not her style. Anyway it's no good bothering about that now. You don't go to America till October, do you? That's nearly five months, and we'll make a plan. We don't want to hurt Miss Pemberton or make her feel she isn't wanted," and then Doris came in to say supper was ready.

"You go in, Harold," said Mrs. Turner. "Listen, Doris, I am engaged to be married to Mr. Downing, but of course we shan't announce it while Miss Pemberton is ill. If I hear anything about it, I shall know where it comes from, so hold your tongue like a good girl for a few days," to which Doris's answer was "Ow," but evidently it satisfied her mistress.

A long acquaintance or friendship made it very easy for Mrs. Turner and her guest to talk, and to Doris's great disappointment she did not find them holding hands, though she made several unexpected forays into the dining-room in expectation of the same. But it stood to reason at their age, and madam married too, they wouldn't carry on like that and she decided to give her present young man the same treatment and see how he took it.

While they were still at supper a car was heard and Mr. Highmore came in.

"Oh, do have some port, Mr. Highmore," said Mrs. Turner, whose first impulse was always hospitality. "It's all right. My husband laid it down," and she named a year and a name, which filled the curate with respect.

"I only came in to say that everything is all right," he said. "By Jove, my mother would like this room, Mrs. Turner. Miss Heath has got Miss Pemberton to bed and was cooking something that smells delicious and I rang up Dr. Ford from the post office—nice people they are and so friendly—and I've told Mrs. Villars. Miss Heath thinks Miss Pemberton may be well enough to come to the pageant, but she mustn't exert herself. But we'll manage all right," and Mr. Downing thought that Northbridge had acquired a useful citizen.

"Do have some supper," said Mrs. Turner.

"Do," said Mr. Downing. "Mrs. Turner has very good port," and the curate was delighted to stay. The middle-aged lovers were so quiet and normal that he had no inkling of what had happened since he last saw them, and if he thought anything, it was that The Hollies was much more comfortable than Punshions. But this pleasant evening could not last for ever. The gentlemen said good-night to Mrs. Turner—though it was still light in a horrid chill grey way—and left together, Mr. Highmore to go back to his lodgings and Mr. Downing to Punshions, where Sister Heath, as we must call her again now, received him with a warm welcome and hot cocoa.

"Miss Pemberton is quite comfy," she said, "and I've been reading an ever so nice book by Mrs. Morland, it's called *In Serious Vein*, about a Russian that tries to give Madame Koska the fashionable dressmaker an injection, so that he can steal her new season's models, but he won't get away with it. That's what I like about Mrs. Morland's books, you always know what you'll find. Not like a book I got from the library last week called *Scented Powder* and it was all about cocaine-addicts, so I took it back at once and changed it for a nice book on bird-watching. Now you must just go on as if I wasn't here. I've put a hot bottle in your bed and a thermos of Ovaltine on the table and if you do wake in the night it will only be me just taking a peep at the patient and Dr. Ford will be here first thing. Can I take a book to bed? I never like to touch anyone's books unless I ask. Could you lend me one about the Troubadours? Miss Pemberton was talking about them and it sounded just what I like, a nice love story."

At this point Mr. Downing did perhaps the most noble and unselfish action of his life.

"Here's one I think you'd like," he said. *"Gaily the Troubadour*. It's by a woman, Professor Gawky."

Sister Heath said she was sure she would like it and went upstairs, calling from the top landing to say she had made the stove up if Mr. Downing wanted a hot bath.

Left alone, he sat thinking of the miracle that had come to him. Warmth, comfort, freedom, and very true love. With Mrs. Turner, with Poppy, he could face America in safety. His lectures were nearly finished and in the last of them he was saying a few pulverizing words about Professor Gawky, whose cheap journalism could not sufficiently be contemned by scholarly minds. Had she not written in *Gaily the Trouba-*

dour that the Vidame des Égouts made his wife eat her lover's heart, when the veriest tyro must know that it was his liver and lungs that were served to her at dinner? Bah! The bath water was hot, the bottle in his bed was hot, the Ovaltine in the thermos was hot. If he did think of Miss Pemberton, it was with affectionate compassion. What she may have thought, no one can know, but Sister Heath had gently doped her and she slept all through the night.

Mr. Downing slept peacefully till about three in the morning, when he woke with the horrid griping inside one that means the Nasty Worrying side of one getting into action. What on earth had he done? He had offered marriage to the most kind and lovable woman in the world and she had accepted him. They could go to America together, where she would take care of him and match American kindness and vitality with her own. But what would happen to Miss Pemberton, the Egeria who had looked after him for so long, had fed him well and worked with him at the B.D.P.? Could he in honour leave her alone at Punshions? Go to America he must, for his word was pledged. Was ever man, he thought, in such a horrid predicament, gnawed by conscience, torn in every direction? He knew where his heart lay, but where did his duty lie? And so did he toss and turn, and get up for a drink of water and knock over a pile of books, that Sister Heath, heralding herself with a discreet knock, came in wearing a gorgeous flowered dressing-gown, her hair in an unbecoming net, clucked with her tongue as if he were a naughty child, produced some more hot milk and was evidently prepared to tuck him in. Under her impersonal eye he got back into bed.

"*Now* we're all right," said Sister Heath, "and you must try to go to shut-eye," with which words she left the room. Such was that remarkable woman's influence that he did as he was told. And though when he woke, to a sense of coffee and bacon from downstairs (for the old wooden floors let every smell come through the cracks), he still felt that if difficulties were ahead, he could now face them with some spirit. Then he wondered how Mrs. Turner had slept and what her thoughts had been, till he made himself imagine that she had repented her words and would never marry him.

"Breakfast, Mr. Downing," said Sister Heath, through the door, "and we've had a nice quiet night," and at these words his gentle timid spirit revived and he went downstairs. The breakfast was excellent (though he noted that the coffee was not so good as Miss Pemberton's) and such was his relief that he listened quite kindly to Sister Heath's artless criticism of *Gaily the Troubadour* and wished Professor Gawky were there to hear it. Then Effie Bunce came in, having heard as she passed the post office that Miss Pemberton had had a stroke and her face all on one side, and was a little damped when she heard that it wasn't. But she was a kind girl at heart and said she dessaid Miss Pemberton wanted her bed-turning and the two ladies went off together. Mr. Downing sat on at the breakfast table, wrapped in thoughts of Mrs. Turner and America, till Effie Bunce came down and clattered the break-fast things onto a tray and took them into the scullery. Sister Heath came down and reported that Miss Pemberton was feel-ing much more the thing, but she thought a quiet day would be a good thing.

"Why don't you ring up Mrs. Turner and go to lunch with her?" said Sister Heath. "I know she's got a chicken today. You gentlemen that write books do worry so much. I was with Mr. Knox who writes those lovely biographies of people once and he worried dreadfully. I'll tell you what I'll do, I'll just run over to the post office and phone Mrs. Turner. Effie's in the kitchen if you want anything," and away the kind creature went. And so shattered was Mr. Downing's world by all that had happened that he found Effie's conversation very soothing and pleasant. Sister Heath came back to say Mrs. Turner would be delighted and went up to her patient. Mr. Downing sat down to his pen and papers, but not one word could he write. To find oneself suddenly in a kaleidoscope may be interesting and agreeable, but it is apt to make one feel giddy.

CHAPTER 11

THE WEATHER, more than ever swift to chide and slow to bless in a year which gave it so many opportunities for showing off, had now settled to Arctic chill and what the poet Gray so well describes as iron-sleet of arrowy shower, hurtling in the darkened air, like anything. Hundreds and thousands of people prepared to spend some thirty-six hours or more sitting on a curbstone with a mackintosh, a thermos, and some buns, to see the world's greatest pageant go by. The whole of what we shall continue to think of and describe as the British Empire was directing its thoughts, its loyalty, its love towards the Queen of England, now awaiting her Coronation. Nor was the weather backward in its attention to Barsetshire, which was afterwards proved, at the Annual General Meeting of the Friends of Meteorology, to have had at least .00217 inches more rain than any other place in England, a temperature nearer freezing than any other place in the United Kingdom, and a wind pressure (though of this phrase we are not quite sure) either higher or lower (whichever is the nastier) than anywhere in Iceland, Faroes, Hebrides, Rockall, Malin, Old Uncle Tom Fastnet, and all. All of which somehow redounded to the greater glory of the Empire and the bulldog breed (though no self-respecting bulldog would have borne one millionth part of what Her Majesty's subjects joyfully encountered to do Her honour).

It is a real tribute to Miss Pemberton that, in spite of the pre-Coronation turmoil, so many people rallied to help her.

Mr. Downing's progress through the town was not unlike that
of Jean Baptiste Cavalletto through Bleeding Heart Yard, with
housewives waylaying him right and left to offer help in the
shape of food, or a bottle of wine, or a nice book, or a friendly
visit, nearly all of which (and especially the last) Mr. Downing had to decline, giving as an excuse Dr. Ford's orders, but
really because he was pretty sure that his Egeria in health
would have declined such offers and he did not wish to press
them upon her in her present condition.

When he got to The Hollies he heard a kind of Revolu-
tionary Tribunal in session, discussing how best to unsettle
everything Miss Pemberton had arranged, with the sole purpose of making things easier for her, but as it mostly consisted
in everyone talking at once no decision was reached and everyone was happy in the consciousness of having discussed everything thoroughly and yet not being committed to any definite
action, so he went to the kitchen, where he was sure of a
favourable welcome, till such time as the committee (if that
was what it was) should have dissolved itself. When everyone
had surged away, Mrs. Turner looked for Mr. Downing. He
was not to be seen and she wondered if Sister Heath had failed
to give her telephone message and felt a little low, but when
she went into the kitchen to see Doris about the laundry,
there was Mr. Downing, telling the fascinated Doris about
Sister Heath and how wonderfully she was arranging everything.

"Now, they've gone, I'll bring in the lunch," said Doris.
"Mr. Downing was telling me Miss Heath does breakfast ever
so nice. She's a lovely lady," which her hearers rightly took
as a tribute to Sister Heath's moral excellencies rather than
her physical appearance—not that there was anything wrong
with that. Lunch was very good and there was some claret
which pleased Mr. Downing, but owing to Doris's exits and

entrances they could only speak of matters of outside interest, though to do Doris justice she was not in the least interested in what they said and only wanted to see that Mr. Downing liked her cooking. But at last they were able to get away to the drawing-room and sit by the fire.

"I've been thinking, Harold," said Mrs. Turner.

"Yes, dearest?" said Mr. Downing, which was very creditable to him, as we think he had never used this word before.

"About our getting married and America," said Mrs. Turner. "I was awake ever so long last night, thinking about Miss Pemberton. I'm going to marry you, whatever happens, but if Miss Pemberton is well enough to go to America it simply wouldn't be fair. I hope she won't, though it's rather horrid of me to say so, but, you see, you need someone well to take care of you, and not you to take care of her."

"I know, Poppy. I was thinking about that too," said Mr. Downing, with simple egoism, "but go without you I simply can't. I cannot tell you what I owe to Ianthe for all her kindness. I can't ever repay it, but if I can't it will be repaid in some other way. The important fact is that you will marry me and come to Porterville and that's that," and he fixed Mrs. Turner with the eye that had quelled his most high-spirited pupils when he was a tutor and Fellow of his college, long ago.

Having said these words, he waited for Mrs. Turner to throw him over in a pet (and even as he vaguely formulated the words, he could see her prettier than ever in the pet, her bright eyes flashing, her silver tendrils curling more madly about her face), instead of which she put her hand in his and said: "Harold, you are marvellous," after which there was no more talk on the subject, except to agree that they would be married in the autumn whatever happened. Which was, we think, exactly what he had wanted.

"And don't worry about the marrying part," said Mrs.

Turner. "I saw to both the girls' weddings, as their parents are
dead, and I know all about it. We must be married here because the Villarses will be so pleased and Mr. Highmore could
help, which I know he would love," and Mr. Downing, overcome by her practical mind, said it would be perfect and perhaps Mr. Highmore would wear his tonsure and he hoped
her nieces would come, which kindly thought pleased Mrs.
Turner immensely and made her cry in a most becoming way.

"There's a lovely record the girls used to play," said Mrs.
Turner, "about Rest in the Lord and He shall give thee thy
heart's desire. I always used to cry when they put it on, but
now I know what it means," in proof of which she cried again
and was comforted, Mr. Downing discovering in his vocabu-
lary a number of endearing epithets that he did not even know
he knew.

"I was thinking about the linen," said Mrs. Turner, whose
practical mind even love could not subdue. "It's a nuisance its
all being marked P.T., but I daresay I could alter the T to D.
It's all a bit Gothic, if you know what I mean, and I could
easily put a half-circle onto the leg of the T and kind of ease
the top of the T into the D," and such is the effect of the
tender passion that Mr. Downing thought it was at the same
time the most beautiful and the most practical suggestion he
had ever heard. Spurred on by the linen (and on Mrs.
Turner's side by the knowledge that Doris was out for the
afternoon), these middle-aged lovers made a careful tour of
the whole house, decided which room Mr. Downing should
have for his study (namely the big room on the first floor
facing southeast) and whether they would have a double bed
or two single beds, all of which might have frightened and embarrassed Mr. Downing quite horribly had not Mrs. Turner
considered everything with a kind of practical simplicity that
he found both admirable and touching. And when it came to

the question of beds, he uttered the dashing words that one might as well try everything once, so that altogether they both felt as if they were quite old married people. After the tour Mrs. Turner got tea and they sat comfortably before the roaring fire that a Coronation summer demanded, remembering the war years and the years between when Mrs. Turner had been away in Norfolk, and feeling quiet confidence in the years to come.

"It is just the question of Ianthe," said Mr. Downing and then wondered if Mrs. Turner would break off the engagement at once.

"Now, you must not worry," said Mrs. Turner. "Not till the Coronation's over, anyway. What shall I have on my cards? Mrs. H. Downing or Mrs. Harold Downing, or just Mrs. Downing? I've got the copperplate of my cards and they can engrave my name on the other side. I think Mrs. Harold Downing, because I want everyone to know who you are," which muddled piece of reasoning seemed to Mr. Downing not only worldly-wise but also—for no assignable reason— infinitely touching. So the afternoon passed and when he got back to Punshions there was a good fire in the sitting-room and he observed that a piece of felt had been nailed across the bottom of the door leading to the kitchen, thus excluding the knife-edge draught that froze the feet of anyone who was trying to get warm by the fire. There was a light in the kitchen, so he looked in and found Sister Heath washing up some teathings. The kitchen fire was glowing and preparations for a meal were on the table, including, as usual, a rabbit.

"Isn't it a lovely one?" said Sister Heath. "Effie's sister Ruby brought it, all ready skinned, and quite a young one. Not like those ones out of cold store. Miss Pemberton was talking to me about cooking and she lent me her cookery book. There's a splendid recipe for casserole of rabbit and I just ran over to the Mitre before Effie went home and got a bottle of cooking wine. I always say a proper kitchen range is better than gas or electricity. The heat seems softer somehow, if you see what I mean. Miss Pemberton is much better and I know she'd like a little chat with you. Now don't go exciting her about the Troubadours."

Mr. Downing felt that he had his congé and almost expected her to add "And run along and play and don't get into mischief." He went up and knocked at Miss Pemberton's door. While he waited for her to say Come In, his mind (the swiftness of thought being no metaphor but an inexplicable fact) suddenly told him this was perhaps the third, or the fourth time at most, that he had been in her virgin bower in all the years he had been at Punshions. Nor had she been in his bachelor bower (unless it were in his absence, to conduct with Effie Bunce an Inquisition into Fluff under the bed, Dust on the top of that Wardrobe or along the Top of the Window). Not that there was any reason for either to be in the bedroom of the other when there was the big living-room downstairs and the garden in warm weather, but the fact did strike him.

Miss Pemberton was sitting up in bed with a knitted shawl round her head and a decayed fur tippet round her shoulders. A wood fire was crackling in the fireplace.

"Well, Harold, here you see me," said Miss Pemberton. "Sit down."

Mr. Downing pulled up an uncomfortable chair and sat down.

"I am much better," said Miss Pemberton, "but I have gone a Step Down. I told Dr. Ford as much and he did not contradict me. I have written to Mrs. Villars to explain that I cannot do any more about the pageant. She came to see me while you were out" (in which last words Mr. Downing felt, or fancied he felt, an implied reproach, though we think his too tender conscience misled him on this point) "and we discussed the question. Mrs. Paxon and Mrs. Turner will carry on. I hope to be well enough to attend the performance, but not as a helper. Nor shall I criticize," at which majestic abdication Mr. Downing felt a kind of respectful awe.

"We shall miss you, Ianthe," he said.

"That, Harold, is as may be," said Miss Pemberton. "But one thing I will *not* give up. I told Dr. Ford that I did not intend to let this foolish complaint—whatever it is—interfere with the B.D.P. As soon as I am about again I intend to go on with it, and while you are in America I hope to make a good deal of progress. Another year ought to see the end of it."

"But, Ianthe—" Mr. Downing began.

"You will have to go to America alone," said Miss Pemberton, who was, we think, taking a masochistic pleasure in her self-flagellation. "Dr. Ford says I must not think of it. In any case, I am much of his opinion. I should only be a clog on your activities, a tie when you wanted to lunch or dine with your admirers. Do not argue, Harold."

"I wasn't going to," said Mr. Downing, his gentle feathers almost ruffled for once. "I expect you are right, Ianthe. But I shall miss you," and this he meant sincerely, almost forgetting Mrs. Turner when he thought of the years he had spent with Miss Pemberton and her devotion to his interests, even if the devotion was apt to take the form of bullying and even of setting him down in public. "I am so *very* sorry, Ianthe. I do hope you will feel better soon."

Disregarding this kind hope, Miss Pemberton said Sister Heath was more than kind and efficient, and metaphorically turned her face to the wall. Mr. Downing got up, put the chair back in its place, and quietly left the room. The least he could do for Miss Pemberton was to go on working, so he settled to his books and was surprised when Sister Heath said supper was ready and why shouldn't they have it in the kitchen and then he needn't disturb his papers and things, which they accordingly did.

It had seemed to the Coronation Committee when it first met that they had time enough, but time had galloped withal, and the day was almost upon them. Frenzied last-moment changes were discussed, made, and unmade, but time went on and then it was Coronation week. Wind, rain, and bitter cold covered the land and we can only hope that the entire disregard for them shown by the whole country put them in their place. But we doubt it. And hearts and spirits were raised to an even higher pitch than before when the Conquest of Everest was fluted through every radio, blared by every newspaper. Something done by Us that could never be repeated. Doubtless the mountain having once been conquered would prove more tractable (as the Matterhorn, once considered unscalable, had been tamed and made almost common property), but no one could rob the Everest Expedition of this achievement and it was considered a gracious act on Everest's part to submit its neck to the yoke at this moment of history.

On Coronation Day practically the whole population of Northbridge (and everywhere else) was glued to the television, or in Horrible Modern English Usage the Telly, though sterner spirits, including those who did not like or had not access to television, preferred to wait till they could see it all in colour at the Barchester Odeon. Even television's most bigoted dislikers (and they are many, though unvocal) had to admit that the job was well done. The grave hieratic dignity of Her Majesty, self-dedicated to God and to Her people, remained like a solemn prayer in the minds of all who saw and heard. There nothing common was nor mean Upon that memorable screen. The pages showed how right was the stage when boys took principal parts: perfectly trained, at ease without self-consciousness, they went unmoved about their business, looking after their elders with serious efficiency. The Mistress of the Robes presided like a guardian angel, never in the foreground, grave, noble, aloof, yet ready at need. A Queen from the far Pacific won every heart. Our Great Prime Minister smiled his acknowledgments of the people's plaudits; the people who owed so much to him and the inspiration of his words and his work, who had trusted him for six long years and not in vain. The bagpipes, played by whatever colour or creed, roused as always a frenzy of enthusiasm among a people who know nothing about them. One or two gentlemen, less used to equitation than to other forms of progress, looked as if they would rather be anywhere else, and then the insubstantial pageant faded. But its memory remained and the world knew that this little England had done what no Asian or Roman triumph could do.

In Northbridge there was an early service attended by quite a number of people. Then silence fell upon most of the town while the television unfolded the pageant in various sizes from about one foot by two in the gentry houses to sets rather larger than a motor bus in the cottages, during which programs everyone ate steadily, this being the English idea of complete enjoyment. The rain also fell steadily, as did the thermometer, and the bonfire was cancelled, though not until several vain attempts to light it had been made.

On the day after the Coronation it was still wet and cold, but the procession to the War Memorial was well attended. Wreaths were laid by the British Legion and other patriotic bodies, and a short prayer for those who had died for their country was read, while representatives of every religion and sect stood by bare-headed, and the little ceremony of remembrance was over.

After lunch there was a Dairy Produce Show in the School Hall, which rather vague term included anything from vegetables and very bad drawings by schoolchildren and equally nasty products in raffia, to eggs and sweets and cakes, all of which were sold at the end of the day.

The tea for the kiddies, originally planned to be on trestle tables in the market-place, had to be in the Church Hall, where the crowding, the noise, the greed, the pushing and shoving were of an unusually high standard. Packer's Universal Royal Derby was in a field behind the Mitre and in spite of the rain was very well attended, and—especially after the tea —the number of children who were sick broke all records. Then Packer took his gaudy caravans away to his next appointment and the children went home to have another tea preparatory to the Entertainment in the Town Hall.

All the tickets for the Entertainment had been taken for some time. Two extra rows had been somehow squashed in, against all rules, and Mrs. Villars, who was rather exhausted by the high spirits, rudeness, and shockingly bad manners of the children, said to Mrs. Paxon that she sometimes felt about children as Bishop Hatto felt about his tenants and then wondered if she were showing off.

"Oh, I know what you mean," said Mrs. Paxon. "I recited it once for the South Wembley Amateur Dramatic.

> "And while for mercy on God they call,
> Set fire to the barn and burned them all,"

"and not a bad thing either," she added, looking at the serried ranks of the audience and thinking also of the other children

who were herded into another room under the doubtful control of Miss Hopgood and Miss Crowder, waiting their turn
to go on and working off their high spirits in whatever damage
they found ready to hand, which included some of the bigger
boys carving their names on the window sills.

Mrs. Turner suddenly emerged from the crowd to tell Mrs.
Villars that Aubrey Clover and Jessica Dean and their accompanist had arrived and she had parked them in the caretaker's
room and there was something about a piano and what was
she to do about it. Luckily Lydia was at hand and volunteered
to deal with the Clovers, whom she found absorbing local
colour from the caretaker hand over fist.

"Divine Lydia," said Aubrey Clover, "though you haven't
a rolling eye, or should it be roving, I can never be sure with
quotations, here we are, ad lib till ready. My accompanist insisted on having a decent upright, so we took the liberty of
having a good one sent in for the evening. I daresay no one
has noticed it. It just happens to be in tune and all the notes
sound, which I do always think rather important, don't you?"

"Excuse me, Mrs. Merton," said the caretaker, "but this
gentleman said we was to have his piano, so I hope that's all
right. I don't know much about pianos, but it looked a lovely
one and the gentleman says all the notes play."

The gentleman, who was evidently Aubrey Clover's accompanist, bowed and said every single note played, even the one
up at the very top.

"But mind," he said, "no one else is going to play it. I've got
the men here and they will take it up before Our Turn and
take it away after the performance," to which Lydia willingly
assented, feeling that things had now got quite beyond her;
but she had every confidence in Aubrey Clover and determined to sit back and enjoy herself. A tall figure who had
been standing in the background now came forward.

"Oh, Ludo!" said Lydia. "How lovely to see you. And I *do* like your tails. *And* the gardenia."

"That was Jessica's kind thought," said Lord Mellings, who gave Lydia an indefinable feeling of being a good deal more grown-up than when she last saw him. "And the tails are my father's kind thought. Oh, father and mother sent you their love and the Coronation was marvellous, especially Queen Salote. I say, Mrs. Merton, I'm feeling horribly nervous. I dreamed my voice cracked last night."

Lydia said firmly that dreams always went by contraries and anyway Aubrey Clover simply wouldn't allow it; which unconvincing and improbable statement appeared to cheer Lord Mellings considerably.

At this point no one was surprised to see Mr. Wickham, who was not expected but always welcome.

"I know you two don't drink before a performance," said that gentleman to the Clovers, "but I thought a little something wouldn't be amiss. Real Advocaat, straight from a pal in Holland. Guaranteed to make you sleep the clock round," and from one of the pockets of his poacher's coat he produced a bottle of that divine, viscous nectar. "No offers? Well, I daresay you're right. Some time later. I say, Mrs. Merton, you remember that jingle I got from old Nandy in the Hop Pole at Marling? Well, it's a rum thing, but it's coming out, like a game of Patience."

Jessica asked what Wicks meant.

"It's a prophecy," said Mr. Wickham. "I got it from old Nandy, who knows more good Saxon bawdy than anyone in West Barsetshire. Not that this is bawdy. It's more like Hotspur."

"What *do* you mean, Wicks?" said Lydia.

"I thought you knew your Shakespeare, my girl," said Mr. Wickham. "It's when Hotspur—I *do* like that fellow—says

what a bore his father-in-law Glendower is, talking about The
dreamer Merlin and his prophecies, And of a dragon and a
finless fish, A clip-winged griffin and a moulten raven, A
couching lion and a ramping cat, And such a deal of skimble-
skamble stuff—sorry, I did Hotspur one Christmas at Malta
in the old *Andiron*. Shakespeare does get one."

Lord Mellings asked, amusedly, what exactly they were all
talking about.

"Prophecies, my lord," said Mr. Wickham, and Lydia knew
that only by a hairsbreadth had he stopped himself saying my
boy; not that Lord Mellings would have taken it in bad part.
"I'll say it to you. It goes like this: Two score year and add
thirteen—that's fifty-three, never mind about the nineteen
hundred; Then a Crowning will be seen—that's the Coronation, at least it can't be anything else; Crowning for a Queen
so good—yes indeed, God bless her, and I'd drink her health
here and now in Advocaat, though it's not usual; Mountain,
Steed, Frost, Fire, and Flood. Well, we've had enough cold
weather this year, God knows, and I'm willing to bet a hundred to one it's all the fault of those scientists and their split-
ting the atom and whatnot. I always said science was no pursuit for a gentleman, but that's neither here nor there. Then
we had the East Anglian floods—poor beggars—and now
here's the Mountain. We've only got to get the Steed and the
Fire and we're set. I'm keeping my eye on Epsom and the
Derby for Steed. But as for Fire—well, I wouldn't mind if one
or two people fell into it. Here's luck," and he took a refreshing
draught of the Advocaat.

Lord Mellings said he had read in Dickens about a slime
draught and Advocaat was about the nearest we could get to
one now, which amused the party. And we think Lord
Mellings was flattered by their amusement.

Lydia then said she was sorry but she must go back to the

Hall, as she was supposed to be chairman and if she didn't see
the Children's Performance, Miss Hopgood and Miss Crowder, the organizers, would be hurt and so would the schoolmistress, Miss Hart, and she went away to her duty.

We shall not attempt to describe the Children's Performance, as it was perfectly nauseating to all but their parents and
their kind, hard-working teachers. We will only say that it
ended with an odious little girl, guiltless of any expression but
greed and idiocy, reciting a Coronation poem composed by a
gentleman who supplied, under the name of Auntie Honey-
bell, very bad occasional verse to a children's paper consisting
of coloured-strip stories that had no beginning within living
memory nor appeared likely ever to have any end. As the
audience was largely composed of parents, the applause was
wholehearted and undiscriminating, and we are glad to say
that a huge bouquet was presented, by the youngest child
present, to kind, hard-working Miss Hart, who said she
couldn't sufficiently express her grateful thanks and retired,
almost in tears with excitement and pleasure.

"Grateful thanks!" said Mr. Villars, an unwilling spectator,
to his wife. "That's what people say in *The Times* every day
about letters of condolence. Tautology! They might as well say
Thankful gratitude," to which his wife replied that when he
died she would answer every letter of sympathy in her own
handwriting, a decision which her husband applauded and
promised he would, if necessary, do the same by her.

There was then, as Miss Pemberton had announced at the
first Committee Meeting, a short interval, during which nearly
all the children in the audience went out—quite unneces-
sarily. But a just judgment fell upon them, for they missed the
delightful spectacle of three strong men, two to work and one
to hover and give advice, pushing the little Town Hall piano
away onto the landing and bringing in its place the upright

piano which Aubrey Clover's accompanist had insisted on having. The green baize curtains were drawn across the stage and exciting sounds of things being moved were heard. Aubrey Clover's accompanist, known then and for ever among the schoolchildren as The Gentleman, took his seat, cast an uninterested look on the audience, and began to improvise on popular tunes of the day, in which the children joined heartily and untunefully. Then the caretaker (briefed to that purpose by Aubrey Clover, on which temporary notoriety he lived for the rest of the year) turned out the lights. Only a small shaded light fixed on the piano shone on the keys. Aubrey Clover's accompanist began to play, softly, tunes from Aubrey Clover's plays, familiar to some of the elder members of the audience. The curtains were drawn apart by the caretaker, who had arranged an elaborate overhead system operated from one side only, so that no one might share the glory with him, and the stage was in full view, with three chairs and a table with a kind of india-rubber plant on it, representing the boudoir of an actress. Here Miss Jessica Dean was discovered, exquisitely gowned (or ungowned), smoking a cigarette in a very dashing way all by herself, and *Two-Step for Three* had begun.

What the darling kiddies thought of it all, we do not know, nor do we care, for the dialogue was not meant for them and was beyond their comprehension, but they were quiet, which speaks volumes for Aubrey Clover's genius. And we may add that the few who did try to speak were at once shushed and silenced by their mothers, who were deep in romance, each seeing herself (as we all, even the oldest and dullest do) as the exquisite woman for whom every man's heart is broken.

To the actress there appear first the shy young man (Lord Mellings) and then the aristocrat (or arístocrat, as Common Usage is rapidly making it, not unaided by the Wahless), whose intentions are far from honourable, but so charmingly expressed that not even Mr. Hopper, the disagreeable cobbler, could object to them. For twenty minutes did the three hold the attention of the packed audience with what is now in Common Usage called sophisticated dialogue. But as the words expressed that most heavenly bitter-sweet of Being In Love, and as no one could guess which gentleman the lovely actress would choose, everyone was blissfully silent, while Aubrey Clover's accompanist let the piano murmur below their talk, reminding the older listeners of the happy days of the silent films and the piano background.

We all know the end of the play. The roué (to give him no worse name) has offered her a red camellia and guilty splendour (only most of the audience, so skilfully did Aubrey and Jessica change a word or an inflection here and there, thought it was honourable matrimony). During his brief absence (unexplained but necessary for the purpose of the play) the young lover has laid his heart and a white camellia at the actress's feet. And at this point the actress and the young lover sing the song that we first heard when the Pomfrets and the Clovers dined with the Mertons. Aubrey Clover's accompanist played the sad, enchanting waltz tune that we know so well. Lord Mellings, against all his forebodings completely master of himself and his voice, sang what still remains one of Aubrey Clover's most popular lyrics.

> "Though I am not twenty, sweet,
> Here is my heart.
> You are sweet and twenty, sweet,
> Where is your heart?
> I'd die for you this very hour,
> (Quiet, my heart,)
> But let me live, just for this hour,
> Deep in your heart."

By this time the audience were perfectly quiet and every mother would cheerfully have murdered a child that raised its voice. The whole hall was hushed, even the coughers forgot to cough, and a good many people were sniffing and dabbing at their eyes. Then, on the last lines, the roué comes in (and if Aubrey Clover chose to wear a cloak and carry an opera hat, who can blame him?) and looks at the couple. The young lover has his back to the door and does not see him. The actress, her hand on his head as he kneels before her, signs with her free hand to the roué to be silent. He opens his opera cloak (which was almost inexcusably lined with red), she drops the white camellia on the table, takes the red camellia between her teeth (a *quite* inexcusable bit of gagging on Jessica's part, as she was afterwards the first to admit) and goes towards him. The roué throws the cloak round her and together they stand in the open door. The young lover rises to his feet, makes a step towards the door, realizes that all his love is but a vain dream and (of course) sings the song again, while the roué sings with him, Aubrey with the promised second, slightly but correctly taken. The curtain was drawn by the caretaker (who nearly forgot to do so in his excitement). It opened again and the three figures were in the same attitude and sang the song again, this time with Jessica's help, who produced a lovely chorister's voice to make a descant (a word of whose meaning we are still not quite sure).

Of course by this time half of the audience were in tears and the whole of it clapping wildly. The curtain was once more opened. Aubrey Clover led the other two actors to the footlights and the clapping died down.

"Thank you all, a thousand times," he said. "This has been a wonderful evening for my wife and myself, and we must thank the gentleman who offered to play the part of the young man at very short notice. He wishes to remain anonymous. Thank you all, and God bless our Queen," at which words Aubrey Clover's accompanist struck a chord with a kind of rolling of drums and everyone stood up and sang *God Save the Queen* and cried and had never enjoyed themselves so much in their lives. The curtain covered the stage, the lights were turned on, and a roar of talking began.

Meanwhile the actors were saying good-bye to Lydia in the little room where they had waited. Jessica flung her arms round Lord Mellings and carefully did not quite kiss his face. Aubrey Clover shook hands warmly and said: "Well done, Ludovic. I knew you could do it. There will always be a seat for you at the Cockspur. And if you don't get into the Brigade of Guards, I'll take you on as an understudy. We'll drop you at the Towers."

"We have *adored* it," said Lydia, whose eyes were still wet.

"I'm glad you cried," said Aubrey Clover. "I shouldn't have been happy if you hadn't. You are, if I may say so, a *perfect* barometer. I apologize for the ending. Too, too *Tales of Hoffmann*, as that little Clarissa Belton would say. I can't think why the people who produce *Hoffmann* always cut the Prologue and the Epilogue. So effective. But that is life."

Lord Mellings lingered for a moment to say good-bye to Lydia.

"You did it all, Mrs. Merton," he said. "Thank you so very much. I simply adored it. You are like that lovely song of Denis Stonor's that I've got on the gramophone, 'You did for me what no one else could do.' " He looked down at her with overflowing gratitude in his melancholy eyes. Lydia saw his father in him and for a moment blushed inside herself (a feeling that every woman will understand) because Lord Pomfret's melancholy eyes had, very temporarily, troubled her. And suddenly she remembered how pretty Mrs. Arbuthnot's looks had troubled Noel in a summer long past and how she had silently grieved. But Noel had not shown any symptoms of grieving, silently or otherwise, and Ludo was a dear boy and his parents would, she hoped, remain good friends of Noel and herself. So that faint romance died on a cold June evening, painlessly, and that was that.

"The play was lovely," said Lydia. "It made me cry like anything. Do ring us up when you are back from Eton and come on the river again," and Lord Mellings said he would and went away after the Clovers.

Lydia turned to say good-bye to the accompanist.

"A very nice bit of work Lord Mellings put up," he said. "I'm not going just yet, Mrs. Merton. I've an idea that I might be useful with your pageant. So long as I'm home before breakfast, Mums never worries. I never sleep away from home unless it's somewhere more than two hundred miles away. Mums doesn't like it. But I wouldn't mind a cup of coffee," so Lydia caught a Wolf Cub and told him to bring some coffee and sandwiches to the gentleman who played the piano, and having seen that all was well, she went back to the hall, where the temperature was gloriously thick and fuggy.

Gradually the hall filled again and a gentle sound as of someone improvising for his own pleasure was heard, which was Aubrey Clover's accompanist amusing himself ad lib.

The curtain was drawn aside, revealing a number of Ancient Britons, which led to exclamations of delight from members of the audience who recognized their dining-room hearthrug, or that old sheepskin we really didn't hardly think worth keeping and what a mercy we didn't send it to the Jumble. The earthenware jugs from the Cosie Tea-Room were enthusiastically recognized as the Britons filled them at the imaginary river. Mr. Downing as Merlin got courageously through his part, inspired by Mrs. Turner's injunction to imagine he was one of the Troubadours, a suggestion whose irrelevance he found quite enchanting.

The cast, who had had several unsatisfactory rehearsals and

one crashingly bad dress rehearsal, suddenly found themselves full of confidence, and the applause was terrific.

"That went splendidly," said Mrs. Paxon, who was helping the actors to undress and simultaneously hustling the next lot into their clothes. "I never thought it would."

"It was the music, I think," said Mr. Downing. "Who was playing the piano?"

Everyone then said it was a funny thing, they thought they'd heard the piano but when you are concentrating on what you are doing you don't always quite seem to take in what's happening, and what on earth could it have been.

"It's Mr. Clover's accompanist," said Mrs. Paxon, who was, in her own words, always one to get to the bottom of things. "He's at the piano just like the silent films and without his notes, the way those pianists used to. I think it's a splendid idea. Here's your tunic, Mr. Clifford," and the headmaster of the infants' school, who had been vainly looking for it in the wrong place, thanked her and said he did seem to think there was music but somehow he was so wrought up that he didn't pay much attention.

"Stage-fright," said Mrs. Paxon, "you'll soon get over it," but her mouth was so full of safety pins that Mr. Clifford did not hear her and was able to tell anyone who didn't want to listen that he seemed to get wrought up like more than other people.

The second episode was the Coming of the Normans, in which the most conspicuous figure was perhaps Mr. Highmore in full canonicals (curtain from Mrs. Dunsford and a dust-sheet from Glycerine Cottage), his artificial tonsure like Henry of Navarre's white plume leading his flock to victory, while the strains of *Glory and Love to the Men of Old* resounded from the piano, and so interested was the audience and so loud was their discussion as to whether he had really cut his hair off that no one noticed Mr. Clifford, the head-

master of the infants' school, being killed till he dragged his
corpse down to the front of the stage and died all over again,
at which moment Aubrey Clover's accompanist quietly played
part of the *Funeral March of a Marionette* and everyone said
wasn't it nice.

After a longish wait, due to the mislaying of Richard III's
hump, which had been mistakenly hung on a peg with the
hats, the Wars of the Roses took the stage, and the destruction
of the bridge (made of some of the banisters from the condemned cottages at Faraway Corner) by Richard Crookback
brought the house down, the children getting quite out of
control till Aubrey Clover's accompanist (who had been
quietly playing tunes from the 1914 war) broke into *Tipperary*
and all the children sang and a great many of the grown-ups
cried.

The Elizabethan episode was a tremendous success, Miss
Crowder in her farthingale and the Pomfret sham crown and
jewellery dancing a pavane most high and disposedly with
Commander Beasley in his tights to the tune of *Greensleeves*
with such variations as Aubrey Clover's accompanist saw fit
to introduce.

"Good gracious!" said Mrs. Paxon behind the scenes to Mrs.
Turner, "Mr. Scatcherd isn't here! I had quite forgotten about
him. He was coming to do the portrait of the Queen in crayons," but even as she spoke Mr. Scatcherd, wearing his usual
dress of Norfolk jacket with belt, knickerbockers buttoning
below the knee, and a deerstalker hat, carrying a full-length
tweed cape, came into the dressing-room.

"Well, ladies, good evening," he said, "here I am and better
late than never, as the saying is. In fact I was just starting
when I had one of my Ideas and you ladies know what it is
when an Idea gets hold of you, so I went to my atterleer where
I work out my Ideas and became quite in a fine frenzy as

Shakespeare says till I became oblivious of the Passage of Time
and had to make a Bolt for it to get the bus, but better late
than never—" at which point Mrs. Paxon said they must hurry
and his cape and kneebreeches would do nicely and she was
sure she had a ruff somewhere and what a mercy the Eliza-
bethans wore their hair short and hustled the artist onto the
stage before he knew where he was.

The drawing of Queen Elizabeth's portrait was a great success. Mr. Scatcherd, by drawing at arm's length, tossing back
his head to get the effect, and generally showing off, made a
deep impression on the audience, while Aubrey Clover's accompanist played *If Those Lips Could Only Speak,* in which
most of the audience joined, for to give credit to those who
shall be nameless, the Wahless has brought back into circula-
tion a number of old songs which are well worth keeping.
Queen Elizabeth then knighted Mr. Scatcherd and the scene
ended.

The final episode, The War in Northbridge, was a success
from first to last. W.V.S., A.R.P., Red Cross, St. John, Townswomen's Guild, Women's Institute, Decontamination Squad,
Air Raid Wardens, Boy Scouts, Communal Kitchen workers,
roof-spotters, and many more were all on the platform at once,
each doing, so far as space allowed, what he, or more often
she, had done during the war. A large white circle of cardboard
with CRATER stencilled on it was marked, which everyone had
to avoid. Aubrey Clover's accompanist played martial and popular airs in which everyone joined. But the final and greatest
success of the whole evening was Mrs. Paxon as a hysteria case,
and never since the war had she enjoyed herself so much,
while Aubrey Clover's accompanist played the *Ride of the
Valkyries.*

There was then an interlude while the whole cast took
breath before arranging itself on the stage for the final tableau.

Aubrey Clover's accompanist, playing some of the old popular songs, found himself leading community singing. Presently he played *The Honeysuckle and the Bee,* in which all the older members of the audience joined with nostalgic enthusiasm, though the children were not so well acquainted with it. Mrs. Villars, who was cheerfully singing with the rest, noticed something peculiar about the accompaniment but had not time to give her mind to it before the curtains were drawn for the last time and the whole company appeared, grouped round Mr. Scatcherd's portrait of Miss Crowder as Queen Elizabeth, which was auctioned by Commander Beasley for the benefit of the Red Cross, finally being knocked down for £5-6-3 to Miss Hopgood's Aunt. Then, with a great scraping of chairs, the audience stood up to sing *God Save the Queen* and all the cast joined them and a great many people had to sniff or wipe their eyes, and the evening was over.

Mrs. Villars, who had volunteered to stay till the hall was clear, went to speak to Aubrey Clover's accompanist, who was talking to the men who had come with the piano and were taking it away.

"Thank you so much for staying," she said. "It made all the difference to have a piano with the pageant."

"Glad you liked it," he said. "It does give a finish. I told Mums I might be a bit late, so she won't worry."

"Do tell me," said Mrs. Villars, "what *were* you playing while they sang *The Honeysuckle and the Bee?* I couldn't make it out."

"Oh, *that,*" said Aubrey Clover's accompanist. "Mendelssohn's *Spring Song.* They go together perfectly. Rum thing. But music *is* rum, you know. I'll tell you another one. There's a Brahms song, one of the *Magelonelieder,* though there's hardly anyone can sing them now, with the same tune as

Gounod's *Nazareth*. And *Danny Boy* is the same as the song in *The Immortal Hour*. I could tell you a lot more, but I must get back to Mums. She likes to hear all about what I've been doing," and he got into a car that was waiting and was taken away to Barchester to catch the late train.

Mrs. Villars and Lydia waited till everything was cleared away, or at any rate neatly stacked to be fetched next day, thanked everyone, tipped the caretaker, and gladly went home, Lydia taking Lady Pomfret's lovely sham regalia with her.

The audience had by now burst out of the Town Hall and was dispersing in various directions. Mrs. Turner, with the other helpers, was still tidying behind the scenes, so Mr. Downing homeward took his solitary way, feeling the reaction from all the noise and the music and the glamour. He went in by the kitchen door, quietly, and found Sister Heath.

"I was just thinking of making a nice cup of Ovaltine for you, Mr. Downing," she said. "Gentlemen need something after a late night," at which words Mr. Downing looked guiltily at the kitchen clock, which said five minutes past ten. "Now, I shan't ask anything about the pageant, because you must be tired and tomorrow you can tell me all about it at breakfast. Miss Pemberton said would you go up and see her for a moment. She seems worried about something and I always say a trouble shared is a trouble halved. I'll have the Ovaltine nice and ready when you come down."

This was the last thing in the world Mr. Downing wanted to do, but gratitude and a sense of duty bade him go upstairs. Miss Pemberton was propped up with pillows and looking even more like one of the less agreeable Roman Emperors than usual.

"Well, I hope you enjoyed yourself, Harold," said Miss

Pemberton, not unkindly, but as a great-aunt might speak to a young nephew who had been to the circus.

"Very much, Ianthe," said Mr. Downing. "Aubrey Clover's play was delightful and the pageant went wonderfully. And everyone asked after you," which last was a pure invention but did him credit.

"Hm!" said Miss Pemberton, which disconcerted Mr. Downing dreadfully.

"I wished to see you, Harold," said Miss Pemberton, "to tell you that I have made a decision. You had better marry Mrs. Turner as soon as is reasonable. Then she can go to America with you, where she will be a great help—and a great success."

"But, Ianthe," said Mr. Downing.

"Do not argue," said Miss Pemberton. "You will do as I say. Miss Heath and I get on very well and a man in the house means a great deal of extra work. That is all. I am tired and shall go to sleep."

"Ianthe!" said Mr. Downing.

"You will come here whenever you need help," said Miss Pemberton, "and as long as I am spared, my help such as it is will be at your disposal. And mind you are kind to Mrs. Turner and don't try to alter her habits. She will be just the wife you need—that you have always needed. That is all."

"Very well, Ianthe," said Mr. Downing, overcome by her generosity and not a little terrified of her determined manner. "And thank you more than I can say for everything," and he took her hand and laid his cheek against it for a moment.

"You needed everything," said Miss Pemberton, with perfect simplicity, "and you must go on having it. Good night."

"Onc moult di lor passoun bielhiez," said Mr. Downing softly; and then gently laying her hand on the bed, he went away, and though we do not know what these words meant, they appeared to satisfy Miss Pemberton.

A fortnight or so later, Lydia and Noel, having answered all the congratulations on Noel's knighthood (which they both agreed they would never get used to and wished he hadn't accepted it if it was to make Palmer so uppish), were sitting on the terrace enjoying what sun there was before dinner, when Mr. Wickham came through the garden. As always he was very welcome and for once he had not brought anything with him and was pleased to have some of Noel's really good sherry. The talk was mostly about the events of the past weeks, and a good deal of local gossip was exchanged.

Lydia said she was longing to see the Everest film.

"Funny thing, your saying that," said Mr. Wickham. "Makes me think of old Nandy's poem."

Noel asked what that was.

"Thought I'd told you before," said Mr. Wickham. "It's a kind of prophecy or something; pure folk-muck. It goes:

> "Two score year and add thirteen,
> Then a Crowning will be seen,
> Crowning of a Queen so good,
> Mountain, steed, frost, fire, and flood."

"And what do you make of that?" said Noel.

"Well, we've got Mountain all right, that's Everest," said Mr. Wickham, "and it's been cold enough this year and floods enough. I had a hunch we'd find something else. Battle of Waterloo, today, June 18th, it is. Makes you sit up a bit and use your brains. What price Steed now?"

Noel said he hadn't the faintest idea.

"What on earth do you lawyers read?" said Mr. Wickham. "What price Gordon Richards winning the Derby? What price Her Majesty's horse yesterday at Ascot? *They* know, all right," though to what unseen powers he was alluding we do not know.

"So there is only Fire," said Noel, whose interest in old Nandy's prophecy was rapidly evaporating. "There is bound to be a fire somewhere."

Mr. Wickham, who was about to help himself to a third glass of sherry, put it down and looked at the Mertons.

"Good Lord! to think I never thought of it," he said, on which Noel's reasonable comment was that he would like to know what the it was.

"I'm not superstitious," said Mr. Wickham firmly, "and I don't believe that what one says can scrizle the luck, as the old people over Chaldicotes way used to say. Look here, Mrs. Merton—mind you, I don't want to raise anyone's hopes, but everything else has come out, and now—"

"What has come out now?" said Noel and Lydia with one voice.

"Well, you never know," said Mr. Wickham, looking round cautiously in case any malign deities, requiring propitiation, were hovering in the neighbourhood. "But—suppose fire meant the Ashes," and at these words they looked at each other in silence with a wild surmise.

THE NOVELS OF ANGELA THIRKELL

AUGUST FOLLY
SUMMER HALF
POMFRET TOWERS
THE BRANDONS
BEFORE LUNCH
CHEERFULNESS BREAKS IN
NORTHBRIDGE RECTORY
MARLING HALL
GROWING UP
THE HEADMISTRESS
MISS BUNTING
PEACE BREAKS OUT
PRIVATE ENTERPRISE
LOVE AMONG THE RUINS
THE OLD BANK HOUSE
COUNTY CHRONICLE
THE DUKE'S DAUGHTER
WILD STRAWBERRIES and HIGH RISING
HAPPY RETURN
CORONATION SUMMER
JUTLAND COTTAGE
WHAT DID IT MEAN?

THESE ARE BORZOI BOOKS,
PUBLISHED IN NEW YORK BY
ALFRED A. KNOPF

A NOTE ON THE TYPE IN WHICH
THIS BOOK IS SET

The text of this book was set on the Linotype in Fairfield, the first type-face from the hand of the distinguished American artist and engraver Rudolph Ruzicka. In its structure Fairfield displays the sober and sane qualities of a master craftsman whose talent has long been dedicated to clarity. It is this trait that accounts for the trim grace and virility, the spirited design and sensitive balance of this original typeface.

Rudolph Ruzicka was born in Bohemia in 1883 and came to America in 1894. He has designed and illustrated many books and has created a considerable list of individual prints—wood-engravings, line-engravings on copper, aquatints. W. A. Dwiggins wrote recently: "Until you see the things themselves you have no sense of the artist behind them. His outstanding quality, as artist and person, is *sanity*. Complete esthetic equipment, all managed by good sound judgment about ways and means, aims and purposes, utilities and 'functions' —and all this level-headed balance-mechanism added to the lively mental state that makes an artist an artist. Fortunate equipment in a disordered world. . . ."

The book was composed, printed, and bound by Kingsport Press, Inc., Kingsport, Tennessee.

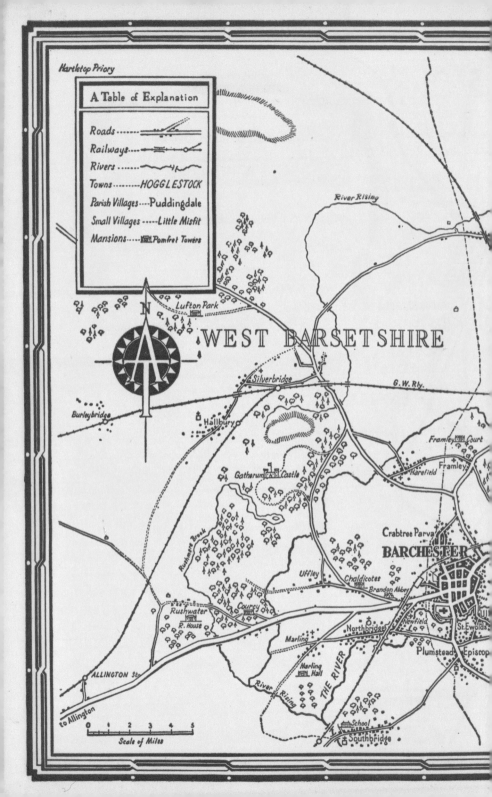